A Cage of Tarred Feathers

Renée Tamsin

ISBN: 979-8-9852465-6-8

Dedication

To the scribblers who wake up and choose literary violence instead of committing actual crimes.

I feel you. I see you. And we can get through it together.

Table of Contents

September 1889

October 1889

November 1889

December 1889

January 1890

February 1890

March 1890

March 1889

Marvelous is the power which can be exercised, almost unconsciously...by one person gifted with good temper, good digestion, good intellects, and good looks
~Anthony Trollope~

1

An Artist with a Feather Duster

Thrones come in many shapes and sizes. Lady Selina no doubt had a rather regal selection of thrones at her disposal, but the one she graced now was of the rich velvet and mahogany variety. Beechbury was the lesser of her castles, but no less elegant and well-kept than it's vast countryside counterpart. In sudden need of a new lady's maid, Lady Selina sat gracefully, paper references in lap, effortlessly intimidating the most promising candidate sitting before her.

Helen Thomas found it difficult to look her potential employer in the eye—not that Lady Selina intended to make much eye contact herself. The lofty heiress thumbed through the paperwork in her hands idly. There was no real need to dwell on the details. She had managed to increase her own fortune since her father's death by relying on her instincts, and not what she'd been told by others.

The women Helen had previously worked for—cleaning house and tending to children—were the flimsier sort. They themselves regularly tread upon, they didn't care much to keep track of anyone else. They hardly remembered Helen's name. Oftentimes she had learned to answer to "Jane" or "Mary" or even simply "Maid". She was expected to keep silent, do her duties, and see that the children did the same. Helen was not four years older than the eldest child in her care, yet she was expected to maintain decorum and mature supervision.

These were much smaller households, of course, with limited staff and very little pay. The middle-class who could afford servants at the time kept help to a minimum, but somehow still behaved as though they were all great barons and lords, simply because they could afford to keep a staff at all.

All of them were nothing to what sat before Helen now. Two homes, one of which being arguably amongst the greatest country estates connected to one of the most successful businessmen in the past decade, and all of the class and elegance that came with such a station.

Helen didn't know what could have possessed Mr. Kincaid, her current employer's business associate, to recommend her to his friend, but here she was. Her endearingly juvenile energy was bubbling inside her, ready to burst. Thankfully, her fear of Lady Selina's judgment kept it at bay—instead, her knee bounced anxiously, allowing small bouts of release.

Lady Selina glanced up and smiled, ever so slightly. "Calm your nerves, Miss Thomas. This is not an interrogation."

Feeling heat flush her cheeks, Helen stilled her bouncing knee. "Yes, ma'am," she muttered.

The heiress flipped to the final page of Helen's references as if she'd been studying them diligently. Helen was not as naive as she so frequently appeared; the wealthy and powerful revel in controlled silence. Lady Selina's smile settled into more of a satisfied smirk. The perfectly crafted bouffant atop her head gave the illusion of a crown. Whether that was the intention or not, she wore it with grace. Not a hair was out of place, not a blemish on her skin, nor a single wrinkle in her fine gown.

She was young for someone so powerful. She couldn't have been more than twenty-seven. Helen supposed the queen came to rule at the tender age of eighteen, so perhaps age had very little to do with power.

"Mr. Kincaid highly recommended you," Lady Selina finally

spoke.

"Thank you, ma'am."

"Don't thank me," she shook her head. "Thank your own merit."

"Of course, ma'am."

Lady Selina paused, placing her hands gently on top of the papers in her lap. "You're quite young for someone with so many past employers. How old are you, Miss Thomas?"

Helen cleared her throat. "Not yet nineteen, ma'am."

Lady Selina chuckled. "Lady Selina is fine."

"Of course, ma—Lady Selina," Helen nodded.

She studied Helen with a gaze so scrutinous that Helen felt the urge to bounce her anxious knee again. "I suppose you were bored with them."

Helen frowned. "Pardon?"

"Your past employers. All claim you started strong and then tapered. Attention to detail waned, pots and pans dropped more frequently, and sheets left wrinkled." Lady Selina set the papers on the end table to her left and leaned forward slightly as if revealing a secret. "I assume they weren't challenging enough to maintain your interest. Laundry and feather dusters are hardly thrilling."

A snort escaped Helen as she impulsively answered, "Yes, they were very boring." Realizing how detrimental her admittance to laziness could prove to be, she quickly amended, "B-but I work very hard, ma'am. And I'm still quite good with a feather duster."

"To be sure," Lady Selina nodded. "An artist with a feather duster, I'd dare say."

"Ma'am?" There was no fault or mocking in Lady Selina's tone, which brought Helen to frown once more.

"This," Lady Selina gestured to Helen's knee—which had resumed bouncing despite Helen's best efforts. "Anxious energy is often found in artistic souls."

Helen hardly knew how to respond; all she could muster was a wide-eyed stare and a mouth slightly ajar, hoping a reply would find its way. As if confused silence was a regular occurrence in Lady Selina's daily interactions, she sat back and continued without pause.

"Everdon is much larger than your previous household employment. The workload will be considerable."

Finally, the words came to her. "Everdon...I've heard that's a castle, ma'am. That seems fitting—a family like the Delameres living in a castle on a hill."

Lady Selina chuckled. "Everdon is on a hill, but it's hardly a castle, Miss Thomas."

Helen shifted in her seat, imagining the possible posts available in a household like that. "What would be my position, ma'am? I have a variety of experience—kitchen, housekeeping, childcare—do you have any children?"

Lady Selina's chin tilted slightly.

"Oh, I'm sorry, ma'am," Helen bumbled. "That was too bold."

Once again reining the conversation as she did, Lady Selina joined her hands together in her lap and moved past the question. "What does an artist like yourself intend to do?"

"Erm...." Helen's heart raced, worried she'd sabotaged any hope of improving her post and working within the walls of such an estate. "Like I said, I am quite good with a feather duster—"

"Not at Everdon," Lady Selina lifted a hand to silence her. Helen's heart dropped to her stomach. "Surely, you don't mean to be a maid for the rest of your days."

Helen's frown returned. "You....you mean, what would I love to do most?"

Lady Selina nodded, encouragingly.

"I'd....um...." Helen's voice started small, but gradually grew as the sentence continued "...I'd love to be a writer."

In almost a decade of doing her part in the workforce to bring an income to her family, Helen had never been asked such a question. Not even her late parents had considered Helen capable of dreaming of any future beyond that blasted feather duster.

Lady Selina's smirk graced her mouth again. "Male writers

have always been deliciously enticing. But perhaps the literary market could use the fresh perspective only offered by the fairer sex, yes?"

Helen sighed in relief and smiled so widely it nearly took her entire face.

"I fund a number of publishing houses," Lady Selina went on. "I hope to one day see your name on a manuscript."

"You think I could, Lady Selina?" The thrill of the thought fell as Helen remembered her place. "I mean….it's a man's world though, isn't it?"

"Nonsense," Lady Selina flippantly waved her hand. "It's only a man's world because that's what we've told ourselves. Those are the words of the defeated, not the victorious. And I, for one, am never defeated. Nor should you be. There are plenty of women now rising to the top with nothing but their words. Besides, it only takes proper connections to pose opportunities necess—"

"Selina!"

The parlor of Beechbury was suddenly stormed by the overabundant vigor of a young lady with features similar to the Lady Selina, but a liveliness that suggested she was much younger—perhaps a year or so younger than Helen herself. The young woman's hair was lighter, her eyes wider, and her sense of decorum somewhat lacking in comparison to the heiress. Lady Selina merely sighed as she entered the parlor.

"Selina," the young lady repeated emphatically. "We've been invited—so we must go! So many people will be there, and my friend has asked us to sit in the front." She moved swiftly to Selina's chair and grabbed her arm. As her face became closer, Selina disguised her sigh of exasperation with a smile.

"Is that so?" she responded.

"He invited the two of us, so you must come."

Suddenly the smile faded from Selina's lips. "*He*?"

Unmoved by Selina's tone, the girl continued. "I told him you wouldn't allow me to go alone, so he said you simply must come as well."

"And you simply must tell me this event to which we've been invited."

"A reading, of course," the girl said, matter-of-factly.

Selina sighed again, gently moving the girl aside. "Penelope, this is Miss Thomas, my new lady's maid. Miss Thomas, this is Miss Penelope Ayres, my ward."

Helen's eyebrows nearly lifted to the ceiling. "Lady's maid?"

Selina nodded. "Provided she accepts, of course. At sixty pounds a year, I should think it would seem ideal to accept."

"Sixty pounds," Helen exhaled. It was double the average salary for a lady's maid—and far more than double Helen's current post. "Um, yes, of-of course I accept."

Lady Selina nodded again, curtly this time, and rose from her chair. She took Miss Ayres' hand with the command of a parent and gestured for Helen to stand and follow her to the door.

"Very good," she said. "We leave for Everdon in the morning. Be here with your luggage at six o'clock sharp and we'll be off."

2
No Merciful Critic

They say the arts, and many things like them, are like sausages; it's better not to see them being made. For once you see how the sausage is made, the appeal declines and your judgment is hardened.

Lady Selina had sponsored many artists and writers throughout the years—a tradition endorsed by her father during her childhood as well. Lord Edward Delamere had taken young Selina to art exhibitions and book readings, more than she could count, in fact. When one has been dazzled by the works of the greatest wordsmiths of their time, it becomes very difficult for up-and-coming artisans of the craft to impress. Selina had seen the sausage made and her taste had become quite refined and particular as a result.

The crowd in the small auditorium eagerly awaited the performance, but Selina sat skeptically. They were placed up front, just as Penelope's friend had requested, and Selina's presence brought the attention of many. Graciously, she greeted all those who passed her—a nod of acknowledgement from her was almost as desired as the author's story.

When the clamor settled, an announcer took the stage wearing a grin as big as his front teeth. In a thickly Cockney-accented and jovial tone, he spoke:

"Ladies and gentlemen, please welcome to the podium our

favorite poorhouse-to-publishing-house success story—the next
Dickens himself: Mr. Darius Royce!"

The crowd erupted, but Selina's frown deepened. "The next
Dickens," she muttered. She sighed and glanced to the ceiling. "My
apologies, Charlie. I suppose the culture of this room isn't broad
enough to see the alternatives."

Penelope, unbothered by her guardian's cynicism, grabbed
Selina's arm in excitement. "That's him! That's him—he invited us
particularly, Selina!"

Selina soaked in the sight of the gentleman who now strolled
across the stage. He was attractive and reasonably aged—only a
handful of years older than herself—and much easier on the eyes than
previous authors she had sponsored. All initial attraction and intrigue
soon escaped her, however, as she saw the elation in Penelope's eyes.
Selina's admiring beam hardened into a critical smirk of disapproval.

"Your friend is Darius Royce?"

"It's starting," Penelope shushed her, patting her on the arm
scoldingly. "Isn't he grand, Selina?" she added in a whisper.

"Hardly," Selina quietly scoffed. "It's offensive to compare
him to a man like Dickens."

"Shhh," Penelope shushed again.

The man's charisma and presence were undeniable. He was
appealing, engaging, and on all accounts, a brilliant storyteller. The
audience—particularly the ladies—couldn't take their eyes off of him.
He moved about the stage as the story progressed, taking on animated
voices that made each character burst with life.

By the end of the excerpt of his tale, his light brown hair was
ruffled and his bright blue eyes glistened with emotion. Within
moments, and after a couple of deep breaths, he regained composure,
his story complete. He straightened his jacket, took a bow, and puffed
his chest with pride as the crowd once again erupted with applause and
praise.

As soon as the audience rose from their seats to mingle with
the presenters of the evening, especially Mr. Royce himself, Penelope

clutched Selina and dragged her through the door to the meeting hall. Congregations tended to part as Lady Selina passed by—thus very little aggression was necessary to navigate the huddled fans— nevertheless, Penelope pushed through with such enthusiasm. It was easy for Mr. Royce to spot her and smile.

The way in which his eyes narrowed on young Penelope, a corner of his mouth lifted and his back straightened gave Selina the impression of a wolf honing in on his prey. His friend, a taller red-haired gentleman standing a short distance from him but occasionally directing a comment or two his way, maintained that same predatory gaze as he scanned the crowds as well.

My how the industry is corrupting, Selina thought to herself.

As Penelope dragged them closer to her intended suitor, Mr. Royce's eyes flashed from the young prey to her beguiling protector. His crooked smirk widened into a congenial smile as he made eye contact with the infamous Lady Selina.

"Ah, my most ardent fan brought a guest. And what did she think?" Though his eyes directed the question to Selina, Penelope didn't hesitate to step between them and reach for his arm encouragingly.

"It was wonderful! You're so brilliant. Isn't he brilliant, Selina?" Dazed with infatuation, she almost neglected the manners in which she had been so trained. "Oh—this is my guardian, Lady Selina."

Mr. Royce grinned, bowing his head slightly. "My pleasure. And what does the Lady Selina have to say of the reading?"

Lifting her chin, Selina respectfully smiled. "Contrived and derivative, she says. But with potential, perhaps."

Penelope gasped. "*Selina.*"

To Penelope's surprise and Selina's amusement, Mr. Royce chuckled. "I see," he said.

"You're charming, sir. Most charming individuals make for the best liars," Selina continued. "And after all, isn't a liar merely a storyteller operating in daily settings? Deceit is their trade."

Mr. Royce cocked his head to one side in consideration. "Lying is, in essence, storytelling, then."

"Mm, yes, but lies are generally fleeting—serving their purpose for a time and then leaving behind scars and wreckage. Very little intention beyond immediate gratification is commonly necessary. Stories, however, require investment and care. Layers must be crafted, to give one the feeling of being enveloped, for better or worse, with a lasting intention."

"Being?" he challenged, tucking his hands in his trouser pockets.

"To inspire hope and fancy, of course," she sighed. "Or to turn a small profit as the case may be."

Mr. Royce's smirk returned with an engaging twist. "And my stories? Am I to assume they didn't inspire hope and fancy in you, Lady Selina?"

Penelope flashed Selina a wary glance. Wealth and social prowess always gave Selina the inclination to speak as she pleased, regardless of the appropriate restraint one would commonly show in public. Tactful though she was, sensitive she seldom seemed.

"Your written words are shallow lies," she said simply. "Your voice and movement make them stories. Your stage presence and physical appeal far outweighed your ability to write truly well."

Penelope lightly but sternly rapped Selina's arm. "Stop it— you must be kind to him."

Mr. Royce rubbed Penelope's hand which rested on his own arm, alarming Selina with the affection but reassuring the young lady's discomfort. "It's quite all right. She's no merciful critic, that's for sure. My agent would cringe."

"But chuckle in agreement, no doubt," his redheaded friend smoothly appeared beside him. He angled himself in such a way that he had the clearest view of Lady Selina.

"My agent, Bernard Abram," Mr. Royce introduced. "Lady Selina."

"Please, my lady." Mr. Abram bowed and held out a hand that

he might kiss hers. To his brief disappointment, Selina merely lowered her tilted chin slightly before returning her nose to the air.

"Hm. A merciful critic is a weak admirer, Mr. Royce," she replied. "I am far more impartial—I am a commentator."

Mr. Royce smiled his surrender. "Yes, you certainly are."

"But she did like it, Royce" Penelope defended in a low tone. Selina's discerning brow lifted at the familiarity in Penelope's voice. "I saw her smile several times. She only pretends to be cross with everyone." Her eyes then met her guardian's and she gave her a coy smile as if she saw right through her façade of snobbery.

"I'm sure she holds a well-balanced opinion, Miss Ayres," Mr. Abram contributed loudly. "Even literary giants need commentators such as the Lady Selina to keep them mortal. Eh, Royce?"

His comment didn't warrant more than a side glance from Lady Selina, but did, however, cause Mr. Royce to clear his throat in mild irritation. Selina's eyes narrowed, still deciphering Mr. Royce's intentions and paying little attention to his cloying agent.

"How did the two of you happen to meet?" she gestured to Mr. Royce and Penelope, who still stood within an inch of one another.

Penelope beamed as she gazed up at Mr. Royce. "We ran into one another in a dress shop the day before yesterday!"

"A dress shop…" Selina repeated, subduing her urge to quickly condemn her ward's foolishness.

"Miss Ayres was the finest woman there," Mr. Royce confirmed.

"And Mr. Royce the finest man," Penelope giggled.

"No doubt the want for variety lent him the advantage," Selina considered aloud. Mr. Abram chortled at a vexing volume.

"It's true," Mr. Royce took the forced humility in stride. "I can't accept the flattery. But I saw Miss Ayres through the shop window and I just had to become more acquainted."

"Hm, I'm sure you did." Selina's expression bore a smile, but Mr. Royce was not the naive girl her ward was—he felt the vitriol beneath the affability.

"I'm sure he'd have thought the same had he seen you through the shop window, my lady," Abram commented. "A fine lady like yourself would certainly stand out on the streets, to be sure."

"Hm." Selina rolled her eyes, but he didn't bother to notice. "It is my greatest intent, Mr. Abram." Subtly pulling Penelope from Mr. Royce's grasp, Selina made a graceful movement easily construed to be a bow. "It was lovely to meet the two of you, but we have some traveling to prepare for this evening."

"But wait," Penelope stopped her, pulling Royce with her toward the door as well. She quieted her voice as Selina's expression became scolding. "I told him he could stay with us at Everdon and attend your birthday ball."

Selina stared at her for a moment. "My birthday ball?" Her voice dropped to a low mutter as she added, "It's meant to be an intimate dinner party, Nell."

As in years past, Penelope Ayres utilized her greatest tool in the manipulation of her guardian: her wide, child-like eyes. "Could we, Lina? Please? I already invited him."

"I have no immediate plans for the next two weeks," Mr. Royce chimed in.

"Two weeks?" Selina's voice rose.

Penelope nodded. "Yes, I told him he could stay for two weeks."

Mr. Royce stepped closer, attempting to soften the shock. "That is, as long as it pleases the Lady Selina."

"Of course it does," Penelope answered before Selina could respond. "Aren't you just completely thrilled, Selina?"

With little energy to contradict, and softened by Penelope's pleading, Selina tightened her jaw and conceded. "Ecstatic."

3
A Deplorable Way
to Make a Living

In a part of London, somewhere near the south bank of the River Thames in which one would never find the likes of Lady Selina Delamere, there was a small tavern wedged between a laundry shop and a blacksmith. Inside the tavern were a handful of less-than-savory gentlemen and some ladies of the oldest profession. A slum of London was among the more colorful destinations for a well-regarded wordsmith after a successful event with his wealthiest patrons and loyal readers, and yet here Mr. Darius Royce strolled. Relaxed shoulders and a confident air would suggest he felt right at home amongst the squalor of the city.

His friend Abram was already seated comfortably in the corner of the tavern, feet perched on the table in front of him, boring a new companion with his chatter. Royce gestured an order to the man working behind the bar as he approached the two gentlemen in the corner with a victorious strut.

"You didn't attend my reading," he pointed at the sandy-haired man sitting beside Abram. He was poring over a folder of papers and scribbling notes in a small book, clearly not paying much mind to whatever Abram had been telling him.

"Fiction bores me," was his response.

Pulling another chair up to the table, Royce sat himself down and sneered playfully. "That's because you have no imagination."

The man glanced, unamused, before returning to his notebook. "I'd rather live the thrill than have someone live it for me and twist the story themselves."

Abram clicked his tongue, leaning forward. "I'm telling you, I could make quite the celebrity out of you, Barratt, if you ever stopped living it and started writing it down."

This prompted a light chuckle. "I wouldn't have you represent me, my friend if you were the last agent left in the business."

Returning the previous disinterest, Abram merely shrugged and settled back into his careless posture, chewing on sardines from the plate in front of him.

"Real human beings," Barratt continued, "are infinitely more interesting in person, rather than pretend people on a page."

Accepting the drink from the barkeep, Royce sipped and sighed. "Yes, but a deep understanding of real people makes the pretend people all the more credible."

Fully engaged now, Barratt closed his notebook and rested his hands, intertwined, on the table. "I suppose your chosen vocations are a testament of that," he gestured to the two of them. "Swindling rich widows out of their fortunes provides both research and pocket money to feed your silly stories."

"Makes for a well-rounded portfolio," Abram casually defended. "As does that cat-and-mouse profession of yours." He chortled. "No doubt you learn a great deal from chasing your imaginary villains."

"Imaginary?" Barratt squared his shoulders. "Villains are hardly imaginary. You read what they wrote on Jack the Ripper— fiction cannot possibly be as shocking as that."

Royce sipped his drink again, considering this. After a moment, he shook his head regretfully. "Hm, rampant killers aren't quite as much the novelty anymore."

"I disagree—else I'd be out of a job." Barratt was one of the more renowned detectives in the Criminal Investigation Department, which had been reorganized only twelve years previous. Having worked through the police strike earlier in that same decade, as well as avoiding scrutiny for the corruption found in multiple detectives of the time, Barratt maintained the trust of his superiors. In order to continue operating under the liberties and securities he currently held, Barratt was the overly-inquisitive sort. Where some saw coincidence and casual happenstance, he saw intent and malice.

"You should travel more," Royce would tell him, but this time with a light criticism. "Get a taste of the more foreign brands of villainy."

"Right," Barratt humored, sighing. "Where then, do you think?"

Royce shrugged. "I don't know. A change of scenery can do one some good. I'm sick of London."

"Lucky we've found your ticket out of it," Abram lifted his glass in applause.

Barratt leaned back in his chair curiously. "You're leaving London. What—did your last mark not prove lucrative?"

Examining his now empty glass, Royce chuckled. "Oh no, Mrs. Grayson was just fine. I've just found a....simpler option."

"I'm almost insulted you didn't consult me first."

"Your last two cases featured nothing but dock boys and bootblacks—too young and poor and no wives or daughters left behind. Besides, I've moved past rich widows."

"What is it now?" Barratt chuckled. "The young and impressionable."

The scheming writer grinned, eliciting just another disapproving sigh from his friend.

"What a deplorable way to make a living."

Royce leaned forward against the table and pointed emphatically. "Is it really any more deplorable than a mourning widow?"

"There are too many variables," Barratt considered. "At least widows are generally isolated from rivals and protective fathers….generally."

Abram took his feet down from the table, keenly listening in now as Barratt posed his argument.

"They're eager to support another man so they delay feeling that sting of losing the first one. The young and naive…" Barratt shook his head. "They're more likely to have a line of suitors ready to expose your materialistic intentions, merely out of aggression. And many of these ladies don't have the control over their fortunes to even give you what you truly want. What sort of scheme is this? It's nonsense — unless you plan to finally marry the dull woman for her pocketbook."

Instead of dignifying the accusation with a response, Royce simply scoffed and sat back into his chair.

"Please," Abram put in. "Where's the sport in that?"

"There is more than one way to strike gold," Royce claimed.

Doubtful, Barratt tidied his papers into their folder. "I take it your book sales are optimistic then?"

"Enough."

"Enough to give you the spare time to hone your *alternative* skills."

"There's no harm in staying in practice, my friend," Royce smiled and gestured for the barkeep to refill his glass.

Barratt looked from Royce to Abram and back to Royce. "And you chose her yourself this time. No help from me or that one?" He pointed airily at Abram. "I'm impressed. What's her name then, eh? Your *practice*." He lifted and sipped his own drink, awaiting the answer.

"Miss Penelope Ayres."

The liquor was nearly spat from his lips. "No, no, no," Barratt shook his head. "Don't be a fool, Royce. You do know her guardian?"

"Lady Selina," Royce shrugged confidently. "I met her earlier today."

"Yes, but do you know her? She's the lady of Everdon. Runs her own estate, inherited by the late Lord Delamere. She's improved her own income threefold since his death. Owns more of London than you can spit at. Her influence goes far beyond her own countryside community."

Royce laughed at Barratt's rebuke. "You don't need to sell me on the mark, Barratt. I'm already satisfied."

"She'll certainly make for an appealing obstacle," Abram contributed, fondly remembering how fine the lady looked early that day. "If you need any assistance in removing said obstacle, I am readily available."

"That's awfully ambitious of you," Royce sipped his newly refilled drink. "The woman would cut you down at the knees."

"Sometimes that's a better view," he lifted a suggestive brow.

Barratt grimaced at his friend's lewdness. "You know why she's in town, don't you?" The other men shook their heads. "She's seeking a new lady's maid; her previous maid was found dead a week ago…under mysterious circumstances."

"Hm," Abram grunted. "That explains why she left her ward's leash so dangerously loose. The lady's preoccupied."

"Miss Ayres is a simpleton, Royce, but don't let that comfort you. Lady Selina is shrewd," Barratt ominously sipped his ale again. "Her county constables are fools with very little training—they hardly gave her a second glance when she reported her maid being found dead in a stream. Suicide, she claimed."

"You think she murdered her maid," Royce assumed.

"I'm being sent to investigate, to aid in the training of the local constables, and I don't want you getting in my way."

Royce laughed again, lifting his palms to show how harmless he supposed himself to be. "No need to worry, I don't intend on meddling in your work—"

"Again."

"Hey," Royce paused his laughter for a moment. "That bank official's case brought me four months of stable income."

"And paid my tavern dues," Abram lifted his glass.

Royce lifted his own as well. "Cheers."

"There are no desperate widows in this investigation. I don't want you meddling with the Delameres—either of you," Barratt pointed to both of them.

Royce leaned back once more, ruminating. "She is the perfect mark….ward to one of the wealthiest women in England…."

The ruminating had the desired effect: creating a rise in the adamant detective.

"I'm warning you, my friend," Barratt said. "Don't go meddling just to win yourself a small fortune."

Royce scoffed. "Small fortune…"

To avoid encouraging any further misconduct, Barratt rose to leave. Royce and Abram did the same but tarried behind just long enough for Abram to grab Royce's arm and pull him closer. In a low and baleful tone, he said, "Don't you forget my share, boy."

The playful antagonist disappeared from Royce's expression. For a moment, the near decade's difference in age and experience between them loomed over him.

"This isn't another novel we're talking about—"

"No," Abram replied sharply. "But that's yet another treasure you owe me. Thank you for the reminder, lad. Perhaps this little excursion will happily make me forgive both debts. I've heard Everdon is a rather inspiring place."

4
The Princess, The Jester, & The Whole Blasted Kingdom

Far from the hustle and filth of the city, the world was so much brighter. With no more dark smoke and grime clouding the atmosphere, one can see the sun, and breathe in the healthy airs brought about by thriving trees and vegetation. The grounds of Everdon were luscious and well-kept. Several gardeners could be seen tending to the bushes and gardens as the carriage rode up the hill to the house.

Helen was speechless for the majority of the journey from London. For the last hour of it, however, Penelope's chattering relaxed Helen's dazed shock and before long, the two of them were gabbing and giggling like school children, filled with excitement for Everdon and the impending ball Penelope had insisted on hosting. In a matter of minutes, the two were fast friends.

While smiles and laughs abounded in the carriage, Selina's solemn contemplation went fairly unnoticed. Distractedly, she stared out the window, only contributing to the conversation to express relief that they had finally arrived.

Awaiting their carriage at the front of the grand manor was a Mr. Lindon, Everdon's land steward. He was a short man with greying hair and a long face. Beside him, nearly a head taller, stood the head housekeeper, Mrs. Melrose. Her dark round eyes, on an even rounder face, searched the driving path for signs of their carriage approaching. Both were aged and loyal servants, commiserating in their lady's absence. She was never gone from Everdon longer than necessary—it was the young Miss Ayres who preferred to stay in town. This particular trip had carried a heavy burden, which concerned both Mr. Lindon and Mrs. Melrose. The loss of a servant to something as tragic as death was never to be taken lightly.

Lady Selina was the first to exit the carriage, and as the two younger girls giggled their way out, Mr. Lindon looked to Selina with sympathy.

"How was your journey?" he asked with a light bow.

Selina's jaw tightened as she glared at him. He understood the expression; it was one to which he had become quite accustomed over the years Selina had been granted guardianship of Penelope.

"It was wonderful," Penelope spoke for her. "I met a friend in London and he's coming for Selina's birthday ball!"

"Birthday ball?" Mrs. Melrose exclaimed.

"*He*?" Lindon repeated softly.

Selina granted both of them a reassuring, yet regretful glance, to which Mrs. Melrose responded with a deep sigh of exasperation.

"How very exciting," Lindon encouraged, before Melrose could question.

"I think so," Penelope nodded with a grin. "Selina doesn't seem very excited, though."

"There's much to do, Nell," Selina brushed the comment aside and reached for Penelope's arm. "Get in the house. Lindon, do see that Miss Thomas is settled."

"Of course," he agreed. As Selina and Penelope disappeared beyond the estate doors, Lindon smiled amiably in Helen's direction. "Hello, Miss Thomas. Welcome to Everdon. I'm afraid your orientation will be a bit rushed—apparently there is a ball to prepare for."

"The princess gets what the princess requests," Melrose

muttered to herself.

"Now, now," Lindon chided. "Let's get Miss Thomas situated, Mrs. Melrose. Perhaps you can show her around before carrying on with preparations."

Mrs. Melrose sighed again, forcing a smile at Helen until it melted into one more genuine. "Of course. Come, dear. Bring your bags."

Fortunately for Helen, her luggage was as minimal as one would expect from one so young and indigent as she. With only a bag in either hand, Helen followed as Mrs. Melrose gave a cursory tour of the more essential rooms of Everdon. She waved an arm one way showcasing the parlor, waved another arm gesturing to the wing where the lady of the house resided, and casually mentioned the guest wing before briskly walking her to the servants' quarters. For a woman of Melrose's age, she moved with an impressive spryness.

"You'll not often linger in this wing, save it be for sleep." She allowed Helen to place her bags on the bed assigned to her in one of the maids' rooms. She was to share with one other maid.

"Lady Selina will need you to tend to her daily needs and routines," Mrs. Melrose explained. "Which should keep you plenty occupied. She's incredibly fair and understanding—I'm sure she'll inform you of the evenings you may be free to tend to your own business. She may even allow you to attend her on her social outings if you wish. She's not nearly as needy as her mother was."

"Oh?" Helen replied curiously.

"I was her lady's maid before Selina was born," Melrose beamed with pride, her hands joined in front of her in reverence. There was a hint of complaint blended with admiration in her tone. "Considerate as she was, that woman worked me to the bone before she passed. That was when Mr. Lindon appointed me head housekeeper. Of course, you're still young, so there's much work to be expected from you. You'll tend to Lady Selina in the morning, preparing her clothes and hair for the day, as well as helping her settle in the evening before bed—though her evenings can be rather unpredictable."

"How so?"

Mrs. Melrose paused. "It's better to expect routine rather than fall short, dear, so I expect you to be where you need to be every evening, understood?"

Clearing her throat, Helen couldn't quite tell if she had overstepped. "Of course, I understand."

With slight hesitation, Mrs. Melrose stepped closer to her. "You'll be working very closely with the lady of the house, Miss Thomas, which means…." her tone deepened in severity, "anything shared or shown to you is to be kept in the strictest of confidence. Not even the maid sharing your quarters is permitted to see inside the confidences of Lady Selina."

"Of course," Helen repeated.

Straightening once again, Mrs. Melrose cleared her throat and nodded. "Good. And you mustn't engage in the gossip of the staff. Best not to tempt yourself with the urge to expel secrets and privileged truths, you understand."

Helen nodded. "Yes, yes, I understand completely." She contemplated this for a moment as she stepped away from her luggage. "I beg your pardon though, missus," she ventured. "Is the Lady Selina not married?"

Mrs. Melrose narrowed her eyes, but softened, remembering the patience required with young hires. "She is not."

"Why is that?"

"We are approaching the turn of the century, Miss Thomas," Melrose offered. "A woman such as Lady Selina needn't explain herself. I myself never married, and there's no shame in that."

Helen frowned at her mistake. "But I thought Mr. Lindon called you—"

"No self-respecting housekeeper would give herself a title less than *Mrs.*, child," Melrose corrected. "I need no defense, and neither does your new mistress. She does very well for herself, I'll have you know." She wagged a finger at the girl. "An admirable philanthropist, a shrewd businesswoman, and a caring guardian to her young cousin."

Mrs. Melrose wiggled her shoulders a bit, regaining composure and considering all the reasons Lady Selina could never be faulted. "Besides, she hardly needs marriage," she went on. "Not the submissive sort. There's not a man in this county or the next who doesn't find her presence and fortune to be equal parts charming and intimidating."

"What happened to her previous lady's maid?"

Mrs. Melrose's distracted gaze snapped in Helen's direction. "My, that was quite the switch, young lady. No wonder Lady Selina hired you on—such a quick mind." Mournfully, the old woman sighed. "When the Lord claims your time is over, He calls you home, I suppose."

"She died then," Helen assumed.

"The poor thing will be missed." Melrose placed a hand on her heart, and then brushed it away. "But let's not dwell on the past, shall we? You'll be sharing this room with Moll, one of the scullery maids. Now, settle in quickly—there's a great deal of preparation you'll need to help with for Lady Selina's birthday ball."

Mrs. Melrose then left her alone to unpack a few of her belongings. The pace of the estate was certainly more stimulating than a dreary townhouse in Charing Cross. Not five minutes later, Helen's solitary settling was interrupted by heavy footsteps charging hastily into the room. The scullery maid who occupied the next bunk over was a curious looking woman, several years older than Helen. Her face was flat and her eyes piercing. Upon rushing into the room, her immediate gaze was skeptical, and then intrigued.

Helen stood quickly from the bed. "Hello, I'm Helen."

"You're the new one," the maid stated. "She's breakin' you in quick then, yeah?"

"Um," Helen shrugged. "I suppose so."

Moll moved past the beds to a small hope chest in the corner of her side of the room. Inside was a small brown bag, from which she pulled a single cinnamon stick. Feeling Helen's eyes on her, Moll stood up and offered her one. "Swiped 'em from the kitchen—want one?"

Helen shook her head kindly.

"Hm," Moll chewed on the end of the cinnamon stick. "She hasn't stopped barkin' orders since she walked through those doors."

"Mrs. Melrose?"

"Lady Selina," she replied in a mocking, high-pitched tone. "Queen's home, time to turn Everdon upside down for one night of fun, eh? Get used to that." Biting off the top half of the cinnamon stick, she turned to return the other half to its brown bag.

Now sensing Moll's candid nature, Helen pressed her inquisitively. "Do they have a lot of parties here?"

"Whenever Miss Ayres commands," Moll muttered. "I wonder sometimes who's running this place."

"Lady Selina seemed to have it well-controlled," Helen frowned.

Moll snorted, loudly and unabashed. "When the princess is in good spirits, yeah. She's a fool the rest of the time—more of a jester than a princess I'd say—so the queen takes her turn."

"Miss Ayres is a bit...childish, isn't she?"

Like a young school girl sharing secrets, Moll sat beside Helen and grinned, lowering her voice to a whisper. "She's a half-wit. But no more than the woman indulgin' her." She snorted again and sat up straighter, watching Helen's shocked expression with glee. "Where'd she find you?"

"I'm...." Helen hesitated, reconsidering her alliance with Moll. "I'm from London."

"Well, Helen from London," Moll launched herself from the bed to her feet. "I'm sorry your first day is nothing but settin' tables and movin' furniture. And I hope you don't get murdered as well." She tipped an imaginary hat toward Helen and bounded for the door.

"Murdered?!" Helen exclaimed. "That's how she—the last one was *murdered*?"

Moll turned quickly on her heel, scolding brows lifted. "Now, now, you didn't hear anythin' of the sort from me, little miss. I wouldn't dare spread rumors like that. Things of that sort don't happen more than once...unless a place is cursed...which I also wouldn't dare spreadin'."

5

A Rather Unfortunate Incident

The county over which the grandeur of Everdon loomed was foolishly believed to be filled with country bumpkins. On the contrary, this particular county was primarily occupied with the tenants and households of many retired businessmen, young gentlemen settling into their inherited estates, and many Londoners who had decided to seek the quiet atmospheres of the countryside. All of the inhabitants of higher social standing, therefore, longed for the sort of parties and assemblies which had treated them so well in the big city.

Everdon hosted some of the most sought after celebrations — even by those still in London. Lord Delamere's political and social reputation made an invitation to Everdon most enviable. Even the parties thrown on impulse were beloved and captivating. One could always tell in whose honor the party was hosted: while Penelope preferred all things in extravagance, Selina was simple, yet elegant.

Lady Selina's birthday ball was just so. The decorations of the foyer, the banquet hall, and the ballroom were all minimal. The menu for the refreshment room that evening was tasteful and understated. The cook was highly praised, as was, of course, Lady Selina herself. She humbly accepted the accolades, graciously bowing her head and granting her admirers a smile or two.

As Everdon's guests funneled in from their carriages, the lowly maids admired from the outskirts. Moll scoffed while Helen awed at the fine colors and elegant movements of the ladies, as well as the nobility and grandeur of the gentlemen.

"Look at these gowns and jewels," Helen breathed. "And how they bow—I wish I was so elegant as Lady Selina. Look at her; so lovely and regal. Like the queen herself."

Moll rolled her eyes. "Yeah, there they all go, lickin' her boots. Like always." Those vexed eyes were briefly captured by the newest face in the room: Mr. Darius Royce from London. "Hm, never seen him before."

Royce bowed to the ladies of Everdon, smoothly kissing the hand of the giggly Miss Ayres, eliciting a slight grimace from the Lady Selina. Lady Selina was raised to hold her head and manners high, no matter the inconvenience—though, her good breeding and proper education often did nothing to offset her rather forthright nature. She saw no need to grant Mr. Royce more than a tight nod when he leaned to kiss her hand as well.

Intrigued by the obstacle she was determined to become, Royce smiled and offered Miss Ayres his arm into the ballroom, keeping a curious eye on Lady Selina as he did so.

"He must be the writer Miss Ayres met in London," Helen whispered to Moll. "Lady Selina doesn't seem to like him much."

Moll scoffed again; apparently it was one of her most favored responses. "Just like all the rest," she spat, seeing his eyes linger. "Ogles the lady of the house, then moves on to easier catches. Not the spine for the bigger challenge then, eh?" She playfully nudged Helen's side, flicking her chin at the general male population of the ballroom. "She sits so high in her ivory tower, no man survives the climb."

Helen chuckled, now noting how few of the men even looked Lady Selina in the eye. From behind her, however, she heard a curt clearing of a throat.

"You'll not be gossiping tonight, ladies," Mrs. Melrose scolded, circling them. "Back to your work. Go on, now."

Moll wrinkled her face in a mocking expression, wagging her finger at Helen as Mrs. Melrose walked away. Giggling again, the girls did as they were told and moved to see to their duties.

Across the ballroom, Penelope was sure to drag Royce to meet each and every one of her acquaintances. Patiently, he nodded and greeted and humored her fancies. He held a certain celebrity in some circles, and Penelope was sure to exploit the attention.

"This is Miss Henrietta Sweeting," she pulled him toward a sweet-faced girl about her age. Much like Penelope, Henrietta's eyes were wide and eager.

"It's an honor, Miss Sweeting," Royce bowed politely.

Giggles erupted from both girls as Henrietta blushed. "I'm a fan of your work, Mr. Royce," she said quickly. "You tell such excellent stories. You must tell us one during your stay at Everdon!"

"I—"

"Of course he will," Penelope cut in. "Selina says he may stay the fortnight. Oh—Mary!"

She frantically pointed at a passing dark-haired young lady, who seemed more determined to find a dancing partner than tolerate conversation with Penelope. However, one look at Royce's grin and she was suddenly inclined to stay.

"Royce, this is Miss Mary Kingston. Her late father owned the largest mine in the county."

"Is that right?" Royce's eyebrows lifted. "The pleasure is mine," he kissed her hand, maintaining her charmed gaze. "There must be something in the air here. I don't think London has half as many bewitching ladies."

To reduce young ladies of a certain age into simpering wreckage was never a difficult feat. In fact, within approximately fifteen minutes, Mr. Royce had given flattering attention to several of the party's more impressionable young ladies, all while Penelope was distracted by her dear friend, Henrietta.

In her usual corner of the ballroom, overlooking the peasants, as it were, Lady Selina fixated on Mr. Royce like a hawk to her prey. She watched him move slyly from one eligible lady to another. Little did poor Penelope realize, she was quickly among the least appealing prospects in the room. Selina's apprehension was eased slightly by Penelope's ignorance, and yet the anticipation of the girl coming to her senses brought tension to Selina's shoulders.

True to form, Mr. Royce's fickle gaze journeyed far and wide, but ultimately rested on the most appealing mark. As the arriving guests settled and Lady Selina's usual circle began to form around her, the prey surreptitiously became the hawk. Royce took note of the uneven ratio of Lady Selina's closest friends.

One lady and three gentlemen.

The lady seemed the delicate type; she stood tall and dignified, yet she glanced at Selina for confirmation after nearly every sentence she spoke. The two smiled in commiseration several times, but their interaction wasn't nearly as fascinating to Royce as the gentlemen. Each of them hung on Lady Selina's every word, but there was only one who captured her full and unyielding attention. Tall, broad-shouldered, well-spoken, aristocratic features, curly dark hair and an amiable grin—but most impressively: he looked her in the eye when they spoke.

"He recommended his friend's housemaid," she said to him. Her body was angled in his direction, excusing the other three in their grouping to converse amongst themselves, which they did with little prompting. It was clear this was routine—comfort in proximity, but with the understanding that there was one she favored above the others. "I must say," she went on, "I was impressed. I hired her on."

A servant passed and offered the two of them drinks, which they both accepted. Selina handed the maid her previously emptied glass and returned her attention to its rightful place: Sir Henry Kincaid of Millhampton.

He downed the drink and sighed. "Did he say anything else when you called?"

"He sends his best," Selina shrugged.

"And Aunt Miranda?"

Selina gave him a wary glance with a peculiar smirk. "Getting brown as a nut with her new lover in Spain."

36

Sir Henry's mouth tightened. Selina lightly touched his arm and sipped her drink.

"I suggested he tell people she passed," she offered. He only lifted a scolding brow, suppressing any chuckle that might've escaped.

"Be kind, Selina."

The lady chuckled. "Oh, be clever, Henry. You know you're simply boiling." She knew her dear friend's temper well; his rigid shoulders struggled to ease.

"It'll do no good surfacing, I can assure you." Desperate to deflect Selina's focus from the rage his family provoked, Henry glanced around until he caught sight of Everdon's newest guest. "I see a lady's maid isn't the only thing you brought back," he nodded in Royce's direction.

Taking a sip longer than was considered delicate, Selina released a deep grunt. "Well, I can hardly be blamed when a tramp follows Penelope home." Henry frowned. "She has a tendency to attract strays," she explained. "Don't worry yourself; it's being handled."

Her reassurance did nothing for Henry's furrowed brow. As susceptible as Selina's ward was, his concern did not lie with Penelope's welfare. "How long is he staying?"

Selina lifted her chin. "If I have my way, not long."

"And you always have your way," Henry chuckled, leaning against her.

"Hm," Selina smiled in return. "You know me better than that, Henry."

Their closeness suggested an intimacy that contradicted the popular claims of the Lady being unattainable. When their eyes returned to one another, Royce safely resumed his distant study. Though her arm wound around his and their eyes frequently locked, when the music changed, she was not the recipient of his invitation to dance. That pleasure went to the only other woman in their ivory corner: Miss Sophie Campbell.

Lady Selina's eyes followed the two of them to the dance floor, but she remained in place, never to abandon her aeries. Curious rogue he was, Royce moved once more toward Penelope.

"Does Lady Selina dance?" he asked her.

"Oh! There you are." She had been looking for her desirable trophy, hoping he would ask for a dance. "What was that?" she wrinkled her nose in confusion.

"Lady Selina," he repeated. "Does she ever dance? I imagine she should have no shortage of partners to choose from."

Penelope turned her head vaguely in Selina's direction and sighed. "No, Selina never dances. She does love the waltz," she shrugged. "But I think that's because it's the only one she knows. An Austrian prince taught it to her once," Penelope's voice dropped to a whisper, only slightly above the roar of the other guests. "I don't think she ever bothered learning another. Her father berated her for it, too— but she said it only added to her allure...you know, being so above everyone in the ballroom."

A small smile of admiration crossed Royce's lips. The more he learned of Selina and her impermeable nature, the more fascinated he found himself. "Certainly effective," he agreed.

Thankfully for Royce's intentions and Penelope's feelings, the younger of Lady Selina's closer friends—a young man named Mr. Andrew Lennox—approached Penelope and requested her hand in the next dance. Royce took the opportunity to slip away and move toward her unwinnable guardian.

"Would you honor me with a dance, Lady Selina?" he posed, even bowing respectfully.

"I don't dance, Mr. Royce," was her response. She granted him hardly more than a glance of rejection as she looked for Penelope's bobbing head in the crowd. "Perhaps you'll find your partner in another corner of the room."

Royce accepted the hurdle, but not defeat. "An overzealous nature is often unappealing to prospective partners," he explained, casually positioning himself in the empty space Sir Henry had left behind.

"Then I suggest you stop winking at the giggles and blushes of every silly girl in the ballroom," she cited. Selina glanced at him from the corner of her eyes and found him once again scanning the crowd before him, presumably spotting eligible targets he had yet to meet. Selina settled her shoulders and sipped from the glass in her dainty hand. "The secret to your sudden success is not one with which I am unfamiliar, Mr. Royce."

"Yes," he nodded in agreement. "I understand you've had quite a hand in the funding of publishing houses."

"As you've had quite a hand in the pocketbooks of wealthy, gullible women," she added, with vague indifference.

His eyes narrowed as his smirk deepened. The dance had begun. "I don't know what you mean."

"Hardly," she exhaled, noticing how empty her glass had become. "There's no denying your experience. It took less than three days to hone in on the greatest assumed target to play patron to your silly stories."

"Assumed?"

She hailed the nearest servant and swapped the disappointing glass for one brimming with a fresh helping of spirits. "With words at the ready, you've hunted many a prey, no doubt," she aimed at him after taking another sip. "Women melt when wooed by an artist of any sort. And I'm sure being so naturally attractive and beguiling lends some advantage to your game of seduction. Must be such a chore to be so cursed."

His smile widened at the praise but twisted at her word usage. "Hm, seduction," he hummed. "Sounds so…shortsighted and filthy. It's not about the seduction, it's about—"

"The money, I know," she finished. "Men of your sort are more common than you may believe. Money or beauty," she gestured offhandedly. "Whichever the woman can manage to maintain your interest."

Royce conceded, getting himself a drink before the servant became out of reach. "Some manage both," he suggested.

"Unfortunately for you, some also manage to outwit—but perhaps not brutally enough to leave you without options."

Not quite grasping her meaning, Royce attempted to follow her gaze as it skirted around the room. Her lips pursed in contemplation as if she was creating a mental list of all those in her sight.

"You won't be doing your womanly duty of turning the scoundrel away from your fellow ladies?" he said slowly, beginning to understand her.

Selina frowned and shook her head. "Oh no," she said. "I care very little about the fortunes of the other eligible women in the room. Keen social parasite that you are, you will go on selecting victims with or without my allowance, so you may as well do it right. In fact, I'll even grant you some exclusive insights."

With her free hand ready to direct Royce in any alternate direction she could muster, she leaned closer to her fellow hawk. Equal parts amused and bemused, Royce responded in kind, leaning in for a valuable education.

"Misses Burton and Halifax are both set to inherit rather sizable fortunes from their fathers' various business successes. Miss Bartlett is the daughter of a baronet, though she seems generally uninterested as of late, and could prove to be more of a challenge than she's worth. Young Miss Sweeting would take too long to even notice your attention—though her late father did leave her with an enviable sum that may prove worthy compensation for the wait."

"And Miss Campbell?" he pointed to Sir Henry's dancing partner.

Selina paused a moment. "If you can pry her from her current suitor, she would be an advantageous mark. But, I'll warn you, Sir Henry is not the man to challenge. No word has been given or made public, but I suspect their union will soon make your game much more grueling than you intend. You'd best set your aim elsewhere. Like Miss Kingston, over there," she gestured.

Noting her deflection, Royce humored her and glanced in

Miss Kingston's direction. "Hm," was all he said.

"Although," Selina paused again, bringing her gesturing hand to her face, re-evaluating. "She would be such easy prey, I'm bored at the very thought of you wasting your energy with such little reward. Though what she lacks in actual wealth, she makes up for in beauty and believed charm."

Royce snickered softly.

"So you see, Mr. Royce, there are many options in the higher society of this county—enough to keep you employed beyond your publishers for years to come. And with a face like yours, and your notorious ability to set a woman in any romantic fantasy she chooses, the other gentlemen are without doubt quaking in their boots." Good-naturedly, she held up her glass to clink his.

"Well, it seems I've struck gold," he sipped.

Selina's contentment in their unspoken arrangement only lasted a moment before Penelope's loud laughter and chatter brought her back to her duties as guardian. "But I must warn you," she started, in an even tone. "Miss Ayres may be naively smitten with your charm for the moment, Mr. Royce, but her wits will inevitably return before you can count her amongst your conquests." Her shoulders squared toward him, forcing his eyes on her and her alone. "Even so, I trust you'll remain an arm's length from her. Otherwise, we would not have such kind words for one another. Take caution—unlike yours, my words can cause irreparable damage."

Without an ounce of fear in his expression, but with a respectful concession to the end of their exchange, Royce maintained his grin. He even lightly chuckled as her intimidating glare bore into him. "Miss Ayres was wrong, Lady Selina." He set his empty glass on the nearest servant's tray. "You do still dance."

"I beg your pardon."

"We've just engaged in a waltz of the mind," he said smoothly. "You simply prefer to lead."

Before Royce could leave Selina in surprised silence, they were interrupted by Mrs. Melrose rushing to Selina's side.

"My lady," she panted. Selina urged her to catch her breath before continuing, but Mrs. Melrose didn't feel there was time for such dawdling. "Mr. Lindon needs you in the library. He's detained a guest." Her breathy voice became a tense whisper. "An inspector from London who wishes to speak with you."

"Inspector?" Royce repeated, not entirely surprised. It seemed his friend had caught up with him. "How interesting."

Selina tightened her eyes in suspicion. "If you'll excuse me, Mr. Royce. It seems I have a rather pressing matter. Do take my insights under advisement."

❧   ❧   ❧   ❧

The Everdon library was among the more infamous rooms in the manor. Lord Delamere was a proud scholar of sorts and insisted on his daughter and ward becoming well-educated and well-read. Lady Selina saw to the upkeep and expansion of her father's collection, lining every inch of wall with shelves. Mr. Croft oversaw their organization and maintenance for decades during his time at Everdon. He was the jolly sort with a fine suit and toothy grin. All who entered his library were offered what he saw as the most ideal story. Every individual has a tale best suited for them, and he prided himself in instinctively knowing just what those stories were.

When Mr. Lindon brought Inspector Barratt to await Lady Selina in the library, Mr. Croft immediately sought out the inspector's story. Mr. Lindon waved him off initially, giving him more time to comb his shelves.

Mr. Lindon and the inspector rose from the armchairs when Lady Selina entered with Mrs. Melrose.

"Who do we have here?" Selina asked half-heartedly.

"This is Inspector Barratt," Mr. Lindon introduced. "He's come with a few questions."

Barratt moved to bow. "Lady Selina, it's a pleasure."

"Inspector," she greeted. "What can I do for you? You do

understand I'm hosting a party at the moment."

"Of course, my lady. I apologize for any inconvenience," he placated. "I'm in town at the request of the county constables to confirm a recent, and rather unfortunate, incident."

Lindon stepped behind Selina to signal for Mrs. Melrose to leave the room. Sensing Lindon's sudden agitation, Selina sighed and took a seat.

"What sort of incident?"

Putting on his most diplomatic smile, Barratt explained, "I'm merely here to confirm the death of Josephine Rodin was indeed a suicide."

In contrast to Mr. Lindon's defensive stance and Mr. Croft's uncomfortable shift in posture, Lady Selina merely expressed slight irritation. However, as inconvenienced as she seemed, there was a cryptic shield put on by her apparent disregard that prompted Barratt's interest.

"Are there not enough savage killers running amuck in the streets of London, Inspector?" she posed. "The poor girl took her own life. Tragic, but not everything is nefarious as those penny dreadful novels make us all believe."

Barratt cleared his throat, taking a small notepad from his jacket pocket. "Yes, well, given that the girl was also with child, the constable thought it best to receive another set of eyes. I'd like to stop any potential speculation in the area, considering its history."

"History?" Lindon questioned.

Selina breathed, "With child." Her tone was riddled with dreaded confirmation rather than shock.

"I understand a dead, pregnant maid on Everdon property has become more commonplace than anyone would prefer," Barratt glanced sideways at Lindon, who only stiffened. "I only wish to confirm the facts, my lady, and eliminate hearsay."

Selina straightened her back. "Did the child survive?" she asked.

"No. I'm afraid it did not."

Selina's eyes closed slowly. Her disregard melted and gave her pause for just a moment. Before she recomposed, Lindon stepped in and gestured for Barratt to rise once again from his armchair.

"Not tonight, Inspector," Lindon insisted. "Nor tomorrow. This is a weekend of celebration, you understand." When Barratt stood, Lindon nudged Selina's arm, lightly lifting her from her chair. "If you have questions for Lady Selina, they may be posed on Monday. She has a party to return to."

Smothering his frustration, Barratt sighed. "Of course, sir. I can certainly wait," he reluctantly tucked the notepad back into his coat pocket. One must properly discern when to poke and when to prod the wealthy and powerful. "I apologize for any indelicacy — I only wish for the situation to be dealt with sooner rather than later."

Selina put a staying hand on Lindon's arm, silently arguing with him in a single glance. "Please join us, Inspector. We have plenty of drinks and pastries to go around."

"Oh no," he shook his head. "I wouldn't want to impose. I shall return on Monday, as instructed." He bowed politely to the lady and nodded to Lindon as he ushered Selina back to the ballroom.

Mr. Croft, who had been anxiously awaiting his moment, book in hand, saw Inspector Barratt's brief awkwardness as his chance. Eagerly, he approached the inspector and offered to escort him to the door, in his own way. "There's a promising young writer in London," he began, "Lady Selina brought back some of his work from her last trip, if you're interested." He offered the book he held in his hand. "They're fast reads, and they may well suit you. Brilliant detective, facing off against a mysteriously worthy opponent. I must say, I was quite impressed. I think this Doyle fellow shows promise."

"Thank you," Barratt graciously declined, "but I hardly need the inspiration."

"Oh, yes, yes, of course," Croft stumbled. He retracted the book and held tightly to the binding as he apologized. "I didn't mean to be presumptuous, sir."

"It's quite all right," the inspector lazily excused, his eyes still on the doorway through which Lady Selina exited.

Mr. Croft, however, continued to babble, despite Barratt's disinterest. "Lady Selina claims I always know the story she wants to read before she even steps foot in the library—calls me a bit of a matchmaker," he added with a chuckle, in spite of himself.

Barratt sighed and turned politely to the older gentleman. "Have you worked for her long?"

"Years, sir," Croft replied fondly. "I worked for her father since we served together in the war."

"Is she an odd mistress?"

The librarian frowned. "Odd, sir?"

"Her habits...her...temperament...?" Barratt baited, hopeful that something could be gleaned from the otherwise useless conversation.

Croft heightened his posture proudly. "She's the finest lady to have dwelt in Everdon. She's quite wise for her age, you know, and has done wonders for the estate's economy."

"Has she ever had problems with her staff?"

"I...I don't know if I should answer that just yet." Croft tucked the book under his arm and placed his hands in his pockets. "Mr. Lindon prefers these sorts of questions to wait for after the weekend. But...I'm sure when you do proceed with interviews, you'll find she's well-loved amongst her employees."

It seemed to the inspector that Everdon would be a much more difficult riddle to unravel. Whether sealed by loyalty or fear, the lips of those surrounding the late Miss Rodin were tightly shut. "Of course, thank you, Mr. Croft," Barratt reasonably bowed before departing.

"Naturally, thank you, Inspector," Croft guided him to the door. "I'm sure we'll see more of each other as your investigation continues. And please, let me know if you change your mind about the detective stories. I'll keep them out for you."

March 1889

April 1889

There is not a crime...there is not a swindle, there is not a vice which does not
live by secrecy
~Joseph Pulitzer~

1

Don't Scare the Horses

The passing of the weekend did little to improve the hospitality Inspector Barratt could expect to feel at Everdon. It was understandable, of course; whatever happened to poor Josephine Rodin, reputations were always at stake. Barratt never understood how the other half lived. They were reserved and guarded, and yet lavish and excessive. Their staff were commonly tight-lipped toward strangers but consumed with gossip amongst their own masses.

The reticent butler welcomed the anticipated inspector once again through the doors of Everdon and left him in the foyer while he fetched Mr. Lindon. As Barratt rather impatiently tapped his fingers against one another in anticipation, the young Miss Thomas passed him from the direction of the kitchen, carrying a tray of piping hot tea.

"You must be Lady Selina's new lady's maid," he spoke, startling the poor girl and nearly causing her to drop the tray.

Helen recovered quickly, steadying herself against the bottom railing of the staircase. Eyes wide, as usual, she suddenly realized his presence. She was uncertain whether she was permitted to greet a stranger in Lady Selina's house, but decided it had to be considered rude to simply ignore him.

"Um, yes, sir," she bumbled. "And, um, who might you be, sir?"

Inspector Barratt smiled. Before he could reply with a pithy inquiry, as he does, Mr. Lindon swiftly came to the bottom of the stairs to rescue the maid from an intrusive line of questioning.

"Lady Selina doesn't like cold tea, Miss Thomas," Lindon prodded. "You'd better hurry along."

Resisting the urge to correct him on the current temperature of the lady's tea, Helen remembered her duties and sighed, nodding compliantly. "Oh yes, of course, sir."

Helen soon scurried out of earshot, prompting Lindon to direct his forthright tone to the visitor instead. As the land steward of Everdon, as well as a close colleague of the late Lord Delamere, Lindon was the dragon who guarded the castle. His scales had an initial appearance of docility about them, like that of a garden snake perhaps, but the moment an intruder such as this graced the castle's halls, his fiery breath proved to be the first line of defense.

"All questions will be directed to me, Inspector Barratt," clarified the steward.

Barratt nodded respectfully. "Of course. I'm sure you will well represent Everdon, Mr. Lindon." Prepared to barter with the dragon, Barratt took out his small notebook and followed Lindon into the parlor for their interview. "You've been with the Delamere family for years, I understand."

"I have," Lindon sat, gesturing Barratt to the chair opposite him. "I was Lord Delamere's oldest friend, and I've been the steward of Everdon since before Lady Selina was born."

Almost on cue, Lady Selina descended from the staircase, finishing the last sips of tea and handing the ensuing Helen the empty cup. When she reached the foyer and caught a glimpse of Lindon and the inspector convening in the parlor, she started toward them. Dismissively, however, Lindon shot her a knowing glance and subtly waved her away, to which she responded with a pause, a slight nod, and then submission. She redirected to the hallway leading to the garden instead, with Helen close on her heels, still balancing the tea tray.

"They are to prepare for a garden party at Lord Rafferty's,"

Lindon explained, excusing any apparent rudeness.

Barratt smirked. "You seem to play a unique role in this household, Mr. Lindon."

"As I said," Lindon turned back to him, "I am the steward."

"Yes, which lends you a broad perspective on the staff in your care, does it not?" Barratt offered. Lindon waited for the remainder of his assumptions before reacting in even the slightest sense. "Past and present, I'm sure, as you've been here for so many years. You've no doubt noticed the similarities between this recent incident and—"

Lindon straightened his shoulders slightly, with a strong air of steadiness about him. "Josephine Rodin was barely four and twenty years old. She started at Everdon as a chambermaid, but Lady Selina quickly promoted her to lady's maid the moment Lord Delamere passed and made his daughter the head of the estate."

Barratt cocked his head to one side and focused his gaze. "Very direct, yet guarded," he said. "You've studied law, Mr. Lindon."

Unmoved by the observation, Lindon's expression remained tight and bland. "I've been a valuable asset to the Delameres in a number of ways over the years, Inspector. This is not the first instance a wealthy family has been confronted with the potential for scandalous scrutiny. I find the facts speak for themselves."

Barratt hummed for a moment, adjusting the grip on his pencil. "In regard to those facts," he pointed, "were Josephine and Lady Selina close?"

"As close as one could expect," Lindon considered.

"She's a complicated woman, Lady Selina," the inspector paused before taking note. "I imagine it's quite the challenge to get close to a woman like that."

Lindon's eyebrow lifted. "Lady Selina was made lady of the house, and inherited guardianship of her cousin, all on her twenty-first birthday. And that was only as far as the paperwork was concerned. Her father passed away when she was eighteen, leaving her three years to learn the various facets of running an estate before she was legally permitted to do so."

Moll quietly moved into the room to set down a tray of tea for the gentlemen before tending to the flowers above the mantle of the fireplace. Lindon reached for a cup, poured some tea for the two of them, and then settled back into his defensive posture.

"The sorts of pressures on any man in that position would be uncomfortable," he continued, sipping from his cup. "I can only imagine the sort of pressure that has been placed on the shoulders of that young woman. Any friendships she maintains would be a luxury, and one she was never expected to gain in her position."

Instead of accepting the tea, Barratt leaned back into the armchair and put his pencil thoughtfully to his lips. "It is rather odd," he mused. "Lady Selina rules her estate as an unmarried spinster. No brothers, cousins, uncles to have inherited it…and no husband forced upon her."

"Spinster, hardly," Lindon cleared his throat.

"The social implications no doubt affect the closeness of her friendships, as well, I'm sure."

"If there be a man who manages to climb to her heights and would also succeed in wooing a woman as unimpressed as Lady Selina, society would be far more disrupted than they currently are with her solitude, I can assure you. The select friendships she has chosen have not suffered."

"Has she ever sought a domestic life?"

"I fail to see, sir, how this pertains to Miss Rodin's death." Lindon set his cup on the table between them and rose from his chair. "I assume that indicates the end of this interview, Inspector."

Barratt glanced at Moll and then rose to follow the steward out of the room. Lindon was no fool. He led him to the door, but not to dismiss him. Instead, they began pacing the garden, which was now emptied of all staff and residents.

"I only ask," Barratt continued as they left the scullery maid's earshot, "because, when I mentioned Miss Rodin's unborn child the other day, Lady Selina seemed…affected."

With renewed privacy, Lindon seemed to settle into a more

forthcoming position. "There's a rather large place in her heart for children," he willingly explained. "There always has been. She never hesitated to care for Miss Ayres, and she donates considerable funds to the local orphanage. Yet, she never seemed particularly motivated to have a family of her own. She's..." he paused, "content."

"Do you have any idea who the father of Miss Rodin's child may have been?" Barratt pulled back to the case, causing Lindon's shoulders to ease.

"I knew only of her professional life, Inspector," Lindon claimed. "I never care to know what my employees do outside the walls of Everdon. Do what you want in private, I say," he chuckled lightly, "Just don't scare the horses."

"But Lady Selina knew," Barratt fired.

Lindon slowed his pace, those defensive scales tightening again. Rarely did Lindon feel the need to breathe fire, but the inspector continued to flirt with the threshold of defensive versus offensive. Sensible man that he was, Lindon inhaled steadily and continued in his original pace. "No one can be certain of that, can we?" he answered simply.

"Women rarely keep secrets like that from one another."

"Inspector Barratt, I understand you've been particularly trained to investigate matters such as these, but might I offer some advice?" Lindon stopped walking and turned to face him.

Barratt closed the small notebook and narrowed his eyes.

"Sometimes things are exactly as simple as they seem." He paused to be clear Barratt had heard him. "Sometimes a depressed young lady who finds herself in trouble—whether brought about by her own actions or misfortunes falling upon her..." he paused again, but this time with heaviness, "...sometimes she feels inclined to regrettably end her life. Devastating as it is, it's often as simple as that."

Barratt's lip curled. The explanation was not nearly satisfying enough. "Ah, but taking one's life is rarely simple. There are always secrets lying underneath the surface."

Lindon's tight smile almost curled as much as Barratt's, and yet his reply remained resolute. "You are an inspector of crimes. The poor girl is deceased, therefore impossible to prosecute. Her alleged success is no longer a crime."

Barratt pointed his pencil. "And murder is not the only sin a man can commit."

"I cannot disagree with you there," Lindon conceded, even chuckling lightly, but without much humor.

The garden path had reached the road leading away from the manor. Lindon may have granted Barratt an extension of the interview while they strolled, but the silent end was now apparent. Before yielding, Barratt tucked his notebook in his jacket pocket and lifted his chin; there was more to be learned before he was ready to be dismissed.

"How long, did you say, you've worked for the Delamere family?"

"A little over thirty years."

"And you yourself never married either," Barratt asserted.

That humorless chuckle returned as Lindon's eyes wandered to the Everdon grounds. "Some are only meant to meet the love of their life once in their life....and I was never fortunate enough to marry mine."

Barratt noted this but didn't dare draw attention by pulling his notebook once again from his jacket. "This...this garden party at Lord Rafferty's. Would you mind introducing me to a few of Lady Selina's acquaintances there?"

The sigh that escaped Lindon gave the impression of annoyance, which Barratt scarcely minded. "I hardly expect any of them to be the father of Miss Rodin's child."

Barratt raised his palms reassuringly. "I will be gracious and tasteful in my questioning, of course. I only mean to resolve that remaining mystery before I rule this tragedy a suicide."

"I fail to see how it's integral to the conclusion of her death."

"As I said, taking one's life is rarely simple. Consider it a formality to avoid any potential noble reputations being unnecessarily tarnished. No need to ruin a man's marriage and good standing by accusing him of impregnating and murdering a young girl."

"Lady Selina's inner circle is filled with respectable ladies and gentlemen," Lindon assured him. "Many are single or widowed, and hardly interacted with Miss Rodin." He sighed once more. "But if you wish, you may accompany our party to Lord Rafferty's."

Grinning, Barratt offered his hand. "Thank you for your time, Mr. Lindon." Lindon shook it politely and returned to the house, leaving Barratt to see to his own exit.

Not far from where the two men bid their farewells, Royce sat on a garden bench, scribbling in his own notebook while awaiting the primping and preparations of the ladies of the house to be finished so they could attend Rafferty's garden party.

"Your line of inquiry could use some work," Royce commented in Barratt's direction, without taking so much as a glance away from his scribbles.

"I know how to do my job," Barratt shot back.

Some distance from them, Helen gathered fresh flowers for Lady Selina's bedroom. Trying as she might to remain removed and proper, she couldn't help but notice the familiarity in the men's tones toward one another. Royce, for example, merely shrugged at Barratt's response.

"What did he tell you about the father of the maid's baby?" he asked.

Helen abandoned her picking and listened carefully.

Walking toward Royce, Barratt tsked, "It's an active investigation."

"So he didn't know," Royce concluded. "But Selina does." He lifted his eyes from his notebook and returned with a smirk of his own.

Barratt stared at him for a moment, deliberating his words. "Shouldn't you be tending to your mark?"

"She's helping Miss Ayres pick a hairpiece to wear for the garden party," Royce waved casually.

Barratt's eyebrows shot to the top of his head and he released a shocked chuckle. "Feeling overly ambitious, are we?" he laughed. "I must say, I was disappointed you started with such a simple target, but Lady Selina might be reaching just a bit too far."

Royce slyly grinned as he stood to meet Barratt's eye line. "Be gentle," was all he said.

"Pardon?"

"Your interviews will get you nowhere if you accuse the most beloved members of this county's society of murdering their maids or having affairs. Trust me," he patted his friend's arm. "Be gentle. Lull them. With the right touch...they'll melt in your hands."

Through the corner of his eye, Royce could see the gawking gaze of Selina's lady's maid. She hadn't heard much, but she felt if she could have a better view, perhaps she would gain a more accurate perspective. She was mistaken. Her better view simply put her directly in Royce's line of sight. The eye contact startled her, so much so that the small shears in her hand slipped and sliced the side of her palm.

Hearing her yelp, Barratt snapped his head in her direction. "Oh, dear."

Royce and Barratt moved to help her, Barratt advancing quickly and retrieving a handkerchief from his pocket. The poor girl's palm bled as the color drained from her face.

"I'm sure Lady Selina cares for blood-stained flowers as much as she does cold tea, Miss Thomas," Barratt chuckled, carefully wrapping her hand in his handkerchief.

Helen mirrored his chuckle but in the more nervous variety. "I'm sure she does. I'm sorry, I was just...." She desperately looked away from the blood on her hand, resting her eyes instead on Mr. Royce. "What were you scribbling there?"

"Oh," Royce held up his notebook. "A story."

"What sort of story?" she pried.

Royce shrugged. "Hm, probably the unlikely-hero-who-finds-true-love-in-the-end sort."

She smiled at him, paying no mind to the detective tending to her wound. "That's my favorite. I do love your stories, Mr. Royce, if you don't mind my saying so." With little encouragement from both gentlemen, Helen's cadence quickened to her natural excitable pace. "I used my first wage in London to purchase one of your books — I read it to my brothers and sisters, as well. I've always wanted to create something like that. Oh — " her eyes jolted to Barratt before returning to Royce. "I'm sorry, I've forgotten my place...."

Rather than agreeing to her sudden awareness, Royce leaned forward slightly. "Well, why don't you?"

"Why don't I...?" she frowned.

"Create something like that."

Her previous shame melted away, lending a new beam in her eyes. "Lady Selina told me to as well. Perhaps I should." She looked to Barratt, who had finished wrapping her hand, as if to ask his own opinion.

"Lady Selina is always right," Royce confirmed.

Barratt rolled his eyes but softened to a smile when he noticed Helen's eager expression. "Your natural ability to notice things that inspire you would be such an asset, Miss Thomas, you'd likely out-sell Royce within a month of publication." He shot Royce a quiet snicker.

Helen smiled widely. "You really think so?"

"Of course," Barratt kindly lifted her back to her feet. "With the stories surrounding you, and the abundance of resources at your disposal here, you just might surpass us all. A fly on the wall can prove to be the most valuable player in any tale."

2
Tantrums & Daffodils

Of the more affluent venues in the county, the home of Lord Colin Rafferty would have been rated one of the most impressive. The Rafferty family had utilized the family fortune much in the same way the Delameres had—purchasing neighboring properties and investing in the ventures of the local businessmen. Colin Rafferty did very well for himself. He married a respectable young lady shortly after inheriting his estate and together they raised three lively children. While Lady Rafferty was alive, she took great pride in the estate landscape and permitted every opportunity to put it on display.

In her honor, her widower continued the tradition. Garden parties were a staple in the county's society. As soon as the sunshine would permit, Lord Rafferty invited the usual gathering of guests, paying particular attention to those eligible to become a potential second mother for his young children.

His favorite candidate attracted a wide array of fans from the moment she exited her carriage, but as the host of the event, Rafferty was given preference. His place beside Lady Selina was guaranteed. The small crowd parted for him so he could welcome his honored guest, while Penelope dragged her own guest to her gaggle of friends convening toward the nearby stream.

The picnic was set up in a lovely clearing on Rafferty's land with chairs and tables and as many sweets and cups of tea as the party fancied. Calmed and directed by Rafferty's signal, the party migrated from the carriages to the clearing, ready to mingle. The younger ladies giggled in their cluster, the older women gossiped on the sidelines and the rest accepted their flirtations and conversation somewhere in the middle.

Until Sir Henry's carriage arrived, Rafferty had Selina's complete attention; the moment Henry joined the group, Rafferty's place was set back to second. He hardly minded, however. There was mutual respect in Selina's inner circle that rarely allowed bitterness to reside.

"It seems you didn't have your way," Sir Henry nodded in Royce's direction.

Selina sighed. "He's done little harm thus far."

Rafferty's scoff disagreed with her. "Aside from casting a spell on every eligible young lady in the county," he muttered. Royce proceeded to make every lady within earshot of him grin and giggle. Selina chuckled. "Has he asked to court Penelope yet?"

"No, he hasn't," she replied tightly.

"Hm," Henry grunted. "I'm not entirely surprised."

"Nor I," Rafferty nodded.

"Seems his eyes are on every woman but her."

Rafferty's stance shifted, angling him toward Royce and Penelope's friends. Miss Ayres was exuberant, as always, but the attention she assumed was not quite as singular as she expected. Royce's eyes wandered wildly in every direction but hers.

"You'd best tell Penelope," he suggested to Selina. "I suspect she's being blinded by her own enthusiasm — oh," he stopped as his eyes scanned over an unforeseen arrival. He leaned in toward Selina and lowered his voice. "That must be the inspector you told me about."

Selina and Henry both looked to see Inspector Barratt arriving in an Everdon carriage. Lindon had brought him as his guest, as promised. Selina made a face, which Lindon promptly disregarded as they approached.

"It seems so," she muttered.

"Well, the more the merrier, I say," Rafferty decided, good-naturedly. Ever the idyllic host, he approached the men before they reached Selina. "Lindon, it's good to see you."

"Lord Rafferty," Lindon nodded. "This is Inspector Barratt. He's investigating that unfortunate incident with Lady Selina's maid"

"It's a pleasure to meet you, Inspector," Rafferty gave a jolly grin. "I hope you find all the information you need to put this matter to rest in your time here."

"I certainly hope so," Barratt shook his hand, his tone somberly contrasting the aristocrat's careless nature.

Rafferty suddenly remembered himself and sighed. "Yes, the poor maid's demise has affected us all. She was a valued part of Everdon."

Barratt lightly touched his pocket containing the small notebook and contemplated the importance of Rafferty's indecisive demeanor. He finally settled to leave it be and put on a smile instead. "That's the impression I've gotten. She seems to be dearly missed."

Lindon cleared his throat. "Inspector Barratt only means to become more familiar with the county before making any definitive conclusions, sir. He wondered if he could mingle."

Without skipping a beat, Rafferty beckoned for Barratt to follow him while Lindon took his place amongst the older generation on the sidelines. "Come," Rafferty said, leading him to where Selina and Henry still stood. "I'm sure you've already met Lady Selina. This is Sir Henry Kincaid."

Henry paused his conversation long enough to politely nod and mutter a monotone, "Pleasure," before returning his attention to Selina. "...my last visit was disgraceful," he went on. "That Litchfield is the most —" His face went red and his fists clenched, contemplating his next statement.

"Curb your wrath, Henry," Selina calmly touched his arm.

"You're overdue, Selina," he told her. "You haven't been in ages."

The lady shrugged. "I know. I'll take care of it." She then mused, "I haven't seen the children since before…." her eyes met Barratt's as she realized he had stopped listening to Rafferty's introductory chatter. "Good afternoon, Inspector Barratt."

"Since your lady's maid passed?" he finished for her.

Selina's mouth twisted as her head cocked to one side. "I can see that London has dedicated a great deal more effort into training investigative techniques rather than the art of conversation."

"Selina," Henry softly scolded.

Barratt, however, was not at all fazed. "Was *the maid* at all connected to the orphanage, my lady?"

Before a snide word could escape Selina's lips, Henry responded, "Miss Rodin always accompanied Lady Selina on her visits, yes. Though, I wouldn't be surprised if she made her own journeys down there as well—I always suspected she was an orphan herself," he added, more to Selina than the inspector.

"Orphans tend to be drawn to lost ones like themselves," Barratt commented, noticing Selina's agreeable nod. "Tell me, how well did you know *Miss Rodin*, Sir Henry?"

Henry shrugged, even glancing at Rafferty before answering. "I can't claim to know her well, but I suppose she was typically close by. She was good, attentive—wouldn't you agree, Selina?" He noted the discomfort Selina was masking in her stance and silence.

"Of course she was," Selina replied with clarity. Her tone was well-controlled, despite the anxiety Henry sensed in her.

"She was a sweet girl," Rafferty contributed. "From what I could tell."

The young Rafferty children giggled and squealed as they ran around with the younger ladies of the party, but found themselves still requiring more playmates. Making their recruiting rounds, they spotted Selina standing with their father and simply had to ask her to play a game of croquet with them. Regardless of her tendency to reject the requests of others, Selina found it nearly impossible to deny any request from a child. Rafferty beamed as he watched Selina join them in the middle of the clearing where the court had been arranged; and Barratt decided it was time he pulled out his notebook.

As was expected, more eyes watched the court than before. One set of those eyes belonged to the crafty Mr. Royce, who saw it fit to find himself a more effective vantage point. Mr. Lennox, who had joined Rafferty and Henry shortly after Selina departed, spotted Royce inching closer to them.

"Are you much of a hunter, Royce?" Lennox attempted.

Henry glared briefly at Lennox, cursing his friendly nature. Royce took notice of the glare, and it only encouraged him.

"I always hit my mark," Royce said. "But I much prefer boxing."

Rafferty pointed at him excitedly. "Ah, I boxed at university." Henry chuckled. "A bit," Rafferty amended. "We should go a few rounds during your stay here."

"Well," Royce smiled. "That would be a refreshing change; the countryside seems to offer more....docile past-times."

Rafferty patted his back with casual familiarity. "It's settled then. We must box. And you should come on a hunt with us sometime, as well."

Lennox laughed. "Perhaps you'll hit something this time around, Raff."

Smoothly, Royce moved away from the gentlemen's playful teasing of Rafferty's athleticism, putting himself within the realm of assistance as it was Selina's turn to swing her croquet mallet.

"Allow me," he offered, placing the ball carefully on the ground before her. He made little notice of the comments of the ladies attempting to recapture his attention.

Selina glanced in their direction and then returned to Royce. "I don't understand what makes you so fascinating, Royce. You have such generic strengths that there shouldn't be anything particularly outstanding about you at all."

Royce rose and chuckled. "You certainly know how to flatter a man, Lady Selina. You see right through me."

She frowned blankly, suddenly putting more than the necessary concentration on hitting the ball correctly. "Artists are accustomed to distraction," she aimed. "Seducing with their art...they never expect their audience to look past the canvas...or the pretty words." She swung the mallet. "And yet, if it weren't for your wolf-like senses honing in on the young and weak, I would have melted at the sight of you, Mr. Royce. I've always been one for pretty words and roguish charm."

Selina stood tall, watching the ball roll in the desired direction. Finally, she looked at him. "But alas, you chose my ward, therefore obliging me to despise you on principle." She gave an enigmatic quirk of the lips, moving past him as smoothly as he had approached her.

"Well, that is a shame," he grinned widely. Seeing Sir Henry's dubious glare fired in his direction, Royce decided it best to return to the gentlemen, lest he risk insulting his host. "This is a lovely estate," he said to Rafferty.

"Thank you—my late wife, bless her soul, was quite a gardener," Rafferty gestured to the landscaping. "She made sure our grounds were the best landscaped in the county, though Lady Selina disagrees."

"I would never disagree," Selina chimed in. "Jane's gardens are without equal, Lord Rafferty."

Rafferty gazed admiringly at her praise, but then sighed. "Hm, she would be devastated to see it so lacking in a woman's touch, though." Royce noticed the man's gaze did not leave Selina as he said this, bringing an amused and conniving smile to Royce's face. "Which reminds me, I've had something added to the east garden that I think you'll love."

Rafferty gestured for his children to snatch another playmate while he borrowed the Lady Selina, and he offered her his arm. "I remember how much you love daffodils," he said to her.

Henry cleared his throat of all discomfort, but as the benevolent prince he was, he made no attempt to follow and interrupt his friend's well-considered attempt. Lennox followed Henry's lead and stayed where he was; Royce, however, was far from solicitous in sparing another's feelings when there was a prize to be won.

"Oh, I love daffodils," he said, proffering his company to the duo as they moved away from the common crowd.

Rafferty tightened his jaw in frustration but was far too polite to reject Royce's interest in the garden. Seeing Royce move away from the party, the handful of young ladies who had been charmed by him sought his attention once more, creating a train of giggling young ladies behind him. Before long, nearly the entirety of the garden party migrated toward the garden itself.

"Poor, Rafferty," Lennox lamented, lingering behind with Henry and slowing his own pace. "That Royce."

Henry grunted. "He's certainly doing his best to maintain a monopoly on every eligible woman in the county."

"And now Selina, it seems."

"I hardly think so," Henry scoffed. "But he is doing his best to isolate her from her usual suitors. Rafferty doesn't stand a chance. I should've known it wouldn't take a man like that long to begin searching the county for the richest pocketbooks. And I should've suspected he would settle on her."

"What does that mean?" young Penelope spoke from behind them. She had only just noticed her friends had left the game of croquet to start for the gardens.

"Oh, Miss Ayres," Lennox stumbled in surprise.

Penelope ignored him, however, and grabbed Henry's arm. "Henry, what did you mean? Why would Royce search for pocketbooks?"

"Nell, not..." Henry began, careful to use a gentle tone. "Not every gentleman who shows interest..."

"Mr. Royce is a bit of a scoundrel," Lennox blurted.

If Henry's sudden glare hadn't stopped Lennox from continuing, Penelope's aghast expression would have.

Penelope's voice became small, but firm. "No, he isn't."

"Move along," Henry said firmly.

Lennox stopped, scrambling to apologize. "But I—"

"Go," Henry asserted. His glare held steady until Lennox obeyed and moved ahead of them. Henry's voice then softened as he took Penelope's arm closer to his. "Penelope, you're a lovely young lady with a powerful guardian. You live in a grand estate and have friends as wealthy and lovely as you are."

"They're not as wealthy," she corrected, slowly registering his sympathy. "Selina assures me we have a greater fortune than Henrietta and Mary combined."

"And sometimes," he went on, "men want that more than they want you…no matter how lovely you are."

Penelope fell silent for a moment as they walked. He knew better than to press for a response as she slowly pieced together all that he was telling her.

"Selina would have told me," she eventually whispered. Her throat thickened and choked ever so slightly. "How dare she lie to me."

"Perhaps she was trying to let you make a decision for yourself," Henry offered. He lightly rubbed her hand, but no amount of coddling can completely protect a broken heart.

The silence of a woman as young and vivacious as Penelope Ayres can cause a reasonable individual to feel some disturbance. The evening's meal was taken in such a silence, bringing quiet alarm to both Selina and Mr. Lindon. Penelope devoured the food on her plate the moment it was placed before her, and deliberately avoided any sort of glance in Mr. Royce's direction while she awaited each following course. He couldn't have minded less; he was perfectly content with his meal and contemplating the revised strategy for the remainder of his visit at Everdon.

"Did you enjoy your chicken, Penelope?" Lindon pressed.

Penelope made little effort to respond.

"How did you like Lord Rafferty's garden party?" he tried again.

"It was well-done," Royce replied instead, wiping his face of sauce from the chicken. "Very well-managed property as well. He seems to be an excellent businessman."

Lindon sat back in his chair, accepting the alternative path of conversation. "Yes, Lord Rafferty and Lady Selina have been partners in a number of financial ventures over the years."

"Our estates, Lindon," Selina clarified. She delicately cut the meat in front of her and lazily contributed to the exchange. "Our estates have been in partnership."

Royce smirked, a knowing eyebrow lifted. "It's a wonder you haven't yet ventured into....other forms of partnerships together."

"Our money is far more compatible," was the bland response.

"And Sir Henry," Royce continued to push as the next course was served. "I assume your money is compatible with his as well."

Selina set her utensils down for a moment and looked directly at Royce's antagonist smile. "Fascinating. You're now inquiring of the men's fortunes as well as the women's, Mr. Royce."

Lindon slowed his chewing as he noted Penelope's head snap toward Royce, awaiting an answer of her own.

"It's a beneficial strategy to weigh the assets of any potential combatants," he shrugged.

"One must settle on a particular quarry before there's a need to weigh contenders," Selina posed. "I believe I granted you all the information you needed; I fail to see what more you could lack."

This time, Lindon set his utensils down as well, glancing rapidly from Selina to Royce, and back to Selina. The lady's words were artfully aimed, but her target sat just as unruffled as he had toward Penelope's silence. He merely smirked and swallowed another bite of chicken.

"How did you enjoy the garden party, Miss Ayres?" Royce idly inquired. The question may have been for Penelope, but his teasing glance remained on Lady Selina.

Flustered by the sudden interest, Penelope's mouth became slightly ajar as she stared, scrambling for a coherent response that properly conveyed her frustration. Unfortunately for her inner rage, the only words that escaped her lips were, "I...I do love croquet."

"You are very skilled at the game," Royce replied, sipping casually from the fresh bowl of soup placed before him.

Rather than the cruel words she intended, Penelope's anger began to leak from her eyes. "You're a skilled player as well," she croaked.

"To say the least," Selina scoffed. "Games appear to be your forte."

Penelope's anger quickly shifted from tears to sobs; after the second release of deep whimpers, she stood abruptly from the table and stormed out of the dining hall. As she did so, Lindon stood appropriately, his paternal glare now directed toward Selina.

Slowly returning to his chair, Lindon cleared his throat. "Selina," he said in a low, scolding tone.

"I didn't..." Selina sighed. After a moment of unspoken compromise between them, Selina set her utensils on the table and rose to follow her devastated ward. Lindon stood once again as she left the room, glancing over at Penelope's apparent problem and noting his maintained blatant disregard. Royce remained contently seated, sipping the remainder of his soup and lightly blotting his lips with a napkin, as the casually cruel commonly do.

Helen knew what was expected of her: tend to Lady Selina. If she needed assistance in calming Penelope, Helen was at her beck and call. She had grown up in such a home that outbursts and tantrums were practically routine. With little children at Mother's heels and climbing over one another for scraps at dinner, feelings were often hurt and fits were thrown. Helen was perfectly capable of handling difficult temperaments, but as she stood outside of Miss Ayres' bedroom and watched Selina approach her in the hallway, she felt the situation far more bizarre than a crying child.

Penelope was a grown woman. Still young, yes, but certainly not a small child. And yet, the shouting and kicking and sobbing Helen could hear was alarming. She'd never heard of an adult having such hysterics unless they were considered entirely mad.

"Do you need me for anything, my lady?" Helen asked.

Selina, already looking ragged before she even stepped foot in Penelope's room, shrugged her shoulders. "Have you eaten yet?"

"No, ma'am. I was preparing your room."

"Have some supper first," Selina ordered. "This will last for some time."

Selina carefully entered the room, after dismissing Helen, but neglected to shut the door completely. Curious girl that she was, Helen took advantage of the sliver of sight she'd been accidentally granted. Penelope was strewn across her bed, sobbing and heaving wildly, only disturbed by Selina's sudden presence sitting beside her. Quiet and patient, Selina reached a hand to stroke Penelope's ruined hair.

"....stupid girl...." Penelope muttered between sobs, unintelligibly. "...a villain, but I thought....supposed to be a prince....why would he trick me...."

Selina didn't need complete sentences to understand her; Penelope hardly had to speak at all. Selina continued to stroke her hair, her expression blank and tired. "You hardly know the man, Nell."

"I did know him," Penelope launched her head from the bed. "He loved me," she insisted. "He said...."

"Pretty words are rarely true."

"I don't understand." From where Helen was standing, she could see an unusual expression flash across Penelope's face. It was to be expected that a heartbroken woman would wallow in denial and misunderstanding, but this was different.

Penelope's eyes were lost. She could hear Selina's words, but their meaning was slow to process. Her naivete was being shattered. It was as if Selina was speaking to a child of no more than eight years old, and Selina's tone gradually began to reflect that as well. Bringing a soft hand to Penelope's face, Selina smiled sadly.

"You can't trust every man to be a prince, darling. And you can't invite a prince into the kingdom without checking with the queen first; he could mean you harm."

Penelope stared at her for a moment, gradually allowing her words to settle. "You would have told me," she understood.

"I would have told you," Selina nodded.

Tears started to stream once more. "I want him banished," she choked. "Banished from Everdon forever. I don't want to look at his face again—never again. He can't stay here, he can't! He can't stay and fall in love with another princess....he can't....you can't let him..."

Selina brought Penelope's head to rest on her shoulder as she continued to run her comforting fingers through the girl's hair. "Don't get lost in your own story, Nell. Royce is hardly a prince, and any respectable princess will see right through him as you have."

"Swear to me, Lina," Penelope sniveled into Selina's dress. "Swear to me you'll banish him."

Her words were as emphatic as her pain was deep. Selina kissed the top of Penelope's head. "Whatever you say, Nell. It'll be done."

Leaving her to rest from the exhaustion of anguish, Selina returned to the hallway to see Helen still peering through the door. Instead of scolding, Selina smirked in amusement.

"Did you eat?" she asked.

"Um," Helen hesitated, scrambling to compose herself. "Um, no, I-I didn't, ma'am. I'm sorry."

The lady shrugged, unbothered. "You may as well help me dress for bed, then."

Helen followed loyally behind her, displaying all the preparations that had been made. While Mrs. Melrose would have argued that Helen's temperament was a bit wild for a lady's maid, she could not say the same for her attention to detail. Selina's rosewater treatment was concocted and set neatly on the vanity, with a clean washcloth beside it. Her nightgown was laid across her bed, with her slippers and robe placed nearby.

Selina glanced around the room, pursing her lips in disapproval. "You forgot my lip ointments."

Helen frowned. While she searched the vanity drawers for the elusive ointments, Selina changed into her nightgown and sat herself in front of the mirror. With a frustrated grunt, Helen found the ointments and handed them to the lady. Selina only chuckled and gestured for Helen to continue on with her duties, namely letting Selina's hair down.

Helen began pulling the pins out of Selina's hair, her brows tightly wrinkled together. "Will...will Miss Ayres be all right, ma'am?"

Selina dipped the washcloth in the rosewater mixture on the vanity in front of her before dabbing her skin lightly. "Penelope suffered a fever when she was a child," she explained. "It...her mind has never been the same. She lost the ability to....well, to grow up."

"Hm," Helen regretfully hummed. Now she understood that vacant confusion in Penelope's eyes. "Poor thing."

"She may be simple, but she knows when she is being ridiculous."

"She does?"

"She can't understand why....she reacts much more intensely than the other girls. But, the intensity is all she knows, so she seeks it out in everything around her. She's insatiable. Being so eager brings a vulnerability for disappointment. Prepare for the dramatics tomorrow as well, Helen," Selina looked up at her through the mirror. "For very soon, the scoundrel will be banished from the kingdom."

3

Rogue Takes Queen

Cruelty rested for the night, only to be revisited first thing in the morning. April's gradually warming weather provided the ideal garden setting of sunshine and chirping birds; Royce settled comfortably in a chair with a cup of tea on the table beside him and a book in his hand.

True to her word, Selina strolled to the back gardens with her usual commanding cadence, but slowed her attack as she noticed the title in Royce's hand. *The Princess* by Alfred Tennyson. Intrigued, she gathered her hands together in front of her. "Of all the Tennyson volumes that grace my shelves, isn't it fascinating you chose that one in particular."

Royce glanced up from the pages, slightly startled by her sudden presence. A playful smile graced his mouth as he turned his wrist to show the book's cover. "A university filled with men-hating women, ultimately charmed out of their stubborn ways. What's not to like?"

Selina cocked her head to one side, advancing another step or two. "Charmed out of their ways?"

His smile shrugged a bit before he nodded. "The comically disguised prince in women's clothes infiltrates the princess' defenses and manages to win her affection. I'd call that rather charming."

Shoulders now squared, Selina took the seat on the opposite

side of the table and leaned her head forward, challengingly. "On the contrary," she said. "Very little charm was needed. The prince disguised himself long enough to intimately *understand* the princess." She then sat back into the seat. "Affection came from understanding, hardly shallow charm."

"Not all charm is shallow," he snapped the book closed and set it between them. "Even so, the prince wins in the end. And, funny you revere Tennyson so. He seems to be quite against the education of women—particularly in this piece," he pointed to the volume.

Selina's lips parted. He was challenging her, baiting her. He lived for sparring and in spite of herself, she could not immediately decline. Remembering her promise to Penelope, Selina inhaled sharply.

"Once again, Mr. Royce, you fail to understand what's in front of you. *The Princess* is not against female education, nor is its purpose to flaunt the prince's alleged victory. It portrays the balance of love between the sexes, highlighting the strengths and weaknesses—their dependency on one another in delicate matters." She stood graciously and smiled at him. "Not everything is a game, as you might believe. In fact, your current chosen hunting ground has expired indefinitely. You'll need to take your sport elsewhere."

"I'm sorry?" he stared blankly.

Bringing her hands in front of her again, with resolve, she exhaled smoothly. "It seems this prince has entered the kingdom *chasing* petticoats, rather than wearing one himself. It's just as well, as you haven't the figure for them."

Royce released an empty chuckle. Their skirmish had reached an abrupt end and the advantage was clearly hers.

"You'll be leaving Everdon by tomorrow, Mr. Royce," she continued to smile. "Perhaps you should have been more delicate in your trivial pursuits while under my roof. The single force keeping you here as a guest at Everdon has finally been offended and requested your absence. If you wish, Mr. Lindon would be more than happy to help you make the necessary arrangements."

Finally, Royce stood, clutching the book in his hand and

looking directly into the lady's eyes. "I'm sorry to hear that," he claimed. "Is there nothing I could do to sway you? Perhaps a story in your —"

"Hm, no. Sadly not," she said, without remorse. "No need to waste efforts in peddling your storybooks here, sir." Her smile twisted into a victorious smirk. "My taste is unattainable, and I am an immovable force."

"Did you enjoy it, Mr. Royce?"

Royce had set the book back on the shelf in the library immediately following his dismissal. Apparently he had been staring quizzically at it for longer than intended, for he hardly noticed Mr. Croft approach him.

"Y-yes," Royce eventually responded. "It was...enlightening."

Croft nodded with a grin. "One of Lady Selina's favorites," he pointed. "She's quite the romantic."

Royce curved his brow and almost chuckled. "Lady Selina is?"

Croft nodded again, but in earnest this time. "Oh yes. One wouldn't know it on the surface, but one glance at her treasured volumes," he gestured vaguely to the room as a whole, "and there's nothing left to wonder. Did you find what you were after?"

"Hm?" Royce grunted, suddenly distracted by the observation that much of the library's selection was chosen by Selina herself.

"Was it what you expected?" Croft clarified. "*The Princess*, I mean."

Royce's eyes wandered to the library window, where Selina could be seen leaving alone for the path down the hill. "Oh, yes, yes. Tell me, where does Lady Selina go every morning?"

The librarian tucked his hands in his pockets and paced slowly toward the window. "Difficult to say precisely," he said. He watched her for a moment as well before turning back to Royce. "She leaves on a whim, most days. Sometimes she fancies a walk to the orphanage to visit the children, as she does. Other days, she finds herself calling on

Miss Downing in town. Lindon's always telling her to take a carriage but I think she rather enjoys the quiet walks alone."

"Miss Downing?" Royce repeated.

"I'm sure you've met her," Croft waved at him assuringly while he made his way back to his desk in the corner. "Mousy older woman. She raised her sister's daughter nearly since the child's infancy. No hopes of marriage, and always incredibly....glum."

He rifled through the ledger in front of him before realizing he had opened the wrong one. As he corrected, he glanced over to see Royce still staring out the window. "An enticing woman, Lady Selina," he commented, testing Royce's attention.

"Indeed she is," Royce murmured.

Setting the correct ledger on the desk, Croft slowly moved back toward Royce, intrigued by the intense interest. "A woman so intimidating and shrewd, she makes others cower with her mere presence." He looked from Royce to Selina's disappearing frame in the distance. "And yet, she manages to raise the most beaten of souls from the deepest of depths, simply by lending a conversation her particular touch. Miss Downing is a wounded bird with dampened cries....but the Lady Selina and her keen hearing won't let the pitiful creature die."

Royce's musing expression turned upward into a smirk. "*Wounded bird with dampened cries.* I do believe I wrote that."

Croft chuckled and gave him a friendly pat on the shoulder. "Lady Selina is not your only loyal reader in this part of the country, Mr. Royce." Amused as he was, the librarian turned away from Royce and returned to his ledger.

"I'm flattered," Royce followed. "I had no idea Lady Selina was a fan."

"She's owned each book since their release," Croft pointed at the shelf across from them, which housed each and every Darius Royce novel in print.

Royce snickered softly. "How interesting." A rush of disappointment fell over him; his worthy opponent had kept the most enchanting parts of herself so close to the chest that it tortured him to have to walk away so soon.

"She's certainly full of surprises, isn't she?" Croft sat behind the desk and took out a fountain pen.

"But I suppose I've seen my last then."

Croft's head snapped back up at him. "I beg your pardon?"

Royce sighed. "I'll be leaving Everdon tomorrow morning."

The librarian seemed almost as dispirited as Royce felt; he even stood in surprise and moved toward him to offer his condolences. "Well then," he said. "Your presence will certainly be missed, sir. Your presence *and* taste in decent literature."

Remembering Selina's snide expressions and well-crafted insults, Royce chuckled. "I'm sure you're alone in that opinion, but I appreciate the sentiment."

"I doubt that's true, sir," Croft shook his head. Suddenly noticing a book or two out of place, he hurried to the appropriate shelf to amend. Croft was not a young man, but his energy impressed Royce.

"Tell me, Croft," Royce tested the waters and took advantage of the man's distracted nature. "What do you know about Lady Selina and Sir Henry?"

His expectations proved correct; while searching for the proper home for the misplaced book, Croft responded with impulse and preoccupation. "Oh they've been thick as thieves since they were children," he said. "It's a wonder they never married."

"Any theories as to why that's the case?" Royce pressed.

Croft finally paused. "Why the sudden interest?" he lifted his brow.

"I've, uh, gained some unexpected inspiration here at Everdon," he shrugged. "I'm only curious."

Croft considered this for a moment and then exhaled. "It's probably not a tale worth your time, Mr. Royce," he confessed, adjusting another book as he passed. "They were betrothed, and then….they were not. And Lady Selina has had many hopeful suitors since, ready to take his place."

"Who broke the engagement?"

Croft stiffened, unsure if they had now entered forbidden territory. "It's...hardly my business to discuss, sir. I should hate to leave an artist lacking in inspiration, however. Perhaps you'd find a great deal more from *this* than Lady Selina's past dalliances," he picked a book from an adjacent shelf and offered it eagerly. *Bleak House* by Charles Dickens. "Some light reading between packing, perhaps?"

Royce acknowledged the withdrawal with grace, but held his chin high, knowing more now than he did before. Politely, he accepted the book he had read several times before; he was not the only one, it seemed, for he noted the corner of a bookmark in the center of the book, tucked between the pages. Smiling at the jolly librarian, Royce started for his room to plan his retreat to London.

Morning passed into afternoon, which melted into late evening as the sun fell. Mr. Royce had missed the call for dinner, but his hosts didn't mind. His absence was enjoyed, and Penelope even smiled once or twice. Everdon felt as if it had gone back to its previous state of contentment, were it not for the sudden burst of energy from Royce's bedroom. With a renewed sense of confidence, Royce flung his door open, snickering to himself and nearly running over Helen as she carried a tray of empty teacups down the hallway.

"Miss Thomas!" he exclaimed. "Where is Lady Selina?"

Helen froze, clinging to the tray and warily watching as a cup came precariously close to the edge. "Um...the library, sir. I believe she's going over some paperwork before bed."

"Excellent," he breathed excitedly.

Helen smiled at his eagerness but settled into suspicion as she watched him bound down the hall to the library. She knew he was to leave in the morning, after the state he inflicted upon poor Penelope. Even so, she did feel a twinge of sadness at the thought of him leaving. She'd enjoyed the presence of a renowned writer at Everdon; he had added to the mystery and appeal. *Ah well*, she thought. *Selina knows best.*

Helen assumed correctly. Selina commonly knew best. Selina did not, however, know what to think of Royce's rushed entrance in the otherwise peaceful library. She was tucked away behind her large desk, in the corner opposite Croft's, and winced a bit in annoyance at the sound of him.

"I assume Mr. Croft turned in for the evening," Royce slowed his pace as he reached the middle of the room.

"You assume correctly," she muttered, returning to her papers and ledgers. Royce couldn't recall ever seeing a woman so studiously at work as Lady Selina. She thumbed through files, scrutinized numbers and scribbled corrections as she saw fit. No doubt her late father would have been proud.

"I only meant to return this book he lent me," he pulled her attention. The lady glanced up at him, as desired, but gestured to the shelves across the room before returning to the work before her. "I'm not quite sure where it belongs."

"I expect Mr. Croft can put it away in the morning," she sighed, growing exasperated.

Royce nodded, still watching her carefully, and placed the book on the nearest shelf. Her eyes flashed in his direction, sensing his disregard for Mr. Croft's order. With another sigh, Selina stood and crossed the room to rectify. Royce smirked as she took the book from his hand and placed it on the appropriate shelf. The barrier between them had been removed and she now stood where he had hoped.

"I wanted to thank you for your hospitality," he started in a sincere tone. "Everdon is…very impressive. The accommodations and grounds are just as fine and enchanting as the lady of the house. It's amazing, the way you so efficiently run your estate—and manage to keep the social stirrings of the county in the palm of your hand. Of course, I expected nothing less from a Delamere—good sense and social grace….it's in your blood." Noting her indifference to the compliment, he added, "Or is it?"

Selina's eyes narrowed as they returned to him, his smirk deepening. "Are you trying to insult me…or my family, Mr. Royce?"

"Oh," he frowned mockingly. "Never the great Lady Selina. I'd only dare to admire her for accomplishing so much…for someone who does not exist."

Her voice hardened. "Since you have never had the privilege of touching me, Mr. Royce, I feel it my duty to inform you that I most definitely exist." Curtly, she turned back for her desk, intent on denying him the satisfaction of another battle.

"Well," he began, determined to pull her back, "I've done a bit of reading during my stay, and I must say, it was all very enlightening. As it happens, the Lady Selina of Everdon, daughter of Lord Edward Delamere and his lovely wife, Angelica....died on the fifteenth of March, *twenty-eight years ago*, before even drawing breath in this world."

Had Selina not reached her desk, she would have had nothing to grip tightly for support. During his rather dramatic pause, Selina's heart stopped beating. When the beat returned, it seemed to match the deliberate footsteps now moving toward her.

"It's as if I'm beholding a ghost," Royce whispered.

"Is there an end to your theory?" she spoke, her fists beginning to form.

"Theories are speculation with little facts," he chuckled. She turned to him, leaning back against the desk as she faced him. "What I have is truth. Truth supported by evidence, in Lord Delamere's own hand," he lightly touched his suit pocket, "which is quite damning."

Selina's eyes widened and her mouth fell slightly ajar. But her opponent only curled his lips and bore his teeth.

"Now that I have your attention," his tone became sinister. "I can't begin to imagine how one is capable of conning an entire community into believing you to be an heiress—nor can I understand how Lord Delamere himself managed to leave his estate to an impostor —it seems you're a much better swindler than I..."

"You are right," Selina's words returned. Her voice was broken and forced. "You understand nothing."

Royce moved in closer until he was inches from her. "But I understand enough to ruin you," he hummed.

"What do you want?" She resigned.

He leaned back, soaking in the power he had finally gained. "What do I want…" he repeated. Slowly, he circled his helpless prey, as if inspecting the use of what he now controlled. "What could I possibly want in exchange for my silence? Money is too simple, too fleeting," he casually waved in no particular direction. "I think a secret of this magnitude demands something much more lasting….more binding. I am a social parasite," he pointed. "You are an impostor. I think it would be most…advantageous to take part in a sort of merger."

"You haven't the faintest idea what you're doing," she fired.

Royce chuckled again. "Oh I can assure you," he slowed and stopped beside her, leaning in for emphasis. "I know exactly what I'm doing. I'm doing what no man has done before. I'm bringing the Lady Selina Delamere to her knees," he gloated. "She will marry me, or risk losing her entire estate."

Selina couldn't bring herself to look at him. After a long moment of painful consideration, the only words that found their way to the surface were, "Very well."

4
Sharp as Shears

Mr. Royce's departure appeared to be stayed for the foreseeable future, but very little was conveyed to the Everdon staff. His carriage was not arranged. His bags were not packed. And he still sat at their dinner table for the next two days. Selina sent an invitation to her only other surviving family member, her great aunt, Lady Philippa Clementine, and planned an impromptu dinner party with no discernible explanation.

The parlor at Everdon was filled with mystified guests, yet Selina was nowhere in sight. Immediately upon her descent from the second floor, Lindon took Selina aside with a firm hand.

"Is there an occasion I'm unaware of, Selina?"

"There often is," she said flippantly.

"Don't be smart, Selina," he warned. His brow was furrowed, which meant the otherwise gentle man was ruffled. "Penelope tells me you planned to *banish* Royce, and yet here he still is."

Selina tightened her jaw. "Penelope is prone to dramatics. You know this."

"And now you've invited your great aunt," he went on, "the London inspector—"

"He's a friend of Royce. He insisted."

"—and half the town for an unprecedented dinner party," he hissed.

Masking the depth of her discomfort, Selina released a breathy laugh. "Half the town—oh please, Lindon."

Nearest the doorway, Aunt Philippa sat equal parts bemused and bored. She was an elderly, pretentious woman with even less of a filtered tongue than her beloved niece. Her upstanding posture suggested there was very little she approved of, but her winking eyes contradicted. "You," she patted Royce's knee across from her. "You ought to attend more of these, young man. This town is in great need of witty, brooding, artistic tripe."

The writer's only friend was perched on an armchair nearby, quick to chuckle and contribute. "He certainly has tripe in spades, ma'am," Barratt agreed.

Royce sipped some sherry, offered the old woman an amiable wink, and promptly ignored Barratt. He wasn't there to join in celebration with him; Barratt need only to witness his recent success and then be on his merry way. Royce glanced over at his prize, noting the arrival of Sir Henry. The gentleman greeted the lady, kissed her hand, and whispered some amusing comment in her ear. Selina stiffened at his closeness, overwhelming regret sinking inside her. She politely nodded to him and to Lindon as she left them to find relief at the drinks table. Smoothly, Royce saw his chance to join her.

"Allow me," he said to her, lifting the decanter to fill her glass. Her eyes were like venom, piercing their way through his. "There's something to be said for happy announcements coming sooner rather than later, Selina."

Gripping her glass, her venom continued to drip, until the moment her face was turned to her guests. The corners of Selina's mouth lifted into a forced smile that defied the heaviness of her heart.

"A toast," she exclaimed, lifting her glass. Everyone followed suit, smiling widely at their hostess. "To my father. Were he here, he would stand before all of you…he'd take my hand…." Lindon's eyes narrowed on her as hers misted. "He would have longed to see this day….in which he could, at last, announce that his daughter's hand has finally been taken….in marriage."

The room fell silent. Hands were frozen against the raised glasses and words were lost. Royce reached for Selina's hand and slowly lifted it to his lips, kissing it manifestly for all to see. Selina's gaze drifted to Henry as he did so, hardening with veiled dread.

The first expression of celebration was Philippa's. She clapped her hands together in surprise, nearly spilling her sherry, and applauded. "How wonderful!"

At Aunt Philippa's exclamation, Penelope's heart burst. She hadn't been mistaken: Selina was marrying the scoundrel she swore to banish. Dismay and betrayal struck Penelope like an anvil, and once again, she quickly stormed out of the room. In concern, Lindon moved to follow her, only to be stopped by Selina's hand.

"No," she whispered to him, "Leave her be."

And so the rush of congratulations commenced. Every man and woman in the room swarmed the allegedly happy couple, proclaiming good fortune and acclamations.

"Well, congratulations seem to be in order, good man," Rafferty kindly shook Royce's hand. "You won the unreachable hand, as it were. One day, you'll have to tell me your secret."

Royce grinned. "One day, perhaps."

"I had no idea you were courting, Selina," Sophie Campbell pulled at Selina's arm. "How happy for you! I should dearly love to be in your shoes—engaged, that is."

Henrietta Sweeting pulled at her other arm. "Could I be a bridesmaid, Selina? Penelope promised I could be her bridesmaid, but seeing as you're marrying first—"

"Henrietta," Mrs. Sweeting chided her daughter. "Your parents would certainly be proud, my lady," she smiled maternally at Selina.

"Thank you, Mrs. Sweeting," Selina strained.

"I daresay, another toast is in order," Philippa stood from her comfortable chair, leaning against her cane and lifting her glass again.

"I couldn't agree more," Royce joyfully added.

"To a new age," she declared. "No doubt Everdon's in great

need of a regime change—with a bit of the classics keeping things in order, of course," she winked at Selina.

"Of course," Selina exhaled.

"To a new age," Royce repeated, narrowing his gaze on Selina.

"A new age," the party concurred.

At the conclusion of the night, the dinner guests funneled back through the doors of Everdon and into their carriages. Royce and Selina stood amiably at the exit, bidding polite farewells with tight mouths.

"You wear your contempt like a sultry gown," Royce whispered to his betrothed after the last guest left and Aunt Philippa retired to her room. "And I must say, it is quite becoming."

With no more reason for pretense, Selina's tight lips twisted. She released her feigned grip on his arm and took a decided step away from him. "You think you have the upper hand, Mr. Royce. You may have pushed me into a corner, but you've overlooked my ladder." She straightened her back, refusing to yield. "You are so determined to acquire your desired wealth and fortune that you've unwittingly chosen to bind yourself to a woman so perfectly capable of making your life a living hell—as it is her way."

"Oh dear, Selina," he continued to grin wildly. "I do believe we're about to create a bestseller."

Had Lindon not made his way toward them, Selina would have no doubt painted a mural of the ways she intended to torture Royce in their dreaded years to come. Alas, her steward had not wished them his best and was too polite to turn in for the night quite yet.

"I'd be remiss if I myself neglected to bid the happy couple congratulations," he approached them near the bottom of the staircase and held a hand out for Royce to shake. "We'll be seeing much more of each other, it seems, Mr. Royce."

"We certainly will," Royce nodded.

Without so much as an acknowledgment of the well-wishing, Selina scowled and turned on her heel to see about Penelope. Down the hall, she charged past a bustling Helen, who had only just finished her own supper for the night.

"Come Helen," Selina called to her. She took the girl's arm and guided her out the back door. Though the light was limited, the two women could see the gardening staff standing like gargoyles near the entrance of the garden, mouths open and brows furrowed in frustration. "Shield this from prying eyes," Selina muttered to Helen. "Send everyone inside to do their work."

Beyond the barrier of angry gardeners, Selina found Penelope in hysterics. It wasn't merely sobbing and weeping into a pillow this time. With sharp shears in hand, Penelope wept and clipped everything in reach. Four bushes had fallen victim to her wrath before Selina marched to her side and snatched the shears out of her hands.

"I'll chop you up too, Selina—give those back!" Penelope shouted at her. Her tone was malicious and aggressive, nothing at all like the broken child Helen had seen a few nights before.

Silently, Selina put the shears behind her back, close to the nearest gardener, who retrieved them before being shooed by Helen.

"How could you?" Penelope wailed. "He was supposed to be banished—I don't understand—I wish you'd die—" Her voice quickly coarsened as the tears coated her throat. Her words became muffled into noises and gasps; Penelope resorted to hitting the bushes with her bare hands, expressing the rage her voice no longer could.

Obediently standing guard, Helen felt her heart sink. All Selina did was watch. She didn't comfort this time. She didn't stroke the girl's hair. She simply watched patiently.

The hateful and irrational words that were discernible brought Helen to tears, despite them being aimed at Selina. Gradually, however, Penelope's punches and kicks against the shrubbery became limp. Her biting insults became seldom. Her breaths were short and jagged. Penelope fell to her knees, clutching her chest with one hand and holding herself up against a bench with the other.

At last, Selina sat upon the bench and reached for Penelope's hand. The girl's breathing began to steady, and her words came back into coherence.

"I don't know…" she stumbled. "I can't understand….what's wrong….I can't understand, Lina." Penelope's cries grew softer, until she rested her head on Selina's lap and suppressed her own noise completely.

She didn't hate Selina, Helen decided.

"It's complicated, pet," Selina stroked Penelope's hair.

"I want to understand," Penelope whimpered. "Help….help me understand. You…you broke your promise."

Helen saw Selina's eyes painfully close. "I love him," she said blandly. "Don't you want me to be happy, Penelope?"

Penelope lifted her head enough to look up at her guardian. "You promised to banish him….and now you're….you're letting him be king."

"It doesn't matter," Selina cupped her face in her palm. "You're still the princess, Nell. Nothing will change that. He'll be a minor disruption now."

Surely that wouldn't put her at ease, Helen imagined. If Selina broke her promise regarding his presence, who's to say she's able to promise how much Everdon will now change?

"Nothing will change?" Penelope repeated, wiping her face. She sounded hesitant, but somehow relieved.

"Nothing you need concern yourself with," Selina assured her. Helen frowned; she considered that she had misremembered the optimism and blind trust of children.

Penelope sat up and leaned into Selina for further support. "But it has to be….you and I?"

Selina forced a smile. "It will be. Only with the addition of the Fool's stories. You like his stories," she reminded her.

Penelope's face began to beam. "And you'll make him tell me more, won't you?"

"To your heart's delight." Selina then beckoned for Helen to join them. "I'll be needing you to prepare Miss Ayres for bed tonight, Helen. There's something I must attend to before my night is over."

The moment Helen's duties were completed—Penelope was rested in bed and Selina's room was well-prepared—Helen rushed back to her quarters and pulled a sloppy manuscript from under her mattress. With the nearest pencil she could find, she scribbled the words:

Interesting concept: a kingdom in which the princess rules the queen. The queen falls in love with a rogue.

Biting the end of the pencil, Helen reconsidered that last sentence. After pausing deeply for a moment, she amended it:

The queen falls in love with a rogue?

Precisely as Selina expected, Lindon had waited for her in the hallway. He had nodded as Helen and Penelope passed him by, but would not move without speaking once again with Selina. Sternly, but gingerly, he reached for her arm and held her back until the hallway cleared.

"Is this your way of ensuring he stays away from Penelope?" he suggested in a somber tone. "Because if it is, I would be obligated to correct you and bring you to your senses, as it will have the very opposite effect in regard to proximity. What brought this on?"

"Whatever commonly brings on engagements?" she shrugged vaguely. "True love and an unquenchable desire to spend the rest of our lives together."

Lindon's shoulders lifted and fell. "I've never heard such passionate things said with such indifference."

With a weak smile, she lightly kissed his cheek and moved past him to her desk in the library. "I want you to fetch Leland Cuddy for me tomorrow," she said over her shoulder, assuming correctly that he had continued to follow her.

"Mr Cuddy has not been paying rent these last few months," he pointed out with a frown.

"I am aware, yes. I need to meet with him on business.

Lindon squinted strangely at her.

"And raise that staff's wages," she added. "Considerably."

"What? All of them?"

"Yes. Particularly whomever you deem Royce's new valet. Price, I'm assuming. He's probably best suited."

"Selina…" he advanced, waiting for her to reconsider.

"Effective first thing in the morning."

If ever there was one between them to yield, it was never Selina. Lindon accepted this much. Oftentimes, her judgment was highly trusted, and always proved promising results. Though there was no reason in sight, Lindon sighed with forbearance. "As you wish."

May 1889

Lying, the telling of beautiful untrue things, is the proper aim of Art
~Oscar Wilde~

1

Josephine's Baby

"I'm profoundly grateful for your willingness to answer a few questions this morning, my lady."

"Hm." Lady Selina sipped her cup of tea, her neck bent slightly in the direction of Penelope and the Rafferty children playing in the yard ahead of her. The front terrace was lively with the bustling of servants and vendors making preparations for the impending nuptials.

Inspector Barratt sat across from the lady, hardly touching his tea. "Your reputation," he continued, disregarding her reluctant cooperation, "is far from meager in this county—and in London, as it happens."

"Old money tends to make its mark across counties, inspector," she hummed, taking another sip.

"Indeed," he agreed. "It's quite impressive. Even without the family name, it seems you've made quite a mark yourself. I understand what Royce sees in you."

Selina's eyes smoothly glided to meet his. She leaned her elbows against the table between them and set down her cup. "Thank you," she said evenly, with the slightest hint of a smile. "No doubt a refreshing change from his usual marks."

Barratt laughed, desperately wanting to dig his claws into that particular line of questioning, but restraining himself. "I understand Miss Rodin served you for years," he focused. "Were the two of you close?"

"She was my lady's maid," Selina sighed. "She was the closest of all my servants. It's an occupational hazard. She wasn't a particularly chatty girl, so I can't claim to have known her well."

"That...."

Selina lifted a brow. "No need to be delicate, inspector. Not with me. This would be considerably more informative if you simply asked what needs to be asked."

"Well, your claim not to have known much of her certainly fits an aspect of the current narrative, I suppose. You wasted no time in finding a replacement. Could you tell me why that is?"

"I said I couldn't claim it," she clarified. "She was a close confidante nonetheless, as lady's maids commonly are. And I'm a very busy woman, you know, who needs tending to—we wealthy women are so fussy. We can't even brush our hair without guidance."

Barratt snorted softly, shaking his head. Selina smiled a bit, but continued quickly.

"In any case, Miss Rodin had been...ready to move on for quite some time.

"And why do you say that?"

She raised her shoulders lightly and took another sip of her tea, which was now reaching lukewarm.

"Were you aware of her condition?" Barratt pushed.

"What better way to ready herself for moving on?" She pressed a finger to her lips contemplatively.

"So you did know. And what did you do about it? Many employers terminate servants who start lives of their own—particularly lady's maids."

Selina considered this, but didn't seem particularly bothered. She poured some fresh tea from the nearby pot into her cup and stirred distractedly. "Well, terminating her would have certainly taken less energy than murder. But I didn't have much motivation to do either, if

I'm being honest."

"Did you expect her to raise the child at Everdon?"

"I expected her to run off with her little farm boy lover and make a life for herself," she answered frankly.

Barratt tilted his chin. "You knew the father?"

"No, I didn't."

"Anyone specifically coming to mind?"

Selina frowned, considering his words once again before shaking her head.

"I find it fascinating the similarities between Miss Rodin and a maid who died here...about twenty years ago, I believe," the inspector commented softly. He glanced up at her response as he scribbled a note in his booklet. "Are we to assume they were both impregnated and murdered by a *passing nobleman*?"

The lady rested an arm against the table and leaned closer to Barratt. "Hm," she said with a bemused smile, albeit tired eyes. "Was the previous maid with child as well?"

"I believe so, yes," he nodded.

"My," she leaned back, shaking her head. "What a striking coincidence."

Sensing the light mockery in her voice, Barratt cleared his throat and made a note. "She worked for the Delamere household as well, I recall. But, of course, you would know better than I."

Selina smiled again. "I must say, you do your research. It's a wonder anyone could ever lie to you."

The children screamed gleefully in the distance as Penelope chased them, pulling attention to the yard. Selina sipped her tea and kept her eyes on the children as she went on.

"Nothing was properly investigated all those years ago, as far as I'm aware. By all means, continue your research—but be wary, inspector," she tapped her nose. "This county is filled with hearsay and stories. Only one thing is certain: a maid died here over twenty years ago. Whether she took her own life or someone stole it from her, there was no knowing whether or not she was with child. And the evidence is long gone. Don't let speculation get the best of you—not every crime holds patterns. Sometimes killers simply kill."

For a moment, Lady Selina might have been the most fascinating woman to ever cross the inspector's path, and he gazed at her accordingly. The succinctness of the facts, the dismissal of rumors as unfounded, and the general studied skepticism surpassed perhaps every other female subject he'd encountered in past investigations. Another childish squeal snapped him out of the daze and returned him to his line of questioning.

"You doubt the child's father is a factor," he assumed.

"My doubts hardly matter. Being an experienced investigator, you're sure to have ascertained that the two most likely possibilities are a member of the Everdon staff or a nobleman who frequented the property. However," Selina adjusted herself in the lawn chair, "Josephine once lived in the village. I cannot confirm where she spent her time off—it's just as likely her lover was a farm boy, or a young man from the shops in town."

Barratt crossed his legs and wrote that down. "With all due respect, Lady Selina," he slowly looked back up at her, "the fact remains that the girl killed herself. That suggests the father was either ineligible...or wanted nothing more to do with her, thus driving her into a mad fit."

Selina's mouth shrugged in consideration, but no rebuttal was posed.

"Which seems more likely?" he prodded.

He watched her take another sip of tea until her cup was empty. Her eyes wandered, but her pursed lips were deeply contemplative. "Snakes exist in all walks of life, inspector. A lowly farmer can be just as cruel as an aristocrat. Both are capable of breaking the heart of a young woman carrying their child. And both are capable of drowning her if provoked."

Barratt couldn't help but smile at the words *drowning her if provoked*. The fascinating heiress was stubborn and contrary, and his amusement knew no bounds. "Mr. Lindon believes murder is out of the question," he pointed out.

"Murder is never out of the question," she replied simply.

With abruptness, his decorum dissolving, Barratt released a chuckle. "You certainly are an enigma. It amazes me that Royce could capture the heart of such a...shrewd lady like yourself. You are far above him; I don't know how he did it."

Pausing for a moment, Selina forced a smile. "He has a way with words," she said. "They simply disarmed me. I had no choice but surrender."

Before Barratt could further explore such a response, Selina's Aunt Philippa called to her from across the terrace. She leaned heavily on her walking stick with an expression of impatience on her face. "Come, Selina. We must get you to your dress fitting. Come, now. Don't waste our time, young lady."

The forced smile melted into amusement as Selina stood from her chair. "If you'll excuse me, inspector. My impending future calls."

2

Poppies Are Fine

The heightened pitch of argument, the tapping of needles, and the cutting of fabric shears overwhelmed Penelope's senses. She leaned her head against the nearest wall in the dress shop and began to drift into a reverie, ignoring Selina and Aunt Philippa's bickering.

"It's only right, dear," Philippa pointed at her niece while sitting comfortably in the corner. Selina stood on a pedestal as she was measured and her new gown pinned by the dressmaker. While her stance was relaxed and accepting, Selina's mouth and eyes were tight. "As the sole reigning parental figure," her aunt went on, "I'm nearly obligated—"

"I am not an obligation," Selina snapped. "I will pay for my own wedding."

"Then consider it a wedding gift," Philippa waved.

"I can't accept it."

Aunt Philippa stood, steadying herself on her cane. Inhaling sharply, she prepared her rebuttal toward her obstinate niece. Their exchanges commonly waded through contention until finding their way to a peaceful resolve. The personalities of the two women were far too similar.

"I've seen your Royce's taste," Philippa advanced to the pedestal and looked up at Selina, pointedly. "You'd do well to accept any generosity offered, young lady."

Selina rolled her eyes. "I can handle Royce's taste," she muttered. "I'm not in need of your charity." Catching the disrespect in her own tone, she corrected and looked down at Philippa. "Your generosity is certainly appreciated, Aunt Philippa."

Philippa's raised eyebrows eased at the apology. She cleared her judgmental throat and sighed. "I know. It is your pride, not you, who continues to scold me." She reached to touch the fabric of Selina's wedding gown, a reminiscent smile stretching across her face. "You must overcome it and allow me to pay for this."

Selina's attention had drifted to her reflection in the mirror on the opposing wall. The deep purple of the fabric framed her figure in a way none of her other dresses had. A smirk tugged at the corner of her mouth as she considered the forthcoming walk to her descent from power. There was perhaps no better color to fool the masses into believing their queen had found her king.

"I need this within the month," she said softly to the dressmaker.

"Oh," she stood upright, widening her eyes. "So soon, my lady." She glanced briefly at Selina's stomach and cleared her throat. "Will….adjustments be needed by the blessed day?"

Selina almost snickered and Penelope's head perked at the suppressed sound from her guardian. The girl's eyes moved to Helen, who stood patiently near the footmen as the business was being conducted, seeking a translation. Helen's jaw fell slightly ajar; it had not occurred to her that the pace of an engagement could imply such a sordid explanation.

"Oh please," Philippa leaned into her cane in exasperation. "There's no need for a woman to have sinned to justify speedy nuptials. Why must we extend engagements simply to fit society's expectations?" She cocked her head to one side, as if expecting an answer from the poor dressmaker. The woman merely dropped her head and proceeded to place pins in Selina's hem. "No, no, no," Philippa continued. "A respectable woman should never have to wait so long to be united with her husband—particularly when they're both such exciting and passionate individuals."

Selina's eyes rolled once more at her aunt's assumptions.

"Hastiness suits my needs," Philippa decided, returning to her seat in the corner, as the excitement was beginning to exhaust.

"It's your needs we considered, of course," Selina hummed, giving the dressmaker an apologetic frown.

"I'm aging, you know, Selina."

Selina nodded routinely; this was neither the first nor last reminder of Philippa's fragile mortality.

"The sooner the better, I say," her aunt went on. Selina mouthed along with the words as Philippa spoke, "I'm so near death's door."

Penelope caught sight of Selina's subtle mockery and giggled. Selina winked at her and cleared her throat. "Of course, aunt."

"There's no knowing how long I could've waited to see this day arrive."

"Do you like this color, Penelope?" Selina changed the subject.

Penelope sat straighter and grinned, always eager to share her opinion. "You know, the queen wore white to her wedding."

Selina smiled, but Aunt Philippa and her much louder input interrupted any response Selina might have had. "No, no, don't be daft, girl. Plum is far more tasteful."

"The queen can't be distasteful," Penelope gasped, looking at her aunt in utter dismay. "She's the queen!"

Philippa dismissed this, waving at Selina's dress instead. "Selina requires a different sort of class. This was a wise choice."

Penelope considered this and leapt from her seat to feel the material. "Oh, I do love this plum."

"We are quite settled then on this color, my lady?" the dressmaker confirmed.

Selina lightly rubbed her hands across the bodice and shrugged.

"Yes, plum, it is," Penelope nodded for her, cutting off any

95

verbal response. "That's my choice. It looks so lovely on her."

Penelope gazed up at Selina in such blind admiration that Selina could hardly hold any sort of irritation or resentment. And so she sighed. "I do love plum."

The dressmaker agreed, "It's a fine color, to be sure."

Penelope spun around to face Helen, practically prancing toward her and taking her hand with newfound energy. "Weddings are such fun, aren't they, Helen?"

"Miss Thomas," Philippa corrected in a deep tone.

Ignoring her, Penelope pulled Helen closer to Selina's gown, encouraging her to feel the material and revel in the thrill of wedding planning. "My wedding will be pink and violet. And my gown will be white, like the queen's—" Penelope shot her great aunt an antagonistic glare before returning to Helen, "but with soft silks."

Helen gasped softly. "You would be beautiful in silks," she agreed.

"Yes, I know," Penelope smiled. "And my groom will be just as handsome—no, more handsome than Royce."

Joining in the rather adolescent daydream, Helen closed her eyes a moment and nodded, imagining the splendor. "Mr. Royce is quite handsome," she said.

The dressmaker pursed her lips, placing another pin in the gown before glancing up at Lady Selina. "I don't believe I know that name—is the groom from these parts, ma'am?"

"Oh no, he's a writer from London," Penelope explained with breathy dramatics.

"The roguish sort—very charming," Philippa concurred. She narrowed her eyes, however, on Selina's reaction as she heard Penelope add,

"As if he could be from one of his own stories."

Selina snorted, disguising it as a clearing of the throat.

"He'll be nearly a brother to me, you know," Penelope continued to chatter. "And writers must always share their stories with family.

"I do believe that's what the law states," said Selina. Helen chuckled, but Penelope failed to see the jest.

"You see?" she said, accepting the encouragement.

Continuing to watch as Selina's gaze settled blankly on the mirror again, Philippa hummed. "It will be greatly stimulating to have a wordsmith in the family."

"Hm, stimulating, yes," was Selina's half-hearted reply.

"Perhaps he'll gain some inspiration."

Helen sat down beside Philippa, forgetting her place as the familiarity Penelope encouraged filled the room and elicited a curious glance from Lady Philippa herself. "I'm sure he will. Your love story alone must be worthy of a novel or two. And Everdon is quite intriguing."

As the dressmaker adjusted the neckline of the gown, she noticed the wearied complexion of Selina's face. "Are you all right, my lady?" she quietly inquired. "You don't seem well."

"She'd better rest well before the honeymoon, I'd say," Aunt Philippa chimed in.

Penelope giggled, but only after a moment after finally understanding her aunt's meaning.

"I've not slept well," Selina muttered.

Helen, remaining seated beside Lady Philippa, nodded. "I've not been sleeping well myself. There are so many noises in the house at night."

Philippa lifted a brow as Helen spoke, but seeing that Selina clearly allowed such outspoken servants in her company, she supposed she would also allow it.

"Noises?" the dressmaker repeated.

Selina turned to look at Helen, encouraging her to expound, but Helen hesitated. "Um, footsteps...."

A coy smile now splashed across her face, Penelope sat on the other side of Helen and leaned in close. "Have you not met our ghost?" Helen shook her head. "A dead maid haunts our halls—"

"Stop it, Nell," Selina scolded, straightening her posture once more so the dressmaker could finish. "It's just a silly story the servants tell newcomers to make them uneasy."

Penelope's shoulders fell in disappointment. "But it is a good story. I wonder if Royce has heard it?" she considered.

Sighing at the silliness of it all, Selina brought her hands in front of her and intertwined her fingers with firmness. "Everdon is no more haunted by spirits than any other old family manor."

"My father was an earl."

All eyes shot toward Lady Philippa and her bored tone. She had leaned against the wall to her left, with a bit more exhaustion than before, and seemed to be idly gazing at nothing.

"His father had an affair with a princess," she continued, "dueled her brother and killed him, but hardly spent a week behind bars before he was declared innocent and returned to his earldom to marry my duchess grandmother within the year."

Selina's brow wrinkled, and then loosened with amusement. "Unless one of them haunts the grounds of Everdon, Aunt, it seems hardly relevant."

Philippa then looked at her audience with the presence of a wise sage finally arriving at the lesson at the end of a long parable. "Old money brings complications. New money...and no money, I suppose...finds intrigue in relics that show them a glimpse of an ancient world they can only dream of being a part of."

The lovely, sunny spring day called for all the respectable gentlemen in town to show themselves outdoors. Sir Henry was always the active sort; always in the mood for a good, long walk through the countryside, taking the long way to town. The scenery was what kept him in the country instead of spending his days wooing the women of high society in the city. That was his explanation, of course. The country was good for his health and mind. The common understanding was somewhat different, what with the implications that Sir Henry preferred certain ladies in the county more than the selection the city offered.

In any case, the jolly gentleman took one of these healthful strolls into town on the very day Lady Selina attended her dress fitting. As was expected, he visited and greeted those he passed along the way. Inspector Barratt noted this and made a point to cross Sir Henry's path.

"It's good to see you again, Sir Henry," he called to him from across the street.

Henry smiled, eliminating the space between them, and shook the inspector's hand amiably. "The pleasure is mine, inspector. I hope your time here has been productive."

Barratt chuckled humorlessly. His morning had consisted thus far of doors being closed in his face, both metaphorically and quite literally. "I suppose that's a matter of opinion. The more jaded inhabitants of Everdon have made progress just a bit slower than I would have liked."

Henry chuckled a little as they proceeded to walk down the road together. He tipped his hat at some passing ladies, maintaining a carefree grin.

Barratt looked at him curiously. "You don't seem the jaded sort yourself, however."

"Lady Selina is never without reason," Henry countered. "I'm certain it's merely her reputation she's protecting."

This time, Barratt chuckled. "You assumed I meant the Lady Selina."

"How could you not? I certainly know how....*jaded* Selina can be."

"Hm, yes, Selina," the inspector noted the slip into the familiar. "You've known her for a good long while, then?"

"Since we were children," Henry smiled again, this time with soft recollection.

Barratt took his notebook out from his suit pocket and scribbled a thought before prying further. From the start, Sir Henry had given the impression of one naturally forthcoming and virtuous. His reputation preceded him as well; in London he was one of the more desirable bachelors—even married women sought him out as a dinner guest. The honesty of his charm was undeniable, and Barratt anticipated a much more illuminating exchange between them. "The two of you are quite close. It's a wonder you never married her yourself."

Henry's shoulders tensed as his pace slowed. Barratt's questioning was already ahead of him.

"I assure you, Sir Henry," he retreated. "I don't mean to pry. I only meant that….it would be perfectly acceptable to feel some bitterness when the woman you love is taken by an impostor."

"Your friend," Henry pointed.

"Acquaintance."

Henry slowly allowed his smile to return, but now without humor or light-hearted intent. "You assume I'm in love with Lady Selina," he nearly grunted.

Barratt fought the urge to write down the return in formality and instead shrugged casually. "I can only imagine...if I had grown up alongside a woman like that, I would certainly be in love with her," he confessed. The glint in Henry's eye didn't contradict Barratt's accusation, but rather his stiffened upper lip suggested his well-bred desire for discretion. Barratt continued, hoping to break the barricade Henry now fought to create. "I would certainly hate Royce for intruding, as he has a habit of doing, but who's truly to blame? The intruder or the woman who chooses him?"

"In this case, the intruder," Henry muttered under his breath. His jaw clenched as the words were released, and Barratt could have sworn he saw a flash of resentment flicker in Henry's eyes.

"In this case…?"

Catching his fury by the throat, Henry stopped in his tracks to recompose. He knew better than to divulge too much to a stranger, but discretion—while always preferred—was not always Henry's strongest trait. "I…." he began, swallowing contempt, "….no longer love Selina the way that Royce ought to."

Barratt tucked his hands in his trouser pockets, content with the success that can often come from poking a bear, so long as one is not the prey. "Why didn't you marry her?"

Henry paused once more, his jaw even tighter than before. "She was a free bird who never gave any indication of wanting to be caged. My initial intent was overridden by..."

"The influence of others?" Barratt assumed. Henry's eyes narrowed on him strangely. "You said, *in this case*. I presume Royce is not the only rogue to attempt to win over Lady Selina. But he is the only one you disdain for it. Who was the other?"

Henry cleared his throat and broadened his shoulders. "It is not my story to tell."

"You're so sure?"

"I do not speak ill of close friends, Inspector. And you'll do well to control your line of questioning," he finally resolved. "Not all are as open and accommodating in this county as I."

All good things must come to an end, so Barratt sighed in acceptance. "Of course. Please, accept my apology, Sir Henry," he smoothly posed. "My curiosity carried me away. I'm afraid my desire for truth gets the best of me at times."

"Naturally," Henry grunted.

"Rest assured, however, we share similar concerns."

"Do we?" His weight shifted from one foot to the other as he calculated the most polite way to end the interaction. Just across the street, through the dress shop window, both gentlemen caught sight of the Lady Selina being fitted in her wedding gown. Her eyes met Henry's and she beckoned him to join them.

Barratt's lip curled. "We both have Lady Selina's best interests in mind. The sudden submission of such a powerful woman is enough to make anyone think twice."

He held out his hand. Henry tentatively shook it as they parted ways.

The company within the dress shop was just as grateful for Henry's reprieve as he was for Selina's. With remembrance of their previous betrothal now fresh in his mind, Henry found himself struck by the sight of Selina in her new wedding frock.

"Ah, Sir Henry," Philippa lazily held her hand up from her seated position for Henry to kiss. "What a lovely, welcomed face."

Henry bowed and kissed the lady's hand, his genuine grin returning. "Ladies. Selina, that dress is beautiful."

"'Tis a shame your vantage point won't be quite as close to it as we'd assumed, isn't it?"

"*Aunt*," Selina hissed as Henry cleared his throat. Philippa merely shrugged at the correction and leaned back against the wall. Her energy for the day was beginning to fade.

Selina anxiously rubbed the soft bodice of the gown again. "Thank you, Henry. Nell insists plum is perfect."

Penelope suddenly appeared by Henry's side, taking his arm. "No," she corrected. "White like the queen. But plum will do, I suppose. Come, look at these silks, Henry." She pulled him away from the bride and toward a wall covered in hanging silk fabric. "Tell Selina to let me choose one for my own dress. She can't be the only one with a fine new gown."

Humoring her, Henry let himself be guided toward the fine materials. He smiled at the girl's excitement, but felt the habitual need to correct her. "Well, it is her wedding, Penelope."

"I know," she shook her head. "But it would be made more perfect if I'm also well-dressed."

"But, of course," Henry conceded, winking at an already chuckling Selina.

The bell of the shop door rang with Selina's laughter, welcoming her fiance and his fine new garments as well. The moment Darius Royce stepped foot in the dress shop, Lady Philippa rose to her feet to greet him. Graciously, he bowed and kissed the lady's hand before pausing to admire Selina's figure and complexion in the trim, plum gown.

"I do hope your new wedding suit is dashing and....complementary," Lady Philippa gestured to Selina's dress.

Royce grinned. "I would settle for nothing less," he assured her.

Philippa giggled like a proud schoolgirl and took his arm. "Of course you wouldn't. If there had only been men like you when I was young...."

As Philippa lamented her past love affairs, Royce noted Henry helping Selina down from the pedestal, and the playful chuckle they exchanged. A grimace settled on the rogue's face which Lady Philippa was sure to catch. She nudged his arm, leaning in as if to share a secret.

"Isn't plum such a fine color on your bride?" she commented, too loudly for any decent secret. It brought the desired effect, however. Selina's attention was captured and Henry became suddenly aware of the eyes on them.

"Any color is a fine color on my bride," Royce was sure to say. His words may have complimented Selina, but his glare was centered on Henry.

Smoothly, Selina stepped away to change into her previous dress before paying. Penelope filled the air with babble that aimed to update Royce on her opinions on matters such as flower arrangements and desserts, all the while neglecting to notice the tense avoidance of eye contact between the two gentlemen.

When Selina reached the counter to pay the arranged amount to the dressmaker, Royce joined her, quietly slipping the bill for his own wedding attire into her hands. Seeing the numbers scribbled at the bottom of the receipt, she inhaled sharply.

"Is the suit lined with gold?" she seethed.

"You said you could handle his taste, Selina," Lady Philippa joined them. She shot her niece a warning glance, silently chiding her for starting a disagreement with her betrothed in such a public setting. "Have you ordered the flowers yet, Royce?"

Royce smiled at the alliance, almost turning his chin up at Selina as he responded. "Yes, I did. Just this morning. And they're as wonderfully extravagant as my bride deserves." With flair, he reached for Selina's hand and kissed it with affection as ostentatious as his claims.

"Oh? And what did you choose? Roses? Lilies?"

"Poppies, actually."

Henry scoffed, drawing attention to himself. "Selina prefers daffodils," he explained.

Royce maintained his hold on Selina's hand as he feigned consideration. "Oh, does she? Interesting."

Henry studied Selina's expression, clenching his jaw as he did so. There was hardly a reaction on her part. Her lips held a straight line and her eyes passively watched Royce as he commanded the room.

"Come now," Philippa abated. "Poppies are hardly traditional, but neither is Selina."

"Traditional for funeral services, I'd say," Henry muttered, adjusting the button on his sleeve. "Which one could deem appropriate."

Royce smirked; the man perceived the humor in it all and Royce appreciated the shrewd perception. Selina, however, did not.

"Poppies are fine," she said shortly, shooting Henry a threatening glare. "They'll do just fine."

Lady Philippa sighed loudly. She was not beyond reading the tension growing in the shop, but she was beyond bored of it. "Perhaps we should convene for lunch," she suggested. "I crave some nourishment and flirtatious banter."

"Yes," Penelope shot up in agreement. "We should. Some tea and cake."

Closing her pocketbook, Selina shook her head. "We need to return to Everdon for your harp lesson, Penelope."

The girl pouted, crossing her arms in front of her chest.

"The harp?" Royce said. "Elegant instrument."

"Of course it is," Penelope looked at him, revealing just a small prideful smile.

Selina maternally secured Penelope's top coat as she agreed and then added, "She's quite talented, but still in need of *practice*." She signaled for Helen to join her in herding Penelope out of the shop.

"Perhaps it's for the best," Philippa followed. "I'll accompany you as well. I'm so near death's door, I should rest my eyes." She linked arms with Penelope and leaned against her to emphasize her fragile state.

"Helen," Selina guided Helen closer to her as the group exited the shop. "Would you ride with them back to Everdon? I'll follow soon. Nell—don't forget to deliver my letter to Mr. Cuddy."

"I won't forget," Penelope assured her, already exasperated with Aunt Philippa's dramatics.

The ladies and their footman moved to load into the Everdon carriage, leaving Selina alone with Royce and Henry. Royce watched Selina expectantly out of the corner of his eye as the carriage pulled away. Fluidly, he reached for the chequebook and receipt in her hand, but just as smoothly, she moved that hand to her side, just out of his grasp.

"Henry, would you excuse us?" Selina forced a smile. "There's some business we must attend to."

Henry and Royce shot daggers at one another, nearly forgetting Selina stood between them until she cleared her throat. "We'll see you at the Sweetings' this evening, yes?"

Jaw still tight, Sir Henry swallowed hard and tore his eyes away from Royce. "Very well," he said to Selina. He kissed her hand with such sincerity that Selina sighed, but did not change her request as he had hoped. "Good day."

"And to you," Royce nodded.

The moment Henry was out of earshot, Selina turned on her heel and clutched Royce's arm. She walked him in the direction of the tailor, but leaned into him threateningly, tightening her grip with each step.

"I don't expect the war to end in a timely manner, Royce," she started, "but as far as this battle is concerned, it's nearly ended, and you've lost." Royce lifted a brow, doubtful. "For until that certificate is signed and my estate belongs to you, the sole ruler of the Delamere fortune is unchanged. I'll gladly open my pocketbook for shrewdly chosen floral arrangements and lavish cakes—but the prince's robes are not my domain." She ended her words with the most genuine smile she's aimed in his direction since the start of it all.

He stared for a moment, slowing the pace and processing her response. "Meaning, you won't be paying for your husband's suit?"

"I won't be paying for my *fiancé's* suit. I do hope you have a few pounds left from your little storybooks, because it seems they'll need to carry you one last time."

Inhaling deeply, Royce heightened his tone with aggression. "Selina—"

"I told you, Royce," she stopped and faced him squarely, keeping her tone even and ominous. "You've bound yourself to a living hell. Allow yourself to roast in it while you wait to assume the throne."

3
Why Not Both?

When one is both among the most revered women in good society and without parents, one tends to attract a multitude of interested surrogates. No young lady could possibly go through with marriage without an adequate number of celebrations in her honor. The weeks leading to the union of Lady Selina and Mr. Royce were filled with dinner parties and luncheons to commemorate the happy couple. The crowning glory of these festivities was hosted by Mr. and Mrs. Sweeting.

Mr. Sweeting had been a particularly close friend of the late Lord Edward Delamere, thus prompting him with obligation to tend to his friend's orphaned heiress. Sweeting and his wife doted on Penelope, as she and their youngest daughter, Henrietta, had always been close. Selina, however, proved a more intimidating duty.

Nearly the day Selina took over management of the Everdon estate, unnecessary business ties were cut. Investments were shifted, and assets were re-evaluated. Sweeting never harbored bitterness toward Selina for ending their professional connection, no matter how cold and methodical she might have been. Bitterness and discomfort were quite different, however. The shrewd confidence in which Selina conducted her business affairs struck intimidation in the hearts of the men with which she often dealt. The aged businessman was no different; Sweeting maintained personal ties to the estate, tending to the girls as was needed and appropriate, but there was little likelihood he'd ever call upon Lady Selina without prompting from his compassionate wife.

"Congratulations, Selina!" Henrietta squealed the moment the betrothed couple entered the drawing room of the Sweeting home. Royce, having recovered from their scuffle over his wedding suit, had resumed his facade of the doting fiance, securing Selina's place on his arm. "Penelope told me about the flower arrangements and the cake— such wonderful choices! The wedding will be—"

"I understand you made most of the arrangements, Mr. Royce," Mary Kingston intruded, stepping directly in front of poor Miss Sweeting to do so. Selina lifted a brow and grimaced. "Such excellent taste; it's a shame Lady Selina managed to steal you away so quickly," Mary stepped closer to him.

"By all means," Selina said, lowering her tone with earnest, "don't let that stop you from trying."

Suddenly aware of how indecently forward she appeared, Mary stuttered, "I-I don't know what you mean."

"With the competition dwindling, there's hardly an excuse for remaining solitary," Selina's sardonic tone held steady as it fired. "I now concede the envious attention of the county's eligible men to you, Miss Kingston. I daresay, with me out of the way, you'll be married within the year."

Royce masked his snicker with a light cough, patting his snide bride's hand encouragingly. Further in the drawing room, Penelope loudly recounted to Mrs. Sweeting the events of the dress shop earlier that day—every detail from the silks to the flowers.

"It's the most wonderful shade of plum!" she told her.

"I believe Angelica wore plum as well. Oh, Selina—" Mrs. Sweeting reached out to grab Selina's passing hand, and Royce could feel her body tense at the mention of Lady Delamere's name.

"Lavender, ma'am," Selina softly corrected. "My mother wore lavender."

"Ah," Mrs. Sweeting gazed affectionately, still holding Selina's hand. "She was just the most divine bride. She would be ecstatic to see her daughter looking just as beautiful on her wedding day."

"She'd also be quite shocked, I'd think." Old Lady Philippa sat perched on the most ornate armchair in the room, settling into a less enthused demeanor than she had earlier in the day. As she had explained to the Sweetings upon arrival, she didn't expect to stay for the entirety of the evening, as she's "been on death's door" nearly all day.

Mrs. Sweeting dropped Selina's hand upon hearing her aunt's remark, but Selina just responded with a good-humored smirk. "Thank you, Aunt."

Though she had little interest in correcting the alleged insult, Philippa did point at Selina with a degree of pride. "From the day you were born, your father claimed no man would be worthy or sturdy enough for you." She paused and chuckled to herself. "I believe those were his exact words as well: *worthy* and *sturdy*."

Mr. Sweeting joined her in light laughter, even slapping a hand to his knee. "Seems Edward expected a farmer," he said. "I do remember that, however. He was over the moon—they both were—the day you were born, Lady Selina."

Selina shifted her weight, as well as her tension; her grip on Royce's arm loosened, but her fingers tightened around her sherry glass.

"Despite praying for a son," Sweeting went on, raising his glass to her, "you were a welcomed blessing. He spoke of the miraculous birth time and time again."

Sensing her discomfort, Royce widened his stance, as he often did when taking a stage. "I'm sure it was a story worth telling," he praised.

Her eyes now warily watching her fiance, Selina forced a smile and sipped her sherry, expecting Royce's onslaught of manipulative mockery. To her surprise, however, it did not come. Royce granted her a comforting glance before turning to his audience.

"There seem to be quite a few of those here," he offered. "The glamour of Everdon is beyond what I've ever dreamt of or written, to be sure."

"Ah," Sweeting grinned, moving in to engage in the shop talk. "But you've certainly spun your share of glamorous tales, Mr. Royce. I'm eager to see what you produce next. Is your publishing house London-based?"

"My current publishing house, yes. I've published through a small number of them in my time."

"Funded by Lady Selina?"

"The one in London is, as a matter of fact," Royce flashed a grin in Selina's direction, but brought Sweeting's attention back to him. "Fate really worked wonders to see we found each other, didn't it?"

It takes very little effort to cause young ladies to swoon, and Royce was a master at such skills. Mary and Henrietta both giggled at the thought of the romantic forces that brought Royce and Lady Selina together. Penelope, however, made a much more puzzled expression. Her idealist nature battled her fickle sense of reason.

In any case, Royce had succeeded in capturing the attention of the room, allowing Selina the vacancy to gather her wits once more, and notice Sir Henry's late arrival.

Sweeting nodded in his guest's direction, "Sir Henry." Henry returned the greeting, but kept his distance from the primary group in the drawing room upon making eye contact with Royce himself.

"Are we to expect any publications in the near future, Mr. Royce?" Sweeting asked. "Or will this wedding delay any sort of progress?"

"If my agent has his way, you'll see another novel before Christmas," Royce claimed.

"And if Lady Selina has her way, you'll be much too busy tending to her, I imagine." Sweeting and the other married gentlemen in the room chuckled in agreement at the understood nature of wives.

With dedicated intent, Sir Henry advanced toward Lady

Selina, only briefly acknowledging those greeting him along the way. "Selina."

"Henry," she addressed, taking a filled glass from a passing servant's tray.

"I take it that matters in town went well?" Henry's hands were in his pockets and his eyes wandered in every direction but hers.

"Yes, they did, thank you."

"Despite your fiance being so determined to make you destitute before your vows are even said," his tone dipped into disdain.

"*Henry*," she fired a withering stare.

Taking a hand from his pocket, he gently pulled her closer to him — a gesture that did not go unnoticed by Royce from across the room. "Did he seduce you?" Henry matched her whisper.

"Oh please," she rolled her eyes, keeping her voice low. "Me? A man like that is capable of many things, but I like to believe I am capable of controlling myself around such charm and appeal. Give me a little credit."

He exhaled in frustration. So much had passed between them over the years, that this sudden secrecy taunted him like nothing else could have. "What sort of hold does he have on you?" he pressed through a tense jaw.

Selina glanced at him, her lips shrugging with a small amount of contempt. "Little did you know, I was still readily available to accept the next handsome man to ask for my hand."

"You never have before."

"The right one neglected to ask for what he wanted."

Henry paused. "Selina…"

"It's a little late to be reciprocating now, isn't it, Henry?" she quietly chided, gulping the remainder of her drink. "No need to worry for Penelope and me. Go. Marry your Sophie. Fill that manor of yours with children and mind your business." Putting on a strained grin, Selina held up her empty glass and stepped away from him to fetch herself a refill.

Henry watched her and sighed. His voice thick with regret, he raised his glass to her. "Then I congratulate you, Lady Selina. And I pray the man endeavors to reach the top of your pedestal without causing it to crumble."

Responding with little more than a glance, Selina reached for a fresh glass of sherry and joined her fiance's side in one smooth movement. Royce may have smiled at her return, but Henry balled his fists. Most eyes may have been on Royce and Selina, but not all. A sympathetic friend caught a glimpse of his tight expression and deep glares.

"I wish Royce would decide on his own character," Lindon lightly hummed, joining Henry in the corner as Royce's arm wound around Selina's waist. Selina took a large sip of her beverage as he did so. "Is he a charming gentleman or is he an impertinent cad?"

Henry gulped from his own glass, mirroring Selina's hidden anxiety. "And why not both?" he suggested. "I think he is, in fact, equal parts charming and cad."

"She knows what she's about, Sir Henry."

"And why would she not?" he snapped at him defensively.

"You seem concerned, is all." Lindon's tone was filled with condolence. He'd worked alongside the Delameres long enough to know Henry's place and how he arrived in such a position.

"And you're not?" Henry gestured his half-empty glass to express the entirety of the situation at hand. "This man's been at Everdon less than a month and she's handing him the keys to the kingdom."

"Perhaps she's in love," Lindon offered.

Henry scoffed, "No. If Selina were in love, she'd be…" He paused, struggling to find the right words. Perhaps he no longer knew them.

"She's not seventeen anymore, Henry," Lindon murmured, noting his hesitation. "And he is no prince."

"No, indeed," Henry agreed, taking a swig from his glass. "I do believe Penelope called him a *rogue*."

"As I said, Selina knows what she's about."

"You will defend her until you die, Lindon," he set his glass down a little too firmly in a veiled attempt to control his bitterness.

"Yes, I will."

Forcing a hand in his pocket, Henry clenched his teeth. "Well, protecting her and defending her are entirely different."

Lindon had gained wisdom in his time on this dark earth and had learned when to respond to frustration with guidance and when to respond to rage with silence. Sir Henry, though a generally amicable man, hardly knew the difference between frustration and rage. His station demanded a certain level of decorum which didn't often allow him the freedom to explore the range of irrational emotions the human condition might trigger. When his hands began to shake, despite their discreet place in his pocket, Lindon knew Sir Henry did not need the negative encouragement of correction.

Across the room, Penelope, eager for the attention Royce had taken from her, insisted on performing a song on the Sweetings' harp. With Selina standing at her side, upon Penelope's insistence as well, she took the stage. She proudly announced the name of the piece and proceeded to play like an angel.

Taking the opportunity to slip away from the spotlight, Royce moved in the direction of Henry and Lindon. Seeing his approach, Henry grunted and brushed past him, claiming a better vantage point to hear the performance.

Royce snickered thinly. "Tempers must run high in the country."

Almost regretting not joining Henry in his exit, Lindon merely shrugged. "Hm, perhaps," he supposed. "I suspect you have a secretly volatile disposition yourself, Mr. Royce."

Royce considered this a moment, then slightly grinned. "Only with men. Women seem to have a more calming effect on me."

"Such a mystery."

"A woman can be reasoned with — much more intelligent beings than men. Most men are better persuaded with a fist."

"Manipulated," Lindon corrected.

Royce wrinkled his nose. "*Manipulate* is such a nasty word."

"Yet it is what you meant. Women can be wooed and controlled by a tender word. Men don't listen to words, they listen to actions." Lindon set his empty glass on the tray resting on the table beside him. "You are a master manipulator, Mr. Royce, and there's no denying you've studied your art. It's no wonder Lady Selina finds you so...fascinating. She hasn't had fresh stimulation in ages."

4
Queen Marries Rogue

Defeated is never a word one would like to use for a bride on her wedding day. Perhaps it should have been used to describe Lady Selina Delamere; however, the lady's chin was held high as Helen curled and set her hair. She was unmoved by Penelope's buzzing around the room; the energetic maid of honor frantically saw to every detail for the big day—well, every detail she remembered. It seemed she had misplaced the bouquet and, contrary to Selina's dispassionate expression, felt as though the rest of the day was now ruined.

"Oof!" she exclaimed, running straight into Lord Rafferty coming through the doorframe of Selina's bedroom.

Rafferty chuckled as the girl recovered. "May I be of some assistance, Miss Ayres?"

"Do you have the bouquet?" Penelope sighed.

"Tsk, I'm afraid not," Rafferty shook his head.

Almost annoyed with the answer, Penelope exhaled sharply, dramatically throwing her hands in the air before disappearing down the hallway to continue her search.

Rafferty chuckled again in amusement before catching sight of Selina sitting in front of her vanity, donning her wedding attire and appearing, even unfinished, as a vision in plum.

"Selina," he nodded to the bride. "You look lovely."

"Thank you," she replied mechanically, forcing a grateful smile.

The gentleman stood awkwardly for a moment, glancing from Selina to Helen and back. Selina felt his hesitance without needing to look at his strained expression.

"Was there something else, Colin?" she exhaled.

"Um..."

"It's all right," she told Helen. Lightly, she waved for her to sort through the assorted hair pieces to give Rafferty the illusion of privacy.

The illusion was enough to bolster his confidence, for his back straightened and he took a step closer. "Henry is concerned..."

"Not you too," Selina groaned.

"Selina," he lowered his tone. "I would like to...this one last time...offer you some...alternative to what you feel must be done—"

"Don't," the lady stood abruptly, alarming her lady's maid. "There are plenty of women in the county better suited for the role of your children's mother. Perhaps that pretty governess of yours."

Rafferty eased into a rather sad smile. "You'd rather it was Henry coming to your rescue. I've never seen the man so troubled."

"Colin," she held up her palm, begging him to concede. "I'm marrying Royce. I need—I want to marry Royce."

He eyed her for a moment, waiting for something in her voice, her eyes, her posture to break. When it seemed as though nothing would reveal even a crack, Rafferty sighed, bowing his head slightly. "Then....best wishes, Lady Selina."

Giving a deep bow, he graciously retreated from the room, once again nearly running into Penelope in the process.

"I found it!" Penelope hurried, panting from the exertion. Shortly behind her was Lindon, amusedly watching Penelope's victorious energy. "Well, Lindon found it, but we have it. It's ready for you!"

Loyally, she set the bouquet on a stand on the bedside table. Selina hardly responded; her eyes stared vacantly at her reflection while Helen finished setting the curls in her hair. The expression troubled Lindon, but he didn't have the heart to deafen Penelope's excitement with concerning questions.

"Penelope, why don't you see to it that the flowers at the church are also ready?" Lindon suggested.

"Of course," Penelope nodded with enthusiasm before bounding off down the hallway.

"Hm," Lindon lightly touched one of the poppies in Selina's bouquet. "The last time there were so many poppies in this house, it was your father's funeral."

"Mother would be ashamed of them. And father..." Selina trailed off before realizing she had forgotten something rather important. "Lindon," she looked up at him through the mirror. "Would you do me the honor of giving me away?"

"The honor would be mine," he told her, kissing the top of her head.

She smiled briefly and then returned to her vacant expression. "It's only right you stand by my side while I stroll toward the greatest moment of my life."

The bland tone disturbed Helen once again, bringing to mind the puzzling scene weeks earlier when Selina spoke to an hysterical Penelope regarding the engagement. Sensing Lindon's deeper intention for visiting Selina's room, Helen cleared her throat.

"I'll wait for you at the church, my lady," she curtsied to Selina, and then to Lindon before leaving them alone.

"Are you prepared for this, Selina?"

Realizing his eyes were on her, Selina straightened her back and pulled her lips into a smile. "Of course, I am. It's only marriage."

Slowly, he paced the distance between them, deliberating his words. "Have you considered...your future, Selina? Any regrets that may develop?"

When he stood directly behind her, he crossed his arms in front of his chest, as he had once done in her childhood. Extracting a confession from Selina was no simple task, and often involved heavy negotiations and patient hours of examining her defenses. She was resolute, and age did nothing to temper that.

"I've come to the conclusion," she started, reaching for her jewelry, "that, should the time come when his face becomes wrinkled and unseemly, I'll send him to live in the townhouse."

"Selina…"

"You've always told me love was complicated," she said dismissively, holding pearls up to her neck before making a decision.

"So," he continued to deliberate, "in settling, you chose a fortune-seeking opportunist who wastes your money and shamelessly flirts with every piece of womanly flesh which crosses his path."

Pointing at him through the reflection in the mirror, Selina smirked. "As the word *boring* was nowhere in that description…yes, I have. It's been some time the county had a delicious piece of gossip to sink their teeth into."

"I only wish it wasn't at your expense."

"My reputation has endured far worse than Royce," she chuckled humorlessly.

"Yes, but this one is resulting in matrimony, Selina." Lindon's tone became more severe, causing her to set the pearls back onto the vanity. "This is more than simply whispers and hearsay, as it was before. Whispers can be disproven. Actions like this lead one to assume the worst is well evidenced."

"I've spent so long living for Everdon," she exhaled. "Perhaps this is the small bit of rebellious thrill I'm permitted to hold on to. I am embarking on something akin to the great romantic adventures I've only read about. How could a woman like me watch such an opportunity go by?"

He furrowed his gaze and tilted his head, but before he could offer a rebuttal, Selina turned around in her chair and reached for his hand. "Trust my rebellion, Lindon," she pleaded. The corners of her eyes tensed as if the girl was preparing her mind for battle. Her words were empty; he didn't trust them. But her eyes were earnest. "Do as you've always done. Take my arm, stand by my side, and do what

Father never could."

For a moment, he saw her as a child dreaming of being a beaming bride with proud parents and a promising marriage ahead of her. But the moment passed. The child he saw before him had a steadfastness that brought more concern than hope. Impulsive though she might have been in her youth, Selina was far from foolish.

"Please," she whispered, tearing at the part of him mourning her childhood. "Please let me do this."

"Then you may fly…" Lindon softly, but hoarsely, conceded. With every ounce of paternal affection he could muster, he squeezed Selina's hand. "And here I will be, ready to catch you."

May 1889

June 1889

A sorrow's crown of sorrow is remembering happier times
~Alfred Tennyson~

1

Derivative Ghost Stories

When being romanced during the obligatory post-nuptial travels, any young couple is expected to become so lost in one another that time escapes them. However, the term *obligatory* might be considered particularly suitable for the new master and lady of Everdon. Not two weeks following their departure, the Everdon staff received word that preparations must be made for the returning newlyweds.

"Is it rather soon?"

Helen lingered in the doorway of Royce's bedroom while Mr. Price, his newly assigned valet, tidied and rearranged. She had begun work on Selina's room, but seeing Price pass her by, and being in desperate need of commiseration, she distractedly followed him.

Price merely shrugged. "Plenty of time for Master Royce to spend all the lady's money, I suppose," he concluded with a mild chuckle.

One look at a man like Darius Royce and one could easily surmise the level of taste to which he had so knavishly made himself accustomed. As Price lifted, brushed and sorted each of Royce's fresh assortment of suits, Helen leaned against the doorframe, a bit mesmerized. Once she had digested his claim of Royce's extravagance, she placed a quizzical hand on her hip.

"Do you really think he would?"

Price lifted a brow; her naivete was certainly endearing, but almost pitiable. "Hm, although, he does seem the romantic sort, doesn't he?" he padded his words gently. "Perhaps returning early was Lady Selina's idea."

Helen frowned. "I don't know what to think of him."

"Mr. Royce?"

"Well, yes. He seems so charming and pleasant. Moll says it's all part of his game—but how can that be true?"

At the mention of Moll's name, Price sighed. No self-respecting employee of Everdon gave much stock in Moll's claims, but her stories were not always completely unfounded. "Mr. Lindon offered me nearly twice the wage I was paid when I waited on the late Lord Delamere," he muttered, almost to himself, as he stood straighter.

Helen narrowed her eyes, waiting for him to explain himself. When he didn't, she said expectantly, "And?"

He sighed again, anticipating his future grievances. "Lindon shrewdly anticipates burdens," he replied plainly. "I feel I've been bribed."

"Ha!" Helen snorted, before realizing there was hardly a joke in his claim.

"There is something he knew from the start regarding Mr. Royce," he went on to explain, "and I suspect he felt the need to overcompensate me into accepting the position."

Helen placed both hands on her hips this time, challenging him. "Or the Lady Selina is generous to her staff," she offered. "She pays me nearly twice the average wage for a lady's maid, you know."

"You know this, eh?" Price laughed at her sudden wisdom. "From all your years of experience in other grand estates?"

Her shoulders settled, sensing the jest in his voice. "You're teasing me now," she pointed at him. "And it's unappreciated."

Price laughed again, this time more playful than mocking. Finishing Royce's room, he gestured for her to follow him to Selina's. Seeing Selina's bed still wearing old sheets, he proceeded to reach for the clean, folded bedding on a nearby chair and gestured for Helen to pull the old ones. Obediently, she did so, but her expression seemed dissatisfied. Price smiled and continued explaining his own assumptions,

"The moment the engagement was announced, Lindon increased household wages all around."

"Oh," Helen's hands returned to her hips, releasing the old sheets. "He did, didn't he? I told you Lady Selina was generous."

Price pointed back to the sheets until she complied and continued her work, albeit with an exasperated sigh. "I'll wager it's more complicated than mere generosity," he said. "With his habits, her money will soon dwindle enough on its own—any shrewd businessman would clamp tight on what he has."

"Well. Lady Selina is no businessman."

"No, she's not. She's a woman, and one who doesn't seem to mind the prospect of winding up penniless."

"You're awfully cynical, Mr. Price."

"An unfortunate symptom of working at Everdon far too long," he chuckled.

"How long have you been here?"

"Decades, Miss Thomas. Decades."

"And you served Lord Delamere."

"For years," was the simple reply.

As Price helped her stretch the new sheet across the bed, she raised her eyebrows and continued her line of questioning. "He was quite different, I imagine, from Mr. Royce."

"Far less interesting, if I'm honest," Price straightened his shoulders while Helen dutifully folded the top of the fine quilt. "Lord Delamere indulged in hunting for sport, with the occasional card game. Royce is the more whimsical sort, as many writers are."

"Whimsical?" she giggled.

"When you spend your spare moments rifling through half-written manuscripts and scribbling stories on scraps, it's safe to assume the term *whimsical* is appropriate. When I prepared his luggage for the honeymoon, he asked me if I was aware of the acidity of swine manure and its effects on a corpse."

Helen froze, dropping the pillow she had just picked up back down on the bed. "And that didn't….disturb you?"

"He's a writer, Miss Thomas. It's hardly unusual. Even avid readers like Croft let their minds stray through dark avenues. Makes for lively conversation. The widely imaginative often make the best company. Though his vices may begin to overpower his initial appeal."

Once the bed was finished, Mr. Price opened the lady's wardrobe and waved for Helen to pick Selina's change of clothes for supper that evening. Helen followed her silent orders and laid the necessary attire across the newly made bed.

"Do you think they went to the seaside?" she continued to muse.

"I couldn't even guess," Price sighed, seeing the topic was not yet resolved.

Helen smiled a little while she imagined the possible sights there were to see in all of the exotic locations she'd only read about. "I imagine they'd have great fun traveling abroad. Having adventures — perhaps riding on a ship."

"They were gone for two weeks," Price reminded her. "You're beginning to sound as fanciful as Miss Ayres, with slightly more sense to you."

"Be kind," she crossed her arms sternly in front of her chest. "She has a condition."

He nodded once. "Yes, some call it spoiled."

"Lady Selina doesn't spoil her," she countered.

Price smirked while he evaluated her work. Then, deciding she had accomplished all of her duties, he ushered her to the door so they could make their way to await the carriage.

"They deserve one another," he mumbled as they passed Royce's room once more.

"Lady Selina and Miss Ayres?" Helen wrinkled her brow.

"No, no, the happy couple."

"Oh," she nodded as she followed his lead down the stairs.

"I'm sure you're right. What's his story? I wonder. We hardly know a thing about him, except his books. We don't even know how long he's known the inspector."

"The inspector?" Price paused before reaching the bottom step.

"Inspector Barratt," she clarified.

"Interesting." His expression became contemplative as he internalized this new information.

"Do you suppose that's why the inspector came to Everdon?"

Price considered this and continued to the first floor. "He did stop sniffing around so much when Royce left on his honeymoon."

"Well, perhaps he's still busy interviewing tenants. He's spoken to me a number of times—and I didn't even know the poor thing. Did you know her?"

They reached the reception area on the path leading to the manor. Price straightened his vest and reached to straighten Helen's apron as well before answering.

"She was a good girl, Josephine," he said with soft remorse. "Did her job, kept her head down. She looked out for others too—all around, just a good girl." He assumed his position and faced the road, staring off into the distance as he continued. "But she grew quite distant toward the end there. I don't know what prompted it, but she did seem ready to go. Though I can't understand why."

"You said she became distant," Helen repeated.

"Lady Selina had just given her a raise," he explained. His tone was reflective and his face tensed as he remembered Josephine's last days. "She took her everywhere with her—connecting her to an obscene selection of eligible young men. Her marriage prospects were more promising than a girl of her station could've asked for. Seemed to be all she wanted."

"To be married?"

He nodded.

Helen fell quiet for a moment, prompting Price to glance at her from the corner of his eye. "Inspector Barratt believes she was murdered," she told him.

"Hm," he straightened his eye line, considering this. "I suppose that's not entirely ridiculous. She could've turned the wrong head...I'm sure the Lady Selina is at the top of his list of suspects."

"You don't think Lady Selina....she doesn't have the temperament."

"Everyone has the temperament," he corrected her firmly. "All it takes is the right reason."

Helen frowned. "What reason could she have had?"

"Jealousy, perhaps," he suggested.

"Is she the jealous sort? I haven't noticed..."

"Hm," he shrugged. "Likely not. Unless it has something to do with Sir Henry—which also seems unlikely. My suspicion: it was the father of the child who did her in."

Helen's voice dropped to a whisper. "Who do you suspect the father is?"

"Whoever he is...he'll get away with it. They always seem to."

She looked up at him with burning curiosity, but any further prying questions were silenced by Mrs. Melrose's hurried interjection as she joined them outside.

"What's that?" she said sharply, straightening the bottom of her dress.

"Nothing," Price assured her. "Just idle chatter." He winked at Helen, who replied with a nervous smile.

Within moments, the carriage came into view, making its way up the dirt path and stopping in front of Everdon's doors. The exorbitant groom and his straight-faced bride dismounted the carriage the moment it came to a stop.

"She doesn't look happy, does she?" Helen observed. Royce lifted Selina's hand and kissed it, but Selina's smile was forced, with far less of a convincing effort than she had exhibited during the engagement.

"It's the long journey, I'm sure," Mrs. Melrose muttered.

"Or the company," Price grunted.

"Oh, hush, you," Melrose playfully nudged his arm as the couple approached them. "Ah, the happy couple," she greeted. "Such a short trip, Lady Selina."

"My chequebook would disagree," was the terse reply.

With little more than a nod, Selina smoothly thanked Melrose and started for her bedroom. Her pace was almost quicker than Helen could match as she trailed behind with the footman carrying Selina's luggage. Helen waited for the footman to set the bags down and exit the room before prying as she did.

"How was it?" she hesitantly asked, seeing Selina settling at the vanity to remove her jewelry. Helen began unpacking the luggage, but only to seem occupied as she awaited Selina's full review.

Selina didn't respond immediately. Instead she paused to stare briefly at each earring; they were new, Helen noticed. She imagined they had been a romantic gesture on Royce's part, but Selina's expression was equal parts skepticism and spite.

"As the beginning of any marriage is expected to be," she eventually answered, in that bland tone she'd adapted since Royce's arrival. She caught sight of Helen's shoulders falling through the mirror. Selina stopped and turned her head to face her. "If you expected something more thrilling, you're free to imagine whatever you wish. No doubt that's what everyone else will do."

"Oh, I didn't mean...actually," Helen stumbled over her words, blushing lightly, "I did, um, while you were away, I sort of scribbled some ideas for a story of my own."

Seeing Helen's cheeks flush, Selina's expression softened. "Ah, you've been writing," she smiled at her.

"Everdon is quite inspiring," Helen's eyes brightened with energy. "I think I'd like to write a story about a heroine living in a haunted castle."

"The castle doesn't need to be haunted," Selina slowly shook her judgmental head. She turned back to the mirror and unfastened her necklace. "Ghosts and demons are so derivative."

"Oh..." Helen's voice dropped. "Um, what would you

suggest?"

Selina tapped her finger against her lips, smiling faintly at the challenge. "Perhaps magic?" she suggested. Standing from the vanity, she turned to face Helen once more. With a spontaneous energy, Selina leaned forward against the back of the chair and grinned. "I've always been fond of stories with fairies and goblins. Magic potions, true love's kiss, all that nonsense."

Helen returned the grin, seeing Selina's eyes slip into a distracted musing. She hadn't seen a smile like that on the lady's face, particularly since her engagement. Helen considered for a moment that the invulnerable Lady Selina was, at her core, quite the romantic.

"I do love magic," Helen agreed. "Perhaps I should see what Mr. Royce thinks—if that would be all right."

Selina's smile faded just a bit before she nodded curtly. "Of course," she stood upright. "He is the resident authority on fabricating stories." She then paused and inhaled deeply. "You know, I think I'd like to read some Charles Perrault tonight, Helen. Could you fetch it for me?"

Ghosts and demons being deemed derivative, Helen took a page from Lady Selina's book and snatched a collection by Hans Christian Andersen from the library before hiding away in her bed. Tightly gripping a candle holder in one hand and the opened cover of the book in the other, Helen read carefully as magic abounded, curious creatures dwelt with humans, and princesses were met with terrible misfortune.

Helen wrinkled her nose and heard an angry hissing voice come from the cot beside her.

"I told you," Moll sat up, her hair a netted mess atop her head. "Blow out the candle so we can both sleep. Ya don't need to read through the night!"

Hurriedly, Helen blew out the candle and settled back into her bed, placing the book on the bedside table. Her mind, however, did not rest when the lights went out. Her thoughts and theories raced around her head, never stopping for breath. With such an overwhelming web of ideas, she simply had to write them all down.

The second she suspected Moll had drifted back to sleep, Helen reached to light one more candle. As she did so, she heard the light shuffle of footsteps from down the hall. Fearing it was Mrs. Melrose, she quickly blew out the candle and hid back under the covers.

There was silence for a moment.

Then the whistle of the wind.

And then the footsteps returned.

They were not in Mrs. Melrose's usual cadence.

They weren't as creaky as the floorboards of the old house while faring against the blistering elements, they didn't patter across the floor the way the rain beat against the shutters; they seemed to glide through the hallway, and then down the stairs.

Fear hastily melted into a curiosity that consumed her, possessing her to light another candle and ever so quietly get out of bed. She crept into the corridor and slowly stepped closer to the staircase. Her eyes struggled to adjust, but as far as she could see, there was no one. All were asleep in their closed bedrooms.

On the first floor, Helen's tricky eyes caught a glimpse of a shadowy movement heading in the direction of the parlor. She lunged as stealthily as she could toward the room, but saw and heard no more than the snoring hunting dogs lying on the sofas, almost in unison with the gently disturbed curtains behind them.

"Calm down," she whispered to herself. "Ghosts are so derivative," she added, hoping to exude the confidence in which Selina had spoken the words.

Despite her realism countering her imagination, she stepped closer to the curtains, reaching a trembling hand to pull the curtain to one side. Through the dark and rainy abyss, the moonlight reflected just enough to reveal the silhouette of a woman standing in the courtyard. Helen couldn't discern features beyond her slender frame, no doubt drenched from the downpour.

Just as she attempted to open the window and beckon the woman to come inside and out of the rainfall, she heard a voice behind her.

"It's a little late for you, isn't it?"

Helen's head whipped around to see Price standing behind her, holding a candle up to her face. "There was—there was a woman outside," she pointed desperately.

He cocked his head to one side, squinting. "It's pourin' buckets out there. Everyone with half a brain is inside."

She looked quickly back to the window to show him the woman who clearly needed assistance, only to see nothing but darkness and silver rain drops blocking all view of the courtyard. In aggravated confusion, she exhaled sharply. "What are you doing out and about, then?"

"I used to work in a shop in London, lass," he placed a hand on her back and led her away from the window. "The night you don't check the doors is the night you get an intruder with less than savory intentions. Now, come on, let's get you back to your room."

Helen nodded as they moved up the stairs. It seemed a reasonable conclusion. "Were those your footsteps then?"

"I imagine so," he assumed. "Everyone else is fast asleep. Now get some rest so you can serve the lady tomorrow without tripping over your own feet."

"I'll be fine, I'm perfectly well," Helen insisted. She didn't dare argue further; however, her hands were still trembling. Clearly, she had been more shaken by the apparition of that poor woman she claimed to have seen.

"Where've ya been?" Moll stood behind the door, hands at her hips, poised for interrogation filled with misplaced concern.

"I-I thought I heard footsteps," Helen mumbled as she passed her to sit on her bed.

Instead of pressing, Moll nodded agreeably. "Seems right."

"I remember hearing them before," Helen rubbed her face, "but they went away, and I thought I was just imagining it all. Why would they come back?"

Shrugging, Moll sat on her own bed and crossed her legs, leaning her elbows against her knees. "The noises get worse when the weather's bleak. Makes the ghosts restless."

Helen shook her head vehemently. "Don't be silly. Ghosts are so derivative."

"They're what?" Moll wrinkled her nose.

"They're just…silly."

"Well," Moll prodded, wiggling her eyebrows. "Did ya find anything?"

"I…" she glanced up to see Moll's teasing expression. Releasing an irritated exhale, she said, "I saw a woman outside in the rain. Perhaps. But that would be ridiculous. It was just a tree—and the footsteps were just Mr. Price checking the doors."

"That paranoid nutter," Moll muttered, shaking her head. "Maybe you did see a tree. Or that dead maid."

"I don't think it was Josephine," Helen waved her hand dismissively. Not wanting to invite any further mocking, she tucked her legs underneath her bedding and attempted to settle herself comfortably for sleep.

"Nah, the first one," Moll continued, maintaining her upright determination. "Before Josephine. Before you were even a gleam in yer mum's eye."

Helen rolled on her side to face her, never one to say no to a story, no matter the source. "How did she die?"

Moll shrugged again, following Helen's lead and tucking herself under her bedding as well. "The ghost isn't too chatty. But she was beautiful, I know that much."

"How do you know?"

Pausing for a thoughtful moment, the jaded maid sighed. "There's a beauty in death, isn't there?"

"There's a beauty in life, too," Helen pointed out.

"Yeah, s'pose so."

"What was her name?"

"No one knows for certain. One a' those stable boys told me he found a little headstone in the woods on the property somewhere. *Sarah Atwood*, it says. I'd imagine that's the dead maid's name."

"Sarah," Helen repeated, reaching for her pencil and parchment. "Lovely name. I'd like to know her story."

"You're better off scribbling one down yourself. No one knows—or the ones who know won't talk." Moll rolled her eyes and her body away from her, signaling the end of their exchange.

"Hm." Helen took her advice; of the many stories Everdon held, the scribbled name of Sarah Atwood should have one too.

2

He Who Holds the Chequebook

"Can I offer you some tea, Mr. Litchfield?"

The round, potato-shaped gentleman with fine clothes that hardly matched his mussed hair and scruffy chin, sat nervously in the Everdon library. His nerves were so loud, he almost failed to acknowledge Lindon's offered hospitality.

"Oh no, I don't want to be of any trouble."

"It would be no trouble at all," Lindon suppressed a chuckle. Everdon guests being of any trouble was becoming a trend, as of late, but the crooked caretaker of the local orphanage had always cast a stinky shadow on the door at every occasion warranting a visit.

As was the usual method, Lady Selina allowed Litchfield's nerves to grow and get the better of him as he sat awaiting his meeting with her. Guilt has a way of bubbling until it manifests itself in one alarming manner or another, no matter how much effort is spent in extinguishing it.

Mr. Croft noted the man's anxiety from around the shelf corner he was straightening. Every soul in the room knew that Selina didn't invite him for a friendly chat. To ease some of the tension, Croft reached for an appropriate piece of fiction and joined Lindon's hospitable efforts.

"Might I offer you a book? Something to read while you wait, sir? I have a knack for knowing everyone's ideal story, if you will. I have a feeling you'd be a *Jane Eyre* sort of fellow."

"Seems a reasonable choice," Lindon agreed.

Litchfield waved his pudgy hand. "No, no. Thank you, but reading has never been of interest to me."

Croft's nose wrinkled in deep disgust, but Lindon was unbothered. "Ah. Lounging with a sturdy mug of sherry is more your speed," suggested the steward.

Litchfield pointed at him in agreement and grinned. "Ah-ha, yes indeed."

"Perhaps some sherry for the gentleman, then, Croft," Lindon turned to the librarian, who still stood frowning in shock.

The thought of any soul preferring sherry over *Jane Eyre* was beyond him. But, obediently, he left the room to fetch a new bottle of sherry from the wine cellar.

"My lady," Croft nodded his head, his expression still bearing hints of judgmental dismay.

Selina was a panther poised for a hunt, her hands deliberately joined in front of her and her chin held high. Royce followed with his hands tucked into his trouser pockets. Viewing the lady in her natural setting was sure to be a sight to behold, and he was practically grinning in anticipation.

"The indolent oaf is here, isn't he?" Selina hummed to her ruffled librarian.

Croft sighed. "Sherry over Brontë…" he shook his head.

Selina chuckled; Croft's disappointment in the taste of guests was routine. He had always maintained the belief that each wandering soul was in search of a story, and was grievously disheartened when any of them preferred a simple beverage over insightful words. Hanging his head in his standard shock, he moved along to fetch more sherry.

As Selina and Royce approached the threshold of the library, Selina turned quickly on her heel, tugging her husband's arm to prevent him from passing through the door frame. Surprised by the abrupt pause, Royce looked to her with wide eyes.

"Legality is allowing you to participate in this meeting, but this is a sensitive matter," she placed a hand on his chest, capturing his complete attention. "I implore you to let me handle Litchfield."

A sardonic brow was lifted as Royce answered, "But, of course. I'm your humble servant."

"I'm warning you, Royce," her tone deepened. "This issue is mine, and mine alone."

Royce mimed the closing of a zipper across his lips, assuring his total compliance, but the lady had her doubts. Tightly she took his arm as they entered the room to meet with Litchfield.

"Mr. Litchfield," Selina greeted with a diplomatic grin.

The man took to groveling nearly the moment she said his name. He stood from the armchair and lunged for her hand, eager to kiss it, inciting a smirk from Royce. "Ah, the lovely Lady Selina."

"And this," Selina moved her hand out of his reach, "is Mr. Royce, my….husband."

"I heard the news," Litchfield bowed. "It is an honor, Mr. Royce. And congratulations."

"Thank you," Royce curtly nodded. He turned his head and visibly tightened his lips, so as to show his wife his continued cooperation.

Selina rolled her eyes and took a seat across from the armchair on which Litchfield had previously sat. "How has the orphanage been running in my absence?"

"Oh very well, my lady. As always."

"Interesting. There are always holes in the walls?"

"Holes in the…"

"And reduced rations for meals…tattered and worn out bedding for the children…"

"I can assure you, my lady, that everything is in pristine order. Those children are well cared for under my reign."

"Excellent," Selina lightly threw her hands in the air in mock relief, letting a hand then rest on Royce's knee. "Well, we should journey into town to see for ourselves then, shouldn't we, darling? It's been far too long since I've seen the children. We should stop by this afternoon, before we write the next cheque."

Royce leaned forward at her touch, carefully watching as Litchfield's panic began to rise.

"Um, uh, my lady…" the caretaker stammered. "Perhaps if you were to-to write the cheque first, then the children would be able to be—um, properly prepared for your visit."

"Properly prepared? Was my last donation not adequate enough to keep them…prepared?"

Royce grinned wildly; it was not simply beauty and wealth that kept Selina in such revered status. She was a craftsman in the art of manipulation. Her shoulders were relaxed, her neck confidently lengthened—there was not a single tell in sight. In fact, he could have sworn he saw a sparkle in her eye as she watched her prey squirm. When Moll brought a tray of tea, along with the new bottle of sherry Croft had requested, Selina idly looked in her direction and accepted the filled teacup she offered.

"Upkeep is ongoing, my lady," Litchfield insisted, wringing his hands. "It's hard work to keep an orphanage in running order."

Royce crossed one leg over the other and leaned back, gesturing lazily to Litchfield. "At least the staff is well-dressed. That's an excellent suit."

Self-consciously, Litchfield adjusted his tie and cleared his throat. "We do business with wealthy donors, sir. Appearances are of utmost importance."

"Oh, of course," Royce nodded, mirroring the man's gesture and straightening his own vest as well. Litchfield smiled in understanding.

"Indeed they are. I've written that assistant I gave you—Mr. Bryant, if you recall," she let her eyes wander, giving Litchfield a momentary rise in anxiety. "He sent me a copy of the institution's financial statement. Costs, incomes, donations, and such." To tighten the tension she'd achieved, Selina paused to sip her tea. "It's fascinating how few donors you've collected over the years. It seems I am the only benefactor who's bothered indulging your…." her eyes finally fell back on him, "appearances."

Litchfield desperately glanced at Royce, seeking affirmation that his appearance was of the utmost importance. He had no such fortune, however. Royce continued grinning and had returned to studying his wife at play.

"It's also fascinating," she went on, "expenses toward supplies, as well as employee salaries seem rather inconsistent. Now, Mr. Litchfield, I expected a swindler to at least excel in his own craft. I can respect thorough cunning, but this is just pitiful. You were too lazy to even forge accounts correctly. Honestly, I'm quite disappointed."

"My lady—"

The lady leaned forward, her eyes narrowing. "Fancy suits and expensive brandy—I can smell it from where I'm sitting," she said in a low, accusatory tone. Straightening her posture once again, she set her teacup on the table beside her. "In light of our recent nuptials, Mr. Royce and I have been inclined to rearrange some estate assets. I'm not entirely sure I'll be able to continue supporting the orphanage for much longer."

Litchfield's mouth fell open, releasing a stupefied grunt. "You'd…you'd abandon those poor children, Lady Selina," he faltered. "They'd—they'd starve without your donations."

Royce snorted.

"It seems they've starved with my donations as well," Selina stood smoothly. "I'll not be funding your wardrobe and drinking allowance, Mr. Litchfield. Good day." Angling herself to exit, she waved her hand for him to follow her out of the room.

"But, I—Mr. Royce," Litchfield stood quickly, forcing assertive resonance. He glimpsed at Selina from the corner of his eye, but narrowed in on the new executor of his fate. "I beg of you to reconsider."

Selina's mouth opened slightly in disbelief, her determined posture never wavering, however. Royce's grin easily released an arrogant chuckle; he even flashed Selina a haughty glance as he did so.

"Please," Litchfield continued the pleading, stepping closer to Royce. "The orphanage is in great need of income. It is *your* decision, good sir."

Selina shifted her weight in growing frustration.

"And just imagine the golden reputation you'd maintain in town," the caretaker lowered his voice. "With such a fresh set of society to impress…"

Royce shook his head, only laughing louder as the man begged. "Aw, now I'm the one who's disappointed." Like all in the room, the fool was now at his mercy—and there was nothing Royce loved more than to play. "But, in point of fact, you're right," he pointed at him. "It is my decision, isn't it?"

He could almost feel his wife's jaw clench, her hands wring, and every ounce of energy radiating from her was sour. Ignoring her threatening glance, Royce stood tall from his chair and lifted his chin, examining the prey at hand.

"My wife has been the loyal donor for years. She's the one with a soft spot for those orphans." Pausing a moment, he wrinkled his nose. "I don't care much for orphans, you know. Being poor and learning to fend for oneself never hurt. Makes them all tough, you see. Ready for the cold, hard world ahead."

Litchfield's eyes widened as he took a step back in retreat. "Um, yes, but sir—"

"You're begging the wrong benefactor. Perhaps you should reconsider your strategy."

Just as quickly as he'd turned his back on Lady Selina, Litchfield returned. Despite her hardening gaze and stiffening upper lip striking no small amount of anxiety within him, he proceeded to grovel yet again. "Lady Selina, I beg of you."

One more burst of laughter was released; Royce could hardly contain himself. "So suggestible!" he exclaimed. "You're not a complete fool, I'll give you that. You've managed to trick Selina into believing you were managing an upstanding orphanage for some amount of time, I suppose. You've just gotten lazy. The cat became the mouse because his effort slid out of control."

The attribution hit its mark, rendering Litchfield dumb for a few moments. He had no defense—and how could he? His pristine wardrobe, liquored breath, and smooth hands betrayed him, and there was no point in wasting the energy to argue. All that he bothered to expel in his own defense was a half-hearted, "I'm terribly sorry, Mr. Royce. I only want what's best for the children."

"Sure, sure," Royce waved a flippant hand. "I'll continue making donations."

"Darling?" Selina said through gritted teeth as Royce pulled the estate cheque book from his coat pocket.

In one swift movement, he flashed it within Selina's blatant view and whipped it open to the first blank cheque. He then stepped toward Croft's desk to reach for a fountain pen. "As long as supplies are provided," he began to sign, "and…all that other nonsense my wife seems to care about…"

Sighing deeply in relief, Litchfield accepted the cheque and held it close to his chest as Royce returned the book to his pocket. "You are an incredibly honorable gentleman, sir," he flattered. "Your generosity is beyond words."

"I'm sure you'll come up with a few," Royce chuckled skeptically, gesturing for Litchfield to make a more complete exit this time.

"I'll see to it that the children are fed and clothed, and that Bryant works harder than he ever has to maintain adequate living," Litchfield swore as he obediently followed Royce's lead to the doorway.

"Of course." Royce glanced behind to see that Selina remained still, frozen in fury and shock.

"And might I say," Litchfield added in a mumble, lightly touching Royce's arm with inflated camaraderie, "it is a delight to see some good sense finally added to Everdon, sir."

In spite of Litchfield's best efforts, Selina heard the insult, as clear as day; the sound of Royce's agreeable chuckle only made her fists ball and her shoulders stiffen all the more. The men shook hands, cementing whatever understanding Litchfield believed he'd achieved.

With sudden ferocity, however, Royce grabbed Litchfield's arm with his free hand, pulling the man in just a bit closer. His eyes were direct and, though his tone was soft, there was no mistaking his intensity. Litchfield stiffened in alarm at the abruptly powerful grip.

"If my wife pays you a visit," Royce muttered, "and sees a single empty bottle, hungry child, or hole in the wall, you'll wish the place had burned down on top of you. Understand?"

The fool should've expected the new lord of the estate would not be the type to mince words—diplomatic threats and poised insults were the Lady Selina's style, and her reign had all but ended as far as Litchfield was concerned. With no more than a thick clearing of his throat, Litchfield bowed to Royce and hastily left, letting himself out and retreating as far from Everdon's doors as possible.

Royce lingered in the doorway, amusedly watching Litchfield scurry away. He didn't notice Selina join him at the threshold until she gripped his arm tightly with her fingers. The feeling of her fingernails about to dig into his skin was a familiar enough gesture that evoked a much more dramatic flinch than Royce anticipated.

"*Never* interfere with my business dealings again," she seethed, forcing his attention back to her.

"Oh, please, Selina," his eyes rolled in annoyance, shaking off her grasp.

But she would not yield. "Whatever fear he once held toward me dissipated the moment you opened your mouth."

"What does it matter?" Royce exhaled. He slackly looked down at her, as if humoring her. "You're getting what you want. He'll clean up his act and those children will be fed. Now let it go."

"Don't you dare tell me to let this go—" her volume rose.

"You see this?" he stopped her. He pulled the cheque book from his pocket once more. "See where it belongs?" he slowly slipped it back into place. Her gaze followed the book from his hand to his pocket, and then narrowed dangerously. "Litchfield's not the only one at my mercy, it seems."

"You meddle in any more business and you'll bring Everdon to ruin just like my father," she warned. Down the hall, Lindon had turned a corner and started in the direction of the library, taking notice that a guest had just left. Selina lowered her voice and sharply added before Lindon was within earshot, "Then we'll both be penniless and all of this *arrangement* will be for naught."

Though he could not hear the words exchanged as he approached, Lindon was sure to notice the mutually aggressive stances of the happy couple while they stood together in the threshold of the library. He was interrupting a lovers' tiff, it seemed.

"Is the Litchfield situation resolved, then?" Lindon innocently inquired.

Selina took a step away from her husband, turning on her heel to walk away so she would no longer have to look at him directly. "We'll see in time, I suppose," she replied with a tightness that concerned Lindon, "if Royce's strong arm proves effective or detrimental."

"Ah," Lindon's eyebrows rose higher than the ceiling. It was unlikely Selina willingly allowed her new husband to conduct a business meeting, particularly one regarding the orphanage; he could only imagine the turmoil between them.

Instead of acknowledging the steward's presence, Royce pushed past Lindon and called out in a commanding tone, "Selina, I wasn't finished!"

She ignored him until the moment he reached for her arm and gripped it with even more tenacity and aggression than she had. If venom had ever shown itself on Lady Selina's face, it was nothing compared to the daggers her glare fired at Darius Royce as she spun to face him. Not one threat needed spoken for his hand to swiftly withdraw.

"What more could you want...darling?" she deliberated.

Clearing his throat, Royce tucked his dominant hand in his pocket. "You remember the Abrams."

"Of course," Selina wrinkled her nose.

"Well, I've invited them to Everdon."

"When?"

"When we saw them in London."

"Ah, well, I'm shocked it took you so long to summon some of your own kind," she lifted her nose in the air.

Royce's jaw tightened at the superiority in her tone. Before he could fire a retort, Lindon chimed in with affirmation.

"Your friends are certainly welcome to stay in your own home, Mr. Royce."

"I know they are," Royce agreed, maintaining commanding eye contact with his wife.

"The standard visit for guests at Everdon is a fortnight," Selina stated firmly. "No more."

"They are my guests, Selina," he took a domineering step forward. "They'll be staying as long as I wish them to. And they'll be afforded every luxury Everdon has to offer."

A long, tense moment passed between them as their venomous stares held tightly. Any other man would've crumbled beneath Selina's unwavering supremacy, but Royce stood even taller. Something between them struck deep concern within Lindon, who observed in anticipation until one of them broke.

"Of course," the lady eventually exhaled, her words robotically submissive. "And why wouldn't they?"

Lindon cleared his throat. "I'll...I'll see to it that accommodations are prepared," he assured them.

"Yes, do that," Royce ordered without so much as a glance in his direction before walking past them.

Lindon watched curiously as the master of Everdon strolled back down the corridor. "Well, I daresay..."

"It's good to be king," Selina finished for him, wringing her hands together.

3

Seduction of the Greatest Caliber

"Selina, dear!"

Elinor Abram crooned as she dramatically dismounted the carriage. Ten years her senior and far below her status and breeding, Miss Abram presumed an oddly imperious demeanor when greeting her hostess of Everdon. From her tone to the way she kissed Lady Selina's cheek, she held no implication of her own class.

"It is absolutely brilliant to see you again, darling. I was telling Bernard after the two of you left us that we absolutely *must* see Royce's little wife again. Didn't I, Bernard?" Her red head bobbed in the direction of her elder brother, who soon followed her out of the carriage.

"She certainly did," Abram confirmed his sister's claim. "And she couldn't have been more right." After straightening his vest at the sight of the lovely lady of Everdon, Abram cleared his throat, flashed a grin, and reached to kiss the half-heartedly offered hand of Lady Selina.

Selina's shoulders tensed in distaste, but soon loosened in relieved frustration at the sound her husband's footsteps coming from behind her. Writers are often haphazard and preoccupied creatures, whether the story forming in their mind is considered promising or not. Time slipped away for Royce as he had mentally escaped for the morning, leaving his irritated wife alone with Penelope and an array of staff to welcome his guests.

"I'm always right. Aren't I, Royce?" Elinor said loudly as she saw him approaching.

When she felt him beside her, Selina mumbled, "Where have you been?"

"Running late, it seems," he mumbled back, putting on a smile that suggested a friendly exchange, rather than the scolding Selina expressed.

"But I suppose you must now say that *she* is always right," Elinor continued, now gesturing to Selina as the couple muttered their bickering.

Penelope smiled politely as Abram kissed her hand as well, but her focus drifted back to Selina as the discomfort settled. "It is true," she told Elinor. "Selina is always right."

"As well she should be," Elinor tightened her smile. "Someone needs to keep Royce right."

The Abram siblings were well-matched in features and complex grins. Only a couple of years apart in age, one could easily mistake them for two heads of the same snake. Both greeted their old friend with a certain ascendant familiarity: Abram gave Royce's shoulder a friendly squeeze, causing Royce to flinch, while Elinor held her hand expectantly in the air, awaiting a kiss.

Lindon, who soon fell in line with Helen and Mrs. Melrose after finishing business of his own, noted Penelope's immediate gravitation toward him. "What did I miss?" he whispered to her, jutting his chin in the direction of the Abrams.

Mrs. Melrose grunted and muttered under her breath, "I think Lady Selina's got her hands full with this lot."

Penelope snorted, only to be nudged by Lindon. "Well, she likes him a great deal, doesn't she?" she whispered, watching as Royce obligingly kissed Elinor's eager hand.

"Hm." Lindon left Penelope with Helen and approached Selina and her guests in time to hear her sardonic chuckle.

Royce's own chuckle was well-disguised, but Lindon heard the uneasy catch in his throat and saw the side-glance in Selina's direction. Selina's mockery was hardly filtered, yet the presumptuous Miss Abram continued to laugh too loudly as she took Royce's arm. "Now, Royce, you *must* show me the grounds." She led him to the edge of the gravel path, gesturing to the grandness before her, which he now possessed in its entirety. "There is so much to see—and I only saw a small portion from the carriage ride. Just how much land is on this estate?"

The sight of the victor lording his winnings over an eager, albeit irritating audience brought a grimace to Selina's face. However, his tense shoulders and clearly mixed regard for the nuisance still managed to bring her some satisfaction.

As if on cue to increase the lady's satisfaction, the carriage of Sir Henry Kincaid rolled up the hill to Everdon's doors. The moment it passed Royce and Elinor, Royce felt prompted to return to his wife's side. However, his attention was forced back to his guest, who continued to interrogate him with questions of tenants and earnings.

Selina smiled in relief as Henry exited his carriage. Finally, a comforting face. "Henry," she greeted, approaching him immediately.

He returned the smile and glanced strangely at the Abrams. "Selina," he kissed her hand softly. "You have guests. I should come back later."

Before he could release her hand and step back toward his carriage, Selina gripped his hand in earnest. "No, not at all," she insisted. Desperate for relief, she pulled him toward her guests. "This is Royce's friend, Mr. Abram, and over there is his sister, Miss Elinor Abram." As she gestured, Abram nodded to Henry in acknowledgment. "This is Sir Henry Kincaid."

"Pleasure, my good man," Abram imposed a handshake and stood just a bit taller.

Dutifully, Henry responded in kind, returning the grip and squaring his own shoulders. "The pleasure is all mine. Welcome to Everdon."

"We're forever grateful for the invitation, Lady Selina."

"Oh of course," Selina discreetly touched Henry's hand,

begging for reinforcement, before stepping away from him to return to the role of involuntary hostess. "Any friends of Royce are welcome here."

"Now, which of the help will be at my disposal?" Abram ran his eyes along the line of servants behind their mistress, until his salacious gaze rested on her lady's maid.

Selina smoothly stepped in his line of sight, her hands joined commandingly in front of her. The silent contradiction and the tension it triggered could be felt by Royce, a stone's throw away, finally bringing him to break any obligation he previously had to continue his cursory survey of the land with Elinor.

"You didn't bring your own?" Penelope blurted in confusion, almost chuckling.

"Nell," Selina hushed her. "Of course you will be lent a manservant during your stay, Mr. Abram," she explained in a rehearsed tone. "Every luxury Everdon has to offer—isn't that what Royce promised?"

Blocking the view of her lady's maid did nothing to dispirit Abram; he much preferred the sight of the lady herself, in any case. Looking her up and down, Abram grinned wider. A glance at Sir Henry's expression, however, warranted a correction in posture and tone. "He's always known how to treat his friends," Abram shot in Henry's direction.

"I'm sure he has," Henry cleared hints of disdain from his throat.

The brazen guest puffed his chest and placed a finger to his lips before pointing it at Lindon. "Hm, you."

"Yes, sir," Lindon dutifully stepped forward. Selina exhaled sharply in disbelief.

"Take my bags to my room and see that I'm settled," Abram ordered.

"Mr. Abram," Selina once again stepped intrusively in front of him, her tone hardening. "Had you more experience with estates such as Everdon, you would have known to wait until you've been given proper introduction to your...help. I can only excuse your presumptions by remembering that you are far from your London flat. Mr. Lindon is not a manservant."

Royce returned to the group as Selina's aggression grew. He nodded momentarily in acknowledgment to Henry and moved away from Elinor's grip. He couldn't fathom how, but he felt the urge to see that Selina didn't offend their guests further. Sensing the discomfort, Lindon lightly touched Selina's arm in reassurance.

"It's quite alright, my lady," he told her.

"No," she shook her head decidedly. Her lips were tight; civility only lasted so long in a Delamere's manners when territory was invaded. "Fetch a footman for him. That's what we pay them for."

Taking little notice to the disturbance he had caused, Abram chuckled. "And what do you pay him for?" he pointed again at Lindon.

"He is my steward," Selina leaned forward with firmness. "A position which demands respect in my household. Do we understand one another?"

Abram grinned at her audacity. "Indubitably, Lady Selina. I wouldn't have it any other way," he bowed.

"Let's have tea," Royce finally spoke. In agitation, he guided his guests toward the entrance

With a wary eye on Abram, Henry lightly reined Selina's arm toward him, slowing his pace as well as hers. "Shall I stay...for tea?" he prodded.

"Please," Selina playfully begged.

"Of course," he winked. Clearing his throat again, Henry thought it best to ask the obligatory question, "How was the honeymoon?"

"As expected," was her bland response.

There was no flutter of her eyelashes, flush in her cheeks, nor a rise in heartbeat—all of which Henry closely awaited. It was an oddly unenthused reaction, bringing a frown to form on his face. His gaze flickered from Royce, leading the party into the parlor, to Selina's evident disinterest. Henry slowed his pace even further, bringing

Selina to linger near the front door. As the sight of Royce and the Abrams faded, Selina's shoulders loosened.

"Sounds romantic," he muttered. "I, uh, called while you were away. To check on Penelope, of course. And, uh, Mr. Croft lent me this." From his coat pocket he pulled out the Everdon copy of *The Mystery of Edwin Drood*.

Selina glanced at it and rolled her eyes. "Frustratingly unfinished," she said. "What did you think of it?"

"That it was frustratingly unfinished," Henry laughed, echoing her review. "Croft's taste is peculiar, but I suppose Dickens is always a middling read at the very least."

"So not a complete waste of your time," Selina joined in the laugh.

The sparkling nature of Lady Selina's laugh carried through the hall and into the parlor where Royce and his unsavory guests resided. Penelope had easily grown bored of their company and left for the garden before the tea had even been served. Helen had seen to the mending of one of Selina's dresses upstairs, leaving Royce and the Abrams to settle into a more comfortable posture of conversation while Selina and Henry took their time to enter.

Elinor watched the doorway with keen curiosity as the men took to their tea. "Does he know your game, Royce?" she whispered.

"My game?" Royce sipped his tea casually.

"He seems the more likely choice for her. Is he absolutely furious with you for stealing her away?" she released a throaty giggle.

"It doesn't matter," Royce waved a hand dismissively, setting his teacup back on the table in the center of the parlor. "She and I have a mutual understanding."

"Mmm," Elinor purred, crossing one leg over the other. "Mutual understanding is seduction of the highest caliber."

Her brother, coming out of his own mind, ignored both the tea and the current conversation, yet clumsily attempted to contribute. "I must say, when you said you meant to target Miss Ayres instead of Lady Selina, I thought you'd settled. Underestimated your own ability." He shook his head and wagged a finger in unison. "But no, sir. Your genius has shown through. You've truly accomplished an insurmountable feat—using the girl to get to the guardian. Well done." Impressed, Abram gestured to the ornate décor of the parlor alone. "What successful trickery this is."

Royce squared his shoulders. "And if there was no trickery?"

"Oh don't bother being coy," Abram snorted. "Not with us. A woman like her is not so easily charmed."

Royce leaned back, bringing a closed fist to his lips and pressing his elbow against the arm of the chair. Regardless of whether or not his claims were unfounded, Abram's doubts stung like lemon juice on an open wound. To further the sting, Selina waltzed into the parlor on Henry's arm, bearing a light-hearted beam.

"Penelope and I will ride in Henry's carriage to the luncheon at Rafferty's," she informed him.

Royce straightened his back, lowering his fist. "I've invited our guests to join us," he gestured to the Abrams."

Narrowing her gaze, but not losing her smile, Selina clicked her tongue. "Then they shall ride in *your* carriage, darling."

He could feel Abram's eyes on him as he stood to face his wife. Lowering his tone and ignoring Henry's presence, Royce gripped Selina's elbow, angling her away from the group. "And why wouldn't my wife ride in my carriage?" he questioned.

Inquisitively, both Abrams stood and moved closer to the growing conflict. They were well-seasoned spectators when it came to the dealings of Royce and his marks, but never had he had such a beguiling subject on whom they could prey.

Still unfazed, however, Selina's smile twisted into a smirk. "I'm afraid there isn't room enough for her. What with your close friends also being extended an invitation, apparently. Henry has graciously offered his carriage."

"Excellent," Royce exclaimed, his voice rising sharply. "Then the Abrams will ride with him, and my wife will ride with me."

"There must be room for the four of us," Abram chimed in,

taking a step closer to the Lady Selina. "Little Penelope can ride with Sir Henry."

"Royce is right," Henry said. He lightly touched Selina's shoulder, smoothly moving her closer to her husband and putting himself in Abram's path. "I shall take you and your lovely sister," he told Abram. "There's no need to crowd the newlyweds. I have plenty of room." With forced enthusiasm, he nudged the man and gestured for Miss Abram to follow. "Come, we can meet the Royces there."

Abram and Elinor both gave Royce a smirk and a wink, respectively, as they passed him to follow Sir Henry to his carriage. Neither, of course, ruffled Royce's feathers quite as much as the commiserating looks exchanged between Selina and Henry. Her knight in shining armor, Henry led the nuisances out of the house and out of the lady's sight. When the knight was out of earshot, the scoundrel scoffed lightly under his breath.

"I don't think I like him flirting with my wife," Royce muttered.

"Oh what do you care?" Selina hissed. "Go buy yourself a new pair of boots."

❖   ❖   ❖   ❖

"Take it slowly, Nell," Selina chided as the girl passed her by, bolting across Rafferty's yard.

Penelope merely giggled and continued on, saying, "but I haven't had nearly enough!" and returning to the servants who held the trays of refreshments. With her hands refilled, she then ran to join the children in the outdoor games Rafferty had arranged in the yard. Her friends attempted to keep up, but easily fell behind and lost interest until she came back around.

Selina accepted her lack of control and helped herself to a tea cake and a glass of champagne. For a moment, with Henry beside her and the sound of laughter filling the garden, she enjoyed herself. And then Rafferty approached her with less than desirable news.

"Your husband's inspector friend is here," Rafferty politely informed.

"Good heavens, why?" Selina exhaled.

"He claims he's needing to speak with you and Royce."

After having greeted Rafferty at the entrance, Barratt immediately started for Royce and the Abrams, hands in pockets and intrusive questions at the ready. Henry's eyes narrowed on the cluster of ingrates and his tone became almost a growl.

"I don't trust him."

"He only means to solve whatever happened to Josephine," Selina said dismissively, taking a bite of the delicious teacake.

"Hm. His questions have been straying. And he was nowhere to be found while you and Royce were away. Seems to have more in mind than just solving a suicide."

"It wasn't a suicide, Henry," Selina softly corrected. "You know that."

"Do I?" he lifted both brows. "Do *you*, Selina? All we know is Josephine is dead. And since her death, we've been visited by a series of unsavory characters."

Rafferty placed a curious hand on his chin. "Is there a connection, do you think?"

Henry and Rafferty both narrowed their sights on the group of them across the yard. The thought of Barratt's intrusion being connected with Royce's devious coercion gave Selina the overwhelming desire for something stronger than a teacake and champagne.

"Of course not," she lied, before walking back to the refreshment tent. "Don't be ridiculous."

At the refreshment tent opposite the one currently attended by his wife, Royce took a fresh glass of brandy offered to him by one of Rafferty's servants and sighed at Barratt's mere presence. "I wouldn't have expected such a standard suicide to take so long to investigate."

Barratt chuckled at his apparent annoyance. "Nothing at

Everdon is standard, even now. You've made a mistake in marrying her, Royce. Kiss all of your previous fun farewell."

"That's what I said, Barratt," Elinor playfully nudged Barratt's arm. "There's no sport in marriage."

"I'm sure I'll find ways to entertain myself," he muttered.

"Indeed," Abram winked crudely in agreement. "Marriage to Lady Selina could be quite...fruitful."

"Yes," Barratt wrinkled his nose. "Well, I'm sure the county society will be enough to keep you on your toes. You have quite a bit of smoothing over with the locals to be done."

"It's nothing I can't handle," Royce straightened his shoulders, looking his challenger in the eye.

"I'd like to see that for myself," Barratt adjusted his vest, "and I'll attempt to stay out of your way as you do so. If you'll excuse me, gentlemen, Miss Abram — I have a murder to solve."

Before Barratt could fully leave the presence of his colleagues, Abram quietly gestured a request to join him. Barratt hesitated, detesting the idea of Abram ruining all hopes of gaining answers, but then considered the benefit of his presence. After quick deliberation, Barratt nodded permission and Abram followed him across the yard toward their first subject.

Noting the fleeting scowl on Sir Henry's face at the sight of both gentlemen heading in his direction, Barratt grinned. "Sir Henry," he greeted, watching a polite smile quickly grace Sir Henry's face. "It's good to see you."

"Pleasure's mine, Inspector," Henry lied.

"I understand you've met my friend Mr. Bernard Abram."

That instinctive grimace attempted to return, but Sir Henry's good breeding and manners kept it at bay. "I have," he replied.

Barratt merely chuckled at the struggle. "Common response, to be sure," he mumbled, so only Henry could hear.

Abram was far too occupied ogling the Lady Selina from a distance to notice the offense. Selina had moved from controlling Penelope's overindulgence to seeing to her social rounds, greeting each lady she passed.

"The dead girl—she was Selina's maid, was she not?" Abram asked abruptly. His attention was limited, but he moved Barratt's cause forward, so the inspector allowed it.

"*Lady* Selina's maid," Henry corrected. "Yes, she was."

Abram frowned contemplatively before looking to Barratt. "And you're certain it wasn't simply suicide?"

Almost dismissing his friend, Barratt angled his shoulders toward Sir Henry, cocking his head to one side. "The coroner has confirmed the poor girl was strangled. There were marks left around her neck, apparently."

"Oh, that poor woman," Rafferty exhaled in shock. He glanced around quickly to ensure there were no delicate female ears overhearing the details.

"From the rope she used, I assume," Abram offered, maintaining his volume, regardless of who could hear him.

Barratt stared ahead for a moment in annoyance before contradicting Abram. "A rope was left behind," he confirmed, "but the strangulation marks are from human hands. There were no rope burns." Barratt noted the way Henry's face wrinkled in disgust. "I apologize for the indelicacy. It's easy for one in my field to forget the decent sensibilities of aristocracy."

Clearing his throat, Henry shook his head. His repulsion could not overpower his curiosity. "That's perfectly all right, Inspector. There's just...a monster like that stepped foot on Everdon grounds. And for all we know, he's still there." He then added in a soft mutter, "As if one monster wasn't troublesome enough."

Barratt chuckled, flashing a glance at Royce from across the yard.

Abram, however, lifted a brow in confusion. "Monster, hm?"

Rafferty stammered at his friend's brash statement. "Not-not entirely what he meant."

Barratt's chuckle transformed into a laugh at Rafferty's apologetic tone. "Oh, you don't have to excuse him, Lord Rafferty, the sentiment is understandable. Many are speculating the reasons for the hasty marriage, and most theories point to Royce being monstrous."

After a short pause, Rafferty sighed. "He does have a way with women."

"And the Lady Selina has a reputation to protect," posed Barratt.

"That's enough," Henry snapped hoarsely, silencing all three men for a moment. "The reason hardly matters. There's no need to leap to the worst explanation. Everyone in the county would continue to kiss her boots no matter what posed a risk to her reputation." His tone seemed to soften in reminiscence toward the end.

Abram snorted in agreement. "Here, here," he exclaimed. "Selina could prostitute herself and gamble away her earnings in the underbelly of London, and everyone in this county would *still* kiss her boots."

Rafferty's astonishment caught in his throat, preventing him from uttering a word. His wide eyes found Henry's, sharing in the alarm at hearing Selina's name spoken in such a way. Henry's eyes narrowed on Abram with a deep malice, and Barratt was sure to feel the tension thicken between them. Barratt never doubted Abram's ability to spoil a conversation; his talent for inciting fury was almost impressive to the inspector.

"Royce is a thrilling danger to any young lady," the oblivious lech continued. "That's why they can't get enough. A woman like Selina, even with all her wealth and grandeur, still craves excitement, I'd imagine."

"Hm, indeed," Henry grunted. His composure, however, was quickly fading, motivating him to find an escape before acting irrationally.

As was common since childhood, his fire sought its balm. Selina had made her way to one whose company was among those she preferred most at social gatherings: Miss Florence Downing. Her most utilized strategy was to find Miss Downing, take her by the arm, and walk with her through her obligatory social rounds. No one felt particularly pressed to keep her long when she had a friend on her arm who was needier than most. Miss Downing was the awkward sort; she was most comfortable with as few interactions as possible. On Selina's arm, she had the opportunity to be seen as a social creature, while maintaining minimal responsibility to carry a conversation.

The two women had far more in common than could be openly seen. If there was ever a reclusive socialite, it was Lady Selina. Selina carried a glass of brandy in her free hand, and guided Florence around the yard with the other, gleefully moving along without draining her own energy in an exchange with one of the many overbearing ladies in the county.

Henry was not the only one calmed and amused by Selina and her discreetly orchestrated social dealings. Her husband, idly listening to the chatter of Mary Kingston, wore an occupied smile while watching his wife take care to avoid particular clusters of women around her. Her attention solely belonged to Miss Downing and the old woman's gratitude was misting in her eyes. Of course, Miss Downing's sneezing suggested to Royce that the pollen from the nearby flower beds may have contributed to her tears. Selina chuckled sweetly and guided her away from the flowers to find her some relief.

Mary followed his gaze and giggled at her own assumptions. "She's had sneezing fits all morning," she said, nodding toward her aunt.

Royce took a small sip of brandy, resisting the urge to roll his eyes. "She's raised you for years and never married? Didn't think she needed help with you, did she?"

"Poor woman's afraid of her own shadow," Mary remarked, missing his subtle insult. "She's only out and about as my chaperone. Once she's married me off, she'll just go back to stitching and painting indoors. Alone and boring."

"She doesn't have friends?" Elinor suddenly appeared beside Royce, teacup in hand and nose upturned.

Mary shrugged. "Lady Selina is her only friend. I suppose she's another reason Aunt Florence feels inclined to come out with me." Avidly, she reached for Royce's arm and lightly tugged at it, like a child. "Would you like to play a round of croquet with me, Mr. Royce? If I remember correctly, you're quite good."

"No, no, thank you," he distractedly brushed her hand away.

Sneering at Royce's disinterest, Elinor stepped to the other side of him, offering mocking condolences to the dejected young lady. "I'm sure there are other gentlemen here who would love to play with you, Miss Kingston."

Realizing the dismissal, Mary sighed and tightened her closed mouth. Despite any resistance she felt, she couldn't deny Elinor's suggestion: there were plenty of other gentlemen to rope into a game of croquet. Accepting defeat, Miss Kingston started for Henry and Rafferty, who stood just outside of the croquet court.

"I thought she'd never leave you alone," Elinor groaned. Glancing around Royce to the young vicar who stood idly nearby, she called out, "Was she always like that?"

Samuel Holbrook, unaccustomed to interacting with the general public, was often encouraged by his employer, Lady Selina, to join in on social events so as to more effectively minister to the masses. He would have much preferred hiding away in his chapel reading the day away, but as it was, he accepted the invitation to Rafferty's garden party. Being so singled out by a lady such as Elinor Abram caught the poor man off guard. He quickly scarfed down the remainder of the pastry in his hand to avoid any mistaken rudeness.

"Um," he cleared his throat after swallowing the refreshment. "Er, she's a very determined young lady, ma'am."

Elinor narrowed her eyes on the girl as she flirted with each passing fellow. "Even with married gentlemen?"

"Ha!" Holbrook impulsively chuckled before remembering Mr. Royce was standing beside him as well. "Well, it's Mr. Royce, he's...erm..."

Royce glanced at Holbrook from the corner of his eye, listening expectantly for him to finish. The clumsy young vicar regretted the beginning of the sentence as much as he dreaded the end.

"….a, uh, married gentleman. I suppose perhaps there's still an appeal," he concluded, clearing his throat again.

Elinor grinned at the man's obvious discomfort, and even giggled softly at the idea of encouraging it. "Come now, vicar. Why is it you think Mr. Royce is so different? Have they all figured him out?"

"I'm afraid I don't know what you mean."

"Elinor," Royce softly nudged.

Elinor ignored all chiding and continued. "I know you're a man of the cloth, but you've surely heard talk of the scoundrel of Everdon."

"I haven't heard a thing," Holbrook shook his head, shoving both hands in his trouser pockets.

"There's no need to be discreet, sir," Elinor lowered her tone suggestively. "I'm well-acquainted with the impression Royce gives."

"Oh, no, no, there's only been discussion regarding the marriage."

With sudden interest, Royce looked up from his brandy. "What about it?"

Royce's interest was far more unnerving than Miss Abram's; Holbrook cleared more nerves from his throat while scrambling to verbally retreat. "Well, it's none of my concern, sir. And I'm not one to pry or condemn."

"Condemn!" Elinor guffawed. "Oh dear. It's never happy when a vicar uses a word like that. What do they all say about you, Royce?"

The jest in Elinor's tone was far from mirrored in Royce's face —Holbrook hardly knew where to look. There was a severity in his new employer's expression that seemed far more troubled than amused.

"What are they saying?" Royce pressed.

The fast-spreading theory was not one comfortably discussed by those of nervous dispositions—nor was it comfortably discussed by those of the religious occupation. Being of both a nervous disposition and a religious occupation, Holbrook struggled to find words. To his relief, Elinor so plainly spat what he struggled to accuse.

"They clearly believe you've seduced the great Lady Selina and sullied her reputation," Elinor sipped her tea so casually. "Marriage was simply the salvaging of it all."

"Is that what you believe?" Royce snapped at the vicar, his tone suddenly defensive.

"I don't know, sir." Quickly, Holbrook reached for a glass of brandy on the tray of a passing servant. "I know so little of women," he gulped, "particularly Lady Selina. I do know she never seemed the sort to be won over and seduced by any man without being appropriately equipped with sense and restraint. Although...I suppose no woman is completely immune. She's been the most sought-after lady in the county since she came of age — no matter how many seasons have passed, and no matter the man in question. I would have thought...."

"You would've thought she would have married Sir Henry," Royce finished for him.

"I can hardly make assumptions like that, sir," the vicar shook his head and sipped the rest of his brandy. "All I know is they were once meant to be and then the engagement was broken. And now she is Lady Selina Royce. Much more than that I cannot say."

"Love is complicated, vicar," Elinor shrugged. "Surely, you've learned that much. There's not always a need for traditional seduction when there are other ways to secure a match."

A knowing glance passed between her and Royce, but his contained considerably more venom, which she ignored.

"Sometimes the seduction is innocent and well-meaning," she went on. "There can be a softness found in chance meetings. And when the connection is found, why wait and watch it grow slowly? All one needs is...mutual understanding. I've said it before: seduction of the highest caliber."

Finally comfortable with her contribution, Holbrook considered her words and nodded. "I suppose I could understand that. Lady Selina has obvious virtues — she's influential, intelligent, generous, witty, and has a uniquely genteel quality to her. It's no wonder every man in the county wanted her."

"Hm, yes. It's no wonder. You see," Elinor pointed at him, "Lady Selina might be just as culpable in seduction as the roguish Darius Royce."

While Holbrook quietly yielded to Elinor's opinion, Royce's eyes wandered back to Selina. Her conversation with Miss Downing had been interrupted by Abram. Royce's jaw tightened and his shoulders rose closer to his ears; there they remained even as he noticed Henry follow Abram to Selina's side to relieve her. Selina angled herself closer to Henry as Abram spoke. She leaned toward him like a ship to a lighthouse.

Ever since Royce was of a more tender age, his attentions were always a matter with which Elinor concerned herself. Seeing his attention now settle on Selina and her overt attachment to Sir Henry, Elinor sighed. "Why are you torturing yourself over your wife's personal life?"

"I think you answered that when you called her *my wife*," he replied, maintaining his gaze.

Frustrated by his distraction, Elinor tapped her finger against his chin until he turned his head to face her. "Perhaps you should concern yourself more with your newfound fortune, rather than her Sir Henry."

As he sighed in concession, she slipped her arm through his and pulled him to face the opposite direction, where young ladies and gentlemen were playing croquet. Loudly, Penelope ran past them, both hands filled with sweets she had swiped from the attending servers in the yard.

"Look at this," Elinor scoffed at Penelope's lack of decorum. "So curious and wild. You clearly craved the chaos as well as the wealth of Everdon. What is it about the Delamere ladies? Vulgarity must be in their blood."

"Miss Ayres is, by name, not a Delamere, Miss Abram," Selina's voice shot through Elinor's mocking with such sharpness that it caused both Elinor and Royce to turn around. "'Tis only I who inherited the vulgarity—and I must say, it happens to be one of my best features."

Now stumbling over her words at the sight of the stone-faced heiress, Elinor let out a nervous laugh. "Oh, of course, dear."

"I'm taking Penelope back to Everdon," Selina stated plainly, now ignoring Elinor's brief attempt to grovel. "She's had quite enough."

Elinor's arm still rested around Royce's, tightening ever so gently as Royce contemplated his response. "Abram's not quite ready," he vaguely waved in the direction where Abram was now playing croquet with Mary Kingston.

"Royce will summon you and the carriage when he sees fit," Elinor told Lady Selina, her chin slightly lifted. "It shouldn't be too much longer, dear."

Sinister was not often a word used to portray the Lady Selina. However, the expression that donned her face as Elinor spoke to her with such audacity could quite easily be described as sinister. It was a smile, yet almost a grimace. It was polite, yet terrifying. It was submissive, yet manipulative.

"Of course," were the first words to escape Selina's controlled lips. "I wouldn't want to inconvenience our guests. So I've arranged for Sir Henry's carriage to take the two of us home. You may stay as long as Lord Rafferty allows."

"Wonderful," Elinor grinned, sipping her tea while maintaining a steady eye on Selina. Without another word, Selina turned on her heel and left to rejoin Henry, who had just beckoned Penelope toward his carriage. "Hm," Elinor sipped again. "Perhaps you *should* concern yourself with her Sir Henry."

June 1889

4
The Appeal of a Married Woman

"What's your game, Royce?"

Royce stood upright, leaning against his cue stick and watching the balls scatter across the green table in the Everdon billiards room. "I'm fairly sure I'm winning."

"No, no," Abram shook his head and poised for his turn. "I mean with the Delamere girl."

"Ah," Royce started to grin, flashing his success around the room for both Abrams to see. "I think you mean Lady Selina *Royce*."

Elinor's lips curled slightly, the forced smile never meeting her eyes, as her brother darkly chuckled. She crossed her legs, leaning against the arm of the chair in which she sat. Their apprentice had grown wings, but only one Abram seemed overflowing with pride. Elinor's smile gained sincerity while her eyes darted around the ornate billiards room, but straightened when they rested again on Royce.

"I'd be more impressed if I knew how you managed to pull it off," Abram continued to chuckle

"Hm," Elinor hummed, intertwining her fingers. "Trickery, I'm sure. You underestimated him, Bernard."

"Trickery and charm," Royce flicked his wrist before gripping the cue stick and aiming across the table. "Isn't that my usual method? Not even Selina is immune to charm." His smile widened as he spoke her name, and Elinor's tightened.

"You can't fool us, darling," she contradicted. "She's not a

162

vulnerable widow with a moderate fortune to exploit. Selina's elegant, powerful, and nearly untouchable."

"She's right," Abram pointed his cue stick in Royce's direction. "You couldn't have possibly charmed the woman. She almost seems to despise you…" He leaned over the table again, just as Royce stood rigid and upright.

With no immediate defense, Royce cleared his throat, shifting his weight from side to side.

"…and yet," Abram frowned in concentration, "she married you. Willingly."

"*Married*," she repeated. Elinor pressed a confounded finger to her lips and shook her head slowly. "You've surprised us all."

Color rising to his face, Royce cleared his throat once more. "And why couldn't I charm a woman like Selina?"

Abram gestured for Royce to continue the game, but quickly noted he had no intention of doing so. Abram sighed, rolling his eyes. "Oh please, man. A woman like that could hardly be taken by a grimy lad from Whitechapel who thinks he's the next Charles Dickens. Writers are romantics, Royce, but Selina is not a romantic. Your well-crafted words have no effect. There must be a catch. What could she possibly gain from marrying the likes of you?"

"She is an intellectual woman." Conceding, Royce continued with his turn at the table. "And, with all due respect, you have no idea of Selina's romantic sensibilities."

Elinor caught the smile returning to Royce's lips as he once again spoke Selina's name; her legs switched places across one another, fumbling back into position as clumsily as her irritation. "Well, I for one would believe Lady Selina is charmed when I stop seeing her gazing, as she does, at another man." Having captured the attention of both men, Elinor widened her eyes, ready to reveal her findings. "Barratt told me they were once betrothed, you know."

"Who?" Abram frowned, this time in confusion.

"Selina and that Kincaid fellow. Something made Selina less desirable to him at the time, it seems. Clearly, he's coming around again."

Royce's grip on the cue stick tightened. "And why would Barratt tell you that?"

She shrugged dismissively. "I'm far less a threat to his investigation—he's more forthcoming to unassuming ladies, and I used it to my advantage. I had to properly evaluate the risks involved—"

"The risks?" he leaned forward with a grimace.

"The risk of losing the woman's favor," Elinor held up her hand, as if the answer was directly in front of him. "If she wasn't charmed—and you refuse to tell us how she agreed to all of this—she could so easily slip away from you." She rested both wrists against either arm of the chair, posed as if sitting atop a throne. "What if she loved another man? A woman's heart can be a powerful thing... perhaps more powerful than whatever hold you currently have on her. Broken hearts between you could bring the entire scheme crashing down." Sensing the masked indignation in Royce's stance, she sighed and slowly rose from the chair, placing a reassuring hand on his arm. "I had to investigate her level of devotion."

Abram scoffed at his sister's concern. "Oh, what does it matter?"

"Just a moment ago, you wanted to know how he's done it, and now you're so comfortable tossing it aside and accepting your share without question?"

Elinor's tyrannical gaze now aimed elsewhere, Royce brushed her hand off of his arm and stepped backward. "I am her *husband*, Elinor," he stated bitingly. "Not a fleeting suitor. It's done. The Delamere fortune is mine, and Selina's wandering eye can't change that. Her heart can belong to whomever she chooses, so long as the cheque book remains in my pocket."

Considering the new space between them, Elinor narrowed her eyes. His words were caked in false calm and emphatic firmness. It was what she and Abram had hoped to hear. But Elinor was far shrewder than her brother. The fool was content collecting Royce's wages and only prying with vain curiosity; Elinor was never so content. No detail escaped her, and no slip of influence could occur without her taking notice.

His words might have appeased Abram, but Elinor's chin lifted with contempt. Where she had only just seen a smile at Selina's name, she now saw a furrowed brow, hardened jaw, and flushed cheeks.

"You see?" Abram blindly waved in satisfaction. "He's cleverly secured a lifelong income while he scribbles away. It's what you wanted, wasn't it? For him to devote more time to his writing and less to sycophantic pandering?"

She maintained a steady, scrutinous gaze as she nodded. "I suppose you're right." Dissolving the space between them, Elinor stepped closer to Royce as he focused on the billiards table. "Have you written much in Everdon, darling?"

Her hand returned to his arm, attempting to calm, but his shoulders only tightened. The feeling of her fingernails through his jacket hardened his jawline all the more. "Here and there," he replied. "I haven't been particularly inspired."

"Well," she stroked the back of his head. "I'm here now. You'll have a novel finished and ready for print in no time." Sensing a servant approach the doorway, Elinor lightly patted Royce's face before stepping back to her chair.

Helen felt her presence was an intrusion the moment she stepped into the room. Her hesitation only increased when Abram caught sight of her as well.

"Um, Mr. Royce," she said slowly. "Your guests have arrived." Her tone eased at Royce's eye contact. "Lady Selina isn't quite ready and asked that you entertain them."

Royce smiled at her and set his cue stick against the nearest wall. "Of course. Thank you, Miss Thomas."

As was routine when invited to Everdon for dinner, Sir Henry and Lord Rafferty were sure to bring the gift of flowers and flattery. Penelope expected nothing less, and she wasn't to be disappointed. The moment she greeted them, alongside Lindon, Henry bowed and presented her their offering.

"For you, Miss Ayres," he winked at her.

Like a schoolgirl, she giggled. "And it even matches my dress," she gestured to her gown for emphasis. "Thank you, Sir Henry. I love it. You always bring just the right thing."

When Henry straightened to greet Lindon as well, he noticed Royce approaching from down the corridor. Straining a smile, he said, "Good evening, Mr. Royce."

"Kincaid," Royce nodded shortly.

Rafferty waited a moment for any sort of prompting, but the tense exchange between the two gentlemen brought anxiety, so he stepped forward. "We thank you for the invitation, Mr. Royce. It's good to see hospitality hasn't changed much since...well, recently." He awkwardly stopped himself, and then welcomed the sudden appearance of the Abrams from down the hall as well. "Ah, Mr. Abram, Miss Abram."

Elinor lit up with pretentious social graces. "Gentlemen," she extended her hands, for either of them to kiss as they saw fit. Only Rafferty complied. "It's a pleasure to see you both."

"You look lovely, Miss Abram," Henry forced.

"Oh, I see why Selina cares so much for your company, Sir Henry," she grinned.

Royce's stance stiffened as he shifted his weight closer to Penelope and lowered his voice. "Why don't you play them your new song?" he suggested.

"Oh!" she exclaimed with sudden vigor. "I learned a new piece." Henry and Rafferty both smiled as she took their hands to guide them to the parlor, where her harp resided, and insisted, "I'd like to play it for the both of you."

The party migrated to the parlor; Rafferty and the Abrams took their seats in the respective chairs and sofas, but Henry stood his guard close to Penelope. She immediately recruited him to turn the pages of her sheet music as she moved melodiously through the song.

Royce, lingering in the doorway, was the first to feel Selina's arrival. When she appeared beside him, his arm promptly wrapped around her waist. Awareness of her presence inevitably spread throughout the room, but in spite of the attention, hers quickly settled on Henry and the harp. Royce looked from Selina to Henry, and then back to Selina, pulling her just a bit closer to him.

"Penelope was playing her new song," he softly informed her.

Selina lightly smiled at Penelope's enthusiasm from across the room. "Of course she was."

With the bearing of a showman escorting his prized pony, Royce guided a subtly glaring Selina into the room and seated her carefully in the chair farthest from the entertainment, and farthest from Henry.

Before long, Rafferty stood to join in Penelope's tune. It was familiar to him, inspiring the lyrics to flow out of him. He had a fine voice and a jolly demeanor, which encouraged Penelope's enthusiasm in her musical interpretation. Now compelled to exhibit her own talents, Elinor stood as well, lending her voice alongside Rafferty's.

Despite the performance before him, Abram's attention lingered on Selina. "I'd like to hear the Lady Selina sing."

"Selina is above such ridiculous things—singing and dancing are so beneath her," Henry flashed her a playful grin, which she returned with a smirk.

"Every woman must do something," Abram concluded, unsatisfied.

Penelope rested her hands in her lap as the disagreement escalated, though she could hardly discern contention in their voices. Feeling the need to contribute, she shrugged and said, "My old headmistress told me a woman is worth nothing if she's not accomplished."

"Thank you for that, Nell," Selina nodded sardonically, almost smiling at the girl's guileless nature.

Abram, however, disregarded the innocent comment and leaned closer to Selina. "What do you do, Selina?" he pressed.

"She's not a performing monkey, Abram," Henry muttered.

"Correct your tone, Kincaid," Royce fired. "Mr. Abram is a guest at Everdon and is entitled to respect."

Henry's questioning glare shot daggers. "He's entitled to insult your wife in your presence?"

Just as Royce's lips parted for their next retort, Selina placed a sharp hand on his knee. "Do sheathe your swords gentleman," she gestured to the footman who entered to announce dinner. "You may compare the sizes of your wit after we've enjoyed a meal without regurgitation."

Everdon had always housed the finest cuisine; Lord Delamere provided only the best for his lovely wife, and her taste was so very singular. And so, Everdon's chef was one of the highest-trained France had to offer. A dinner invite from a Delamere was a guaranteed culinary treat. Everything was set just so: the lovely hostess was poised at the head of the table, with her ward to her right and her guests to her left, while the host was placed at the foot of the table, surrounded by his own guests.

As the footmen presented the first round of appetizers to the eager guests, Penelope whispered to her guardian with less discretion than she anticipated. "Could I tell them about the lake?"

Selina humored her and leaned over to respond in an equally loud whisper. "Of course."

"You're going to the lake?" Henry contributed, eyeing the appetizer in front of him.

"Yes," Penelope smiled and leaned forward against the table. "Boating and wading would be perfect with this weather. And we're inviting all the gentlemen in the county."

"And ladies…" Selina quietly corrected.

"Well, yes, and the ladies as well. I told Selina we should plan more water excursions since it's been so warm. And Royce has never been boating before. Can you believe it?"

Abram's eyebrows rose as he glanced doubtfully to Royce, at the foot of the table. "Never been boating, eh?"

"No, I haven't," Royce glared, choking down a bite and then smiling in Penelope's direction. "It should be good fun."

Penelope settled back in her chair, bringing a buttered dinner roll to her mouth. "And everybody loves a good picnic."

"Hm," Rafferty nodded from the center of the table. "They certainly do. Picnics are my favorite outings."

"You must bring your children, Rafferty," Penelope encouraged. "The north lake has the best hiding places for hide-and-seek."

"You enjoy the water, Miss Ayres?"

"Of course, I do," her speech slowed a bit as Abram addressed her.

"My sister here is an excellent swimmer, you know?" he pointed his fork in Elinor's direction.

"It's true," Elinor smiled, accepting the attention. "I am. I'm very quick."

Penelope fought the instinctual scowl at the sound of Elinor's voice when she saw Selina's chiding expression. "I'm not a very proficient swimmer," she sighed instead. "Selina only lets me boat."

"She keeps you close to her own strengths, Nell," Henry explained, signaling to the footman for another serving of vegetables. "Isn't that right? Selina is an impressive sailor. I've never seen a woman so comfortable on a boat."

Royce watched the exchange of regarding glances between Selina and Henry. There was a glint in Selina's eye as she reminisced.

Holding her utensil pointedly, she concurred, "I've only fallen once."

"And, that wasn't entirely your fault," Henry chuckled, mirroring the glint in his own eye as he too remembered her tumble.

With a full mouth, Abram waved a finger across the table. "It's a wonder the two of you never married. You seem to get on so well."

Royce pushed food around on his plate before taking a bite and mumbling, "She's no doubt more appealing to him now as a married woman."

Selina's jaw fell slightly ajar; Henry forced his eyes on his food, but couldn't stop them from glancing incredulously at Royce. If Selina had stared aghast any longer, her food would have become cold to the touch—the silence hung in the air with widespread discomfort at Royce's assertion.

Rafferty set his fork rather loudly on his plate, all of a sudden, recapturing the attention of all. "Do you know who's a talented swimmer?" he posed, wearing the dowdiest grin he could force under the circumstances. "My eldest, Margaret. I can hardly keep her away from the water. I'll bet she could outdo you any day, Miss Abram. And she'd dearly love the challenge."

Pulled from an amused daze, Elinor chortled. "Mr. Rafferty, I'm sure I should love to prove you wrong." She lightly dabbed the corners of her mouth with a handkerchief. "Tell your Margaret we must race at this lake outing."

"Naturally!" Rafferty exclaimed too loudly. His distraction had been indulged. "Do your worst, madam." He laughed, good-naturedly, and prayed with all of his might that the discomfort had passed.

Lady Selina Royce could hardly stand to look at her husband for the remainder of the meal. When all had dined to their satisfaction, the guests were excused. Farewells were curtly given, the Abrams retired to their rooms for the night, and the remaining gentlemen were escorted to their exit. But not by Selina. Before Rafferty and Henry departed, Selina told Helen she had had enough for the evening. While the lady dismissed herself, Helen hurried to the kitchen to gather Selina's nightly cure of all ills. As she did so, bottle in hand, Helen was caught by the menacing postures Henry and Royce maintained as they walked side-by-side to the front doors.

"We seem to have succeeded in upsetting Selina," Henry regretfully acknowledged.

Royce rolled his shoulders back and tucked his hands in his trouser pockets. "An apology is unnecessary."

"Good," Henry tilted his chin. "It wasn't offered."

Pleadingly, Rafferty patted Henry on the back, moving him through the open door and toward their awaiting carriage. "Henry, we should—"

Dodging his friend's restraint, but still moving through the door, Henry kept his face inches from Royce. "It takes a man of a certain….*breed* to bring himself to harm a woman like Selina."

Helen inched closer down the hallway, burning with interest. There was a fearsome edge to Henry's voice that she had never before heard. Moll had told her whispers of the conversation from dinner, but Helen hardly believed her claims.

"Harm?" Royce repeated, unfazed.

Henry stood taller, looking the man in the eye. "Publicly humiliating her, so soon after exploiting—"

"Henry, please," Rafferty begged again. Helen could no longer see him, as night had fallen. "Not here, not now."

Royce stepped farther past the door, encouraging Henry's physical challenge. "Exploiting?"

"You come to Everdon as her guest," Henry seethed, "take advantage of her, coercing her into marrying you for the sake of her reputation—"

"I never laid a hand on Selina. I'm a scoundrel, not a brute. How dare you—"

"And why not both?" Henry took a step back, opening his arms as if inviting Royce to accept the gauntlet. "What else could possibly move her to marry a man like you if not to protect her own virtue and honor?"

Hands still in his pockets, Royce stepped forward, scoffing and lightly shaking his head. "You know, it takes a man of a certain *breed*, as you say, to cast a woman aside as a disgrace, and then suddenly come to his senses only when she's become vulnerable and so taken in by another man."

Before Rafferty could temper his friend's wrath, Henry's fist was thrown in the direction of Royce's head. Those acting in rage, however, are not always well-aimed; Royce easily dodged the attack, blocking the blow with his left arm while he countered with a properly aimed fist of his own. Royce's hit landed against Henry's clenched jaw, knocking the tall man backward and into Rafferty's arms, which prevented him from reaching the ground.

With a short flex of his experienced hand, Royce sighed in contempt before turning away. "Tighten your form the next time you throw accusations, Kincaid."

Mortified from what she had just witnessed, Helen hid behind the staircase, clutching her stomach. She flinched as she heard Royce's footsteps make their way up the stairs. The ease with which he had struck Sir Henry was alarming. He was clearly a man accustomed to violence, Helen had no doubt. It wasn't easily construed who was in the right—from the claims she'd heard cast between them there was no knowing who was truly at fault.

Lady Selina cared for one and married the other. Helen's elevated concept of romanticism was shattering, while her youthful inclination to cling to hope was beginning to tread water. She was not so naive as to think Price had been wrong in assuming there was more to the recent marriage than what was shown on the surface, and yet, there was still something curious between them that kept Helen's interest. It was a story that was clawing and grasping and begging to be told.

Lindon, emerging from desk work in the library around the corner, brisked past her hiding place and then stopped a few steps away before turning back to check on her. "Are you all right, Miss Thomas?" he gently asked.

"Um." She didn't know the answer herself. "Yes," she supposed. "I-I think so."

"How was the dinner party?"

Helen suddenly released a nervous laugh, scrambling to remember Moll's account, rather than reveal the aftermath she had seen. "From what I've heard, horribly awkward."

"Well, that was expected," he chuckled in complicated

amusement, before turning on his heel to continue on down the corridor.

"Mr. Lindon…" she stopped him. "I'm not accustomed to the habits of wealthier couples….but did Lord and Lady Delamere share a bedroom?"

The question took Lindon aback, but Helen's innocent demeanor worked to her advantage. He gave a small, patient smile and deliberated. "I suppose your previous employers would have. I believe it depends entirely on the couple. Lord and Lady Delamere kept two rooms, but more than often they shared one with the other. They were a very affectionate pair."

Her searching eyes moved to the side while she considered the answer. "Hm," she grunted softly. Then, more in observation to herself than to Lindon, she almost whispered, "I don't believe Mr. Royce and Lady Selina have shared a room since they returned…"

"Ah." Lindon caught her curiosity by its wings and pulled it back to earth. "Marital affairs are none of our concern, Miss Thomas," he gently chided. "Lady Selina is quite private and unpredictable. There's always been a bit of a wild streak beneath the glamour she portrays. You'll find yourself much more at peace if you stop worrying yourself over business that is not your own. Besides, not every married couple can be expected to have the same habits."

"Hm. I suppose not," she shrugged. "Everdon is such an odd place, isn't it?"

"It certainly can be," Lindon chuckled and gave her arm a paternal pat before returning to his original path down the hall.

"Um, Mr. Lindon," Helen stopped him again.

Patiently, he sighed and turned back around. "Yes?"

"Do you remember Sarah Atwood?"

The man's mouth tightened at the name. A sudden depth in his eyes gave Helen a taste of the answer she'd never receive. Steadily, Lindon squared his shoulders and cleared his throat. "You should stop listening to Moll, Miss Thomas," he told her. "You're above that."

The lanterns in the library were dimmed, but not extinguished. A bottle of brandy rested on the table beside the oversized armchair which sat in front of the fireplace. A full glass of the dark amber beverage was cupped securely in the delicate hand of Lady Selina. It was all Royce saw of her from the threshold, but he could sense her vexation.

In an endeavor for levity, Royce leaned casually against the door frame and pointed out, "There was wine with dinner."

"This is still my house, Royce." Selina's voice was low and hoarse. She didn't turn to look at him, nor did she need to. Lightly, he pushed himself from the doorframe and slowly approached her. "I am still permitted to drink whatever I wish whenever I wish it, and be free from the judgment of others. I'm *entitled* to a bit of numbness. Isn't that the word you used…"

"Selina, I—"

"Did you know he's a barrister?" She stopped him. He caught a glimpse of her expression: she was resigned, not scolding. "A gentleman and a barrister…"

Royce knew better than to speak. Her voice was layered in tired deliberation and her gaze was wandering and unfocused. "Your temper…" she went on, "your behavior has done nothing to stave off the suspicions of the county, particularly my close friends. You've won my money, Royce, but you have one remaining obstacle. You antagonize a man like Henry, and he may just find a way to take away that fortune you've lifted a couple of fingers to obtain."

Royce snorted. "Is that a threat?"

Finally, her eyes moved up to his. She took a sip from her glass. "It's a warning," she said. "I have nothing to gain from Henry's suspicions coming to fruition. A legal battle only brings to light everything I've kept so well hidden." Again, she slowly sipped. "You were so amiable, even charming before….your success has made you lazy. The master of Everdon must now act as if he belongs—with decorum and civility."

"I embarrassed you." His eyelids closed as he verbalized the truth of it. His intentions had been less than honorable, but she was the unwitting target.

Selina swallowed the remainder of brandy from her glass and reluctantly set it back down on the side table. Royce watched her hand roll off the glass and hang off of the end of the armchair. The hand that once held the scepter.

Trickery and charm, he had said. The truth was much darker, and the evidence of such darkness sat before him, in all of her beautifully bested glory. His throat thickened. "Well," he croaked. "I can't have the lady of Everdon unhappy."

"Oh, stop pretending you went into this coercion with a mind for my happiness. The certificate has been signed, you have your fortune." Her limp hand now gestured generally to the hallway. "I'm no longer your mark. They are. So don't trouble yourself with my happiness and take care of Everdon. Plenty of married couples slip out of liking each other after marriage. No one will think twice if the two of us despise one another."

Royce wrinkled his nose, remembering Abram's observations. "Do you even like me, Selina?"

"No," she moved to stand. "But a continual liking is not part of our arrangement, so don't let it break your heart."

5

Hearsay & Headstones

The local magistrate building resided in the general center of Everdon village. It was built decades previous with funds provided by Lord Delamere himself. It was easily one of the finest structures in the county. The staff who tended to the justice of the county were well-meaning constables with hearts larger than their brains, at times. Inspector Barratt was used to the sort. They were quite commonplace in London as well.

Marley, the head constable, was gracious enough to let Barratt occupy his office while in town on investigation. Barratt didn't hesitate a day before making himself at home. His witness statements and various notes were strewn across Marley's desk—those from the initial set of interviews as well as those conducted while Royce and Lady Selina were away.

Barratt rubbed his temples. His scribbled notes only created more of a web than he intended. Tenants of Everdon were much more forthcoming after discussing the wedding of Lady Selina Delamere first. It was such a to-do that curiosity and gossip had peaked. Simple minds were always more malleable after being opened by idle chatter, Barratt found.

Josephine Rodin had been seen by several witnesses in the days before going missing. She had been believed to be missing days before she was discovered near the river. Her last sighting was in the area between Everdon village and the manor itself.

Barratt had tracked that property over and over again for hours at a time. He rubbed a hand across his eyes as he attempted to envision the dead girl's final hours.

Her dress had been muddy.

She was in a hurry.

Mr. Cuddy, the last to have seen her, supposed she had simply been running late to some engagement with Lady Selina. The orphanage was nearby, and Lady Selina was ever so particular about seeing the children.

But there was no Lady Selina.

Just Josephine.

Josephine and her muddy hem. Running. On foot. It hadn't seemed strange to the old man until Barratt brought up the subject of her death and disappearance.

To whom was she running? Or from whom?

She was never seen without the lady of Everdon. From what Barratt gleaned, she had been treated more as a lady-in-waiting than a lady's maid. Her involvement in Lady Selina's affairs—particularly the orphanage—were almost equal to Lady Selina herself.

So why, then, was she alone?

Lady Selina.

There was something more the woman knew, but she'd never disclose.

Barratt frowned.

Lady Selina didn't strike him as the murdering sort, nor the sort to ever truly get her hands dirty, as it were. But the exposure to her inner circle, which she seemed to grant to the young lady in the last few months of her life, could prove to be the vehicle needed for the true murderer himself.

A pregnant lady's maid.

That was the result of the exposure Selina granted her.

And the company to which Josephine was most exposed was that of Sir Henry Kincaid. Lady Selina's closest friend.

The man had a streak of fire in his countenance, though he

masked it with good-natured smiles and calm charm. Barratt saw it for himself in the street before the wedding. At the mention of Royce's despicable weaseling of his way into the halls of Everdon, Sir Henry's blood boiled.

But would his blood boil over just enough to strangle a woman whose condition could threaten his reputation and way of life?

The thought was not so outlandish to Barratt as he remembered Sir Henry's suspicion of Lady Selina's own reputation being spoiled. Appearances were so amusingly important to the aristocracy. None of them were above acting rashly to preserve what they'd taken generations to create.

And that is why Barratt had sent Constable Marley to fetch Sir Henry on the morning following the Everdon dinner party. There was something to be said for a change of scenery when aiming to throw a subject off their course. Barratt had encroached on Sir Henry's natural setting so many times as of late that it had practically become routine.

But instead of Marley returning with Sir Henry, Barratt's first visitor of the morning was a courier carrying a letter tied in a deep maroon ribbon.

"What's this?"

The courier stared at the inspector for a moment. "A letter for you, sir," he answered obviously.

Barratt sighed. "Yes, from whom?"

The gangly young man shrugged his shoulders nearly to his ears. "Couldn't say, sir. Was just left with the postmaster and said to be delivered directly to you."

Barratt impatiently snatched the letter from the courier's hands and examined it. There was no return address on either side, only a calligraphic number "7" written in black ink. When the inspector untied the maroon ribbon, he found that the inside was just as sparse. Scrawled along the interior was the word "WRATH".

"Hm," Barratt grunted. The courier slinked away as the inspector's grin curled across his face. He sensed a riddle at play.

Wrath. A common drive for murder most foul.

"Sir Henry was unavailable, sir."

"Hm?" Barratt grunted again, looking up to now see Constable Marley standing in front of his desk. "Unavailable?"

Marley nodded once. "His staff suspect he stayed the night in the Everdon guest house. Dinner party last night, apparently."

Barratt lifted his head from the papers before him. "He didn't return home?" he squinted.

"Seems not," Marley shrugged.

"Hm," Barratt grunted, stuffing the cryptic letter into his jacket pocket.

"What next?" Marley inquired as the inspector rose from behind the desk.

"Apparently I'm needing to call on the master and lady of Everdon."

On the occasion that Lady Selina had a scheduled brunch with Miss Downing or Mrs. Sweeting in town, Helen would have the morning to herself. The morning after the Everdon dinner party was just such an occasion. Helen had finished her chores and decided to take advantage of the mild summer day by taking a long walk on Everdon's grounds.

With notebook and pencil in hand, Helen attempted to sort her thoughts into discernible words. She found that expressing her unfinished ideas to the other maids only resulted in mutual confusion and periodic annoyance. She supposed not every mind was capable of understanding her own.

And so she strolled farther and farther from the manor where her fellow maids scurried to and fro and escaped into the gradually thickening forests of Everdon. In the distance she could see the distinguished Everdon cemetery on a hill with fencing and a small building for the keeper.

A headstone, she remembered.

Moll had mentioned the headstone of Sarah Atwood.

Ghosts and dead maids might have proven terrifying in the dark of night, but during daylight they only added to the manor's allure.

Perhaps if she walked far enough, she could find Sarah's headstone, Helen thought. Ideally, the headstone would be in a corner of the cemetery where she could perch herself atop a stump or rock and scribble pieces of her own story while enjoying the ambience.

Not an hour later, after wandering the cemetery hill, Helen realized the grave of Sarah Atwood must have been nothing but Moll's silly legends. In frustration, she started back down the hill toward a stream closer to the road. There she found a large rock that suited her need to rest and write.

Woman mysteriously dies on castle grounds.
A princess lives there now.
Perhaps the woman was a witch who helped the princess.
Or cursed the princess.
Yes.
The dead witch had cursed the princess somehow.
But why would the witch be dead?
The witch was a sorceress who lived with the royal family.
She tried to stop the curse.
That's why she's dead.
Who set the curse? Who killed the sorceress?

Helen stopped for a moment, frowning at her incoherent jottings. They made very little sense; it was no wonder to her that the other maids often stared blankly in confusion. Lost in the depths of her own bewilderment, Helen hardly noticed the footsteps approaching her until they were within arms reach. Suddenly, she dropped her pencil and spun her head around.

Barratt held up both hands, in a gesture assuring peace. "I didn't mean to startle you, Miss Thomas."

"Oh, you didn't," she lied, and then paused to reconsider. "Well, you did. But it's quite alright; I was only writing."

"I came to call on Lady Selina this morning." Barratt paused, awaiting a response that didn't come. "Do you happen to know if she's at home?"

Helen pointed generally toward town. "She's out having lunch with Miss Downing. But Mr. Royce should be home, I believe." She pointed back at the manor, but then brought the finger to her mouth and lightly bit it, questioning her answer. "Though, I'm not entirely sure. I've had the morning to do as I wish."

Barratt chuckled. "Writing compelling dramas, I gather?"

Helen blushed, looking down at her hands. "Hardly compelling, sir. Mr. Royce and Lady Selina encouraged me to write a story of my own…"

"It's fine encouragement. I'm sure you could craft a better story than Royce himself."

"Oh no, I hardly think so." Her cheeks burned, and it only worsened as she realized she still lay lounging on the rock beside the river, legs sprawled and her dress nearly up to her knees. Hastily, she shot up from the ground and straightened her now-dusty dress. "Um, sorry. I thought finding that headstone would give me proper inspiration."

"Headstone?"

Suddenly remembering that Barratt was not in fact privy to her mental narrative, Helen sighed, exasperated with herself. "Um….Sarah Atwood's, sir."

"Oh!" he exclaimed. "I passed a headstone just a few days ago, when I interviewed Mr. Cuddy. I'd be happy to show you, if you'd like." He gestured past him, inviting her to join him.

"You did?" she grinned. "Yes, of course, I would love to see it! Do you have the time?"

"I'm free to meander until Lady Selina returns," he assured her.

As they started walking, it occurred to Helen that Barratt was not the sort to make social calls. In the excitement of the headstone, she had almost forgotten the investigation he was currently pursuing,

and how that might involve Lady Selina. During his long months in
Everdon village already, he seemed to have overstayed his welcome,
though he had not bothered the Everdon staff directly since before the
wedding.

"You have more questions for her?" Helen pried.

Barratt slipped a thoughtful hand in his pocket and stepped
carefully to avoid the occasional rock and branch. "Hm, regarding Sir
Henry. He seems to be absent from his estate this morning."

Helen shook her head. "Oh, he isn't at Everdon. I saw him
leave last night. Perhaps he went to Lord Rafferty's," she suggested.

"Perhaps." He noticed her tuck her notebook against her side,
self-consciously. "Now," he said, "this story of yours: what sort of
inspiration do you think this headstone could offer?"

Nervously chuckling, Helen rolled her eyes. If residents of
Everdon were no help, she doubted an inspector from London would
be any different. "No one will tell me all that much about her. Only
that she's the ghost of Everdon."

"Ghost of Everdon, eh?" he ruminated. "I assume, then, that
Sarah Atwood is the maid who died all those years ago."

"Yes, sir," she nodded. Their information was aligned thus far.
Helen let out a frustrated sigh. "When I have no answers, my
imagination tends to run a bit wild."

"I see."

Within a few steps, she began to slow her pace; her mind and
her feet were out of sync and Barratt studied this carefully. "If I were
writing her story," she suddenly told him, "I should like to make her a
mystical being charged with protecting the castle, even in death."

"That would be more fascinating than the truth, to be sure," he
agreed, watching the hand that held her pencil begin to tap against her
side. "Why did she have to die?"

"Well, as I said, she protected the castle. When a curse was
aimed at the princess, she died so the princess could live."

"Hmm." Barratt shrugged his mouth in interest. The plot was
certainly more unique to him than the nonsense he had always heard

from Royce. "Only one of them could have survived."

"Sometimes that's the nature of magic, you know." Helen brought the pencil to her lips, continuing to tap as if feeling for a goldmine of ideas to eventually rush forth.

"What has she to protect the princess from after her own death?"

"Well the fiend who attempted the curse would undoubtedly try again," she supposed. "So she must continue to accompany the now cursed princess in spirit."

"Can a spirit lend much protection, I wonder."

"Well," Helen stopped. She looked past him for a moment, her face twisting in confusion. "Hm, no, you're right. Perhaps the princess doesn't need protection, only good company." She shrugged and continued walking. "Now all I must know is what sort of villain cast the curse to begin with. That's why I'd like to know Sarah Atwood. I'm sure whatever happened to the poor girl would inspire the perfect answer for me."

"I'm afraid the inhabitants of Everdon are not the most forthcoming."

"And that's why you're still here," Helen guessed. When Barratt nodded, she sympathetically frowned. "I'm sure it's hindered your investigation."

"There is more than one way to obtain information, however," he told her with a grin. "I've found the tenants more willing to discuss a nearly thirty-year-old crime more freely than the loss of Miss Rodin."

"What have they told you?" she asked, before quickly adding, "If you don't mind my asking."

"The usual story, I suppose. A wealthy woman's maid had a scandalous love affair with some nobleman, fell pregnant, took her own life—much like Miss Rodin. Though there are conflicting reports. Some claim she was never pregnant. Some say she fought with the nobleman because he refused to abandon his wife and his estate. Some say she didn't even die, just disappeared."

"Is that at all helpful to you? For Miss Rodin's sake, I mean."

This time, Barratt stopped. With both hands in his trouser pockets now, he looked ahead at the horizon which was interrupted by Everdon manor. Light shone through some of the windows of the building, but not all. The grim estate was just as curious in the daylight as it was in the darkness, he thought.

"Patterns fascinate me, Miss Thomas," he finally answered. "I'm bothered by similarities I can't reconcile."

"Could…" Helen started. She squinted carefully before continuing. "You don't think the father of the first child could have struck again, do you?"

"Is that a theory you'd believe?"

She inhaled sharply, disgusted at the thought. "Mr. Price claims that, whoever he is, he'll get away with it. They always seem to."

Barratt chuckled. The peculiarity of Lady Selina's staff never ceased to amuse him. Story matchmakers, idle scribblers, unassuming negotiators, and now amateur detectives.

"But how could it be the same man?" she frowned again, doubting her own theory. "Surely a different man fathered Josephine's child, right?"

Barratt shrugged, considering this. "Miss Atwood's body was never found, nor was her death recorded. For all we know, the tale was fabricated by bored fools who thought it amusing to give an old manor an interesting ghost story. I don't base investigations on rumors. However," he pointed suddenly at her, "a killer would be shrewd to take advantage of such a story. I know if I wanted to kill my pregnant mistress, I'd utilize the superstitions of the area to distract the investigation against me."

The young maid stared at him, not in fear or disturbance, but in strange wonder. "You are a lot like him," she exhaled after a long pause.

"Who?"

"Oh, Auguste Dupin. Mr. Croft recommended *The Murders in the Rue Morgue*, and he said you reminded him of Mr. Dupin. He's right. You're awfully clever like he is, aren't you?"

"You're very kind, Miss Thomas," Barratt puffed his chest, while feigning a humble smile. "I certainly do my best."

As they approached the road leading to Everdon manor, they came upon a small ditch that wound along the outside of the path. From the road, one couldn't see much of it, but from the grounds it was quite apparent. Barratt politely offered his arm to Helen so she could step across the small obstacle. Before she could do so, however, Helen abruptly halted, clinging to the inspector's arm with eyes wider than her opened mouth.

In confusion, Barratt gently pulled her back and leaned forward to see what had caught the poor girl's disturbed eye.

Lying in the ditch, limbs sprawled and shoulders slumped to the side, was the bent and broken body of Sir Henry Kincaid. The side of his face was horribly bruised, from his chin to his temple, his neck apparently broken.

"Oh."

Both of Helen's hands covered her mouth, smothering her soft screams of horror. Torn between his gentlemanly sensibilities and his desire to confirm what he already supposed, Barratt placed firm hands on her shoulders and looked Helen directly in the eye.

"I'm sorry, Miss Thomas, but I must know....was that what Sir Henry was wearing at the dinner party last night?"

Helen resisted the urge to shut her eyes, even hesitating to speak for fear she'd become ill. Slowly, she nodded. "Is...is he dead?"

"Yes, I'm afraid he is," he began to mutter, crouching down and reaching to feel for the poor man's pulse. He found none. "For over twelve hours, at least." Barratt shook his head at the shame of it all, ignoring the retching noises the poor girl was suddenly making behind the nearest tree.

Then, sighing deeply, he said, "It seems even the mightiest can fall."

June 1889

July 1889

I think the greatest rogues are they who talk most of their honesty
~Anthony Trollope~

1

A Violent Origin

Birds freely flew and sang on the grounds that afternoon, unaware of any tragedy or misfortune. Croft and Penelope strolled the garden, with a botany book between them, identifying flowers, while Selina and Elinor sat on the terrace awaiting afternoon tea. The book perched in Elinor's hand was one of Royce's bestsellers, and all Selina could force between them was a strained smile of acknowledgement.

Seeing a lack of refreshment on the table between the two ladies as he passed the door, Lindon promptly returned with a tray of tea from the kitchen. A few moments later, whether induced by Abram's compulsive need for female company or Royce's compulsive need to follow, the gentlemen left their game of billiards to join the ladies on the terrace.

Royce matched his pace to Abram's and side-stepped around him to tenderly kiss his wife's head and claim the seat beside her. The gesture was well-received, as it spared Selina proximity to the unpalatable closeness of Mr. Abram. Selina gave her husband a small smile of gratitude before reaching to pour herself a fresh cup of tea. To her surprise, Royce's hand was much quicker, gripping the teapot first and placing an empty cup in front of her.

Behind them, in a steadied, but scolding tone, Lindon placed his hands on his hips and remarked, "Where's Miss Thomas? I've been looking for her all morning."

"Well, I was out," Selina watched her husband in quiet bewilderment as he poured her a cup of tea. His demeanor had a gentleness to it that curiously contrasted his behavior at the dinner party. "I told her she could have a few hours to herself," she further explained.

"She was expected back hours ago." There was a paternal concern in Lindon's voice that made Selina smile; it was one with which she was well-acquainted.

"I'm sure she's just fine, Lindon," she sipped her tea. "She's wildly imaginative — perhaps she took a walk and lost track of the time."

Disregarding Selina's reassurance, Lindon scanned the property from where he stood. Elinor began praising Royce of his past publications, only to be interrupted several times by her brother, who seemed keen on complimenting Selina's skilled gardening staff. Both conversations went ignored as Lindon squinted to see a carriage and a lone horse rider make their way up the path to Everdon.

"Ah, there she is," he said, spotting the young maid through the window of the carriage. When the carriage halted in front of the manor, the door was opened and her traveling companion could be clearly seen.

"What the devil is Barratt doing here?" Abram derided under his breath.

He and Elinor both glanced at Royce, who only focused quizzically on Selina and the sudden alertness of her posture while the rider came close enough to identify. Rafferty rarely called at Everdon without the company of Sir Henry, and he certainly wouldn't make a social visit with Inspector Barratt. Rafferty dismounted his horse and joined Barratt and Helen as they exited the rented carriage.

Selina smiled at Rafferty as they approached, but it quickly faded. The expression Rafferty wore continued to alarm her. His hands were wrung in front of him, his eyes darting everywhere but in her direction.

"Good afternoon," Barratt nodded respectfully to Selina.

But it was Lindon who replied. "Inspector," he took a step forward, watching Helen's nerves continue to erupt beneath her thin poker face.

"Why the grim look, Barratt?" Abram leaned his arm against the back of his chair, angling himself toward what he sensed would be a fascination.

"It appears there's been a tragic development," Barratt spoke. His voice was less remorseful and more intensely curious.

"You've found the devil who killed that poor girl!"

"Let him finish," Royce groaned, vainly attempting to conceal contempt with a sip of his tea.

Barratt soaked in the suspense; all eyes were now on him, so he paced himself. After a drawn out sigh, he looked to the lady of the house and stated, "Sir Henry Kincaid was found dead this morning."

Selina's teacup dropped from her hand, spilling across the table. Relieved by the distraction, Helen hurried to her side to soak the tea with a handkerchief.

"You can't be serious," spat Elinor. She sounded more disappointed than dismayed, as if it was all a stage production taking a less than satisfactory turn.

Barratt paid her no mind, instead narrowing his focus on Selina, whose sudden grief, despite the spilled tea, was expertly contained behind a blank stare and rigid shoulders. "It seems your dinner party had a rather dark ending, Lady Selina."

Her composure would not yield, only slightly breaking through her misting eyes. Barratt's prodding nature brought Royce to his feet. His concerned hand on her shoulder was all but ignored. The inspector's probing gaze meant nothing to Selina. She had faced much crueler scrutiny and had been left unruffled.

"Has Miss Campbell been informed?" she finally spoke. "They were…they were courting."

"I thought it best to come here first. He was found on Everdon grounds. I've spoken with Lord Rafferty and Miss Thomas," the inspector gestured to the two of them, "and their testimonies have suggested a fairly prominent explanation. In fact, I'm comfortable making an arrest — "

"You suspect murder," Selina assumed. Her shaking fingers curled into a fist. "There's no possibility it was an accident of some sort?"

In obligatory regret, Barratt shook his head.

"Well?" Abram pressed. "Who was it then?"

The suppressed smirk on Barratt's face welcomed its cue. He took no pleasure in disparaging old friends, but Abram's impatience triggered the satisfaction of knowing the Abram family trust would soon run dry. The inspector's eye's dramatically moved to Royce.

"Personal acquaintance cannot set anyone above suspicion."

It was not an apology, it was an accusation, and neither Royce nor Selina mistook it for anything less. All eyes flashed to Darius Royce, none doubting. Immediately, Royce turned to Selina, even reaching for her hand.

"I didn't," he said, to her, and to her alone.

"Let's not make a scene," she exhaled sharply.

Despite Royce's expectations, she did not pull away from his touch. While her gaze would not meet his, her acceptance of his claim of innocence appeared to be unmoved. The stiffness of her words, however, brought a sudden indignant edge to his panic.

"What proof do you have?" he shot at Barratt.

The outrage had little effect on the inspector. Barratt calmly placed both hands in his trouser pockets and straightened his emerging smirk. "Two witnesses who claim you struck Sir Henry in the face last night, hours before he was presumed to have died."

Rafferty, the expected accuser, looked down at his hands with remorse. Helen, the avoidant accuser, anticipated Royce's threatening glare and slipped behind Lindon, praying she was well out of view.

"You have a temper, Royce," Barratt pointed out, almost flippantly. Abram grunted in agreement, warranting a derisive glance from the inspector. "There's no denying that. You argued, threatened, and then physically assaulted him."

"You hit him?" Selina withdrew her hand from her husband's, looking at him now in disturbance.

Selina's sudden movement drew the attention of Croft and Penelope from across the garden. Hesitantly, but curiously, they both moved closer to hear the cause of the commotion. Croft did his best to slow Penelope's pace and not contribute to the scene at hand, but his own curiosity was just as overpowering as hers.

Abram nudged Royce's arm, causing him to flinch and flash a glare as he stammered.

"I—"

"He did," Barratt finished. "And he was seen leaving the house around the time we suspect Sir Henry was killed."

"What?"

"This is preposterous!" Elinor exclaimed.

"I have a witness," Barratt simply shrugged his shoulders.

Delicately, Rafferty took a step toward the silent Selina. "Perhaps," he suggested in a hushed tone, "Miss Ayres should be sent to Beechbury until the investigation has passed."

"No!" Penelope suddenly burst onto the terrace, and Croft hardly lifted a finger to stop her. "No, don't send me away, Selina. I won't stand for it!"

Selina raised a calming hand to the girl. Penelope was only occasionally well-trained, and given the stress of the situation her adherence to Selina's hushing was quick and still. "I think Miss Ayres is much safer here than she would be on her own at Beechbury," Selina concluded.

Rafferty glanced at Royce from the corner of his eye. "Here?" he whispered, not at all quietly. "In the same house as the man who—"

"The man who did what?" she suddenly challenged him, her volume lifting ever so slightly. "Killed Henry? He's already being accused of murder, Rafferty. Do you really think he'd be foolish enough to kill twice under the same roof?" Selina leaned back in her chair and rolled her eyes. "Penelope will stay at Everdon with me and the alleged murderer, as long as she wishes."

Selina's backhanded support was an odd comfort to Royce. His desperation was not wholly abated, however, for just as soon as Selina declared her decision, Barratt strolled past Rafferty and placed a victorious hand on Royce's shoulder. Every muscle in Royce's body tensed, with Abram and Barratt on either side, and neither completely benign.

"No need to trouble yourself over the safety of the ladies, Lord Rafferty," the inspector assured the anxious lord. "Mr. Royce will be returning with me to the jailhouse." With a menacing arrogance, Barratt muttered in Royce's ear, "Will you be coming willingly? Or shall we….as your lovely wife would like to avoid….make a scene?"

Elinor stood abruptly, slamming her cloth napkin so forcefully beside her teacup that all of the dishes on the table trembled. "If he won't make a scene, I will. Barratt, you'd better get more evidence than that if you expect to arrest the master of Everdon."

"I go where the evidence takes me, Miss Abram," Barratt shrugged. "Regardless of the man's current social status, Royce will be imprisoned until he can be taken to London for a fair trial."

"And what physical evidence do you have to substantiate this arrest, inspector?" Selina calmly joined her hands together on the table in front of her. Her unusually controlled tone thrilled Barratt. "How was he….killed?"

"His neck was snapped," the inspector said bluntly, hoping to get a rise from the lady. To his disappointment, Selina merely cleared her throat. "Presumably caused by a blow to the back of his head. The two witness testimonies will be enough to start. If you'd like to call upon representation for your husband, you are more than welcome." He paused, leaning forward. "Or, perhaps, you'd be better off letting fate take its chosen way."

It was not the tacitly broken Lady Selina Royce who watched as Barratt pulled his arm toward the carriage out front, it was Abram. The cold glare, lifted chin, and broadened shoulders led an observer such as Lindon to assume this was not the first time Abram watched his young friend apprehended. This twisted game between them sickened Lindon. From the triumph expressed on Barratt's mouth to the passive acceptance of Abram's shrug.

As Royce was loaded into the carriage, however, his eyes did soften and search for Selina's, but they were avoided. All Selina could bring herself to look at were her intertwined hands.

Moving quietly but suddenly, Selina stood from her chair, passing Helen as she started for the house. "Sherry, Helen," was all she mumbled.

"Of course, my lady." Helen was sure to avoid hesitation and turned to promptly follow Lady Selina inside, but not before Lindon lightly caught her by the arm, not hearing Selina's request.

"Where are you off to now?" he asked.

"Lady Selina has a headache, I'll tend to her."

"Are you all right, Selina?" Lindon called out, but she quickly disappeared through the doors.

"How do you think she is?" Abram slurred, as if he knew the answer himself. "Lost a friend and gained justice in the same day."

Notwithstanding the poor girl's nerves, Mr. Croft never tolerated spilled sherry in his library. As he passed Helen in the hallway and heard the glass in her hand shaking from the spectacle on the terrace, he kindly took the bottle and glass and gave her a comforting wink.

"Allow me."

Selina had made herself at home, as she did, in the oversized armchair in the library. Her hand dangled over the arm, waiting for Helen to fill it with her usual remedy for such stress. When it was Croft's hand which held out her glass of sherry, she hardly noticed. She simply hummed a 'thank you' and continued blankly staring ahead of her.

Swift on Croft's heels, and much more imposing than the librarian's gingerly approach to the mourning heiress, Elinor Abram stomped her way into the room. Had the large oak doors to the library been closed at the time, she would have theatrically flung them open, posed for a moment in her anger, and then proceeded to waltz toward Selina's chair.

"Well," she exhaled dramatically. "Such a stoic expression for a woman whose precious paramour was just locked away for murder. I would think such a powerful lady as yourself wouldn't hesitate to march down to that jailhouse and demand her husband back, no matter what the cost."

Selina barely granted her a glance. "Such a presumptuous tone for a woman who's so dangerously close to overstaying her welcome."

With much more deliberation than she intended to contribute to the interaction, Selina sipped her sherry and awaited its effects to heal her throbbing head. Unfortunately, the arrival of Abram's voice in the library undid whatever relief the sherry was lending her.

"Now, now, ladies," Abram hummed.

Selina closed her eyes, steadying her breathing. "Is there no more privacy in this house?" she whispered, for only Croft to hear. The librarian chuckled, but remained by her side—his seasoned instincts doubted facing the Abrams alone was good for the lady's nerves.

"Say the word, Selina," offered Abram, walking past his sister to gain a better view of Selina. "We are at your service—whatever you should need," he pointed at her.

On the contrary, Elinor stood out of Selina's sight, demanding she face her with an explanation. "We will sit here and do nothing, then?" she tossed.

Croft watched Selina with widened eyes as she did just that. Nothing. Eyes still closed, she allowed the hysterically entitled woman to carry on.

"Will you at least see to it he receives representation?" Elinor continued. "This is all ludicrous."

Abram grunted and glanced up at her. "Not entirely, Elinor. Just calm yourself."

Selina's eyes opened, narrowed on Abram now. "You think

Royce did it," she said.

"I think any man is capable of killing," he shrugged.

"But Royce," Selina pushed herself into a straighter posture. "Your dear friend. You truly believe he killed Sir Henry?"

Abram paused a moment, pouting in thought, and then nodded. "I don't see why not."

"You shut your bloody mouth, Bernard," Elinor spoke the feelings of the room.

Selina and Croft exchanged baffled expressions as Abram poised himself for thorough clarification. With overstated comfort, he sat himself in the chair opposite Selina—her eyes followed him and he relished the thought.

"Royce comes from an upbringing where violence was fully utilized," he explained. "It stands to reason that, when provoked, his nature would take over."

Elinor moved closer, staring at her brother, incredulously infuriated.

"Poorhouse to publishing house..." Selina recited his previous sales pitch.

"Well," he spread his arms in consideration. "I wouldn't say poorhouse exactly."

Slowly and with derision, Selina sat back in her chair, rolling her eyes toward Croft. "And I thought your marketing of his rise to fame was completely accurate, Mr. Abram. How silly of me."

"He was a dock boy in Whitechapel," Abram reasoned. "It might as well have been a poorhouse—just with more pistols and clubs."

"Whitechapel?" Croft breathed. "Good heavens."

As if only now realizing the librarian's presence, Abram glanced at him in surprise. "Have you been there?"

Croft shook his head emphatically. "Heavens, no."

A degrading smile stretched across Abram's lips. "No," he said. "I wouldn't expect a respectable librarian to find himself in a place like that." He crossed one leg over the other, flashing a grin at

Elinor. "Royce has come far, but there's no ignoring his violent origin, his makeup. There's something in the water there…"

"Would you stop, you fool?" Elinor finally reached to slap her brother on the head.

"Come now, Elinor," he said again. "There's no point in defending him now. He's lied to the poor woman enough." Abram gestured to Selina, the vainly painted victim. "As he does to them all."

Croft's nose wrinkled; the gossip of Royce's womanizing nature had not yet reached the library, it seemed.

"Perhaps he hasn't." Elinor gritted her teeth. "After all, Bernard, this one is his *wife*."

"In any case," Abram brushed her off and leaned forward. "I only regret he turned monstrous in the company of such a lady. I'm very sorry for you, Lady Selina."

Without acknowledging the sympathies, Selina stood from her chair. "If you'll excuse me," she said bitingly before heading for the door.

"Ah, my lady," Croft hurried after her. Once they reached the hallway, she vaguely turned to him. "I don't mean to be presumptive," he began slowly, "but considering this alarming development, perhaps….oh dear, I can't believe I'm suggesting this….but perhaps, given the circumstances, Mr. Royce is the sort of man who might have left behind some sort of…"

"Evidence," she finished.

Croft angled his head back toward the library where their tasteless guests still sat. "Protection," he corrected in a whisper.

2

Box Clever &
Keep Your Mouth Shut

Less than two days behind bars might seem like very little, however, when one is accused of killing one of the most respected and beloved gentlemen in the county, kind treatment is not expected. The cells in the magistrate building were filled with pickpockets and thieves, the drunken and disorderly— no murderers. But the handful of inmates didn't take much notice; it was at the hands of the local constables by which Royce suffered.

His hands were bound and he had been tossed in an isolated cell in the corner of the holding area. Face bruised, lip bleeding, and sleeves torn, Royce had felt the wrath of each angry officer in the station. Not all were as patient and honorable as Constable Marley; in unfortunate cases, evidence was hardly questioned when emotions ran high.

Sir Henry had contributed, alongside Lady Selina, to the welfare of most institutions in the area, and the magistrate station was no different. Only the year before, he had provided them with updated equipment and supplies, as well as suggesting to their London counterparts that they receive continual training.

Though his accusations were to blame for the suspect's mistreatment, Barratt's sympathies were virtually nonexistent. He strolled down the corridor of cells and casually halted when he reached Royce. Holding his finger and thumb less than an inch from each other, he complained,

"I was *this* close to escaping the county."

Royce's sunken shoulders and hanging head hesitated to rise. "You said the maid's death wasn't a suicide," he muttered.

Barratt crossed his arms in front of his chest. "Yes, well. You just killed my best suspect, so now we may never know the truth."

A scoff escaped Royce's lips as he finally strained to look up at the inspector. "You honestly believe Kincaid could've killed a young girl," he mocked. The tenderness of his cheeks and jaw prevented any further laughter at the thought, but the sentiment was felt.

Barratt shrugged, unbothered. "He nearly killed you. Why not?"

"He didn't—"

"No," Barratt stopped him. "Because you got to him first. I certainly hope you've gained the desired inspiration with this one, Royce," he shook his head. "I'd offer a recommendation for representation, but I'm certain if your rich little wife actually cares about you, she'll be more than capable of buying the best help in the country. Though, I noticed...she has yet to do so."

Royce lightly scoffed again. Barratt watched doubt overtake the man; without the pomp and circumstance in which he had recently reveled, Royce appeared as lowly as the young boy from Whitechapel Barratt once watched trail behind every opportunity he could find. Helpless, hopeless, and clinging to the last shred of self-preservation left in him.

"You never know," Barratt said adversely. "Perhaps whatever your leverage over her may be might prompt her to toss you a life jacket."

Defeated, yet defiant—that was the expression Barratt often saw on Royce's face, and as the prisoner propped himself up against the wall with his head upright, he saw it once again.

"Is it so impossible to believe she cares for me of her own

accord?" Royce murmured.

"Yes, Royce, it is," Barratt replied simply. "You can fool Everdon, but you can't fool me." He took a step closer to the bars of the cell, his tone becoming gritty. "I don't know what you intended with this one, my friend….maybe it was the size of her fortune, maybe the power….but you've gone just a bit too far."

Royce's eyes snapped to him with intensity. "I wouldn't do this to Selina."

"You didn't kill your bank roll," Barratt pointed through the bars. "You killed her dearest friend. Your romantic sensibilities won't be a strong enough defense. You can't talk yourself out of it all this time around. You've gone just a bit too far to keep yourself entertained."

Through clenched teeth, Royce muttered, "When can you recall my killing a man for entertainment?"

Barratt narrowed his gaze, leaning back slightly in contemplation. "You're a fighter, Royce. Perhaps killing him wasn't the intention," he offered. "Perhaps it was entirely accidental. The trial will no doubt reveal that."

"I've boxed for years," Royce countered, rubbing his palm. "I know how to strike a blow without causing permanent damage."

"You're also hotheaded, which can override any amount of experience."

Royce leaned his head back and allowed his eyes to stray away from the inspector. "The back of the head…." he grumbled. "You know that's not my style."

Grinning, Barratt stroked his short beard. "That surprised me as well," he confessed. The contradiction of evidence gave him odd satisfaction. "But we have two witnesses, Royce…"

"I haven't denied throwing a punch. That's all they witnessed."

"That and your apparent motive."

Royce glanced back up at him, brows pulled skeptically together. "What motive?"

Barratt's own brows rose incredulously. "Any man would've been riled by the way the fair Lady Selina looked at Sir Henry. I can't say that I blame you. Particularly considering their affair."

Shoulders now alert with alarming energy, Royce sat up straighter. The distraction caused by the bruises and abrasions now dissipated. "What?"

"That's what they're saying at least. But you know how busy-bodies seem to get everything wrong. Still, it's curious isn't it? They were meant to marry. Youthful folly separated them, and they've lived with regret ever since. It only makes sense that they'd reconnect. A villain like yourself—Kincaid viewed you as a threat coming along to take away his dear Selina. The friction between you has been evident to everyone, you know."

"That's your theory," Royce almost smirked, but the lesion on his cheek tempered him. "Selina and Kincaid had an affair and I offed him to end it."

"Careful, my friend," Barratt smiled. "That sounds like a confession."

"If I'm the villain you think I am," the scoundrel spoke slowly, attempting to internalize each word, "I wouldn't be bothered by my wife's infidelity. What was hers is still mine. Henry Kincaid posed no threat to my fortune."

"I'd suggest you encourage whatever overpaid barrister Lady Selina hires to push that exact point," the inspector clicked his tongue. "Confessing to being a gold-digging sycophant is much less horrid than a reckless killer. Let your representation do the talking. Box clever and keep your mouth shut—no matter how much of a challenge that may be for you."

Royce's eyelids closed as he exhaled, leaning back against the stone behind him. Selina's shaking hands when she received the news wouldn't leave Royce's memory. Walls of propriety and composure disguised a crumbling foundation. His sympathy for the deceased himself might not have held sincere, but some emerging part of Royce possessed him to ask,

"Has Kincaid's family been notified?"

Barratt squared his shoulders at such a question being posed from the jealous husband. "Seems his only surviving family is an aunt in Spain, an uncle in London, and two cousins, heaven knows where. I've contacted the uncle." Barratt chuckled for a moment at the thought of overeager aristocrats climbing over one another to collect the fallen gains of their own blood. "As he now inherits Millhampton, I'd imagine his arrival will be rather speedy."

3
The Effects of Charm & Breeding

Aristocrats scurry to family money like rats to cheese. Whether in London or in the country, it was all the same. The Honorable George Kincaid, regardless of estrangement from his dearly departed nephew, hastily made his way from the bustling streets of London to claim his rightful place in the halls of Millhampton. Had his elder brother sired a daughter instead of a son, the estate would have been his years ago. But where money is concerned, emotional bonds can be easily broken. As Sir Henry inherited, George Kincaid disappeared from the family estate.

At the request of Inspector Barratt, as stated politely in his letter of condolences, Kincaid was asked to make an appearance in the magistrate building to meet with the inspector as well as officially identify his nephew's body. Making his way down the streets of town, he was met with a familiar face. Her hair was perfectly pinned, her bodice tightened, and her polished shoes clicked against the cobblestone. She was poised for an attack he had seen many times in years past. A fierce business meeting awaited her, he imagined.

"Ah, Lady Selina," he called to her.

Selina's pace slowed at the sound of his voice, until finally she stopped and faced him with a friendly smile. "Kincaid."

"It's lovely to see you."

"I wish it wasn't under these circumstances," she looked to her hands, but then peered back up at him."Though, it seems, you'd come for nothing less than something as important as the passage of property."

His grin widened at her derisive wit. "Just look at you, Selina," he gestured to her elegantly feminine frame."You've become quite a woman. And I understand you're married now. I never thought you'd ever wed, and now here you are....married to a murderer."

Selina's lip curled venomously. "How is dear Francesca?"

Following a brief but playful glare, Kincaid burst into a jovial laugh. "Well played, my lady. You're sharp as ever." He leaned closer to her as they both continued to walk. "Since you want to know," he went on, "I seem to be missing an alarming amount of jewels and silverware."

"Clever woman," Selina nodded in approval. "She couldn't wait for the divorce hearing to tell her what she's no longer entitled to, so she decided to take what she could and disappear."

The two of them passed Mr. Litchfield's assistant from the orphanage, Mr. Bryant—a strapping young man with curly dark hair and wide eyes. Selina glanced at him, subtly attempting to make eye contact, but he looked away, even angling his head shamefully from her view.

Lifting her chin and pressing forward, Selina added to Kincaid, "Now I understand why you're so quick to come to Millhampton."

Kincaid chuckled again. "Oh Selina. I see why Henry admired you. I'm very sorry for your loss. And even more sorry at whose hand it's come."

Her upper lip stiffened. "There's very little evidence, George," she muttered. "One shouldn't be so quick to settle on the easiest explanation."

"The easiest? That Barratt fellow's letter suggested the evidence was strong enough to take Mr. Royce to London for a trial." Kincaid suddenly noted in which direction the lady's feet were still pointed. The magistrate building, as his were. "Of course you're not content with that."

"Hm," was all she said.

He wasn't in the habit of withholding criticism, but considering the circumstances, he thought it prudent, just this once. "I've seen his name around London. Brilliant writer, I'm told," he commended, instead. "Though I'm not much of a reader. Friends of mine have attended his book readings and told me he's a sensational storyteller. I should dearly love to meet him."

As they reached the entrance to the building, Selina paused and gave a small smile. "How lucky for you that his time of penitence is now ending."

An amused grin crossed Kincaid's face again. "How lucky for him that you've put on your crown and waltzed down to his rescue."

"Tsk, tsk," Kincaid clicked his tongue. "I take it you're her Mr. Royce."

"He usually looks much better," Selina patted Kincaid's arm.

There was a pinch of sorrow in her eyes as she peered through the bars of his cell, but Royce wasn't certain it was at all related to the sight of him.

"You look terrible," she proved him wrong.

"Are you going to hit me too?" he hardly lifted his head to ask.

Notwithstanding the slight satisfaction she felt at seeing her blackmailer in such a state, an anger grew within her that he was struck by any hand but her own. Slipping her arm smoothly away from Kincaid's, Selina cleared her throat and called to the young officer who stood behind her.

"When was he last fed?" she demanded. The color in Royce's face had drained since she last saw him, as any starved man's would.

The young sergeant adjusted his coat as she addressed him. "Erm...." he hesitated to form an answer.

"Sergeant," she turned on her heel to look him in the eye. "If you're about to mumble something about his last meal being at Everdon, I can assure you your future in law enforcement will be meeting its share of complications."

Kincaid chuckled heartily, in total awe of the spectacle. The spineless young man facing the mouthy heiress—it was as if they had stepped back in time to Selina's youth. "Oh I've missed you, Selina."

"Be quiet, George," she hushed, directing her authoritative smirk at the stammering sergeant.

"The-the constable said—"

"Get him up—*gently*," she gracefully barked.

Upon seeing the Everdon carriage just outside of the magistrate building, Constable Marley scurried as quickly as he could to see his sergeant lifting and releasing Mr. Royce. Marley breathed deeply for courage, which Selina was sure to disregard.

"My Lady Selina," he attempted. "With all due respect, Inspector Barratt has ordered this man to be transported to London for trial by morning."

Selina turned to him with a softer smile, but maintained a high chin which brought anxiety to form in the constable's throat. "Where is the inspector now?" she challenged him.

Marley coughed lightly. "Getting Lord Rafferty's testimony in writing, ma'am. There are still details he'd like to confirm."

The lady squinted doubtfully, sparking another cough from the constable.

"And here I thought the case had been closed," Selina hummed.

"Well, I mean—"

"Mr. Royce is taking up unnecessary space in your jailhouse, constable," she told him plainly, taking Royce by the arm and guiding him past Kincaid and the constable. "If Inspector Barratt has concerns, he may speak with me directly regarding my husband's alibi for the crime in question."

"I was told he had no alibi, my lady," Marley retorted with strained confidence.

Selina stopped and turned on her heel. "Of course he has an alibi," she corrected him, her tone low and poignant.

"He does?" Kincaid's question reflected in Royce's expression as well. Marley, however, stood by his previous answer.

"We have a witness statement putting him out on the grounds —" he tried to explain.

"Gardeners and gentlemen all look alike in the dark, constable," she crooned. Her hand wrapped tighter around Royce's arm as she leaned into him. "Mr. Royce was in my bedchamber during the time of the murder."

Marley's jaw fell ajar at the implication, but stammered to confirm her claim. "In your bedchamber....?"

"He is my husband, after all," Selina shrugged acceptingly. "Would you care to transcribe the details of that testimony, or are we quite finished?"

"Ha!" Kincaid exclaimed, amused to his wit's end. "Excellent."

"No, ma'am," the red-faced constable coughed. "I'll inform the inspector. You are free to go."

Selina smiled amiably at him as she guided the tired man on her arm out of the building. Surprised as he was by the ordeal, Royce had only energy enough to lean against Selina and accept the rescue as they made their way to the door.

"Brilliantly done, Selina," Kincaid whispered in her ear as the three of them departed. "Let us both hope you've not just released Henry's true killer."

Selina looked down her nose toward him. "I think you have an estate to be auditing, don't you, George?"

Grinning in agreement, Kincaid kissed her free hand and nodded to her husband. "Always a pleasure."

The carriage ride back to Everdon was silent. Cold tension hung in the air, and Royce didn't dare break it. Their arrival at the homestead was not announced or met by servants. It was as pedestrian as a walk through the yard. The master had come home, but greetings were withheld, eyes were averted, and not a word was spoken.

Royce thought it best to hide himself in his room until he was presentable enough for dinner that evening. His hair hadn't been brushed since he left Everdon, and Price was sure to find the state of his shirt disgraceful.

Rather unexpectedly, Price was waved off by a pursuing Lady Selina as she followed her husband up the staircase and into his bedroom. Without question, Price stepped aside and waited to be needed in the hallway outside. When Royce heard Selina's heels click and the door close behind him, he stopped unbuttoning his shirt and his head perked up from its bowed position. Cautiously, he turned to face her.

Her mouth was a straight line, but her eyes were searching. Royce waited a moment for her to speak, but when she said nothing, he sighed.

"Should I be thanking you? Or was all of that done out of fear that I would expose you?"

Tightening her gaze, her hands joined in front of her, she stated plainly, "I found your revolver."

Royce's fingers combed through his hair on impulse and his gaze strayed, but he said nothing.

Selina took a step forward. "Was that your plan then?" she pressed.

"My plan?" he squinted at her.

"Marry me, secure the estate, and then do away with me?"

This time he took the step forward; he held his palms in the air in earnest. "No. That revolver is only ever—"

"It was meant for Henry, then?" she continued, her volume spiking with each emotional breath. "Anyone who got in your way?"

"Oh please, Selina," he snorted, turning away from such a ridiculous notion. "I didn't snap his neck with a bullet."

"Have you ever killed a man?"

Royce froze. When he glanced back at her, she was wringing

her hands, her face feigning fearlessness against whatever answer that awaited her. The setting sun through the window beamed and reflected the mist in her eyes, but she held firm. He imagined not a tear had escaped her since hearing of Henry's death. And why would it? There was no longer safety behind the walls of Everdon. He had robbed her of that—and his absence meant nothing as long as his guests remained.

"I did not kill Kincaid," he said at last.

She lightly cocked her head to one side. "That was not the question. Are you claiming you are incapable of killing a man?"

He mirrored the gesture, angling his head in the opposite direction, while releasing a labored sigh. "No. I can't claim that. But I promise you this: while I may be perfectly capable of taking a life—I would *never* kill an innocent man," he shook his head vehemently. "Especially Kincaid."

"You hated him."

"But, you cared for him." He spoke the defense so quickly that Selina's lips parted. Seeing her surprise, Royce cleared his throat. "I may seem heartless," he explained, "but I could never do something like that. Not to you. And if you're worried for Penelope's safety—"

"I can take care of Penelope," she cut him off with a hand in the air. "And when I can't, there are others who can. Besides, you have nothing to gain from shooting her."

"That revolver is for protection," he insisted once again. "Nothing more."

"Yes, I'm sure a man of your....background would feel a constant need for it."

"My background..." he repeated, tasting her meaning as he said the words.

"*Poorhouse to publishing house.* I had no idea the poorhouse included the docks of Whitechapel. I've heard talk of smugglers, stranglers, and all sorts of filth that linger there."

"That's enough," he warned.

"Abram told me—"

"Abram?" His temper burned in his cheeks and ears. Any

amount of time away from Everdon meant influence lost; his absence appeared to have allowed Selina to be tainted.

"Found you in the gutter and brought you to fame and fortune," she glanced at the ceiling in exaggerated recollection, "throwing you in the paths of every wealthy patroness you could get your hands on. It's perfectly reasonable for you to take such violent measures to secure your own future." She then shrugged flippantly. "At least, that's what he claims."

"And you believe him?" his voice choked.

"Why should I not?" Selina threw her hands in the air. "He's your *friend*, yes? He seems to know you quite well, and claims you're capable of killing….Henry…." His name caught in her throat. It was a name she'd only refer to in the past tense, and the truth of that was sinking into her heart. "You've done your best to keep me compliant thus far, Royce. You're not above playing mind games…but through the entirety of your time at Everdon….through every manipulation and coercion…you have never once lied to me. You have always made your intentions clear."

"Selina…" he steadily crossed the room. "I am a scoundrel and a villain. I hit Henry—I hated the man. But I wouldn't…I couldn't do that to you. I could not kill him."

"He was figuring you out," she whispered. Her hands gradually moved toward her face, first clutching her stomach, and then rubbing her neck, before reaching her trembling mouth. "He was too clever for his own good."

"That's not why he died."

"Then *why*?" Her sobs burst through. She tried to quickly turn her head from Royce's view, but it only prompted him to move toward her.

"There's a reason Barratt hasn't closed the case. He'll dig until he finds the answer that fits—he'll solve it, Selina." He only vaguely believed his own words, but his empty faith softened her enough for her to allow him to pull her closer. Gently, holding his breath, he cupped the back of her head with his hand and gave her a shoulder to catch her tears.

4
Broken Wings

Those accustomed to the affluent environment of an upper-class manor were quick to find it quite dull to lie around the parlor on a fine July morning. The heat was not unbearable, but the only one who seemed to enjoy the warmth was Penelope, who awoke early to spend the day with the Sweetings in town.

Meanwhile, the parlor was filled with the lounging Everdon guests. That is, until Mr. Royce could be heard tenderly inviting his wife on a stroll across the grounds. Her mourning had kept her indoors, and he felt it was his husbandly duty to encourage fresh air and sunshine. To his chagrin, Miss Abram caught wind of the suggestion and was all too eager to join them. And, naturally, any movement of Lady Selina was sure to catch the attention of Mr. Abram as well.

And so, the four of them embarked on a good long walk along the dusty paths of Everdon—but not before, however, Selina made Mr. Croft swear to send her reinforcements as soon as Lindon became available.

The Everdon walking paths were infamous in the county. After years of the active, young Selina coming home from a day's play with muddied shoes and hem, Lady Delamere saw to it that paths were made throughout the forests leading to and surrounding the road at the bottom of the hill. This never stopped Selina from making a mess of herself, of course, but it did provide her with some much needed direction.

Early in their walk, the party approached a small, muddy rivet in the path. Abram hurried to hold a helpful hand to Lady Selina, as the fancied gentleman he was. With Royce preoccupied with the needy Miss Abram, Selina accepted the assistance with a straight-face and the minimally required politeness.

"Thank you, Mr. Abram," she said blandly, stepping past him.

Abram grinned at the touch of her hand. "Of course," he returned. "We wouldn't want mud splattered on that lovely bodice of yours."

Selina couldn't stop her lips from curling downward in distaste—nor did she attempt to. Rather than wasting energy on a forced smile of politeness, she stepped ahead of Abram and sought her husband's arm, even steering him from Elinor's grasp. Abram and his sister paused a moment in surprise and then slowly conceded to follow behind.

"How long will the Abrams be staying at Everdon, darling?" Selina uttered softly, pulling Royce's arm closer to her side.

His lips parted at the term of endearment, but then straightened again at the sound of Abram's cackle behind them. "Selina," he sighed reluctantly, "he's my friend and my agent. I'm sure he intends to stay until I produce the next manuscript I've promised him."

Selina grimaced at the thought. "And how much longer might that take?"

"I haven't written a word since they've arrived," Royce confessed.

She would have chuckled more heartily if she had not been so disappointed. "What," she scoffed, "with all their constant demands, I can't imagine what could be distracting you so."

"Stop it," he softly but firmly chided. "Elinor may have extravagant taste, but she's instrumental in my publications."

Royce could feel her stiffen beside him. Curtly, she cleared her throat. "Then it's a wonder her inspiring presence hasn't helped accomplish what her brother needs from you."

As if her ears were burning, Elinor interrupted the couple's conversation with a boisterous, "You're being ridiculous—come now, Royce, settle this for me." She pushed ahead, her brother still on her arm, to take her believed place on the empty side of Royce. "Bernard has gone mad…"

Selina felt she'd had more than her share of Elinor's presence, and so she allowed the shrew to advance and move Royce ahead while she herself slipped out of Royce's reach. Royce's eyes trailed after her until she met and took the arm of Mr. Lindon, at the rear of the party.

Lindon smiled warmly at Selina, happy to see her in the sunshine. He sobered, however, as he offered an explanation for his tardiness. "Barratt requested I write down my own testimony of the night Henry died," he informed her. "You've forced him to look from different angles of that night's proceedings."

"In the name of justice, of course," Selina smirked.

Lindon caught Royce's lingering gaze until his head was forced back to face Elinor and her babbling. A strange smile of contemplation stretched across Lindon's face. "You're defending your husband now. I confess it's unexpected."

Suddenly, Selina slowed her pace. As soon as Elinor's giggling began to fade ahead, Selina lowered her voice. "He knows, Lindon."

Lindon blinked. "He…"

She didn't feel the need to complete his baffled sentence. "How do you think he managed to marry me?"

His smile faded at an alarming rate. "Blackmail…the cad," he swore.

"He thought we were both out for a prize, and he simply wanted to be part of it."

"And you still don't believe he killed Henry?" Lindon's teeth gritted.

"He has his money," she decided, disregarding the threat she once threw at Royce. "He has nothing to gain from killing Henry. A thief traditionally retires once he has achieved his greatest con; stepping back at the height of his career."

"Yes..."

"Everdon is the greatest con in his career," she went on, gradually convincing herself as well. "He'd be a fool to throw away his prize. And he is no fool."

There was a peculiar admiration in her tone as she said this. From the corner of his eye, Lindon could have sworn he saw a fleeting smile. "Is that all you are to him? His prize?"

Selina inhaled contemplation and exhaled surety. "I believe, in a marriage, it is important to be perfectly honest about one's feelings. Neither of us has been shy regarding where our affections lie. He loves my money, and I don't hate his face."

"And you are both content with that...as if nothing else is necessary for the functionality of this arrangement?"

The answer she'd recited to herself for weeks escaped Selina's lips: "As long as he has his money and his mistress, he'll stay content."

Lindon lifted a skeptical brow. "You think Miss Abram is his mistress?"

"He's made it clear he doesn't keep them at Everdon for Mr. Abram's company."

Resisting the urge to roll his eyes, Lindon asked, "Did he say as much? Or are these your own assumptions?"

"Well, you've met Abram, haven't you?" Selina snorted, quieted only by Lindon's nudge to her arm. "Horrifying as Elinor is, she's infinitely preferable company."

Lindon joined her in the laugh. He couldn't deny her assessment. However, as he watched the way Miss Abram careened against Royce's side when she spoke to him, and when he remembered the lingering gaze he'd seen as Selina left Royce's arm, Lindon's laugh settled. "I think you've been far too close to all of this," he deduced.

"What do you mean?"

"You've lost your keenly objective skills of observation.

You've never been so in the thick of things. Miss Abram pines, but Royce is disinterested...despite his apparent conditioning," his voice lowered to a grumble.

"Conditioning?" Selina followed Lindon's shrewd glare. Elinor vied while Abram bullied. Royce was a horse with two masters, led along the path in conflicting directions. His posture was rigid and almost pained at being so surrounded. No creature could function properly with such constant antipathy encompassing it—not even a beast like Royce.

"He still seems preoccupied with studying his recent catch." Lindon now glanced back at her. She was softening with sympathy, and that was far from his intent. "Please be wary, Selina," he warned. "I don't think any of this is quite so simple. I hate to see you so confined."

"Confined? Please," she scoffed again.

"He's clipped your wings."

"This is not a new state of being, Lindon." Her correction came with a dispassionate truth. "Broken wings often go unnoticed on those who seldom used them anyway."

Lindon's gaze fell to his feet. She was only a few years from thirty and already speaking like a world-weary soldier. "You've been burdened too young," he murmured. "We should have never told you. You wouldn't be in this mess if you were none the wiser."

"Nonsense," Selina clicked her tongue. "I've taken care of things so far, haven't I? His upper hand is an illusion....though only sometimes I suppose. We seem to be taking turns being at one another's mercy."

That faint glint of admiration returned to her expression, and only brought deeper worry lines to Lindon's. She would never admit her enjoyment now, as it all came at the expense of her livelihood and even the lives of her loved ones, but since childhood Selina had dearly loved games. "You will keep fighting for the upper hand over the other until you both end up with the same hand. The Abrams presence here was his move, and I take it your saving him from rotting in a cell was yours."

"If I'd left him there, he wouldn't have hesitated to reveal what he knows," she reasoned, though she sincerely doubted he'd play such a gamble.

"I think he's capable of more damage within Everdon's walls than he is behind bars."

Selina lowered her chin and lifted her brow. "Even with the evidence against me?"

"Evidence?"

"He has a letter."

"Impossible," Lindon shook his head with resolution. "Edward and I destroyed the evidence. There was no letter left." He pursed his lips, running through the memories for any possible indiscretion. "Have you seen it?"

She strenuously shrugged. "I don't need to see it." In truth, she had almost been too terrified to ask. But her fears were in check, and far from something in which Lindon needed to concern himself. "The details were far too accurate for the evidence to not exist. He learnt it somehow."

Gradually, Lindon's pace slowed until they both came to a stop. Then, with great deliberation, Lindon asked the question she had since ignored. "Are we certain he's kept the information to himself?"

Dinner was a bit quieter, Selina's nerves were a bit tighter, and her attention to the Abrams was a bit closer. Every whisper and nudge they cast in Royce's direction brought her to question just how much of their awareness was possible. It would not have come as such a shock to her if a man like Royce was sure to secure an army before attacking the castle. The growing anxiety manifested in more forced niceties and accommodating than she had willingly given earlier that day.

Later that evening, gathered in the drawing room to hear the full account of Penelope's day with Henrietta, the residents and guests of Everdon seated themselves comfortably for their tea. If Selina hadn't known better, she would have suspected Royce of sensing her uneasiness, for he took the seat beside her on the sofa before Abram had even entered the room. He rested an arm along the back of the sofa and crossed one leg over the other, discouraging anyone else to assume a place beside her. With the cesspool of thoughts swimming around Selina's mind, however, the gesture was more foreboding than it's potentially helpful intent.

Realizing the only conversation in the room was hers, Penelope paused, mid-sentence and said, "Um, Royce. When you married Selina, she promised you'd tell me stories…."

"Did she?" Royce lifted an eyebrow at his wife, who simply straightened in her seat while Penelope went on.

"Yes, she did. Like the one you told in London."

"Which one did he tell in London?" Elinor squinted to recall, as if she'd been there herself.

"The one with the crooked naval captain. Have you heard that one?"

"Yes, of course," she nodded presumptuously. "I've heard his stories many times before."

Selina could hardly bear it; the day had been far too long for her to be expected to control the expressions of her face. And so, she turned her head away from Elinor and allowed herself to roll her eyes and wrinkle her nose in distaste. In turning her head, however, she noticed Helen and Moll sneak into the room with trays of evening tea. Just as she had hoped, her lady's maid had developed the habit of including just a small decanter of sherry as well.

"Of course, you must have," Penelope replied snidely, with complete disregard for volume. Selina chuckled lightly, amused to hear her own sort of words escape Penelope's lips. "Well, I think you should make a new one."

"Here, here," Abram lifted his tea in the air. "The girl speaks sense. It's about time you've come up with a fresh one, Royce."

Penelope wagged a finger at him, before he became too

carried away. "But not for you," she told him."

"Nell," Selina breathed.

"He should write one for me," Penelope held her hands out, as if challenging someone to correct her. When no one else spoke, she leaned against her elbow closest to Royce. "You always put ladies in your stories, don't you? Well, Helen and I came up with some ideas before the wedding, and I've been dying to tell you."

Moll's eyes snapped to Helen, who was pouring a cup of tea for Elinor when she finally felt the attention shift. Seeing Royce suddenly look at her, she swallowed hard. His glance seemed harmless, but all she could see was the man she put behind bars, for however brief a time.

"And what might those be?" he asked.

To Helen's relief, Penelope grabbed the reins of the conversation and pulled everyone back to her. She leaned forward and touched Royce's knee for emphasis. "We were thinking, perhaps, a story like yours and Selina's. An artist and a lady."

Selina couldn't tell if Elinor grimaced because of Penelope's familiarity with Royce or the mention of the artist and the lady, but it brought apprehension to Selina's posture. "You could do better than that, Nell," she told Penelope, her voice hoarse.

"No, no, hush," Penelope waved a dismissive hand at her. "The story is about me, it's just—there should be a princess. And she lives in a castle."

Selina smiled; she was beginning to see the wide reach of Helen's budding story. "How original," she glanced at Helen.

"A princess, eh?" Royce started to grin. "What sort of princess? The damsel sort?"

Penelope looked at him the way one looks at a pitiable fool. "The powerful sort," she gently corrected, "with mysterious friends— perhaps with magic." She began counting on her fingers as she listed the heroine's virtues. "She's confident, shrewd, well-respected, and fiercely beautiful."

Royce loyally scribbled her description into his notebook. Only looking up to add, "Hm, and what does she look like?"

Penelope pursed her lips and leaned back on the couch. "She wears a great deal of purple, I think."

"Indeed, purple," Abram exclaimed. "Color of royalty."

His contribution to her creative process was unwelcome, and Penelope's vague remembrance of manners weren't enough to stop her from flashing him an irritated glare. "Yes," she curtly agreed.

"And what of the conflict?" Royce then posed.

Taken aback by the question, Penelope looked over to where Helen was refilling Selina's glass. They clearly hadn't discussed that aspect of their story. "Conflict?" she prodded Helen to lend her assistance.

Royce followed her eyes to the lady's maid. Having not noticed her much since his previous arrest, Royce's stare was unsettling to her. "Every good story has a conflict of some kind," he explained to the two of them.

On the couch beside Royce, Selina stirred her drink in her hand, throwing her words half-heartedly. "Perhaps the hero is a criminal."

"Yes," Helen agreed, her volume rising. "A highwayman."

"Excellent choice," he pointed his pencil and gave her a soft smile. At his approval, Helen's shoulders eased; they were friends again. It was all it took for Helen to melt into the seat beside Penelope and forget all propriety.

"How romantic it would be if the highwayman fell in love with the princess he's trying to rob," she suggested, reaching excitedly for Penelope's hand. "Roguish love is the greatest kind."

Elinor shifted uncomfortably in her seat, flashing a disinterested Selina a side glance.

"Yes, Helen, that's brilliant!" Penelope shook Helen's hand, returning the enthusiasm. "What an unthinkable ending it will be."

"Unthinkable," Selina sardonically applauded. "Never been

done before."

Royce lightly tapped Selina's knee in reproof, flashing Penelope another smile. "It's a good choice, yes," he scribbled in his notebook. "Purple dresses....highwayman…"

Helen joined Penelope in leaning forward, pressing her hands against her knees to get a better view of Royce's notebook. Both girls corrected his details and added more for him to note, regardless of their merit in the actual story. Royce good-humoredly wrote down their every word, treating every note as a monumental decision they've made. Selina, lowering her teacup, found herself smiling at his enduring patience.

"Will there be romantic intrigue?" Helen innocently asked him. "The easy romantic stories can be quite boring."

"Yes, of course," he glanced up at her. His eyes then moved to Elinor, whose grimace had settled on the easily smiling heiress, as he added, "Easy is always boring." When he looked back to Penelope and Helen, he snapped his notebook closed. "But," he enunciated, "you ladies will just have to wait for the story to be ready. We should rest for the night and let the creativity restore itself before we get overexcited."

He rose from the couch and offered Penelope his arm. Penelope looked up at him, glanced at the darkness through the windows, then looked at Selina in mild protest before finally sighing in acceptance.

"Oh, all right," she said, standing to take his arm. "I suppose we must let the artist work."

July 1889

August 1889

And yet to every bad, there is a worse
~Thomas Hardy~

1

Her Gilded Cage

Summer was nearing its end, and in following tradition, Lady Selina treated her household and guests to a trip to the nearby traveling menagerie. It passed through the county at that time every year, and Selina herself was quite fond of the annual outing. She and Penelope had frequented menageries since they were both small children, often bonding over their favorite exotic animals and imagining journeying far and wide to the animal's native land.

At the suggestion of the outing, Elinor insisted on acquiring a new hat, as it was a fresh occasion and all of her current hats had been well-worn all summer. Selina posed little argument as Royce footed the bill for Elinor's new menagerie outfit. She merely rolled her eyes and made arrangements for the day. She had even invited Helen to accompany them as a guest, as it was her day off and the idea of exotic animals greatly intrigued her. She and Penelope were practically giddy with excitement, almost giving Selina the feeling of having two wards to govern.

"You brought that with you?" Penelope suddenly noticed the notebook tucked under Helen's arm.

"Well…" Helen felt a flash of embarrassment. "Mr. Royce says there's art everywhere. I might as well capture it." Her embarrassment passed as Penelope caught sight of the Rafferty children ahead of them within the menagerie. She grabbed Helen's hand, ignoring her answer, and pulled her along to meet the little children, leaving the other four in the party behind.

Selina watched the two of them prance toward the entrance, wearing an amused smile and a hint of her own childlike wonder.

Penelope was not the only one to notice the presence of the Rafferty party. Abram narrowed his sights on Rafferty's young governess tending to the children. She was a well-endowed, pleasant-looking woman with a quiet smile and unending patience as the children loudly exclaimed and bounced around her.

Abram nudged Royce, humming salaciously. "Hm, Rafferty's governess."

"She is beautiful," Royce grinned in agreement. Selina followed their gaze and rolled her eyes, slipping her arm out of Royce's. An unfamiliar feeling of shame rushed over Royce as he watched her walk ahead of them.

Having just purchased tickets of his own, Selina was approached by none other than the pervasive Inspector Barratt. "Well, Lady Selina," he greeted her as soon as he found himself in line with her pace. "What a pleasant surprise."

"I'm not against seeing your handsome face, Inspector," the lady sighed and stopped to face him, "but I must say it's beginning to feel rather intrusive."

"Forgive me, my lady," he dutifully bowed. "I tend to immerse myself when there's a tricky case to be solved. It happens to be my day off, but it is serendipitous that I should run into so many subjects in one day."

Deciding his company was preferable than that from whom she had just escaped, Selina complied. "I understand your list of suspects has expanded," she commented.

"In a sense," he shrugged.

"And that Lord Rafferty was among the first to be questioned, despite having no motive," Selina angled her chin, narrowing her eyes. "Along with Mr. Lennox and my vicar, Mr. Holbrook."

"That's right."

"Even Mr. Abram over there—questioned, and yet, no motive. It seems your list should be dwindling, not growing."

"Do you truly want your friend's murderer brought to justice, my lady?"

"Certainly, but not at the expense of every handsome face in the county being accused," she gestured to the moderate crowd of passersby, which happened to contain a handful of handsome faces.

"My list has, in fact, expanded beyond the gentlemen in your company, Lady Selina." The inspector narrowed his own eyes as his lips tugged upward in an amused smile. "You yourself are not above suspicion."

Selina pulled her hands together in front of her, both pensive and challenging.

"A delicate touch is needed, you understand," he hummed.

"I fail to see how I'm a suspect."

"It seems you can't avoid people dying around you. And I find that greatly intriguing."

Selina chuckled humorlessly. "The earliest death in which you've shown interest happened nearly thirty years ago—I couldn't have possibly murdered a woman in my infancy. Josephine Rodin was a tragedy—something clearly happened to the poor girl—but I'm hardly a candidate for the murderous father of her child, and I certainly had no reason to do away with one of my best maids. Good help is so hard to find."

"And Sir Henry?"

The lady's mouth tightened with her tone. "How could I possibly take the life of my dearest friend? If I were to kill a man, it would certainly not be a man who's done well to protect me since childhood."

Barratt lifted a brow. "Some deaths may be more justified than others. But you are right, Kincaid's is not the one in which I'd wager you had taken part."

Selina's hands tensed, a suspicion gnawing inside of her.

Abram appeared suddenly beside her, bringing a renewed

tightness to her shoulders. "Oh stop targeting the poor woman, Barratt," he chided. "What could you possibly have to suspect?"

"There have been rumors of an affair, even so young in the marriage." Barratt continued to look to Selina. She almost scoffed, until Barratt clarified, "Between yourself and Sir Henry."

"What?" Selina froze.

"Potential motive for you or your husband, if I'm being honest. But as you've assured me Royce had nothing to do with Sir Henry's death, I can only explore the alternative—if Royce didn't kill him in a jealous rage, perhaps you killed him because of some lover's tiff."

Abram chortled, causing Selina's nose to wrinkle at the sound.

"Do you usually base your investigations on rumors, inspector?"

Barratt shrugged away a smile, utterly amused. "Not typically, no. But this one was particularly titillating."

"Now, listen here, Barratt," Abram squared his shoulders, stepping closely in front of Selina. "A woman like Selina has far too much class to be ruining her family's good name. You'd do well to remember that."

Seeing Abram's sudden step from the corner of his eye, Royce left a chatty Mr. Sweeting and approached the growing conflict. However intensely Barratt and Abram may have stared at one another was nothing compared to the discomfort shifting Selina further from Abram's proximity.

"Come, Lady Selina," Abram turned and offered the lady his hand. "Let's enjoy the menagerie as intended, instead of listening to these silly accusations."

She glanced at his hand, cleared her throat as she promptly ignored him, and glanced once more at Barratt. "It's your day off, Inspector. Enjoy the birds."

As Selina once again left the gentlemen, Barratt shook his head. "I'd watch my assertions if I were you, Abram. You're not cleared of this investigation either."

Abram puffed his chest threateningly at hearing such accusations. "You have such nerve being here, throwing about dangerous ideas like that." He reached to nudge Royce as he approached, for solidarity. "He's accusing your wife of murder, Royce, as well as infidelity."

Royce, still unaware of what prompted Selina to leave just as he neared, frowned in confusion.

"I simply explained that she was a person of interest, as are most of you," Barratt continued.

"You don't think a dainty woman like that could kill a grown man—come on, Barratt!" Abram guffawed too loudly. "You're better than that. You're just getting bored. The dead maid killed herself, and there's nothing left to investigate."

"A man's dead, Abram. Might I remind you—you were there, as a matter of fact. There is most certainly something to investigate."

"He's right," Royce gestured to Abram. "You are bored. Perhaps Kincaid tripped and fell."

Barratt glared aloofly. "While it's perfectly typical of you to agree with him, Royce, it's not any less despicable."

Abram put a hand on Royce's shoulder in support. Royce lightly pulled his shoulder away, disguising his flinch as a smooth shift in position.

"Don't harass the boy, Barratt," Abram defended. "You haven't investigated the possibility of an accident. Hit his head hard enough, and it's bound to snap his neck. And he had been drinking, as a matter of fact."

Remembering the letter of WRATH he had received, Barratt frowned doubtfully. "Hm, unlikely."

Stepping around the two of them, Royce cleared his throat and poised for his own escape. "Well, if you'll excuse me, I'd like to join my wife now."

As he walked away, Barratt grabbed his arm and muttered. "Heavy is the head that wears the crown; heavier still for the thief who wanted to try it on for size."

Royce grimaced.

"How long will those crown-snatching vultures circle their kill before collecting, do you think?" Barratt smoldered smugly.

"I don't know what you mean." It took considerable energy for Royce to resist allowing his eyes to flash toward Abram. "Excuse me."

Royce brushed past Barratt, soon meeting Selina in the next wing of the menagerie, where the more exotic birds were held in cages all their own. Selina observed them, slowly moving from one to the other, quiet and pensive.

"Is it true?"

"Is what true?" she mumbled, flickering her eyes in his direction for a fleeting moment.

"The affair. Were you having an affair with Kincaid?"

Her gaze dropped away from the cages and slowly moved toward him. "Those are not the sorts of games I play," she steadily assured. "Disdain is no excuse for infidelity. Marriage is sacred, even if the man is not."

It was an answer Royce believed; vindictive as Lady Selina could be, she had her own conscience to which she always answered. He was quiet for a moment, contemplating his next question. Before he could articulate, however, Selina continued to ruminate on her late friend.

"You know he never loved me," she softly said.

"Who never loved you? Henry?"

Her lifted brows confirmed her pain.

"Selina…"

"He didn't. Not then. Not when it would have mattered." Her fingers fidgeted with the fan she carried between her hands. "My reputation was in question, and he couldn't risk attaching himself and his family name to a spoiled union."

"The Austrian prince?"

Selina stared at him in surprise.

"You waltzed. I assumed."

"How did—"

He leaned in with a slight grin to expound on their now-shared secret. "I doubt Penelope understood why your father berated you the way he did."

"Youth makes fools of us all," Selina sighed, accepting her ward's indiscretion on the matter. "Reputations are a fragile thing. Even the slightest word can shatter them, regardless of the truth of it. The Delamere name is resilient nonetheless, though Henry's father had his misgivings."

Royce's face wrinkled in disgust. His opinion of the deceased remained steadfast. "So he did the noble thing, abandoning his ladylove to preserve his family's honor."

"He was a good man."

"But a coward," Royce maintained. "And yet, you loved him."

The bird before them continuously attempted to fly, but was just as continuously stopped by the cage. The repetitive sound of wings against the metal bars of the cage echoed throughout the menagerie, however, in that moment, it was as if only Selina's ears could hear. The Lady's expression as she watched the bird fell deeply somber, almost pained. Despite the clamor, Royce's gaze did not move from his wife.

"Only so much energy can be spent on the unrequited," she muttered. "I gave up marrying for love years ago."

Royce sighed, preparing to wax poetic. "It's an oft-written affliction…unrequited love."

"And I'm sure an oft-felt symptom of your well-trained dalliances—no doubt something you're accustomed to seeing, so there's no reasonable excuse for that gobsmacked expression."

Royce laughed, realizing he still looked mildly surprised that someone like Selina could ever be found on the losing end. "I'm beginning to think you've never truly been loved."

"What a heart-warming sentence to hear from my husband's lips," she cocked her head to one side.

"Not properly, at least. Kincaid wouldn't have known how to properly love a woman if he tried."

"Don't you dare—" her head snapped in his direction, and her finger lifted in warning.

"Why?" Royce challenged. His eye contact was suddenly intense as he sensed her temper flare. "Because you think he could have?"

"Many women prefer a certain temperance, tenderness, and reliability."

He suppressed a scoff, angling his head slightly, almost pitying. "But do you really see yourself as that sort of woman, Selina?" he said in a lower tone.

"As you said," Selina vaguely gestured, "I've never truly been loved. So I suppose I'll never know."

Royce paused, his eyes following her as she moved ahead of him once more. Slowly, he turned to look at the bird she'd been watching. Its body was a vibrant blue, with orange wings and a black band that stretched across its eyes like a mask. Lightly it pecked at the cage, fluctuating in aggression until it realized there was no moving the bars blocking its path.

Helen wandered aimlessly back toward her mistress, until she hesitantly approached the now-lone Royce with her notebook, wrestling with the idea of initiating conversation as she noted the intensity of Royce's concentration.

"How is that story of yours, Miss Thomas?" he startled her.

"Oh," she exhaled. "Um, fairly well, I think. I just…I'm having trouble deciding on a conflict. As you said before, every good story needs a conflict. Perhaps a kidnapping? Or a ransom?"

"Yes, if the context is adventurous, those are good choices. There's something to be said, however, for subtlety."

"Subtlety?"

"Look there," Royce nodded toward the bird. "How do you suppose he got in there?"

"I expect someone put him there."

"He was probably lured in with food, I suppose. Or distracted, watching his friends lured in with food. Then, before he knew it, he was trapped. The cage was not always the enemy. Wasn't an immediate threat or even seen as dangerous….even seemed safe, perhaps….and just like that," Royce snapped his fingers, "it became a monster."

Royce's eyes, as he spoke, smoothly moved from the bird to Selina, who'd been approached by Abram once again. But Helen hardly noticed; instead her eyes were on the bird.

"An impossible cage would no doubt be a more triumphant overcoming, I would think."

"Yes, exactly," his eyes snapped to her. "The most cunning of birds have overcome cages. Some overpower the door and break it loose." He jutted his chin in the direction of the bird, who pecked at the cage once again. "Some lull the enemy into a false appearance of submission, and then slip past when the door is left open by the lazy captor."

Helen scribbled in her notebook — *queen is in a cage* was scrawled, but *queen* was soon scratched out and replaced with the word *bird*. Imagery of kingdoms and queens began to melt away and transform into a cage with a lowly bird. She then paused. "Well, which is best?"

A moment or two passed as they both watched the caged bird eventually sit calmly perched on its stand, appearing to have given up on the cage door. Royce then answered, softly, "I've always been partial to feigned submission."

2

Don't Leave the Cage

"You must have more by now."

Penelope had made a daily habit of pestering Royce for any and all developments in his ever-building tale he was crafting for her. She bounced to his side after everyone convened in the parlor, following their evening meal. He had just sat himself in an armchair and poured some brandy when she tugged at his arm.

"Perhaps he needs a break," Elinor lazily suggested, allowing Royce to pour her a glass as well. "We don't want him getting burnt out, now do we?"

Penelope shot Elinor a nasty scowl, but was quickly and quietly rebuked by Selina in a single scolding glance.

Suppressing a chuckle, Royce cleared his throat and sat back in his armchair. "Why don't you pick a story already written for me to tell tonight?" he amiably suggested.

The compromise seemed to appease Penelope. With content resignation, she squared her shoulders and bounded for the library. Royce smiled at her tenacity and stood to follow, glancing first at the remainder of the party and gesturing for them to follow.

"What?" Elinor exhaled loudly in exasperation. "We have to move?"

"What better place to tell a story?" Royce waved his hand

theatrically, masking his irritation with a tight chuckle. Then, offering his arm to his wife, Royce turned on his heel and led the party to the next room.

Selina could feel Elinor's eyes on her, as well as Abram's, the moment she took Royce's arm. As soon as the decanter table was visible, she slipped her arm away from her husband's and poured herself a drink. Abram watched her, hovering just behind the assortment of chairs and sofas until the lady herself chose a seat.

Penelope was concentrating fully on the bookshelves before her, with Mr. Croft loyally at her side as she scrolled through the titles. "Tell me a story...now which story shall we choose?" she mumbled. "Mr. Croft, you're the keeper of stories. Which story should Royce tell?"

"Oh, Royce," Elinor pointed decidedly as she took her seat beside him. "Tell *The Lady of Shalott*."

Croft spoke softly to Penelope, not wanting to contradict Miss Abram too loudly. "I think you'd rather enjoy the *Goblin Market*."

"Which do you prefer, Selina?" Abram continued to hone his hawklike focus on the lady. He remained standing, but had his eye on a prospective seat, only waiting for Selina to make the first move.

Lindon had joined Selina at the decanter table and the two muttered in commiserating conversation, removed entirely from the story debate at hand. In fact, Selina had hardly noticed Abram's question until she caught sight of Royce's gaze from across the room. His expression urged her to play tiebreaker. Just as Selina parted her lips to respond, Elinor straightened her back and exclaimed,

"*The Lady of Shalott* has such a tragic elegance. That's Royce's forte."

"Yes it is, isn't it," Lindon muttered, discreetly lifting a brow as he sipped his drink.

"Just do *Shalott*, darling." Elinor waved her hand dismissively as if Selina's input was of little matter.

That wave of Miss Abram's hand brought a spiteful smile to Selina's mouth. With deliberate pace, Selina advanced to the empty sofa and finally took her seat, crossing one leg over the other, poised for battle. "I don't recall *Shalott* having quite the character dynamic that would capture Miss Ayres' interest, Miss Abram." She leaned forward slightly, gesturing to Penelope, who now sat in the armchair beside her. "The storytelling is at her request, after all."

Elinor and Selina stared intensely, waiting for the other to yield. While maintaining challenging eye contact, Selina casually sipped from her glass and leaned back into her chair, settling comfortably. She was not one to be rattled, and the battleground on which she stood was immovable; Penelope would not be a casualty.

Elinor cleared her throat in mild frustration, but sighed in feigned cooperation. "Perhaps both. Why don't you tell both stories?" She leaned toward Royce, placing an encouraging yet dominant hand on his knee. "That would be grand. And I'm sure we'd have no complaints from Miss Ayres, would we?"

Penelope shifted awkwardly in her seat, particularly upon seeing Royce's uncomfortable grimace. The pressure of choosing a story had quickly plunged from enticing to dreadful. For solidarity, Penelope turned her head toward Croft once again. "There's no harm in more stories, I'm sure."

"That seems the diplomatic solution, miss," Croft nodded approvingly.

"Very well then," she sighed. "Royce will tell both stories. I don't remember *The Lady of Shalott*. Selina, is that Tennyson?"

Selina nodded, holding her glare on Elinor, only breaking it when Abram slithered onto the empty seat beside her. "Yes, it's the one with Sir Lancelot."

"That seems appealing enough, I suppose. Knights and ladies are always interesting. What more is there, Royce?"

"Well," he exhaled dramatically. Everyone settled into their seats as Royce took center stage. He stood in front of the fireplace, capturing all attention. "The poor, beautiful lady was cursed."

Penelope shrugged. "Curses are good."

"She could never look out of the window in her tall tower and see the outside world below."

"What happens if she looks out of the window?"

"She hardly knew," he released an exaggerated sigh. "She only knew she wasn't permitted to do so. All she was left to do was weave a tapestry, all day long. Alone in her tower prison, only dreaming of the world beyond her walls."

"That's ridiculous," Penelope scoffed.

"That's how curses work." Quietly, Helen had slipped into the room, unnoticed, and stood behind the couch, eager for the story. Selina wasn't the least bit startled at the sudden sound of her voice, but both Elinor and Penelope flinched just a bit in surprise.

"Who cursed her?" Penelope asked. She was far from satisfied with the lack of explanation Royce had previously given.

Royce paused. He glanced at Croft for some assistance, but Croft simply shrugged while pouring himself a drink and taking a seat on the sofa, near the other side of Selina.

"That's not really as important, I think…." Royce brushed it off.

"A witch," Helen suggested. It was said with such a confidence that one would have assumed she actually knew the story.

Royce glanced at her with a lifted brow. "A witch," he accepted.

Helen anxiously intertwined her fingers, but cleared the nerves from her throat before confidently responding, "Well, surely there are witches in this world of knights and ladies. I mean, there were sorcerers, weren't there?"

"I suppose you're right."

"A witch it was, then." Selina settled it, lifting a decisive glass in the air.

Penelope wrinkled her brow. "Hang on, how did she keep herself from looking out the window."

Elinor groaned softly, sipping her drink in irritation of the constant interruptions. Royce, however, smiled amiably at Penelope with endless patience.

"Well, the lady's only view of the world was through its reflection in a very large mirror she placed across from the window."

"How backward." Selina mumbled into her drink, loud enough for only Croft to hear. The two of them chuckled quietly and clinked glasses, causing Lindon to stiffen.

"Oh, she cheated," Penelope nodded in understanding. "I see. That's clever."

"One day, she saw the reflection of a dashing knight traveling on the road down below."

Penelope and Helen sighed dreamily as Royce continued.

"His reflection was so beguiling, so magnetic that the Lady of Shalott decided—*hang the curse, he's just far too handsome, I simply must leave this tower.*" Royce's high-pitched impression of the Lady of Shalott elicits laughter throughout the room. Even Selina cracked a smile. "She boarded the small boat at the bottom of the tower and embarked across the lake to the handsome knight."

"And then he broke her curse and married her." Penelope rushed the ending decisively.

Helen watched Royce's expression change from dramatic to hesitant; who was he to correct her?

After taking a swig of her drink, a bluntness settled in Selina's throat. "She died before the boat even reached land."

Penelope looked at her, expecting her to be joking as she did. But Selina merely shrugged off each of the surprised glances. Helen and Nell looked to each other in devastation, but the Abrams both smirk in mild amusement.

"Sometimes the heroine loses, no matter how pretty she is, Nell."

Penelope shifted in her seat. Regret for allowing Elinor to choose the story washed over her and revealed itself in a nasty scowl across her face. "You said it was elegant."

"*Tragic elegance* is what I said, Miss Ayres," Elinor corrected. "When he recites the prose, it's an intoxicating tale."

"Not if she still dies in the end. What sort of story is that?"

"Well, perhaps she didn't truly die on the lake," Croft offered.

Selina realized her glass was empty, but intrigued by Croft's input, she turned her full attention to him.

"Go on, Croft." Penelope lifted her eyebrows and leaned forward as well.

"It's entirely possible that it was simply part of the curse she needed to overcome for herself. As Miss Thomas said, this is a land of magic, is it not? Who's to say there's no possibility of a rebirth of sorts?"

"A rebirth."

Lindon sipped his drink and subtly challenged Croft. "How can a woman come back from such a curse forced upon her?"

Croft looked to Lindon, acknowledging the challenge, a slight iciness between them.

"Redemption is possible in any curse. And often that redemption leaves the lady stronger and more resilient against any other curses that might come her way."

"I like that." Helen refilled Selina's glass as she smiled lightly at the idea of rebirth.

"Who's telling this story?" Elinor mumbled.

Selina grimaced at the rationalization of reality. "She died. There's no reversing it. It's a tragic tale of warning. Sometimes it's dangerous to leave the cage."

"Well…" Helen started, pausing only a moment when all eyes moved to her, "…a cage is merely an obstacle for a bird, not complete doom and defeat. There's always a way out of it." Her gaze flickered to Royce for confirmation, drawing Selina's attention to him as well.

Selina sipped from her new glass with an amused glint in her eye. "Someone has been listening to far too many of Royce's stories."

Munching on one of the tiny tea cakes on the plates beside the tea, Penelope waved dismissively. "Well, Selina, Royce is the storyteller, not you. So let's hear his ending. Did the lady die and then come back stronger?"

Royce looked Selina dead in the eye. "No one's fate is ever

final—especially in the legendary land of Camelot. King Arthur himself couldn't be kept dead, so certainly the Lady of Shalott stands a chance. Cages can be opened and curses can be broken."

Lindon noted Royce's maintained eye contact with his wife. She was not, however, convinced, despite his best efforts. Gradually, Royce's eye contact softened.

"With true love's kiss and all that. That's why Lancelot must break her curse." Penelope decidedly chose her favorite ending.

"He can't." Selina argued, shaking her head. "Her love was unrequited. He loved Guinevere."

"This isn't your story, Selina. Let Royce tell it his way. Maybe it was a different Lancelot."

Royce pointed at Penelope. "Precisely. Different Lancelot. Certainly it was a common name in Camelot. And so, the lady didn't truly die, she only thought she did. Deep, dormant, and seemingly defeated sleeps can often imitate death—ask any physician!"

Never had Penelope nodded more emphatically.

Royce continued, "The lady's boat washed up on shore, after she's believed to have died, and whose attention does she happen to capture—"

"Lancelot's."

Elinor grunted again, but before she could utter a complaint, Selina's glare seared into her.

"He finds her boat and realizes who the woman truly is. His true love. He hadn't noticed in times past—riding along the road and seeing her up in the tall window could only leave him assuming she was some mysterious, powerful sorceress far too above him to come down from her tower. But now, oh now, here she was. Helpless and broken."

"Just the way men like them best." Selina held her empty glass, prompting Helen to fetch another. Hesitating briefly, with memories of her previous, over-served employer, Helen conceded with a sigh.

"Ah, but some prefer the powerful sorceress high up in her

tower." Abram sat just a bit closer to Selina on the couch.

"You mean, while she was cursed with confinement."

Penelope waved her hand frantically for silence.

"And he kisses her."

"Yes. But it doesn't work." Royce slowed, producing the desired dramatic effect.

"What?"

Helen suddenly remembered their previous discussion. "That would be far too easy, and easy is boring—isn't that right, Mr. Royce?"

Royce glanced at Elinor. "That's right. We can't have it be easy to break a curse like that. As it happens, she was Lancelot's true love....but he was not hers."

"But you said she pined for him from her tower." Elinor pointed at him with a bitterness.

"Things look very different up close. Pretty, shiny things may be more of an acquired taste when they're close enough for their flaws to be so apparent."

"But Sir Lancelot is Prince Charming. Surely, she could grow to love him, even if he is irritating at first." Penelope frowned. Selina almost smiled at Penelope's naivete.

Royce chuckled. "In an ideal world, Lancelot would be just as charming up close as he is far away. But, of course, if that were the case, it would all be too easy. It's far more interesting if Lancelot and the Lady of Shalott were at odds. Miss Thomas was right: true love shouldn't be easy."

"What a deterring thought." Elinor's tone was snide and venomous.

Royce continued, "Why should Lancelot have such a smooth time of it, just because a beautiful woman is delivered to him so conveniently? He's not entitled to her."

Selina peered up at him from her glass.

"He kisses her, to be sure, but when it fails—when the curse remains and she continues to be helpless and broken, despite his best efforts—there isn't much left to be done."

Penelope's impatience escalated. "Well then, how does she break the curse?"

"It has yet to happen. Her fate is not final, but much like King Arthur himself, the great lady will one day return….overcoming her curse….her cage…with the power of her own strength."

"That's beautiful," Helen exhaled.

Abram scoffed. "That's sadistic. And ridiculous. He should've just taken the girl to his castle and paid another witch to wake her up."

Selina angled her legs farther away from him.

Lindon noted Selina's revulsion and lifted his glass to Royce's surprising chivalry. "I think Mr. Royce's ending was lovely."

"Better than Tennyson's," Helen nodded.

"I'd have to agree." Selina granted Abram a disgusted side glance before clearing her throat and shifting once again away from him.

Seeing the exchange of subtle smiles between Royce and his wife, Elinor wrinkled her nose and rose from her chair. "Well that was exhausting. I think I'll retire for the evening."

Abram gulped the rest of his drink. "I think I will as well. Perhaps read myself to sleep with a story that has a bit more resolution, eh?"

The well-mannered librarian stood as Elinor rose to leave, and quickly he reached for a book before intercepting Abram's path to the hallway. "Perhaps this one, if I might suggest, sir? I think it would be to your liking." Amiably, Croft handed him a well-read copy of *Pamela* by Samuel Richardson.

A skeptical brow lifted, Abram humored him and accepted the book. After a cursory glance at the cover, Abram sighed. "Couldn't be any worse, could it? Thank you, Croft."

"Of course, sir."

"I'd like to hear the goblin one now." Penelope wiggled deeper into her seat, making herself comfortable now that the company of the room quickly improved.

"It's getting late, Nell." Selina nudged her, as she herself stood to retire as well.

"But, I…"

Royce lowered his voice, directing it to Selina alone. "I can tell it. It's the one she preferred anyway."

"I liked the *Lady of Shalott*, Royce, but it didn't feel like it was quite ready to end…but this one has an ending, doesn't it?"

"Of course it does. And goblins always have the most diverting voices, don't they?" Royce slipped into a high-pitched, hoarse tone, making Penelope giggle.

"You can turn in, Selina. I want to hear his goblin story."

"Helen, prepare my room."

Obediently, Helen left to prepare Selina's bed and nightgown. Lindon aimed to follow her into the corridor, but paused as he caught sight of Selina's lingering eyes on Royce. She lightly smiled as he animatedly created mannerisms and voices for each goblin featured in the story. The smile was not forced; it came as easily as Penelope's giggles.

3
Fair Vanity

Helen woke up, prepared for the day, as she routinely did, and started for Selina's room to begin her duties. However, when she reached the lady's bedchamber, she was startled to find it quite empty. The bed was sloppily made, as if Selina had tossed her quilt over her mussed sheets, and her night clothes were strewn across the chair by the vanity.

Helen heard Price's familiar gait from down the hall and called out to him in confusion. "Um, Mr. Price—what time is it?"

"It's not half past seven."

Helen frowned. "I'm not late."

Price mimicked her puzzlement. "So what's the problem?"

"Lady Selina, she's gone up and left. And so early." Helen bounded downstairs to the library, to search Selina's usual hiding place, but only found Royce standing behind the desk and staring down at some open bookkeeping ledgers, nonplussed.

Helen hesitantly approached, not wanting to break any necessary concentration. "Mr. Royce?"

"Yes?" he acknowledged, but hardly granted her a glance. His tone was low, clearly deep in thought.

"Have you seen Lady Selina this morning? I can't seem to find her."

Royce continued to study the papers in front of him, occasionally flipping a page or tucking one aside. "Have you checked the garden?"

"Erm, not quite yet."

He crossed his arms in front of his chest and finally glanced up from the papers. "What do you know of a Mr. Cuddy?"

"Oh, Mr. George Cuddy? He's a lovely man." Helen advanced to the desk with a smile of acknowledgment, nearly forgetting her initial purpose. "He's one of Lady Selina's tenants. My first week at Everdon he brought the ladies flowers, and he even gave me one. He's very kind. Why? Is something wrong?"

Royce closed the ledger, stepping out from behind the desk. "No, of course not. Let's find Selina, shall we?"

The two headed toward the garden where Lindon and Elinor sat separately, ignoring one another as they sipped tea and idly turned pages of a book. When posed the concerned question of Lady Selina's whereabouts by Helen, Lindon calmly reported that he had seen Selina leave for a walk just as he was coming in for the day.

"You see?" Royce comfortingly patted her on the back. "She's only out walking. Lindon, I have a matter I need to discuss with you."

Lindon nodded dutifully and rose from his chair, but noticed Helen's face fall, like a lost puppy. "Why don't you serve Miss Abram some tea while you wait for Lady Selina to return? I do believe this pot has gone cold," he suggested, gesturing to the tea set on the table before them.

"Oh, yes, of course." Helen hurried to fetch more tea from the kitchen.

Upon her return, Royce and Lindon had finished their discussion of business and Lindon had moved on to carry out his duties for the day. Royce now sat across from Elinor, notebook out and pencil in hand. He scribbled wildly for a few moments as Helen poured the fresh tea. Suddenly, he sat back and stared at the page, biting the end of his pencil in frustration.

Elinor playfully nudged him from across the table. "You look so intense, darling."

"That's because I'm stuck."

"How so?"

He began bouncing the pencil against the knuckles on his non-dominant hand, shaking his head. "We know plenty about Penelope's princess. Confident, shrewd, elegant. But I know nothing of the highwayman. His....his motivations aren't as....I don't know, straightforward as I hoped they would be."

Elinor smirked a little. "Don't hurt yourself. There's no harm in leaving him two-dimensional, is there? Penelope would want a story that's as simple as she is."

Helen grimaced, and even cleared her throat, at the insult toward Penelope, but she continued serving them tea.

Royce shook his head. "Unacceptable. It doesn't matter how simple the patron is; the story needs depth or there's no point. He needs a motivation of some kind. Stealing would be standard—he's a highwayman for heaven's sake—but why on earth would he stay? To hold the princess for ransom?"

"Calm down," Elinor reached to calm his bouncing hand. "I've helped you before, and I'll help you again. Let your muse do her work."

Helen wrinkled her nose; the thought of such a disturbing muse for someone so brilliant rattled Helen's romantic sensibilities.

Elinor eyes narrowed and her head angled to one side—an expression so deeply pensive, it was as if her input would solve every plot hole. "Your standard archetypes would make for a simple solution. Is it so ridiculous to assume it was something like love at first sight?"

Helen made another face. Elinor noted this and smirked again.

"Your *accuser* seems to think so."

Nearly dropping the cold teapot she was removing from the table, Helen shifted uncomfortably, prompting a chuckle from Royce.

"Sit down, Miss Thomas," he gestured to the empty chair. "What would be a proper motivation for a highwayman to abandon the highway life?"

Helen eyed Elinor with bitter anxiety as she sat and responded. "Not love at first sight."

Royce shook his head in agreement. "No. That's far too fleeting to make a man abandon his way of life so easily. What then?"

"Perhaps there's something more valuable—another treasure in the castle more valuable than what he's already stolen."

Elinor narrowed her eyes, but maintained a tightly playful tone. "A man like that is only interested in two things: gold, because of his lifestyle, and women, because of primal instinct."

"Those aren't the reasons men go to war."

"War?" Elinor lifted a brow in surprise at the escalation in terms.

Royce leaned back in his chair and watched, waiting for Helen to explain.

"I mean," she slowed her speech, but gained more confident footing from Royce's encouraging expression, "sometimes they are, but they're surely not the only reasons. There could be a threat of some sort….greater than whatever evil is within the highwayman himself. Whether he loves the princess or not, the thrill of danger and the desire to protect what he's claimed….that could be enough motivation for him to linger. Love for the princess could always grow and encourage his need to face the bigger threat. I imagine."

Elinor lifted a lazy hand to challenge the notion. "What greater threat is there than a man with a knife forcing priceless jewels from a woman's neck?"

Helen almost started but paused in hesitation.

As if on cue, Croft entered the terrace to offer contribution. "Perhaps the highwayman brought more trouble with him than merely a desire for jewels. Like a plague. Or even a curse."

Helen's eyes widened at the suggestion. "Magic is always a nice touch, I think. Like your story last night—there could be a curse the highwayman brings and has to then break."

Croft shrugged. "A curse or an accomplice."

Royce finally glanced over at Croft, after studying Helen for a moment. "I think you're right, Miss Thomas. Magic does sound more appealing."

Elinor scoffed. "Certainly for a girl like Miss Ayres, it would prove more engaging. Fairies and witches and such seem to tickle her juvenile fancies." Royce chuckled in agreement; Elinor leaned over and placed a hand on his knee before making the quiet snide comment, "Be sure to keep it short, darling, lest she lose interest and feel a bit overwhelmed."

Helen shifted uncomfortably again, wrinkling her nose at the mockery Penelope's name endured in her absence. Before she could leave the terrace, Croft stopped her.

"Oh, Miss Thomas, I meant to come and ask you—do you know where your mistress is this morning? I just got a few new books from town I'd like to show her."

"She took an early walk, I'm not entirely sure where. And I'm afraid I don't know when she'll return. I'd assume before the assembly ball tonight. I have her dress set out and everything."

"It's no matter. Perhaps the lord of the house would like to take a look at them as well—I think you'll find them interesting."

Royce scribbled distractedly, but perked his ears at the mention of his own name. "Hm, what are the titles?"

"*The Woman in White, The Tenant of Wildfell Hall, Vanity Fair*—I do believe you'd like that one a great deal, Miss Abram…." Croft continued to chatter titles while Royce looked up at him with a raised eyebrow, smirking in knowing approval.

"Show me the new books, Croft." As soon as they were out of the ladies' earshot, Royce added, "I trust your judgment; you appear to notice far more than you reveal."

"It's one of my hidden strengths, sir," the librarian winked.

As they made their way indoors, starting for the library, they passed a corridor through which Selina had just entered. She walked briskly, her eyes darting nowhere in particular and her hem muddied.

"Oh, the Lady Selina has returned," Croft exclaimed at the sight of her. He smiled widely, paying little attention to the state of her dress and expression. "My lady, I have some new titles for you to enjoy."

Looking as though she had been fully startled at the sound of Croft's voice, Selina cleared her throat to regain composure. "Oh of course. Let me get cleaned up and I'll be right there." Without so much as glancing at her husband, Selina hurried past them for her chambers.

"Hm," Croft sighed. "She must have had quite the excursion."

Royce frowned, wrinkling his brows together as he turned to watch her walk away. "Yes, it appears so."

Later that afternoon, well approaching evening hours, Barratt returned from a walk and the constable greeted him at the station door. Marley stood anxiously, but Barratt expected nothing less from him as of late. After seeing very little crime in nearly thirty years, a community was bound to feel an ominous stress continue to hover over them when faced with not one, but two deaths among them.

"There's a message left for you," he told the inspector.

"Who delivered it?"

Marley shrugged. "I didn't see anyone."

The letter on Barratt's desk was of a familiar sort. It bore the number 6 and was folded as all the others had been. Before opening it, Barratt tightened his grip on the parchment and shot Marley a glance with a mixture of excitement and dread.

"Wonderful," Barratt exhaled.

He unfolded it to read the word *LECHERY*.

"What does that mean?"

Barratt sighed, slowly folding the letter once again, and casually responded with a question of his own. "Have we had any word of another murder in town?"

"Another murder? What is this? You think there will be more?"

Marley was horrified, which made Barratt correct his enthusiasm, becoming a bit more somber.

"I don't believe Miss Rodin and Sir Henry were the last. Has anyone else called for me today?"

"No, not outside that message, no. Did your walk help you figure out the murder weapon?"

Barratt thoughtfully shook his head. "The trauma to Sir Henry's skull was most likely done by a solid rock. Judging by the setting, there are one or two possible culprits....both half-buried in the ground. Although, that's not to say the killer couldn't have taken the weapon with him..." He examined the letter pensively.

"Could it have been an accident? A trip?" Marley offered.

"His body was found away from those rocks—too far away for him to have tripped and hit his head on one."

Marley slipped his hands in his pocket, his mouth shrugging. He never liked the idea of a killer wandering around his town. "An animal could have moved him?" he suggested. "Or he stumbled a bit before he fell?"

"I suppose that's a possibility...."

The constable then frowned with consideration; as promising as an accident might have been, there were variables favoring Barratt's theory of malicious intent. "It's a wonder you've had such a hard time getting honest testimonies if the answer could simply be a bad tumble on a rock."

Barratt glanced over at him, his lips curled ever so slightly into a smirk. "I suspect there's a good deal more to hide than a good friend tripping over his own feet."

The Everdon household bustled for the duration of the afternoon, in preparation for an assembly ball hosted by the Lennox's in town. At Penelope's request, and Selina's insistence, Helen assisted her in selecting the best gown and hairstyle for the evening. Royce paced the halls as he waited on the ladies, anxiously awaiting one in particular.

Royce stopped Elinor as she casually passed in the hallway. "Where's your brother?" he asked with mild curiosity.

She shrugged. "He's been scarce all day. I'd suggest you check on that pretty wife of yours." She tossed him a rather salacious wink.

Resolving to aim his pacing more deliberately, Royce continued toward Selina's bedroom. Just inside, Selina sat in front of her vanity, staring at an open drawer; distant was her expression, her eyes nearly vacant. As Royce slowly opened her door, she shut the drawer abruptly and her eyes snapped up at him in the mirror. Quickly, she fiddled with her necklace and stood as if she's done getting ready.

"You look beautiful."

She cleared her throat and moved to the jewelry box on the dresser to grab a different set of earrings.

Royce decided to press. "Where were you this morning?"

"I may not be running the estate, Royce, but I'm still a rather busy woman. Will you be requiring a detailed account of my daily schedule?"

He leaned against the doorframe, crossing his arms in front of his chest. "I'm beginning to see how rumors can be circulated, Selina"

Distractedly, Selina continued to rifle through her jewelry. "Rumors?" she parroted the only word she truly heard.

"About Henry…" he gently lifted himself away from the doorframe and stepped toward her. "You skirting off in secret. I'm sure there are other options for affairs if you're unhappy. Rafferty, Lennox —even Abram."

Selina suddenly stumbled over the chair beside her.

Royce reached for her arm to steady her. "Are you unwell, Selina?"

Her eyes suddenly pierced his as she straightened and collected herself. "Don't be ridiculous."

"Well, then. Are you ready?" He offered her his arm. She cleared her throat and accepted it, accompanying him down the staircase where Elinor, Penelope, and Lindon eagerly awaited.

Taking notice of Selina's bland expression, Lindon stressed a smile. "You look lovely, Selina," he said.

Penelope moved to link arms with Selina, simply gushing. "I told Helen to pick the green dress. It's Selina's best color, isn't it? What do you think of mine? I decided purple might be fun for the night."

"You look beautiful as well," Lindon assured the young lady.

"What do you think, Royce? Loads of eligible young men will be there tonight."

"Stunning, of course," Royce chuckled, gesturing for the door. "Shall we?"

Before the last of them could make their way through the door, Elinor stopped and held a demanding hand in the air. "Where's Abram? Did you find him upstairs?" She looked expectantly to Royce, who felt Selina's arm tense against his.

The corners of Royce's mouth shrugged. "No. But he didn't seem particularly enthused this morning at the idea of an assembly ball so I assume he's made his own plans."

Penelope sighed impatiently, urging the rest of the party to move along. "Let's leave, or we'll be late."

The carriage was filled with incessant chatter and humorous banter as the Everdon household and guests journeyed into town. Penelope hardly needed contribution to maintain a conversation, but Elinor was not the tolerable sort and was sure to force her own involvement. Lindon watched Penelope in amusement, occasionally chiming in as a buffer amid the tension. Elinor periodically glanced in Royce's direction, eager for him to participate. Royce, however, had no attention to spare. His concern was wholly turned to Selina. She stared out the carriage window for the duration of the journey, with a new depth in her expression that alarmed him.

When they arrived at the assembly building, Royce quietly touched his wife's hand, causing her to flinch. "We're here."

She recovered and straightened her shoulders. "Oh, yes, of

course."

Penelope darted out of the carriage and into the assembly hall, dragging Lindon behind her as her chaperone. Elinor dismounted, with the assistance of a footman, and waited just a moment for Royce. At the realization that his pace was entirely reliant on Selina's, Elinor huffed and moved ahead on her own.

Royce guided Selina gingerly out of the carriage. "You didn't have to come tonight, you know. We can send the carriage back."

"No, don't be ridiculous. I'm perfectly capable of...." Selina trailed off when she heard something popping in the distance.

"You don't seem well. How did you sleep last night?"

She grabbed his hand abruptly, silencing him. "Do you hear that?"

Royce paused and narrowed his eyes. Horses and carriages rode past, shop doors closed for the evening, and down toward the end of the street, Royce could see children playing in the yard of the orphanage, on the farthest end of town. Nothing seemed particularly out of the ordinary.

Before Royce could dismiss Selina's overactive imagination, attributing it perhaps to sleep deprivation, Litchfield's assistant, Bryant, ran out of the building and shouted for the children to follow him, just as the roof of the orphanage suddenly collapsed. In seconds, crackling flames became visible through the windows, consuming the building gradually, but with an alarming pace.

Mr. Bryant shouted at passersby to grab any children they could see and pull them to safety. With an overpowering instinct, Selina lunged toward the orphanage to help the children, but was stopped by Royce's quick grip. Men from the nearby shops and inns bolted from behind their doors and ran to Bryant's aid. Even Barratt emerged briskly from the police station to recover survivors from the crumbling wreckage.

Selina shouted at Royce in desperation, struggling to escape his grasp, but it was hardly effective. Just as he kept her from the danger, children screamed from behind the flames, unable to escape the second floor. Hearing the children and Selina cry out and without a single thought of safety, Bryant braved the flames and ran back inside the burning structure. An innkeeper and a farmer from the other side of town called for Bryant to return to safety, but to no avail.

Not two moments passed before the entire building collapsed, bringing Selina to her knees, collapsing in Royce's arms, defeated and sobbing.

September 1889

The world is full of obvious things which nobody by any chance ever observes
~Arthur Conan Doyle~

1

A Still Mourning

That night and following morning were hauntingly silent. Not a word was spoken, save by Elinor. She had been fretting over her brother's prolonged absence. Even if he had spent the evening in the local tavern, as she had speculated, he ought to have been home by now. She paced the house in concern, repeatedly inquiring to each passing soul if Abram had yet returned to Everdon.

During midmorning tea, Elinor continued her fretting aloud. "What if he became bored and just abandoned me here? Or, I suppose he would've been the sort to run into that building and save those poor orphans."

"Nonsense, he would've gotten his boots dirty," Selina mumbled while stirring her tea.

Elinor ignored her. "He's probably burnt to a crisp now." She sniffled, her eyes sure to well at the thought of it. "Why must he be a hero?"

"Cheer up, Miss Abram," Selina stated flatly. "He most likely abandoned you."

Elinor slammed her tea spoon on the saucer. "Control your wife, Royce. This is quite a serious matter."

Royce smirked a bit, as if he dared to interfere.

Reluctantly, however, Lindon had begun to agree with Elinor. "He has been missing for some time, Selina. Perhaps we do have reason for concern."

"Or rejoice," the lady suggested, shrugging her shoulders. "He could have likely moved on to bigger and better things than little old Everdon."

Elinor glared, but Royce only smiled at Selina. They were in agreement for probably the first time in their marriage.

Selina only responded with further spite. "Oh come now, Miss Abram, the tavern in town is quite nice. There are more interesting matters than your brother's likely bender."

"Yes, indeed, like those dead orphans of yours." Elinor's tone had equal venom.

Selina's mouth tightened and her eyes shot daggers. Elinor successfully silenced her.

"Elinor." Royce softly corrected, apprehensive to scold too harshly.

Helen approached Selina's table, bringing the lady's preferred cure for her routine headaches: a sparkling glass of sherry. "Lady Selina....have we heard if the children are all right?"

"We've not." Selina was suddenly reduced to a monotone, sipping her sherry. "We don't yet know who...who was still inside."

Lindon noticed Barratt arrive from around the corner of the house. "Selina, I do believe we might have news."

Barratt approached the group in the garden out back, and his expression was deeply pensive and troubled.

Helen burst, "How are the children, Inspector?"

Barratt hesitated to answer her, first sorting the sensitive explanations that have now arisen. "Well, Miss Thomas...I'm afraid I have rather unpleasant news." Selina gripped her glass tightly. "Among the expected casualties...five children, we believe, along with the maid and the cook...it seems we've also found the body of Mr. Bernard Abram."

Elinor gasped. Royce frowned. Selina swallowed hard. Lightly, she sat down her glass, avoiding the sudden glances being exchanged across the terrace.

"He's being examined by the coroner as we speak, but based on initial findings, I'm comfortable assuming he was in the building before it caught fire and collapsed. We were able to recover most of the children, along with Mr. Litchfield."

"And Mr. Bryant?" Selina croaked.

Royce looked to Selina questioningly, his eyes begging to know if he had been the reason for her frequent visits to the orphanage.

Barratt shrugged. "He survived as well, though I'm not entirely confident he'll recover—"

"How did this happen?" Elinor dramatically grabbed Royce's arm for consolation.

"I'm very sorry for your loss, Miss Abram," Barratt's voice is bland and obligatory, as if he wants to move on to the true purpose of his visit. "I assure you, when I have answers, you'll have answers."

"I was right." Elinor began sobbing. "He was saving those poor children."

Barratt looked doubtfully at Royce, who responded in kind. "As I said, it seems he was in the building before the fire started. But I suppose it's not entirely impossible to assume he tried to help children get out when it came down. I'm deeply sorry for your loss as well, Lady Selina."

Selina snapped out of her avoidance and looked up at him. "Thank you, Inspector." She rose to leave, face stoic and fists clenched. "If you'll excuse me."

As Selina slipped away from the mourning crowd and disappeared inside the house, Elinor wept on Royce's shoulder; Royce lightly patted her back in consolation, still in shock himself.

Lindon muttered to Barratt, "It seems every time you come to Everdon, Inspector, you have tragic news to share."

"It seems every time something tragic occurs, it somehow connects to Everdon, Mr. Lindon." Barratt glanced at Royce. "If you don't mind, once the ladies have recovered from the shock, I'd like to return later for interviews."

"What? No immediate suspects to arrest?"

"It's hardly worth the effort as of yet. Lady Selina would only pay off my jailor anyway. I might as well show restraint and patience this time around. Besides, accidents do happen every now and then. Though hardly, I think, at Everdon." Barratt bowed graciously and bid them all farewell.

Penelope, who'd been uncharacteristically quiet while eating a tea cake, finally shifted in her seat, visibly disturbed. "I don't want to be here anymore."

Lindon moved toward her with paternal concern. "Are you unwell, Penelope?"

"I can't...all of this is....I don't like it. Will you take me to town, Lindon? I'd like to get something to calm my nerves."

"Of course. Perhaps a walk would do you well."

Helen liked the idea of an escape of any kind. "I can take her, sir."

"No, I think you should stay in case Lady Selina needs you."

"I'll walk with her." Royce moved toward Penelope as well. Lindon looked at him in surprise.

Elinor quickly stood, realizing the attention was now flickering away from her inflated grief. "I'll go along—I need to get away from this cursed house."

Royce wasn't the only one slightly irritated by Elinor's presence. Penelope watched the way Elinor kept clinging to Royce's arm for sympathy, and it made her uncomfortable for the same reason Barratt's visit did. It brought on confusing and upsetting ideas and feelings. The moment Royce paused and turned away, casually slipping away from Elinor before continuing, Penelope seized her chance and took Royce's arm instead.

"Don't forget: we're not to tell Selina. She's already upset enough as it is—she wouldn't want to hear how many sweets I've gotten. She thinks I eat far too many, but I don't see how she expects me to limit myself to just one."

Royce chuckled. "Well, she won't hear it from me."

They entered the shop and Penelope immediately grabbed her favorite sweets. The shop owner encouraged her to get more. She was his best customer.

"I just know she'll ask what I've spent my pocket money on. I should come up with a clever answer. She only gives me so much at a time, you know. I think it's her way of controlling me."

Elinor clicked her tongue in disapproval. "That's despicable. A woman should do what she wishes with her own money."

"I think it shows good sense. No need to gorge yourself right away. There's something to be said for savoring sweets at a reasonable pace, so they're not all gone too quickly. Eat one or two, but save your sweets and your money, should you need them later."

Elinor glanced at him in surprise. "Funny coming from you, Royce. Suddenly so keen on saving money?"

As they approached the counter to pay, Royce stepped ahead of Penelope, handing the shopkeeper coins from his own pocket.

Penelope's eyes widened in surprise. "Well, thank you."

"We can't have you lying to Selina," he winked in reply.

Penelope grinned because he bought her a few more than she had initially chosen. On their way out of the shop, she ate one or two, but tucked the rest in her little bag, which Royce took to hold so she could control herself. They could see the burned down orphanage from the shop. While they waited for Elinor to finish purchasing her own sweets, Royce and Penelope studied the wreckage with morbid curiosity and surprising sobriety.

"How long did Selina put money into that orphanage?"

Penelope considered for a moment and cocked her head to one side. "I don't remember a time she didn't. I played with those orphans since I was a child—she's always done business there."

"I wonder how that Bryant fellow is doing."

"Oh, I liked him."

"He's not dead, Nell."

She ignored his correction. "He was such fun—could I have another from the bag? I promise I'll save the rest for later."

Royce looked doubtful but handed her one anyway.

"What happened to the children who escaped?" Penelope shoved some candy in her mouth.

"I don't know."

Cuddy passed them by and stopped. "The children have been housed in the hospital for the moment."

Penelope smiled with a mouthful. "Mr. Cuddy. Royce, this is Mr. Cuddy."

"Ah, Cuddy."

"He gives me flowers every time he visits with Selina, you know." She snuck another piece of candy from the bag, taking advantage of Royce's wandering focus.

"It's a pleasure to finally meet you, sir." Cuddy cordially shook Royce's hand. "Excellent choice in candy, Penelope."

"It's nice to meet the face behind the name I've seen so many times in my ledger. We've apparently sent you so many checks, it's as if I know you already."

Cuddy grew visibly anxious, shifting back a little and placing his hands in his pockets. "I've, uh, I've had a rough go, since my daughter passed, sir. And age has not treated me well. But the Lady Selina never faulted me for that. She knew I was lonely and struggling —I'll admit, her checks have bordered on the obscene, but I'm forever grateful."

Royce chuckled. He was beginning to understand Selina's cleverness. As Elinor finally rejoined them with her own comfort food, he settled into a grin. "How old was your daughter? Miss Ayres' age, I assume?"

"Just about, yes."

"Of course."

"Lady Selina and Miss Ayres have always visited regularly when she got sick, and even more after she passed."

Penelope's sugary and satisfied expression downturned into a reminiscent frown. "I don't know how often it will be now, without the orphanage. Walking there was Selina's motivation for visiting people along the way. I don't know how much she'll like us walking now."

"She'll come to it again. Lady Selina has a big heart. And she knows I enjoy seeing you."

Royce actually smiled in agreement. "I imagine so. You're quite likable, Penelope. She can hardly keep you locked up at Everdon."

"Although, she did dearly love those children. When it was properly used and not squandered by Litchfield, her funding did wonderful things for that place." Cuddy glanced back at the ash of the orphanage. "Do give her my deepest sympathies."

Penelope nodded the promise as he wobbled away to finish his errands. Royce slowly started in the direction of the orphanage wreckage and Elinor took his arm while Penelope munched quietly behind them — she succeeded in taking the whole bag from Royce.

Elinor muttered. "A few orphans die and suddenly Selina is the most pitied woman in town. My brother was demolished by the tragedy and not a word of sympathy for his surviving kin. It's disgusting. After all he did for those children…"

Penelope's sweets occupied her attention far more effectively than Elinor's dramatics. Knowing this, Royce glanced around wearing a mocking frown.

"What are you doing?" Elinor wrinkled her nose in confusion.

"Trying to find the most likely audience for this performance of yours. Have you shed a single genuine tear for the man?"

"Have you? He was your agent for heaven's sake. And your friend, as a matter of fact."

"But he was no hero. You know that. Whatever he was doing in there before he died, it wasn't to save any children," Royce seethed, quietly enough to avoid eavesdroppers.

"Then what was he doing there?"

"I don't—"

Mrs. Sweeting saw them and crossed the street, calling out,

"Mr. Royce! Oh, Mr. Royce, I was just going to call on Lady Selina, but I thought it best to give her some time. Would you deliver this message to her?" She handed him a letter. "We were planning a fundraiser for the children before....all this." She then turned to Elinor. "My greatest sympathies, Miss Abram."

Elinor tried not to smile too much at the attention, prompting a deep eye roll from Royce. "I thank you. Truly, thank you."

"We've decided to raise funds for the hospital instead, as they've been housing the orphans for now. We'll be throwing a festival in town for the children. We're hoping the funds will be enough to rebuild."

Elinor frowned doubtfully. "Couldn't Lady Selina fund the reconstruction herself?"

Mrs. Sweeting, slightly put off at Elinor's response, forced a smile and maintained the upbeat nature of the conversation. "Well... yes, I suppose she could. But the festival will be good for the children too. Carnival games and such. Monetary funds are essential, Miss Abram, but so is morale."

Elinor placed a falsely humble hand on her chest. "Of course it is. Forgive me. I've not been myself since my brother..."

"No need to apologize at all."

Royce rolled his eyes again, as Elinor continued to elicit sympathies from the amiable Mrs. Sweeting.

Selina hadn't let Helen into her room for most of the day. Finally, later that evening, she called for her to draw her a bath. Helen obeyed and filled the tub with hot water. While Selina bathed, Helen decided to get her a good book to fall asleep with, once she'd finished soaking away her nerves. And so she found herself browsing endless titles in the library, until she was rescued from the depths of options by the eager Mr. Croft.

"Can I help you, Miss Thomas?"

"I'm looking for something.... something.... good?"

"That opens a very wide variety, Miss Thomas," he smiled sweetly. "Might I suggest narrowing your search?"

"Lady Selina....she's not been well," she softened her voice as she explained. "All these terrible things happening and all. That fire at the orphanage really affected her, I think. She's not been the same....disturbed rather than her usual shrewdly aloof self."

Croft chuckled sadly. "Yes, she was quite attached to that project. Lucky for you, I know all of her favorite stories. Come, come." He beckoned her to follow him to the first shelf he had in mind. "When she was a child, the only book that could cheer her was *Gulliver's Travels*. But then she found herself drawn to stories like *The Adventures of Arabella, the Female Quixote*."

"She was quite the adventurer, wasn't she? Did Lady Selina ever travel much?"

"Not nearly as much as she wished."

"What stopped her?"

Croft shrugged. "Who's to say for certain? I only occupy myself by properly stocking her shelves with as many worlds as she wishes."

"I admire your devotion. You seem to greatly enjoy working for Lady Selina."

Croft smiled widely. "Of course I do. As do you."

"What girl wouldn't? Working so closely with aristocracy, her gowns, her parties, her charm, her fascinating husband..." She caught herself. "Not that I'm in love with Mr. Royce."

"I would never accuse you of such a thing," he winked at her.

"I only meant their marriage—such a roguish mind falling in love with such an elegant heiress. Could you ask for anything more romantic? I confess sometimes I wear her jewelry while she's out and imagine for a moment that I'm part of her story instead of my own."

Croft chuckled, searching for Selina's recent literary obsession. "I have noticed she's been considerably more distressed as of late. Her night walks have become more frequent."

"Her night walks?"

"Your Lady Selina is an insomniac, my dear. Been like that since childhood, I'm afraid—particularly when she's overwhelmed." Helen suddenly understood the cause of the footsteps at night. It wasn't Moll's ghost who haunted Everdon after all. "A good Dickens novel has always soothed her—though, lately she's taken more to Tennyson."

"Oh Tennyson is good. He wrote *The Lady of Shalott*."

"Well-remembered."

Helen carefully studied another shelf. "She does seem to own a good amount of volumes written by women, doesn't she?"

Croft's face lit up. "She most certainly does. I understand you're quite the wordsmith yourself, Miss Thomas."

"I try to be, at least," she shifted her weight self-consciously. "I hope one day to be a writer. It would be the next-best thing, I suppose."

"Next-best to what?"

She then sighed dreamily. "Well, I've always dreamed of being told I was secretly the daughter of a baron or something. I'd inherit loads of money, move to a castle with closets filled with gowns, throw lavish parties, and marry myself a charming rogue."

Croft chuckled again. "I see why you find Lady Selina so appealing. Though, it's not all lovely to live like she does," he gestured to the shelf with Royce's books on it. "It seems his pages have started to spill like tar...all over our lady's pure white feathers."

Helen sighed again, this time at the daunting titles and remembers reading some of Royce's darkly written yet intriguing plots. They all seemed too interesting to be real, but it seemed he'd brought some of that dark plot with him.

"Well....I've always liked the stories where the pure female lead is bathed in tar, as it were....and is then seen still standing in the end. Her wings are just that much stronger; she'll fly out of the tar, molt her damage away, and leave it all behind."

Croft smiled. "With a little help, she might just be strong enough. It's in her blood after all, is it not?"

September 1889

2

A Drunken Confession

Motivation to solve the mysterious passing of a man like Bernard Abram was fleeting. The fire could have easily been ruled accidental—fires happened every day. However, the letter which sat on Barratt's desk, bearing the word *LECHERY*, was far too enticing for him to ignore. Abram's body had been discovered among the wreckage with a bullet wound in his chest. Even the simplest constable could see that it had been murder. As soon as the coroner's report found itself on Barratt's desk, the inspector learned Abram had likely been dead long before the fire finished him.

All surviving witnesses were being held in the town's hospital. Children occupied the majority of the beds, with the exception of Mr. Bryant and Mr. Litchfield, both of whom were the last to be recovered. Bryant had been barely breathing when Barratt and Sweeting pulled him from the debris, and Litchfield hadn't stopped hacking since he stumbled into the street with an understandable head injury.

Critical wounds never impeded a Barratt investigation before, and he was hardly going to allow it this time. And so he began his interviews, with Constable Marley at his side, starting with the shriveled and singed caretaker of the orphanage himself. "Mr. Litchfield," the inspector began.

Litchfield grunted.

"How are you feeling?"

Litchfield grunted again.

"Do you remember what could've started the fire?"

Litchfield mumbled something incoherent.

"What was that?" Barratt leaned forward.

Litchfield cleared his throat and croaked. "I did."

"Why would you do something like that to your own orphanage?"

Litchfield shifted in discomfort and tried to clear his throat again. "Am I dying?"

"Most likely," the inspector replied frankly.

Litchfield sighed deeply. "Did you find the gun?"

"What gun?"

"I had to hide him. I had to..."

Marley stepped a little closer. "Did you see who shot Mr. Abram?"

"I did."

Barratt frowned doubtfully. "Why would you shoot Abram?"

Litchfield's mouth turned downward, as if he was ready to weep. "I'd been drinking. I went down to see if Bryant had gotten rid of my good scotch, and there he was."

"You found him that way. So why do you believe you killed him?"

"I just did it. I just...I just must've shot 'em and left him and forgot and then after the tavern...he was just there and I—what was I supposed to do? I had to hide him, so I-I burned the place down."

"Logically."

Marley shrugged. "Makes sense to me."

Barratt looked up at Marley incredulously; he had confirmed the inspector's working theory of the intelligence of Everdon's working class. "I'd like to know where the gun is now, Mr. Litchfield. We didn't find it in the wreckage."

"I don't remember."

"Where did you get the gun?"

"I...I don't remember."

"He was drunk, Inspector," Marley reminded him.

"Yes, drunk," Barratt slapped his knee. "So drunk that he believed, with no perceivable motive, that he shot a man with an invisible gun and then burned the place down while still inside himself. Was there anyone else visiting the orphanage at the time?"

Litchfield painfully shrugged and coughed some soot out of his lungs. He had no genuine memory of the night's events, and Barratt saw no further need to press. Glancing away from the fool, the inspector noted one of the older boys from the orphanage, sitting a few beds away and watching the interview with keen interest.

Barratt stood and curiously approached the boy. "Do you remember who was visiting the day of the fire?"

The boy tightened his mouth, but nodded. "Mr. Abram, sir."

"Anyone else? Anyone with him?"

Looking the inspector boldly in the eye, the boy replied, "No, sir."

"Do you know who shot Abram?"

"Mr. Litchfield, sir," he answered simply.

Barratt was impressed by his tenacity; they stared at one another for a long moment and the boy's eyes were unyielding. There was an air of protection in his answers—curt, decisive, and firm. Barratt slowly smiled. Whoever the child protected was clearly in good hands, for this boy was far from confessing his secrets.

"Thank you for your cooperation, son," the inspector nodded politely to him before turning back to Marley. "Get his statement in writing as well. I'll meet you back at the station."

"Yes, sir," Marley nodded and handed the boy a pad of paper, only to be received with confusion and recoil to record the account himself.

Barratt left the hospital with new theories ruminating in his mind. As he started for the crime scene to once again examine the remnants, he noticed Royce doing the same, with a cheque book tucked under his arm. "Royce." He nodded in acknowledgement.

"How's the Lady Selina holding up?"

Royce shrugged. "As well as she can be, I suppose."

"Must be traumatizing, seeing her pet project go up in flames." Barratt's tone struck Royce as suspicious, so he held back his response and instead nodded slowly. "I would've expected you to be home tending to your mourning wife's every need. What is it you're doing in town?"

"Visiting tenants."

"And spending more of your wife's money." Barratt pointed to the chequebook.

Royce ignored this, gesturing instead to the foundation of the orphanage. "Do you know how it started?"

Barratt turned to face the ruins as well. "Litchfield confessed. Says he killed Abram and set the fire to cover it up."

"Hm."

"I'm not entirely convinced. He doesn't seem nearly intelligent enough..." Barratt stopped the sentence.

"It doesn't take intelligence to shoot a man," Royce pointed out.

"How did you know he was shot?"

Once again, Royce shrugged. "People talk. I assumed."

"Interesting. This is the second tragic occurrence that's been brought on since your arrival at Everdon."

Royce considered for a moment, his jaw tightening just a bit before relaxing again. "Coincidence."

"Hardly. First your rival, then your agent."

"Oh please," Royce slipped his hand in his trouser pocket. "That's too easy, blaming me. And derivative at this point, don't you think? I don't even have a gun—you're welcome to check."

"Oh no, you didn't kill Abram," Barratt shook his head resolutely.

"Thank you."

"You'd have shot him in the head." Royce glanced at him in surprise, but let Barratt finish, "This kill was hasty, inexperienced, panicked. You're too steady."

His jaw clenching again, Royce chose his words carefully. "Yes, you're describing Litchfield perfectly."

"But he had nothing to do with Kincaid."

Royce frowned. "What does Kincaid have to do with this?" Gathering his own assumptions, he squared his shoulders to Barratt, looking to his face and not his words for the answer. "You think it's the same killer?"

"I didn't say that," Barratt shook his head again. "But there is undoubtedly a connection. And I'm determined to find it. The fire was the drunk fool, but the murder….I think it's something entirely different. Not that your wife's loyal orphans will be of much help. So I'm left to my own devices, investigating this curse of Everdon."

3

To Snare a Fox

To offer a distraction from the recent tragedies, Rafferty and Lennox thought it best to orchestrate a pleasant outing for their circle of county society. Naturally, being the sporting sort, the two gentlemen decided on a fox hunt. Though Everdon was the more ideal venue, Royce adamantly refused to host such a gathering. Good-natured Rafferty instead offered his own estate for the hunt. His tenants set up obstacles throughout the property and his servants prepared a well-crafted luncheon.

When faced with an invitation, Royce didn't show particular interest, but was keenly more receptive than Lady Selina. Her hesitation and failure to accept social invitations were becoming more common as of late.

"Some fresh air would do you good, Selina," Lindon gently suggested.

Royce watched her pour a small flask of alcohol into her tea, when she thought attention had turned elsewhere. "He's right. Fresh air and sunlight would do us all some good. Let's all go."

Selina did not look happy at the suggestion. "You should take our guest, Miss Abram, along with you. She should certainly be enough to keep you happy on your hunt."

Royce didn't grant Elinor a glance, and instead shook his head emphatically. "No, I'll be accompanying my wife on the hunt."

Elinor clenched her jaw, but forced a smile. "Yes, do come, dear. It wouldn't be much fun without you."

Selina was no less thrilled. On the day of the hunt, the coercion of Selina's social involvement was underway. All guests were gathered, dressed and properly armed. Then men, along with Elinor, were mounted on their steeds with rifles in hand. With her natural assortment of nerves, Sophie Campbell gravitated toward Selina and joined her in declining the offer of direct participation. They both claimed just as much enjoyment from watching.

Just as all of the participants were mounted and ready for the hunt, the usual intruder was announced as having just arrived. Inspector Barratt was walked to the party by the butler, who informed the good-natured host.

"Inspector!" Rafferty gave a warm smile. "What can I do for you?"

Barratt waved congenially, ignoring Royce's annoyed and mocking reaction to his arrival. "If I could just have a moment of your time, Lord Rafferty."

Lennox, who rode beside Rafferty, frowned. "Should we cancel the hunt?" he suggested.

Rafferty shook his head in unison with his hand. "No, no, nonsense. Go on without me. I'll catch up shortly. It shouldn't take long."

Rafferty dismounted and waved the rest on. And so the party complied and rode down the hill to prepare for the start of the hunt. They took their time trotting down to the starting point, attempting to bide Rafferty a little time to join them. But the fox and the dogs grew antsy, and the men grew eager.

Before Lennox decided to signal the release of the fox, Sophie leaned over to speak to Selina, her voice nearly a whisper. "Selina."

Selina mimicked her leaning whisper and replied, "Sophie."

"I've missed you," Sophie laughed. "We haven't been out like this since….well…"

Selina stopped chuckling. "I'm so sorry about Henry," she added with gentle sincerity.

"I'm sorry," Sophie shook her head quickly. "That's what I'd like to tell you…"

Selina frowned. "What?"

Sophie shifted in her saddle, fidgeting with the reins in her hands. Lennox signaled for the release of the fox, Selina flinched at the sound of the starting gun, the dogs howled and the hunters rode. Sophie and Selina lagged behind as Sophie attempted to gather her words.

"I've, um," she started, and then stopped. After taking a deep breath, she then went on, "I seem to have healed quicker than I thought I could. Um….Colin actually has, um, asked for my hand. And I've accepted him." Selina slowed her horse, causing Sophie to hesitate once more. "Is-is that all right?"

Recovering from the sound of the gunshot, Selina forced a chuckle. "You hardly need my permission to marry Rafferty, Sophie."

"I meant….so soon after…I mean I was only just engaged to Henry and—"

"Engaged?" Selina repeated in disbelief.

Sophie looked at her hands on the saddle, instead of at Selina. "He was afraid to tell you. And so was I. He asked me shortly after your wedding. I don't want to disrespect his memory….but I do care deeply for Colin and his children."

"As well you should," Selina began to smile. "Rafferty is a very good man."

"I could not live with myself if I couldn't have your blessing, Selina." There was a desperation in her voice that saddened Selina. To have one's happiness depend so wholly on the opinion of another was something Sophie and Henry always had in common.

"I don't understand," Selina said slowly as their horses broke into a light trot. "You didn't seek my blessing to marry Henry. Why now?"

"I don't….Henry's gone. You've been dearer to both him and

Colin for years. I just thought — "

"Marry him, Sophie," Selina slowed her horse's gait. Her tone was decisive and calmed Sophie's nerves. "Marry that man before he changes his mind." Thankfully for Selina's own growing nerves, the dogs bolted past the pair's idle stroll, pulling Sophie's attention from the conversation.

Lennox shouted at them through the trees. "It's coming your way, ladies!"

"Oh how exciting!" Sophie smiled widely, with excitement and relief.

The fox was spotted and two shots were fired. The first shot brought the light-footed fox to his knees. The second knocked Sophie from the top of her horse. Selina and Sophie had stopped a short distance from the fox's path, to avoid interference. And yet, a bullet found its way directly between the two ladies. Though her neck was only grazed, the moment Sophie fell from her horse, her head struck a thick log which lay partially concealed on the ground. Royce and Selina lunged toward her in perfect and frantic unison.

"Sophie!" Selina jumped off her horse and ran to Sophie's side.

Lennox shouted. "Who fired?"

Royce was suddenly right beside Selina, peering over Sophie. "Don't be ridiculous, we all fired." While his hands applied pressure to Sophie's wound, his eyes were more concerned with Selina's visible horror.

"Are you all right?" Royce asked her quietly.

Selina, incredibly shaken, swallowed hard, but nodded.

"You were standing next to her?"

Selina nodded again. Royce's accusatory glare shot toward Elinor whose hawklike stare was directed at Lady Selina.

"Someone's a horrible shot. But it looks like one of us hit the little bugger." Lennox paused as Selina looked at him incredulously, then he quickly corrected, "I meant the fox! Of the three guns, one of us hit the fox, one hit a tree, and the other..." he gestured helplessly to

Sophie.

Royce held pressure on the wound and wrapped her neck gently but firmly with the torn sleeve of his jacket."Keep her awake." He looked to Selina, but seeing her shock he quickly changed his tone. "Selina, darling." He lightly touched her arm to get her attention. "Keep her awake."

Selina's voice was small. "Yes."

"Nice work, Royce." Lennox applauded.

Royce directed his orders, pointing authoritatively at Lennox. "Get your horse. Take her back to Rafferty."

"Of course."

When Lennox obediently brought his horse, and mounted it, he held his arms to accept Sophie as Royce lifted her into the saddle. Following further orders, Lennox rode the horse safely back to the house.

"Selina." Royce tried to lightly touch her arm again, but this time she flinched as if startled.

"I'm fine. Is she....is she going to be all right?"

Royce waved for the servants to come to them. "One of you take the fox to the house. And you, fetch a doctor." He then turned to Selina. "She will be, if we can stop the bleeding."

Invasively, Elinor appeared at his side with an insistent hand on her hip. "Is a doctor entirely necessary, Royce? You could patch her up in no time."

Royce snapped. "She needs a doctor, Elinor." One of the servants called back for further instructions from Royce. Before responding, Royce peered over at Selina, whose focus faded in and out with her visible shock. "Selina, come with me."

"No," she suddenly gained the lucidity to protest. "Don't be silly. I can take my horse."

Royce took one of her hands, better capturing her attention. "I'll walk ahead to give them instructions and then I'll escort you back to the house, all right?"

Her distracted gaze settled on him and she finally nodded,

walking away from him to fetch her horse. Royce glared at Elinor and snatched the rifle from her hand before walking ahead.

When Royce was out of earshot, Elinor decided to disguise her malice with flimsy concern. "That bullet was awfully close, dear. Are you quite all right?"

"Fine." Selina brushed her off, focusing straight ahead.

"I'm so relieved Royce was there," she went on. "He's a bit of a veteran with battle wounds. He always has been, for as long as I've known him. In all our years together, I've never seen him squeamish from blood. Comes in handy, to be sure. I'd trust the man with my life, you know." As she failed to evoke the desired response from the lady, Elinor smirked and chose a more transparent approach. "We're terribly dear friends. I don't know if I've made our history quite clear to you, Selina—"

Selina was not sniffling and sulking. There was no apprehension, nor a shred of intimidation in her eyes. With a sudden fierce aggression, she turned on her heel to face Elinor. "I am fully aware of my husband's feelings, Miss Abram," she seethed with well-harnessed fury, "as I am fully aware of your history. But before you crow too loudly, do consider the possibility that you remain unmarried because he loved my money more than he loved you."

The state of Rafferty was unlike anything Selina had seen in him since the passing of his dear wife. Riddled with concern, he paced near the couch where an exhausted and drained Sophie lay awaiting the local physician.

"We should have canceled the hunt," he muttered, his throat thick with regret. "You were right." He looked over to Lennox. "She wouldn't have been harmed…"

Selina touched his shoulder comfortingly. "This is not your fault."

Sophie was barely conscious. "It's not…Royce was there," she managed to wheeze.

Rafferty immediately shot a glare at Royce.

Selina, seeing Rafferty's expression harden, stepped in front of Royce. "He helped her, Colin. He stopped the bleeding. She's alive because he was there."

Rafferty stepped back and digested that bit of news, and then suddenly shook his head. "Thank you, Royce. I am eternally grateful. I've thought such terrible things…"

"Stop," Royce insisted, seeing Barratt approaching. "It's fine. Consider our slate clean."

"You didn't kill Henry. You didn't. He must've tripped."

Royce glanced at Barratt again.

"It would seem so," the inspector shrugged.

Royce's eyes narrowed; his innocence was hardly confirmed. Barratt merely stated the theory. He didn't trust the suspicion that remained in Barratt's tone.

"It's why I interrupted your outing for the day, as a matter of fact." The inspector straightened his suit coat. "The Honorable George Kincaid has insisted on Sir Henry being embalmed for immediate burial and funeral proceedings. Our investigation has been forced to reach a tentative end."

Selina lifted a brow. "Tentative?"

"Circumstances dictate that an accidental death is entirely possible. And now that I've also ruled out Lord Rafferty's suspicions, the investigation rests."

When Doctor Davies arrived, he was immediately escorted to Sophie's side. Barratt took his leave, as the physician did his work, and started for the front door. As the attention shifted to the good doctor, Selina took Royce aside quietly.

Selina almost whispered. "Thank you, for tending to her."

He smiled, without another word passing between them, and kissed her forehead before seeing to the doctor's full report.

Elinor stopped Barratt, grabbing him by the arm. "When will my brother be released for burial?"

Barratt kindly placed a hand on hers. "You have my word,

Miss Abram. As soon as my investigation is over, he is all yours to pay necessary respects."

"How interesting it is that so many horrible things are happening around the Lady Selina."

Barratt chuckled. "You form your theories, Elinor. Just don't neglect to account for the involvement of your lovely Bernard while you theorize."

September 1889

4
The Depth of Grief

All the traditional family funeral proceedings took place at Millhampton as soon as Henry's body was released for burial. The Honorable George Kincaid summoned his adult children for the process. The state of poor Henry's body by the time the investigation had ended, prevented the usual turn of events. No family photos could be taken, and Kincaid even requested cremation of his nephew's remains. The wake at Millhampton lasted four days—none of which Selina attended. Her absence was hardly questioned, and Kincaid didn't allow speculation.

The day of the funeral a grand procession was arranged to journey through the town, ending back at Millhampton for the burial. With the exception of Sir Henry himself, the Kincaid clan had hardly been in the county over the last several years. Since Sir Henry had been so beloved, Kincaid took the opportunity to ingratiate himself back into the county society by making the arrangements as extravagant as possible. Nearly everyone in the county had been invited, and those who weren't were sure to watch the procession go by.

The first carriage hosted the clergy and pallbearers—which included Rafferty, Lennox, Henry's cousin, and three other friends from London. The hearse followed directly behind them, succeeded by Kincaid and his two children in the third carriage.

The Royces rode directly after the family carriages, fourth in the procession line, at Kincaid's insistence and despite Selina's protests. Selina and Royce sat on one side, Lindon and Penelope sat opposite them. Once they had arrived at the Kincaid family cemetery, Lindon and Penelope exited the carriage, but Royce stopped at the notice of Selina's hesitation.

"Selina." Royce took her hand.

She almost flinched when he reached for her hand, but then relaxed and allowed him to take it. "I don't know if I can," she murmured, unable to look at him.

"Sure you can. Just put your hand on my arm," Royce wrapped her hand through his arm, resting it on top so as to continue holding it, "and it will be over soon."

She finally brought her eyes to his, pained but forcing a smile. She let him help her down from the carriage and even leaned into him as they walked to the graveside service.

The weather was beautiful so the service was held outside as well. The only true tears shed were those of Sophie, Penelope, and a few of the older women. All other guests bore matching solemn expressions, bowing their heads with respect and maintaining their stoic decorum.

While the vicar spoke, though, several times Selina tensed, Royce gently rubbed her hand. What seemed for an ordinary onlooker to be a casual act of comfort between husband and wife came as long-needed affection to the quietly surprised Lady Selina. The more he rubbed her hand, the harder it was for her to hold back her tears, but she managed. Her lips tightened and her eyes closed every now and then, suppressing guilt as it built.

When the service ended and everyone began to mingle and share condolences, Selina pulled away from Royce and strolled in the opposite direction to be alone with her thoughts. From a short distance, Lindon immediately took notice and stopped Royce from following.

"No, no, sir," he warned, reaching for Royce's arm. "The best part of her childhood was just put to rest. Let her be."

George Kincaid approached, unaware of his interruption. "Royce, so good of you to come." He offered a hand for Royce to shake.

Royce nodded politely. "Of course."

"I know it would mean the world to Henry."

Royce smirked; Kincaid wasn't nearly as aware of his nephew's dealings as he believed himself to be. Royce glanced at Lindon to share in the amusement, but Lindon continued to watch Selina slowly disappear into the distance.

Kincaid glanced around. "Where is Selina? I thought I saw her as well."

"She's grieving privately at the moment, sir," Lindon answered for Royce.

"Ah, yes I can understand that," Kincaid nodded agreeably. "The two of them were inseparable for years. Despite, I understand, growing apart these last months. Can't imagine what could have caused such a friendship to decay. Excuse me." Kincaid then moved to the next grieving guest.

After a silent moment of standing alone, Lindon's voice hummed, lower than before. "I should hate you for what you've done to her."

Royce didn't look at him. He didn't need to; he could feel the disdain. "I would."

"Then why do it?

"I'm an opportunist, Mr. Lindon," he tucked his hands in his pockets. "We're not all selfless saints, like the company you seem to keep. What's done has been done."

Lindon exhaled anger, but did not reply.

"Lindon."

Lindon gritted his teeth. "Yes, sir." From the corner of his eye he could see Royce swallow hard before continuing.

"Could you..." he worked through a catch in his throat, "could you tell Selina that I can either summon the carriage to take us back to

Everdon, or meet her down by the road to avoid being seen in her current state?"

Lindon glanced more fully at him, and then back at Selina's path. "That's very considerate of you. I'll see that she knows."

Obediently, and with a heavy dose of paternal concern, Lindon started for Selina, walking the path further down the property. When he found her chosen hiding place, she'd settled on a rock in a small nook by a creek, hugging her knees. She didn't bother looking up when she heard him approach; his finding her was inevitable and expected.

"We played here," she stated faintly.

Lindon nodded. "I remember."

Selina stared at the water, her cheeks dry, but her mouth twisting with anguish.

"They say that weeping lessens the depth of grief," he gingerly told her.

"It hasn't so far."

"One day, it won't hurt quite so much," he promised.

"You can't fool me," she muttered. "You're still miserable."

Lindon smiled sadly. "I'm a cautionary tale, Selina. When you lose what you could never have, you must be strong enough to accept and move on to greater things...well greater for you. Fate decided Henry wasn't meant to be the lord of Everdon. Whatever the reason for his death, we must believe it's all for the better."

She glanced up in his general direction, almost smirking in spite of herself. "Is this your idea of comfort?"

"No, but I know how you dearly hate being coddled. Your husband, however, seems to be far more sympathetic. He'd like to know if you're ready for the carriage or if you'd like him to meet you by the road to avoid prying eyes."

"Leave me; I'll walk."

"It's quite a walk to Everdon."

Selina looked directly at him as she stood upright. "I'll walk."

She received no argument from Lindon; he knew better than

to question Selina's method of grieving. Instead, he delivered the message to Royce and saw to it that Penelope returned home safely.

An hour or two passed and Selina started to finally walk back to Everdon alone. As she neared the road, much to her chagrin, she saw a parked carriage with her husband disobediently leaning up against it.

"Was I not clear?" Selina lightly lifted her arms in disbelief.

Royce casually glanced at her. "It's a long walk."

"That was the intention, yes.

"I sent the others ahead in one of Kincaid's carriages."

"I can see that," she grumbled as she approached.

"Come," he beckoned her. "Ride the rest of the way."

Selina glared, walking past him dismissively. Royce signaled for the driver to follow them as he walked after her.

"Selina, you're in no state to walk that distance."

"You have no idea what state I'm in. And I wanted to be alone." Just as she thought she had gained distance, she slightly stumbled. Though she caught herself, her ankle twisted and instantly throbbed with pain. When she glanced back at Royce, he raised his eyebrows.

"Uh huh."

Spitefully, she pushed on and continued walking until finally she stopped and turned around, still glaring at him. He offered his arm to help her in the carriage, but she pushed it away and climbed in herself.

"Selina...what you're feeling is to be expected."

"No, it isn't," she stifled a sob.

"Yes, grief is entirely expected."

Selina choked, smoothing her dress to provide herself a distraction."But relief isn't." He felt his curious but sympathetic gaze as her eyes welled. "He was my dearest friend. Yet here I am...relieved. I had as much to lose with him learning the truth as you did. This is what you've done to me. And for that I can never forgive either of us."

"Don't be relieved. If he'd known, Selina...you weren't the

one he wanted to hurt. He would have protected you...he would have saved you."

"No one could have saved me," her eyes fell to her hands, laying helplessly in her lap.

Royce took one of her helpless hands, stroking his thumb lightly across the top of her hand. "You don't believe that," he said softly.

"I do," she nodded, her tone matching his softness.

"No villain is unbeatable, just as no heroine is untouchable."

"Even you?"

His eyes widened slightly as he watched her defeated expression deepen. "There are villains out there," he said, "just begging to be beaten."

"Why?" her voice became barely audible.

"Some victories are more satisfying than others. I never wanted this — I never wanted Kincaid dead. I never wanted you — "

"No, not me," she exhaled gradually in an attempt to steady herself, "just my money. Henry was merely collateral. Accidental collateral."

Royce paused, not initially certain how to respond. "I only wish he had been....I wish, now, that he had won."

"And taken your precious treasure." She gestured vaguely in the direction of Everdon.

His eyes did not follow hers to Everdon; they remained steadfastly on her. "He was certainly more deserving."

5
Bare-Knuckle Bluff

About a week after the funeral, the festival fundraiser was in full swing. The Sweetings orchestrated the majority of the labor, avoiding troubling the still-grieving Lady Selina. But, despite their efforts to spare her the burden, Selina soon saw the festival as a welcomed distraction, throwing herself into the planning and preparations. She spared no expense, and Royce didn't dare lift a finger to stop her. Working with Lady Selina's budget enabled Mrs. Sweeting's extravagant ideas to come to fruition, and the town was better for it.

Carnival games lined the streets, with a small petting zoo and food vendors dispersed throughout as well. The orphans who were well enough roamed freely and the ones too injured to play were carefully seated on benches along the road, so as to still feel they could participate and partake in the sweet treats.

Toward the end of the main street running through town, there were activities and games better suited for the adults in town — particularly the pig races and a boxing ring. Royce himself lingered near the boxing ring with keen interest. One of the more notorious street boxers in his part of London, Royce had relied on boxing a release only rivaled by his writing..

Also lingering and observing the match at hand was Rafferty, with Miss Sophie Campbell on his arm.

"Miss Campbell," Royce turned to notice Sophie's surprising presence, "it's good to see you out and about."

Sophie smiled at him, leaning a bit more into Rafferty. "Thank you, Mr. Royce. I just had to—they put so much work into this, I had to come and see."

Rafferty chuckled, placing an affectionate hand over hers, resting both on his arm. "And she hates feeling caged."

"Most women do." Royce agreed, his eyes flickering across the festival at Selina.

Seeing a friend of hers, Sophie politely excused herself. As she strolled away from them, Rafferty cleared his throat, rather loudly, and bowed his head shamefully.

"Something wrong?" Royce squinted.

Catching his expression, Rafferty shook his head and cleared his throat again, his eyelids fluttering. "I don't…I wept like a child when she was shot."

Royce bit his lip to prevent himself from smiling before he nodded a reassuring, "It was perfectly understandable."

"Yes, but now I feel….less….less of a man…."

"Because you wept?" Royce frowned.

"I should have been strong for her," his volume rose slightly, "but it was her comforting me in her time of need. It wasn't…it wasn't right."

"There's no shame in tears, Rafferty. I'm sure you're mistaken. She doesn't seem to view you any differently."

Rafferty wrinkled his forehead, doubtful.

Royce's smirking eyes glided from Rafferty to the boxing ring. "Although if you wish to regain some masculinity, you appear to be presented with an enticing solution."

"Hm, and what's that?"

"An expression of physical dominance and bravado, my friend." Royce lifted his arm to dramatically present the boxing ring before them.

As was expected at events like these, young Penelope ran wild. She played with the children, played mother and scolded them when she deemed necessary, took more than her share of sweets and pastries, as well as paid little mind to the state of her dress by the end of the night. Selina made little effort to correct her. The children adored her—her juvenile nature made her quite relatable, while her occasional flashes of maturity caused them to hold her with a certain level of respect common from young admiring children.

One of these admiring children scurried frantically past Selina and Lindon as they strolled, before quickly turning on his heel to hand the lady a sample of his meal.

"Lady Selina, here!" he shouted, too loudly. Within the brown paper in his hand was what seemed like a doughy, ball-shaped pastry with raisins.

"What is this?" she politely accepted.

"Plum duff!" the child exclaimed before running off without accepting thanks.

"Oh, well thank you," Selina muttered, examining the common street food.

Lindon laughed, squinting at the pastry with faint familiarity. "I don't need to point out to you, Selina," he then said, "that Penelope's hem is now torn as well as muddied."

"Oh let her be." Selina began picking at the plum duff in her hands and deciding the best way to partake.

"Where's your husband?"

She shrugged. "Somewhere admiring young flesh, I'm sure." She then attempted a bite of the plum duff.

"Hm," Lindon narrowed his eyes on the boxing ring and almost chuckled. "I believe he may be the young flesh being admired."

"Hm." She hummed, commenting more on the food than her husband's whereabouts.

Toward the end of the street, a crowd had gathered around

Mr. Royce and Lord Rafferty. Men shouted suggests and women giggled and exclaimed the name of their preferred winner. Expectedly, Elinor was the loudest spectator.

When her attention finally peeled away from the pastry in her hand, Selina cocked her head to one side in light surprise. Sparking Lindon's interest, however, was the faint smile that formed on her face at seeing Royce in the ring. Suddenly, however, Selina's eyes quickly found Sophie in the crowd.

"Sophie, you came!" Selina exclaimed as she quickly approached her friend.

Sophie grinned and embraced her. "Yes, I did. Being cooped up for over a week takes its toll. I feel fine, just a small bandage left." She gingerly turned down her collar to reveal the remaining cotton dressing on her neck.

Lindon smiled warmly at her. "It's good to see you, Miss Campbell."

"Thank you, Mr. Lindon. I missed everyone." She brought a tender hand to her chest. "Especially the children. Colin didn't want me to be overwhelmed, so I haven't seen them since the accident. He's been ever so sweet, tending to me in my recovery. He even shed a few tears, he was so worried."

"Yes, he seems to be trying to recover himself as well," Selina light-heartedly gestured to the spectacle behind them.

Sophie spun her head back to watch the men continue to spar. "Isn't it exciting? He told me Mr. Royce is quite experienced, but he seems to be pretty evenly matched—I didn't know Colin could box."

Selina considered the claims as she watched for a moment. Despite Elinor's shouts of encouragement, Selina noted Royce's muscles tense when struck, but become almost limp when his own punches were thrown. He was a skilled boxer, to be sure, but Selina was no fool. He was also a bit of an actor. Smoothly, she went to the mediator and placed a bet. "Three guineas on Rafferty."

Royce's ears pricked as he heard Selina's voice come closer. Noting her bet, he then smirked at her disregard for his experience.

Even the mediator himself released a short laugh, knowing well the sort of odds to be expected from a boxer like Rafferty.

Elinor circled the lady and clicked her tongue. "You're making a mistake, Selina. I've seen what Royce can do."

"Yes, so you've said," Selina replied dismissively.

"He's an exemplary boxer."

Selina cocked her head to one side. "Perhaps. But Lord Rafferty has a particular investment. One always goes farther when one's heart is in it."

Elinor looked at her strangely. "His defensive maneuvers are adequate, but his throws have no power or aim."

The corners of Selina's mouth shrugged, but she didn't respond.

A few more punches were thrown until Rafferty threw the final blow. He would have missed Royce's head entirely, had Royce not bobbed himself directly in his path, allowing himself to fall to the ground. The mediator counted, and in a few short moments, Rafferty was declared the winner.

"Hm, imagine that," Selina muttered, so softly it was nearly a whisper.

Elinor frowned deeply, determined to harass the mediator until she received her money in full. Selina, however, collected her winnings with a grin and leaned against the railing to playfully taunt her defeated husband, who sat rather contently on the ground of the ring.

Royce suppressed a smile. "You bet against your own husband."

"Shame you didn't prove me wrong," Selina revealed a hint of a smirk, paired with a lifted brow.

"The great Lady Selina must always come out on top."

Her smirk softened into an amused smile, until she noticed Elinor approach with a vengeance. "It seems you have some explaining to be done." And she winked playfully before leaving him to be scolded.

As only ladies were granted private changing tents, Elinor found it quite accessible to intrude as Royce cleaned himself up and changed into a fresh shirt. Meanwhile, Rafferty was still being congratulated by dear Sophie, and therefore in no particular hurry to clean or change. So, with limited privacy, Elinor leaned against a nearby post and studied Royce with suspicion.

"I had money on this, and you threw the match. Why? To impress her?" Elinor jerked her head in Selina's direction.

"How would losing impress my wife?"

"She's an observant woman," she practically snarled. "You hoped she'd notice how generous you are and suddenly melt with affection. Despicable. You have her money, Royce. You don't need to continue wooing the woman."

Royce rolled his eyes and glanced over at Selina as he changed into a fresh shirt.

Elinor murmured, nose wrinkling in spite. "There were plenty of rich women in London. And you wouldn't have had to marry them."

"Seems my taste has become a little more refined."

"How did Bernard choose her?"

"He didn't."

Elinor frowned, taken aback. "What?"

"He didn't choose her." He finished buttoning and began to walk away. "I did."

Walking away was hardly effective; she only followed and continued her chattering. "And when am I to expect my cut of the winnings?"

"If you remember correctly, I lost."

"Not from where I'm standing." Elinor glanced over at Selina, who was approached by Helen.

In Helen's precious attempt to mind Penelope during the evenings events, she had found herself unable to control Penelope's impulses, causing the girl to act out when refused additional servings of pastries from one of the street vendors. Helen was at a loss. She clearly wished to help protect Penelope, but was uncertain how to protect her from herself. Cool and calm, Selina assured Helen and recruited a nearby Lennox to help assist the wrangling of Penelope.

"No," Royce replied to Elinor firmly.

Elinor grabbed his arm to make a point. "We made you what you are—you don't think Bernard was around for the same thing? We're entitled to our share, just like every other win."

Royce brought his face inches from hers. "You're brother's dead, Elinor. He may have earned a cut of his own, but you're not entitled to a single cent."

"Well, my, my," she was shocked by the venom in his gumption. "It's not like she doesn't have wealth to spare."

"It's not about the—"

"The money," she finished sharply. "Yes, I'm beginning to understand that now."

From the opposing end of the street, Royce suddenly heard Penelope raising her hysterical voice to Selina, who had dragged her to a more private place to argue. "Excuse me."

Elinor muttered, her glare shooting daggers toward Selina. "Yes, dear, off to her rescue you go."

Penelope's volume escalated well beyond Selina's liking. Her guardian's scolding glare became intimidating enough for her to gradually correct herself, but the obstinance in her tone was no less menacing.

"He can't tell me what I can and can't do, Selina."

Selina's jaw was clenched as she struggled to maintain composure. "He can, because I told him he can."

"I'm sorry." Lennox's palms rose in defeat. His best efforts were proving to be in vain.

"Don't be," Selina touched his arm reassuringly. "Nell, apologize to Mr. Lennox and go to the carriage."

"No, I won't. I'm a grown woman, Selina—"

Selina scoffed with elevated pitch.

"—and I can do what I wish. We paid for this festival, so I can have as much as I please."

Lennox slightly lowered his hands, the hero in him desperate to still be of assistance. "It's all right, Miss Ayres."

"No, it isn't," Selina snapped, just as Mr. Cuddy approached to lend assistance as well. It was not the first time he had seen Selina struggle to control her ward; Penelope was quite like his late daughter, wild and obstinate. "You've had enough. Mr. Cuddy, would you fetch us a carriage and escort Miss Ayres?"

"Of course. Come now, dear Penelope, I might have some of my share of sweets left. You're welcome to have some of mine."

Penelope was almost tempted by that, but shook her head. "You can't treat me like a child."

Selina lowered her voice and grabbed Penelope's arm. "I can when you're acting like a child," she seethed. "Mr. Cuddy has fetched us a carriage." Selina then muttered, "I should tell Royce we're leaving."

Penelope dug in her heels. "I'm not leaving, Selina. I've told you. I'm a woman and you can't control me, so I'm staying as long as I want."

Royce came up behind them, grabbing Penelope's other arm with a firm grip. "No, you're not." Penelope looked up at him, starkly alarmed at his assertion. "Come, Penelope. We're leaving. Thank you for your concern, Barratt. If you could see to it that Miss Abrams gets back to Everdon, it would be greatly appreciated."

Mouth slightly ajar in pleasant surprise, Lady Selina followed as her husband escorted the two ladies to the carriage, abandoning Miss Abram to find her own way back to Everdon.

October 1889

No one is useless in this world who lightens the burden of it to anyone else
~Charles Dickens~

1

Curious Clockwork

Like clockwork, the moment Barratt received news of Litchfield's succumbing to his wounds, he was delivered yet another letter, this time bearing a large number 5. Scrawled on the inside was the word *SLOTH*.

"Curious," the inspector mumbled to himself.

"What's curious? He was in a nasty state. I'm not at all surprised." Marley hadn't yet noticed the letter in Barratt's hand.

"Marley, how familiar are you with the seven deadly sins?"

The constable thought for a moment, then shrugged his shoulders. "Only what I've heard in church. Why? What's that?" Marley finally pointed to the letter.

Barratt held up the receipt of the recent death.

Marley frowned. "My, that is curious. What does that mean? Sloth?"

"I've received two letters exactly like this one. Wrath and lechery..."

"Oh, I see. Wrath, lechery, sloth...all recent dead are sinful. What's that mean for the rest of us, I wonder?" Marley chuckled, but stopped at seeing Barratt's contemplative stare.

"Someone is counting their sins."

"Well, that's the Good Lord's job, I believe," Marley shook his head resolutely. "No one has any business —"

Barratt silenced him by raising a hand. "Someone is counting the dead and tracking their sins. We may not be dealing with a killer…"

"What does that mean?"

"It means," Barratt clicked his tongue, "the sender of these letters is not necessarily killing, but merely arranging, watching, and evaluating. We don't have a murderer, my good man, we have a master manipulator."

Marley's face wrinkled, struggling to grasp Barratt's theory. "How could he arrange accidents? Sir Henry tripped, Mr. Litchfield inhaled too much smoke—I don't see the foul play."

Barratt shrugged. "Can't forget Mr. Abram."

"Ah, he got a letter as well."

Barratt put up a finger. "Before he was found. Before the orphanage was even burned to the ground. Someone knew he was dead, long before anyone else…"

"Perhaps the culprit killed one and simply watched the others."

"I don't think so." Barratt crossed his arms in front of his chest and lifted his nose in the air. "But I think whoever sent these letters is someone very close to the person around which they seem to center."

"And who's that?"

Marley's clueless, vacant eyes gave Barratt the amused arrogance he had hoped to gain before posing the most enticing portion of his theory.

"Sir Henry being found in a ditch on Everdon property," he began, slowly pacing the floor of the station. "The orphanage funded by the Delamere estate being set ablaze, slowly killing the wretched caretaker. And the body of a guest of Everdon being found shot inside. I've said it before, but it seems far more concrete now—every crime thus far has revolved around the Lady Selina Royce."

Marley's eyes widened. "Do you suppose she's next?"

Barratt looked carefully at the letter in his hand, briefly uncertain.

The inspector's silence made Marley anxious. With shaken confidence, he sought confirmation, "Surely she's not the one sending the letters…"

"Oh no, I'm sure she's not. But it is curious. It's a wonder what other crimes have been committed against her." Marley frowned at him in confusion. "I'm going to call on Everdon today. Hold any of my messages—unless they look like this one." Barratt waved the letter in front of him.

When Barratt arrived at Everdon, he was welcomed by the butler, routinely so. Mrs. Melrose hardly blinked an eye at seeing him arrive yet again. Politely, she escorted him to the drawing room, once again routinely, and offered him tea.

"You can wait here, Inspector, while I fetch Lady Selina," she told him. "Mr. Royce appears to be out at the moment."

"Of course. I don't want to be a bother," he lied, "but could you fetch Miss Abram as well? I have something I would like to discuss regarding her brother's passing."

Beyond questioning, Melrose nodded congenially. "If you wish it, of course."

Within minutes, Lady Selina and Elinor entered the drawing room. Barratt stood when the ladies entered, making a particular effort to kiss Selina's hand, merely bowing to Elinor.

"Lady Selina, Miss Abram. I hope you are both well."

Before Selina could answer, Elinor held her hands in front of her and demanded an explanation. "I hope you've come with answers about Bernard. It's taken much too long, Barratt. Disgraceful."

Selina accepted the lack of attention and comfortably chose a quiet seat to observe the interview with detachment. However, Barratt would not allow her to go so unnoticed.

"Have you been well, Lady Selina?" he asked, ignoring Elinor's demand.

Selina granted him a smile. "I am well, thank you."

"Quite interesting, considering…"

"What?" she prompted. "Considering handfuls of my own money have just gone up in flames? It's become a trend from the moment I wed. It hardly troubles me any more."

Barratt chuckled as Elinor tapped her foot ferociously.

"Why are you here, Barratt?" she pressed. "Do you have news, finally?"

"No need for false outrage, Miss Abram," he mockingly frowned. "You're in knowing company."

Selina wrinkled her eyebrows at his insinuation, which also caused Elinor's head to snap in Selina's direction before focusing once again on the inspector.

"What on earth do you mean?"

"You've been at Everdon for months, and Lady Selina is no fool. Polite as she is, she's no doubt as familiar with yours and Abram's facade as I am."

"You're impossible," Elinor huffed, sitting back in her chair with exaggerated exasperation.

"Be that as it may," Barratt compromised, "I have some rather difficult questions for you. Did Abram have any notable debts?"

"Of course not," she clipped.

"Who were his most recent marks?"

Elinor's eyes tightened on him; Selina's back stiffened. "I don't know what you mean."

Barratt looked to Lady Selina for a more finite response. "Have there been any other guests here at Everdon since you've arrived?"

Elinor answered for her. "No."

"Did he and Royce have any disagreements of any kind before his death?"

"Royce didn't—" Selina quickly interceded, bringing Barratt's curious attention back to her. Self-consciously, she cleared her throat. "I'm sorry. I hadn't noticed any disagreements between them. I beg your pardon, Inspector—am I truly needed for this interview?" she attempted to rise from her chair to dismiss herself.

"Oh yes, I'll get to your questions in a moment, my lady," he gestured for her to once again take her seat before pointing back to Elinor. "Miss Abram, when was the last time you saw your brother?"

Seeing his insistence, Elinor became just as tireless as her tone. "The morning of the assembly ball," she finally responded. "He left to take a walk on the grounds."

"Did you know he meant to travel as far as town?"

"No," Elinor frowned. "He didn't say so, at least. He didn't even take a horse."

"Why's that?"

She sighed. "It's as I said, he meant to only walk the grounds."

"What do you think would have taken him to town?" Barratt jotted a few notes in his notepad before hearing her answer.

"How am I to know?"

"Was there anyone in town who had recently caught his eye?" he continued to jot.

Elinor glanced at Selina from the corner of her eye. "How do you mean?"

Selina shifted in her seat, but Barratt ignored this and kept his attention on Elinor. He smirked a little with derision. "We both know Abram was a bit of a rake. Perhaps there was a…jealous husband or something this time around?"

"Well if there was, he didn't say a word of it to me," Elinor crossed one leg over the other, shifting haughtily in her seat.

"Was there anyone Royce introduced him to that he seemed to speak to more than others?"

"No one worth mentioning."

"It's usually the other way round, is it not?" Barratt peered at her from the top of the notepad. "Was there anyone he introduced Royce to in London that could've developed, I don't know, a conflict between the two of them?"

Elinor leaned forward intensely. "Why don't you ask me what you mean to ask me?"

In opposition, Barratt leaned back with arrogance. "I know

the sort of people the three of you surrounded yourselves with in London; unsavory people have a way of showing up when they're least wanted."

"You believe a mark did this?" Elinor scoffed; never had she doubted Barratt's investigative abilities more."You think a woman is capable of shooting my brother in the chest? There can't be proof of this."

Barratt shrugged, considering the possibilities. "Abram had a knack of picking the most interesting ladies London had to offer, but he was transparent. It seems likely that if Royce's charm wore off when he turned his attention to the lovely Lady Selina here, Abram's clumsy affection would lead the spurned lady to assume she'd been used. A woman is capable of a great deal when provoked. Hell hath no fury, as they say..." he waved his pencil artfully.

Elinor avoided Selina's glare, straightening her back. "Abram had no one that I knew of."

"How did Abram find you, Lady Selina?" Barratt angled his head slightly in Selina's direction.

Before Selina could answer, Elinor spat with distaste: "He didn't, apparently."

Barratt looked to the true lady of the house for confirmation. Selina, however, posed no argument, merely a shrug as she rose from her own chair. "I'll walk you out, Inspector."

The inspector graciously bowed and thanked Elinor for her time, despite her deepening grimace, which only elicited a smirk on his part.

"I hope you've learned what you've needed, Inspector," Selina said quietly, with a hint of amusement.

"Thank you, my lady. I can assure you, the misfortune that seems to drown you will soon be gone. Or I shall die trying." Barratt placed his hat on his head and politely tipped it. "And if you should ever need me, please, don't hesitate to call on the station."

His sincerity surprised her, bringing a warm smile to her face. Outside, by his carriage, two unfamiliar carriages making their way up the drive, carrying small mounds of what appeared to be furniture.

"Have you ordered new furniture?" Barratt peered curiously.

Selina sighed. "Not to my knowledge, but that's hardly my decision."

Barratt touched her arm, with sympathy. "As I said, Lady Selina, if you should ever need me."

"Thank you, Inspector."

He boarded his carriage and was set on his way. In the distance, Royce ran out to meet the carriages, stopping both to better direct their paths. One he sent to the top of the hill toward the manor, while the other seemed to be directed back down the path and onto an entirely different part of the estate property. Selina watched him in confusion as Royce jumped in the back of the one bounding for the house.

Elinor suddenly appeared beside her, making her flinch. "What in heaven's name is he doing?"

Selina muttered, after recovering from the startle. "I don't know."

The carriage stopped and Royce hopped off to help and direct the furniture being unloaded.

"What have you been doing?" she asked him.

"For the drawing room." Royce gestured to the furniture.

"I wasn't aware the drawing room needed new furniture," she faintly argued.

"And the bedrooms." He then pointed to the bed frames being moved, as well as a new mattress for Selina's room.

"Why do we…" she caught sight of the new sofa, "Oh that's….that's actually lovely."

Royce followed the furniture movers in and Elinor, exasperated, followed him just as Lindon made his way outside to see what the fuss was about.

"What is this?"

Selina crossed her arms in front of her chest, guarded and confused. "Another arrogant power move, I'm sure."

Lindon watched the bed frames as they were unloaded from the carriage. Frowning thoughtfully, he cleared his throat to correct her. "They're to your taste, Selina, not his."

He peered through the open doors and down the hall to see Royce dictating where it all was to be placed.

Selina placed an admonitory hand on her hip. "Isn't it you who argued his propensity for mind games?"

"Initially, perhaps. But what I see now is something entirely different. I see a man confused by his own motivation. I don't think he knows his own game anymore. It's almost poetic."

"Poetic?"

"What do dreamers do, Selina?"

"Reach for the unattainable," she skeptically mused.

"Until they attain it."

"Then what do they become?"

"Realists. Even so, the romantic in them never dies."

Royce retreated to his room to wipe the dirt and sweat from his face as Elinor advanced past the border of his open door.

"Barratt is telling her far too much," she hissed, sitting herself on the end of his bed.

"What?"

"That Barratt," she pointed out the window, "is giving your little wife enough information to ruin us."

Royce smirked. "No, he isn't."

"He suspects one of the two of us killed Abram."

"Come now, Elinor. Being a murder suspect isn't all bad." Royce wiped his face, chuckling as he tossed the used towel into a small hamper.

Unbeknownst to Elinor and Royce, Helen passed by after putting Selina's laundry away and upon hearing the words *murder suspect* she stopped and started listening.

Elinor hissed again. "How can you be so calm?"

"Because I didn't kill him. Why? Did you?" He looked at her

with a lifted brow.

"How dare you. My own brother." She grabbed his arm, her nails digging. "Barratt thinks one of us killed him for a bigger cut of the profit."

He shook his arm out of her grip. "Well, you aren't getting a cut, so killing Abram would have been a waste of time, wouldn't it?"

"You're so confident that none of this can be lost to you."

"You mean, my estate? My fortune? My wife?"

"She could divorce you," she pointed fiercely at him, determined to strike fear. "Grueling process, but not unheard of these days—and certainly nothing too grueling for a woman like her. What would you do then, if the great Lady Selina got wise to your scheme and left you?"

"She's not nearly as oblivious as you assume," he exhaled, "and she wouldn't leave me."

"You're certain of that?" she challenged.

Royce turned to face her with ferocity. "Yes, I am."

2

The Lady & Her Demons

After a night of scribbling by candlelight, Helen awoke with hardly a wink of sleep. In her exhaustion, she had neglected to properly stash her manuscript safely in the hope chest at the end of her bed. When she returned from preparing Lady Selina for the day, Moll had found the wrinkled papers strewn across the bedsheet.

Helen's eyes grew wider than the moon when she saw Moll's hands all over her story. "What are you doing?"

Moll slyly peered up at her. "I think someone's in love with Mr. Royce."

"What? Give it back!" Helen lunged to take it from her.

Moll smoothly moved out of her reach and waved the manuscript mockingly in the air. "Maybe if you spent less time daydreamin' about being the Lady Selina and more time doin' yer job, he might notice you."

"Stop it. I'm not in love with Mr. Royce."

"Oh yeah?"Moll bolted out of the room, manuscript in hand, as Helen chased after her down the hall. They ran into the main part of the house, Moll taunting all the way, but Helen was faster and gained on her quickly, snatching the manuscript out of the thief's hands. "Oi! Give it!"

In the midst of the scuffle, the two were so distracted that they hardly noticed Lady Selina curiously approach them. "Give what?" she asked.

Moll froze, her eyes widening. "I'm so sorry, Lady Selina," she stammered. "We were only jokin'."

Angrily, Helen panted and forcefully straightened the pages of the manuscript against her dress.

"Miss Thomas doesn't seem to understand the joke." Selina gestured to Helen's fury.

Moll made a face at her colleague, scolding her for not immediately supporting her claims.

Selina took a step closer to Moll. "I think you should get back to work before Mrs. Melrose sees you running through the halls....joking."

"Yes, my lady. Of course." Moll scurried away.

Helen tried not to let her eyes mist in embarrassment and rage, but she was unsuccessful. "I'm sorry, my lady. It won't happen again."

"You must learn to hide your manuscript better," Selina told her, leaning forward with sincerity. "Why was she so determined?"

"She wanted gossip....about you. I'm so sorry it caused so much trouble."

Selina straightened her back, smiling just a bit. "I'm in your manuscript?"

"Well, notes....yes." Helen's cheeks suddenly burned.

"You chose to base your story on Mr. Royce and myself," Selina's hands came together and rested in front of her—a gesture which only added to the intimidation overwhelming Helen's already humiliated sensibilities.

Helen looked to the ground, confirming the lady's assumption. "The story keeps changing. I hardly know anymore."

"How so?"

Helen sighed in frustration. "It started with an elegant lady and a charming rogue, but then it turned into something about a bird in a cage, and then somehow there was a gun involved, and then a ghost story, and now I can't seem to—"

"A gun?" Selina attempted to control the alarm in her tone, but Helen paid no mind in any case.

Adorably, Helen threw her hands in the air. "I don't know. How is this done? How do novelists make sense of all of this? How could Mr. Royce do this half a dozen times without going completely mad?"

Selina laughed, considering the struggle of a creative mind, and immediately remembered the various scribbled nonsense currently strewn across her husband's own room. "I'm sure maintaining a constant state of madness certainly helps." Seeing that Helen only slightly smiled amidst her overwhelming frustration, Selina sighed. "Would you mind if I gave it a good read? I'm not Darius Royce, but I've read my share of books. I know a good story when I hear one. Perhaps I could lend a fresh perspective."

"Would you? It wouldn't be too much trouble?"

Selina shook her head, smiling while Helen sorted the crumbled papers and handed them to her.

"Thank you, my lady. I would be forever grateful if you could make sense of this." Helen turned to continue her chores, mumbling on about the ridiculous nonsense that will inevitably be found in the sorry excuse for a manuscript.

The weather was particularly fine that day, so the lady decided it would be providential to take Helen's manuscript along with her on her usual jaunt through Everdon's grounds. She didn't imagine it would be difficult to find somewhere peaceful to read it. Her anticipation, however, prevented her from waiting, and so she read as she walked.

Helen's anxieties were not entirely unfounded; the manuscript hardly made any sense at all. What began as a classic love story soon became a clumsily constructed epic poem about a bird cage. Selina squinted in confusion as she deciphered the scribbles along the bottom of each page.

Ghost of Everdon, Helen had written. A few pages later, she repeated the words, but with the addition of a name: *Sarah Atwood.*

Selina's pace slowed.

Suddenly Helen's story gained coherence. Her heroine was trapped. Was it a castle, was it a cage? Helen couldn't be sure, but she clearly suspected, in her clumsy way, that this trap, this cage, this alleged castle, was somehow put there because of a ghost named Sarah Atwood.

"Well," Selina muttered to herself, "girl's cleverer than she seems."

Lost in the revealing tale, Selina had reached the end of the property, where Mr. Cuddy's barn once stood. It had been burned down during an accident caused by Cuddy's fluctuating health. When Selina glanced up from the pages, she expected to see the barn's ruins —her usual sign to turn around. However, as she neared that particular clearing, there was no ruined barn.

Instead, Cuddy, the older children from the orphanage, and a seemingly recovered Mr. Bryant were bustling around a mostly reconstructed structure now built in the old barn's place.

Selina stopped in her tracks, expressing her previous confusion of the manuscript in her hands but directing it toward whatever she now witnessed. She then heard a familiar voice from the other side of the building. The voice varied as words were spoken — changing from the one she knew intimately to a strange assortment of pitches and cadences.

It was Royce. The younger children gathered around him with wide and eager eyes as he animatedly regaled a story with which Selina was equally familiar — *The Emperor's New Clothes.*

In a gruff, decrepit voice, Royce spoke, "Those would be just the clothes for me. If I wore them I would be able to discover which men in my empire are unfit for their posts. And I could tell the wise men from the fools. Yes, I certainly must get some of the stuff woven for me right away," He then switched to normal narration. "And so he paid the swindlers handsomely for them to start work at once."

One of the children giggled. "But there was no work."

Royce placed a finger against the side of his own nose in understanding. "When the swindlers brought him the invisible clothes, the lords and ladies of the courts all looked at one another." He put on a funny voice, "I can't see a thing, can you?" He then heightened his pitch to play a lady, "Don't let him hear you say that, or we'll be branded impostors, darling."

The children all giggled, wildly entertained.

"The swindlers held up the invisible clothes and asked the emperor what he thought of them, but he was confused and frightened. He couldn't see anything either. Was he, himself, unfit for his position?" The children's eyes widened even more in anticipation as he returned to the gruff old emperor's voice, placing comical hands on his hips. "Perish the thought! I must maintain my position at whatever cost. Of course they're positively splendid clothes, the finest I've ever seen!"

Royce danced around a bit as if trying on and parading new clothes. The children laughed and so did the Lady Selina. The familiar melody of Selina's laugh caught Royce's attention, bringing realization that he had expanded his audience. Hastily, he cleared his throat and clapped his hands. "All right, back to work."

The kids mumbled about wanting another story, but obediently returned to Bryant and Cuddy to receive further orders.

"So, this is why you've looked so filthy by the end of the day." Selina mildly applauded.

Royce smiled, placing accusatory hands on his hips. "You don't usually walk this far, Selina."

"I wasn't supposed to see you….rebuilding Mr. Cuddy's barn?"

"Remodeling," he corrected, bringing his hands back together in front of him.

"Remodeling for what?" Selina advanced curiously, suspecting his answer.

Royce gestured to the children scurrying to and fro around them.

Selina angled her head to one side before clarifying the words aloud. "You're....you're building an orphanage."

"For some reason," he shook his head in mock disbelief, "you seemed to care so much for that last one."

Instead of immediately revealing how tenderly the sentiment touched her, Selina forced a smirk. "You could've hired a building crew," she commented.

Quickly, he shook his head again, even wagging a finger at her before bending to retrieve a long hammer from the ground beside him. "You would've noticed and been suspicious. Just as you would have been of the furniture, had I not replaced pieces at the house. Besides," he stood and looked at the other men, "we have it handled. Cuddy and Bryant are good workers. And thankfully, your staff think very highly of you. Several of the stable boys and gardeners have lent a hand and been discreet." He winked at her, gesturing to the property as a whole, and added, "I thought the location was ideal—away from town, shorter commute for your weekly visits. And Cuddy will be an excellent caretaker. I assumed if you trusted him to be Penelope's escape plan, you'd trust him with the orphans."

"Penelope's…" she slowly repeated.

Royce stepped toward her with a revealing tone. "You've funneled a small fortune to him since our engagement was announced, Selina. Give me some credit. You made certain Penelope was cared for, should I squander your fortune and make ruin of Everdon, and you with it."

"I didn't…" Selina stammered a moment before settling on his smirking eyes. Slowly, she finally smiled. "I should've known you'd catch on."

"It's very clever," he laughed. "I should've known you'd make such an arrangement. But don't worry—to keep the orphanage safe from my dastardly grasp, I've given Cuddy enough funds to keep the orphanage afloat for the next decade, at least."

She looked at him in continued surprise, becoming more speechless by the moment. He turned casually to peel a strip of useless wood from the side of the new orphanage, and she simply started. "You have?"

"Yes," he confirmed, still facing away from her. "And now I can waste the Delamere fortune with my extravagant habits and vices, and those children will be left unaffected."

Selina's eyes fell down to the manuscript in her hands. Perhaps Helen's heavily romanticized idea of the hero she vaguely based on Royce was not as entirely fiction as Selina had dismissively believed.

Breaking her from her brief reverie, Royce finally turned around. "What are you doing all the way out here, Selina?" he asked.

"Um, I was…" she stammered again, "reading this. Miss Thomas' manuscript. It's lovely weather, I thought I'd also walk and visit…"

She placed a hand to her chest, as if physically stopping herself from finishing her sentence. Royce continued to gaze at her until her eyes finally met his and she sighed in resignation.

"You picked a place so dangerously close…" she exhaled.

"Close to what?"

Her hesitation caused him to set down the hammer and step toward her. At last she sighed and gestured for him to follow her past the building and further into the trees behind it. They were away from the curious eyes and ears of the busy children, and they continued until they came to another, smaller, clearing. In the center of the small clearing there was only a quaint bush and a single headstone.

Sarah Atwood, 1842-1861, it read.

"Is that you?" Royce inquired softly.

Selina bowed her head respectfully before answering. "She never gave me a name. All I ever learned was hers."

Royce suddenly remembered whispers of a ghost story. A poor, dead maid. A maid named Sarah Atwood. "So she's the ghost of Everdon. Your mother."

"A disgraced, dead maid," Selina murmured.

"And your father?"

She chuckled humorlessly. "Don't you remember? Lord Delamere is my father. That's what the papers say. I never cared to know what genetics claimed. She wouldn't dare expose him. But he was a well-respected gentleman, I do know that much." She tightened her grip on the manuscript between her hands. "And it was not what she wanted....I know that much as well."

Royce closed his eyes briefly, disgusted by the implication, like any respectable man would be.

"Broken bodies and broken hearts don't stand much of a chance. Within...twenty-four hours of bringing me into this world, she...she took her own life."

"And Lady Delamere..."

"Her stillborn broke her heart the same day I broke Sarah Atwood's." Selina's voice was broken by the onslaught of memories. Her own truth, which had been seared into her remembrance for years. "A mutual friend of theirs brought us together and the lie was born. They so desperately wanted a child...and my new father wanted to guarantee my future without speculation of the circumstances of my birth. So I became Selina Delamere."

"You fill the shoes beautifully."

Selina shrugged. "It's all I've known. I have no other shoes to wear."

"How long have you known?"

"Nearly fifteen years now. Lord Delamere never wanted me to doubt where I came from and just how much he fought to keep me where I am. I've never felt unwanted, because I know my story. And after they brought Penelope to Everdon, he wanted to ensure that her future remained just as secure as my own."

"Did Sarah have any family?"

"No. No, she didn't," Selina almost whispered. A slight expression of tragic relief flashed across her face. "But she had....well, she had...I suppose even a knight-in-shining armor doesn't guarantee the fair maiden is saved. Sarah and Josephine met the same fate. Sarah's knight was only able to save her child...while

Josephine's...well, I only wish Jo had found herself a Lindon before her end came."

Royce began to smile. He had always suspected a degree of Lindon's involvement. But the steward's intentions were never out of personal gain; his heroism was inspired by the sort of love Royce only fabricated on paper. "She had a Lindon. Perhaps Josephine had one of her own, he was simply too late."

Selina slowly looked up at him. "How would you know?"

"Stories have a way of presenting themselves to me," he lifted his chin with confidence. "Just as I know Barratt is wrong. Henry wasn't the father, and Henry didn't kill her."

"He believes Henry and Josephine…"

Royce was suddenly aware of Selina's ignorance of Barratt's suspicions against her late friend as her lips parted, appalled. "I said he's wrong," he emphasized. "Someone did kill the poor woman, but it was not Henry and it was not the father of her child."

"You just continue to become more dangerous with your access to information, Royce."

Royce grinned, flashing teeth. "You think I'm dangerous?"

"Hm, fairly," she patted his arm, teasingly. "You're fairly dangerous, I'm a great pretender — it's the cornerstone of our arrangement."

Royce maintained the grin as she teased, but softened into an expression with a pinch of soberness. "I was mistaken, Selina," he then said. "You're hardly a pretender."

"And what makes you say that?" she challenged.

Royce scoffed and gestured to all of her. "I'm a decent charlatan, Selina, I am. But what might have started as a hoax turned into something quite natural. No pretender could increase her own fortune in a matter of years through legitimate business dealings, while maintaining unbelievable influence over society reaching as far as London. If you're pretending, then my own skills are utterly disgraceful." He mockingly bowed his head in the presence of her greatness.

Selina smiled at the praise and blushed just a bit. "I think you've been in the sun too long," she dismissed.

Royce chuckled, and before turning to resume his work, he tipped an invisible hat to the lowly headstone. "I thank you, Miss Atwood, for producing such a beguiling and lucrative mark for a scoundrel like me to exploit." He turned to leave, but stopped to peer over Selina's shoulder. "You might suggest to Miss Thomas that she'd amend any hint of ghosts in her story there," he added, pointing to the manuscript. "It's not a ghost who haunts the halls of Everdon. It's the Lady Selina. The Lady and her demons. Which is, on all counts, a far more enticing tale."

3

A Brandied Cynic

"And what did you think?" Helen grinned eagerly as she brushed Selina's hair before bed. "About the manuscript, I mean."

"You were right," Selina sighed, staring at herself in the mirror with a troubled frown. "It was a jumbled collection of notes, rather than a story."

Helen suddenly flushed and looked downward bashfully, ashamed of the chaos of her own mind. "I'm sorry, I knew it wasn't ready to be read through."

"Nonsense. You needed an outside eye. I was actually quite impressed."

"You were? Why?" Helen paused.

"Well, it showed your own growth. The development of style, the changes in the story. You thought it was a simple fairytale, but that's for children."

"Not all fairytales are for children."

"No, but yours was. It was incredibly naive and fantastical."

Helen nodded and then remembered her task at hand and resumed brushing. "It was, wasn't it? The rogue pursuing the lady and the two falling in love….well, I thought they were falling in love. Until it all became a cage."

"It was always a cage. The story just didn't know it yet. It had to grow up first."

Helen set the brush down, nodding in agreement as she started braiding Selina's hair in a long braid down the back. "You could be right. The love story wasn't what it seemed. But I don't think the love was the cage."

"Oh?"

"After Sir Henry died, I felt....I don't know, stuck. Nothing made sense; I couldn't move forward."

Selina nodded.

"But then Mr. Royce told me something about birds with wings and their cages and being tricked and such and then it finally fell into place. And that's why I don't think much of the love itself being a cage..." Helen fastened the braid in Selina's hair and straightened her back to look at Selina through the mirror. "I never thought someone's voice could inspire a story."

"What do you mean?"

"The way Mr. Royce told me about the bird at the menagerie —how it was lured into the cage and was forced to either use brute force or trickery to escape. Something in his voice. I don't know. I don't think the princess in my story was ever free and in love. I don't know if this is a story that intends on being about love. It could turn into a love story, to be sure—I think any story could—but I think it actually starts off as a different kind of story altogether. The tone in Mr. Royce's voice when he spoke of the bird....the way he tells any story, really. He can make you feel the pain or the joy or whatever he wants you to feel. And with that bird in that cage....I felt utter devastation. He had such pity, such regret in his voice. It hurt so much —I had to change the story. I had to understand how the bird could be freed."

Helen held up nightgown options. "Would you like me to lay out the blue or the red?"

Selina was lost in thought, dwelling on that comment about Royce's perceived regret. "Um, the red. I think I'll go fetch myself a book for the night."

"Do you want me to get it for you?"

"No, no," Selina waved her hand. "You get some rest. Dream up the ending for that story."

Helen obeyed and headed to bed while Selina journeyed down to the library. Croft was finishing up his work for the night, returning books to their rightful place and closing his ledger.

"Ah, a bit earlier than usual, I see," he lifted a brow and pointed playfully at her.

Selina smiled and sighed. "What story do you have for me tonight, Mr. Croft?"

"What mood do you find yourself in tonight? I've just received a new copy of *Far From the Madding Crowd*. I've heard good things of that one."

Selina took a copy from him and sat herself in an armchair. She began fingering through the pages but hardly read the words.

"Difficult to see the story when the words are moving so briskly past."

Selina ran her fingers through her hair, clearly restless, and shut the book. Without looking up at him, she exhaled, "I'm afraid my husband might love me."

Croft was suddenly pensive. "My, my. Such a scandal that would be." His warm smile slowly returned, but only in the moments Selina glanced his direction. "That is becoming a more common reason to marry these days. Why else would he ask for your hand?"

"Because he—" Selina momentarily forgot she wasn't speaking to Lindon, so she stopped herself and sighed again. "He loves me, I suppose."

Croft chuckled. "No need to be so ambivalent, dear. Even a blind man could have seen the distance between the two of you. The clever man weaseled his way into Everdon; it doesn't matter how. Though, I've been around long enough to know to assume your grand fortune was a matter of interest."

Selina placed a thoughtful finger to her lips. "He is a clever man. And now he is a rich man."

"And you feel he's now seeking redemption." He chuckled

lightly at her blank stare and moved to pour them both a drink from the decanter table. "That highwayman story he's scribbled....his rendition of the Lady of Shalott....we all make stories personal, Selina. We place ourselves inside them, connect to the horror and the accolades alike, and then suddenly decide we are above them. Mr. Royce speaks in stories—I find that quite relatable, in fact."

She accepted the drink he handed her, still staring pensively ahead. "I confess I once thought him such a sadist."

"It doesn't take a sadist to find beauty in someone else's pain," Croft corrected. He sipped the brandy and pointed at her with profound intent. "It takes a human. They've been so beaten down, so belittled and broken—and that is what gives artists such beauty. That damage provides the most depth and character that can be captured in a story, painting or a song, and can reach out and touch another damaged soul. It's what makes Mr. Royce's novels so appealing. He reaches the very bottom of society and raises them up to find a place in our hearts, because we're all vermin, deep down."

"Aw, not all of us," Selina winked at him. The two clinked glasses and sipped.

"Of course," he smiled at her. "Some of us are the Lady Selina of Everdon and are far above such abominations."

Selina laughed, nearly spilling the brandy. "The Lady Selina might be the worst vermin of them all."

"Nonsense. None of us deserve you. Particularly Mr. Royce."

Selina's forehead wrinkled at his shift in tone when mentioning Royce. With a new gentleness, Selina took another sip and almost smiled. "He's become quite endearing, you know."

"Endearing, eh? Is it the way he assaults your dinner guests?" Croft sardonically offered.

"Did you see it?" Selina immediately challenged.

"From the window, yes. It was such an outburst, I fully believed the accusations against him. Though, I understand now that we were all mistaken. Shame, too. You almost broke free of him."

Selina shook her head in mock scolding. "You get so terribly harsh when you drink, Croft."

"I apologize, my lady," he set down his glass. He smiled good-naturedly and defused his criticisms with a chuckle. "This brandy brings out the cynic in me. I'm sure there is much to be admired in Mr. Royce. As I said before, he can certainly spin a beguiling tale, I'll give him that."

Selina stared at the drink in her hand and tapped her fingers on the cover of the book in her lap. "I was drawn to him from the beginning."

"Hm, were you?"

"Handsome, charming....and no one....challenges me quite the way he does."

Croft chuckled. "I suppose women of your intellect enjoy a good power struggle every now and then."

"Not that he ever needs to learn it," she shrugged, "but if he hadn't wanted Penelope first, I would have loved him nearly at first sight."

"The fool."

"He's building me an orphanage."

Croft paused for a long moment before reacting. "Is he? With what ulterior motive, I wonder."

Selina looked over at him to see a rather solemn expression, containing only a hint of the playful tone that had gradually dissipated.

"Oh dear," the librarian said. "Lady Selina, I'm afraid your husband might love you."

October 1889

November 1889

It's necessary to have wished for death in order to know how good it is to live

~Alexandre Dumas~

1
Final Dues

Selina's sleep was restless, as one would expect. She rose earlier than Helen, which was becoming a habit of hers, to take a morning stroll and clear her bustling mind. The sun had barely risen and only a select handful of the estate staff were seen carrying out their duties. Just as Selina assumed she was off to a peaceful and quiet start to her promenade, a shrill voice called to her from the top of the staircase.

"Selina, dear!" Elinor exclaimed too loudly. "I'd love to join you, if you don't mind."

"Actually, I was—"

"Splendid." Elinor hurried to the bottom step and immediately linked arms with Selina. "We must have a chat."

"Splendid," Selina muttered.

As they started for the path which started in the garden, Elinor tightened her arm around Selina's and leaned into her. "You mustn't let Barratt's assumptions of us trouble you, dear," she began.

"What might his assumptions be?" Selina blandly inquired, with little interest in the answer.

A vindictive grin tugged at the corners of Elinor's mouth. "I know you're not in a position to expose Royce for what he truly is, without risking yourself as well."

Selina slowed her pace, suddenly quite aware of how quickly Elinor had been leading them.

"But you must understand that I am not my brother," the snake assured the lady. "Abram was...not quite as decent and upstanding as I am. And Royce has always been above all that as well. I need to know that rumors and false accusations won't spoil this thing you have going with the dear boy."

"This thing?"

"Your...arrangement."

Selina's jaw slightly dropped and her eyes widened. The thought had not yet occurred to her that Royce could be capable of sharing his leverage with an accomplice. "What sort of arrangement do you believe we have?" she kept a steady voice, though her heart was quaking. "The union of husband and wife is fairly standard."

"Oh please, dear," Elinor sneered. "I've made it clear how close Royce and I have been. You think he could keep something like this from me? From Barratt and Abram, of course—but me?"

Upon hearing the ladies had ventured on a stroll through the garden, Royce was keen to spot them making their way down the path. When he saw they had stopped in their tracks, and that Selina's hands were wringing with anxiety, he hastily made his way to her side.

"Seems we all had the same idea this morning," he tried not to pant from exertion. Smoothly he took Selina's arm, creating a barrier between her and Elinor. "When we return to the house, Elinor, I've arranged for a paid room for you in town."

"You've done what?" Elinor cocked her head as if hearing him incorrectly.

Selina looked at him strangely as well. "You've done what...?"

"You'll be leaving Everdon by this evening. The duration of a guest staying at Everdon has been exceeded." Selina still stared at him with a surprised smile. "But you won't be without boarding. It's all arranged."

"Royce, don't be ridiculous," Elinor protested.

"I'm sorry, Elinor. But I've made my decision. And the only one who can overturn that decision is the lady of Everdon herself."

Royce and Elinor both looked to Selina for any sign of contradiction.

To Royce, Selina finally spoke, still riddled with surprise, "Well, no. I respect my husband's judgment."

"There you have it," Royce clapped his leg with finality. "Mr. Lindon will direct you to the inn."

The shock of the sudden dismissal stung. Miss Abram's bags were packed that afternoon. No further questions were asked, but Elinor spewed her share of profanities as she slammed her belongings into suitcases. Amongst her things, she came across the copy of *Pamela* that Mr. Croft had left the late Abram. Continuing to swear her way through her dismay, Elinor marched downstairs to the library, the book firmly in her hands.

"I believe this is yours." She slammed the book on the desk in front of the unsuspecting librarian.

"Ah, yes, thank you," he glanced up from the pages of his ledger, hardly noticing her rage right away. "I'd begun to think it was lost forever." Suddenly seeing the red in her cheeks and the scowl on her face, Croft slowly closed the ledger and reached for *Pamela*. "Is there something the matter, Miss Abram?"

"It seems I'm leaving Everdon," she huffed. "I've not even buried my brother and I'm already tossed aside like a worn out shoe."

Croft narrowed his gaze, as confused by the sudden nature of the dismissal now as she was. "Oh dear. Where will you go?"

Elinor groaned. "I hardly know," she threw her hands in the air theatrically. "Apparently I am to find Mr. Lindon. Do you know where he is?"

After thinking a moment, Croft considered. "I do believe he was upstairs looking for Mr. Royce. I'd look in Mr. Royce's chambers."

Elinor paused at the thought. "Thank you, Mr. Croft. It's been a pleasure."

"The pleasure is mine," he politely stood to bow, "I'm sure, Miss Abram."

Royce's room proved seemingly useless, however. Lindon was nowhere to be found—as Royce had been out, she assumed Lindon didn't linger long. Elinor, however, intended to linger. The fury within her was begging for an outlet. Royce would regret wronging her, as he had in the past, and she intended to articulate just what his misery would entail. Seeking parchment and a pen, Elinor formulated her threats. Unfortunately, her hunt for supplies was just as fruitless as her hunt for Lindon. She rummaged through drawers and shelves, to no avail.

"Calls himself a writer....there's no paper..." She caught sight of a locked drawer in his desk.

Elinor glanced around and then pulled a pin from her hair to pick the lock. Her well-experienced hands opened it easily, enabling her to peer in to see a book from the Everdon library.

Bleak House.

And inside was a letter, not written in Royce's hand.

She quickly tore it open and scanned the contents. Her eyes widened and a menacing laugh escaped her lips. The sudden sound of Croft and Lindon's idle conversation made its way down the hall; Elinor quickly shut the drawer and tucked the letter deep into her bodice.

Seeing Elinor emerge from the room, Croft gestured to Lindon. "Oh, I've found Mr. Lindon for you, Miss Abram. He should be able to make those travel arrangements for you."

"Thank you, Mr. Croft," she sighed with exaggerated gratitude. "I'd be lost without you."

Lindon wrinkled his forehead. "Is everything all right, Miss Abram? I've heard this is all rather sudden."

"Far be it for me to assume, Mr. Lindon. You'd better ask your master, after I've been fetched a carriage." She aggressively moved past him to get her luggage.

Lindon's mouth shrugged. "Oh I certainly intend to."

Royce stood dutifully at the door to see that his unwanted guest left without causing any further conflict. When her carriage was loaded and her presence was finally lifted from the estate, Lindon lingered by Royce's side.

His tone was somewhere between a chuckle and a mutter. "I

never liked you much, Royce. But it's nice to see you coming to your wife's defense."

"She overstayed her welcome," Royce stated simply.

"I'm fully aware of the lines that woman crossed. I'm just pleasantly surprised your spine seems to have strengthened in your time here." Lindon gave Royce a congratulatory pat on his shoulder before turning away, a new sort of smile on his face.

2
A Rather Dramatic Shift

Henrietta Sweeting had begged for weeks to have another dinner party, so her parents finally complied and invited her usual circle. Politely, they had also extended their invitation to all of Everdon, which included Elinor. After coming upon her in town, their invitation was given in person, unwittingly as they had not been made aware of her recent dissent from Everdon. In any case, she eagerly accepted.

When Penelope and the Royces arrived at the Sweetings' that evening, the sight of Elinor Abram brought tension to Royce's shoulders. She stood in the corner of the room chatting with Barratt, but with an eye scanning the room, prepared to hone in on her newly targeted prey. Instinctively, Royce pulled his wife closer.

"What a lovely pair." Selina commented, noting both Elinor and Barratt. She felt Royce's muscles tighten, so she stroked his arm lightly until he looked to her and smiled with assurance.

Mr. Sweeting, out of morbid curiosity in fact, invited Inspector Barratt, in hopes he could pick his brain regarding the recent happenings. The Royces and Penelope soon found their social position in the drawing room — Penelope immediately pranced toward Henrietta while Selina was approached by others. Little effort was usually needed on her part; all flocked to Selina.

"Hm, such a chill." Barratt noted the intensity in which Elinor watched Selina and Royce.

Elinor grimaced. "Perhaps you should stand closer to the fireplace, then."

"Curious you didn't arrive together."

She tightened her lips, her words dripping with disdain. "It seems the master of Everdon felt my time as his guest had ended."

Barratt raised his eyebrows. "Oh dear."

"No doubt she's made her way into his head."

"You mean, his wife. His wife is in his head. I believe the law implies that's where she belongs."

Elinor grimaced again, sipping her drink; Barratt chuckled at her response.

"I never thought I'd witness that expression, Elinor. Cheers." Barratt held up his drink, mockingly toasting her.

"I beg your pardon."

Barratt observed how closely Royce kept his wife. It was likely the closest proximity they'd kept for the longest time since their wedding. The deliberation was clear on Royce's part, particularly when paired with his wary eye on Elinor. But now, the inspector noticed, there was a curious way in which the lady now leaned into her husband.

"He doesn't need you," Barratt observed. "He chose her all on his own. Suddenly your vulnerable plaything has grown into a con man of his own right. He no longer needs the Abram name to make his way in the world. He has Everdon now. He has her now. And he's ruling his new empire without you."

Elinor scoffed. "Empires collapse all the time, Barratt. Look at the Romans, the Austrians—a great fall is inevitable."

"I suppose that's true, but their falls came at the hands of an even greater force. And I'm afraid your numbers are dwindling. She despises you, but you're hardly a threat. The woman faced rumors of your affair with Royce and Lady Selina was unmoved. Nothing irks a woman like yourself more than failing to intimidate a rival."

Slowly she sipped her drink. "Is it so inconceivable that his numbers begin to dwindle as well? One only needs to inspire the proper amount of fear."

"Come now, Elinor. Violence has never been your preference. You're not Bernard; you're better than that. Methodical. Calculated. You've never resorted to striking Royce's marks in the past. Insanity is your weapon. Did it fail you this time? Did your plan crumble the second you realized he chose one too high above you to be broken?"

Elinor scoffed again, this time tilting her chin upward so as to look at Selina from the tip of her nose. "Too high above me?"

"As he also is now."

"Well, prepare yourself for a rather dramatic shift."

Henrietta and Penelope chatted louder nearby, regarding Henrietta's recent trip to London with her father on business. "And Father commissioned another painting while we were there and it's simply stunning. I must show you. Come—Selina, you too! You'll love it; the artist was absolutely brilliant and so charming."

"They often are," Selina nodded in agreement, winking at Royce before allowing herself to be dragged by the hand into the other room. As Royce moved to follow, he was regrettably stopped by Mr. Sweeting who was eager to converse.

"Mr. Royce," the kind man started, "I ran into your publisher in London, while I was there. He hadn't heard the news of Abram, poor fellow…"

Henrietta's portrait was housed in the music room down the hall, right above her pianoforte, where she felt it belonged. Dramatically, she gestured to it as soon as her audience had convened —which included nearly every woman present at the party.

Penelope giggled in excitement. "My, Hettie, you look like the queen."

"Do you think so?"

Selina humored her with a sweet smile. "Very regal, indeed. Is that your dress?"

"No, no, the painter's friend is an actress," Henrietta gushed. "She let me borrow it for the portrait. She was lovely too—says she knows you, Selina. Lillie Langtry. I believe you met her at one of her plays."

"It's entirely possible," Selina shrugged. As her presence in London was well sought, Selina had spent many years in city society meeting a wide variety of faces. She hardly remembered.

"Lillie Langtry?" Elinor was bitterly impressed. Selina almost scowled, realizing Elinor was standing so close to her, but upturned her lips into a smile for Henrietta instead.

"Yes, she got the dress from a past lover." Henrietta winked suggestively.

Selina hummed reminiscently. "Hm, Prince Edward has excellent taste."

Penelope sighed. "That's why you look like the queen. Was it his mother's old dress, do you think?"

The two girls giggled and speculated the dress' origins while moving out of the room with linked arms. Just as Selina moved to follow them, Elinor stepped directly in her path.

"Lady Selina."

Selina tensed, but complied. "Yes?"

"I'd like to speak to you privately for a moment." Elinor continued without waiting for Selina's consent. "I wanted to thank you for your hospitality at Everdon. I'm forever grateful. I wonder if there's anything—"

Selina chuckled humorlessly. "You've studied the same script."

Elinor dropped the false pretense of gratitude. "I imagine he approached you in a similar fashion."

"But he was much better." Selina started to move again toward the exit.

"I've learned my words have less of an effect on you than his do, so I'll trim the frill and pleasantries, dear. I hardly need to adorn my threats in pretty words." Elinor pulled out a folded piece of scribbled parchment.

"What is this?"

"No doubt the secret to dear Royce's success. We once shared everything, you know. It was only a matter of time this fell into my hands." Elinor opened the letter and dangled it in front of Selina.

Selina studied the handwriting a bit and then snatched it to get a closer look. Slowly, Selina glanced up from the letter. Her lips tugged downward, but then smoothly straightened as she calmly and pensively folded the letter.

"I can't imagine what more you could be after. My fortune is no longer my own—Everdon and all its assets belong to Royce."

Elinor smirked. "I've always managed to get my hands on what I need."

"Interesting. I didn't get that impression when Royce dismissed you from his property. Nor do I understand what more you could want from me." Selina's tone was almost mocking.

"You know exactly what I want."

Selina's smile grew smug. "Royce loves money. I assume he always has. Mr. Abram loved the women Royce's greed brought him. And you, Miss Abram, you thrive on the control he naively granted you. A sickening arrangement that clearly lacks sustainability. I've learned that the moment you grow too comfortable in a position of power, you set the stage for your own downfall. I'm afraid you're threatening the wrong Royce. The control you seek now belongs to the very man who banished you to the inn. You and I must accept that our power has waned. He is as untouchable as I once was."

"No one is untouchable. Tangible treasures are at greater risk of being taken or destroyed."

"Yes," Selina lowered her chin and peered up at Elinor with a pointed hauteur, "but the imagined treasures are far more maddening when lost."

Jaw clenched, Elinor inhaled sharply. "Spoken so arrogantly, while you yourself are on such a brink of loss. Yes, Royce has procured your estate, but according to law, he has no more need of you. If you were to be exposed as a fraud, an impostor, who would the courts favor? The man who fell victim to the ploy or the harlot who tricked him into believing she was more than she was? Royce is awfully good at playing the heartbroken sop. He'd maintain his fortune and you'd be imprisoned, left alone to rot in a cell for the rest of your days."

As she spoke, she advanced. Royce, searching for Selina,

quietly entered the music room, slowing as he perceived Elinor's seethed threats. Neither woman noticed his presence, which suited his quickly developing intent. Tacitly, he moved toward them, grabbing a candlestick from an end table as he passed it.

Elinor grabbed Selina's arm, startling her. "He'd have power and wealth to spare, while you become a disgrace, a pariah. No kingdom can properly operate without a queen. I'm not my brother, dear, I don't run on impulse and instant gratification. I can patiently await Royce seeing reason in his loneliness and restoring me to his good graces. You see, this is the dangerous part of treasuring only the tangible." Elinor squeezed Selina's arm, as a painful reference. "Makes one vulnerable and ripe for the return of a puppeteer."

And that's when the candlestick struck her.

Her temple was pierced, her body falling limply to the floor. Almost instantly, the life was drained from her.

Selina screamed, dropping the letter of blackmail, before properly perceiving what had happened.

Almost as quickly as the letter had hit the floor, Selina fell to her knees, frantically checking the hateful woman's pulse. It wasn't more than a moment or two before she realized Elinor was dead. Her eyes misted in shock as they moved from the body to Royce's steady hand which held the candlestick.

Trampling footsteps, heavy with concern, soon sounded from down the hall. Swiftly, Royce picked up the fallen letter and tucked it into his pocket before rising again.

Selina's voice was breathy and strained. "You weren't the one she wanted to hurt. You would have kept your fortune."

Royce looked at her directly and calmly. "I know."

Selina exhaled with emotion. His response touched her, but the sight of Elinor's body prevented her from feeling the affection.

Penelope was the first to enter, and rightly so, she screamed at the spectacle. Immediately, Selina stood and smoothly took the candlestick from Royce's grip, moving away from him just in time for Barratt and Sweeting to enter the room.

"What's happened?"

"Good gracious." Sweeting exhaled in shock.

"Who did this?" Barratt eyes and accusations immediately snapped to Royce.

Selina posed no hesitation. "I did."

"You?"

"Miss Abram attacked me. I reacted. I didn't mean to kill her; I was only acting defensively." Selina waved the weapon in the air for Barratt to see.

Barratt studied her for a moment, as did Royce.

Sweeting was in a state of naive shock. "Why on earth would Miss Abram want to attack you?"

"I hardly know." Selina shrugged off the lie.

"Did you witness this, Mr. Royce?" Barratt eyed Royce suspiciously.

Selina didn't let Royce answer. "If I am to be charged with murder, Inspector, I'll ask you send word to Mr. Lindon."

Barratt looked at Royce, then back at Selina, and then sighed. "That won't be necessary, Lady Selina. If a woman such as yourself claims self defense, who am I to argue? Besides, I had a rather troubling conversation with Miss Abram not an hour earlier."

"Troubling, eh?" Sweeting frowned.

"She was not a violent woman," Barratt confessed, "but her recent state of mind was starting to cause doubts."

"She was a friend of yours, Royce. Could it be jealousy toward the Lady Selina?"

Penelope squinted. "Why would she be jealous of Selina?"

"I'm sure it was grief. She had recently..." Selina started, "lost her brother, if you remember." Selina's tone shifted as she cleared her throat. "If you don't mind. I think I'll be going home now."

"Of course, my lady. You need rest after something so traumatic." Barratt attempted sympathy, but it wasn't his color. His suspicion flashed in Royce's direction, despite Selina's claims. Briskly, Selina walked past him and down the hall, but he soon caught up. "If you don't mind, Lady Selina, I'd like you to accompany me tomorrow. I intend to visit the orphans in the hospital and interview a few of them regarding the fire. Mr. Abram's case is unfortunately still open."

"Mr. Litchfield already confessed." Selina snapped. "Shouldn't you be focusing on Miss Rodin's death?"

"I'd like a more well-rounded perspective before settling on a resolution. The children would be forthcoming with you; I only need to learn Mr. Abram's comings and goings from the orphanage before he was shot."

Selina inhaled and exhaled, but with struggle. "Of course."

"I apologize, my lady. For everything. Particularly Miss Abram. Something like this should never happen to a woman in your situation."

"No matter what the philosophers say, inspector, even the deadliest of sins don't discriminate based on social class or breeding."

"Hm, the deadliest of sins."

"Everyone has a little of each in them. That's what makes them human. Miss Abram was no different." Selina paused. "Nor am I."

3
Smoking Gun

Lindon was surprised to see the three of them home so early in the evening. They'd only been gone a couple of hours and the Sweetings' dinner parties were often considerably longer. Selina's stone face alarmed him, supported by Penelope's puffy eyes as she leaned desperately on Royce's arm.

"Is everything all right? Penelope, are you ill?" Lindon asked, anticipating a tale of dramatic proportions.

Selina ignored any kind of interaction and continued up the stairs to her room. Lindon anxiously watched her pass him by, looking then to Royce for an explanation.

Royce's tone was very matter-of-fact, but distracted as his eyes also followed Selina. "Miss Abram has died. Cut the evening a bit short for us."

Lindon's eyes widened. "What?"

"Selina killed her," Penelope suddenly took on Royce's straightforward tone, expressing little sorrow for Elinor's death.

They could hear Selina's door close, bringing Lindon and Royce to exchange glances. Lindon's glance soon shifted to a glare. "Selina is not a violent woman."

Royce slowed and then said with deliberation, "It was self defense." Lindon lifted a brow. "It was in Selina's defense."

"Miss Abram attacked her. Why would she do that?"

Penelope moved away from Royce and toward Lindon, seeking both comfort and a more reasonable explanation than she'd been given. She lowered her voice and added, "Who would want to hurt Selina?"

Lindon frowned curiously, allowing the glare to slip away as he looked once more to Royce.

"You should go to bed, Penelope," Royce gently encouraged.

"Yes, let's get you to bed. You need to rest." Lindon agreed, taking her upstairs.

As the steward had expected, Royce aimed for Selina's room. He almost helped himself through the door before pausing to consider some degree of sensitivity. Softly, he knocked his fist against the wooden door. She didn't hear the door open as he peeked in; she sat at her vanity, glass of wine in hand, her fingers shaking as she sipped. Several times, her unsteady gaze flickered down to an open drawer of the vanity. When Royce took a couple of steps in the room, she snapped her head in his direction, startled again.

"Are you all right?"

"Yes, I'm fine," she claimed, quickly shutting the drawer.

Royce gently stepped toward her and took the glass of wine out of her hand. "I think you need some rest."

"Give me my wine," she demanded.

"What's in the drawer?"

"Brushes and pins and such." Selina attempted to reach for her glass from his hand.

He dodged her and reached to open the drawer himself, only to see his own gun. He hardly minded the possession, until he suddenly noted a blemish or two.

"Selina...it's been fired," he told her.

"Is that so suspicious? Are you telling me you've never fired your own gun?"

"I clean it."

Selina hesitated and couldn't look him in the eye. Her shaking hands grew worse, and the shaking soon traveled to her shoulders and quivering lips. "I didn't...I didn't..."

Royce set her glass on the vanity. "What happened?"

"He...I never meant to fire it — I-I don't even know why I took it, I just—"

"Didn't trust me. Selina, who's he? Abram? Did you—you killed Abram?"

"He-he—he came after me and I....I shot him."

His voice quickly thickened with faintly controlled rage. "Did he touch you?"

Selina bit back tears, her eyes welling, but neglected to give a definitive response. Then, compelled to explain herself in some way, she nodded, then shook her head, before settling into an indecisive shrug as if she hardly knew the answer herself.

Royce suddenly remembered Abram telling him about what he thought he was owed; the thought stiffen his jaw more than ever before. "He tried to," he hated the words as they came from his lips.

Selina could do little to prevent the tears, so they began rolling down her face. "I didn't...I didn't know what else to do."

"Why didn't you tell me?"

"He was your friend—"

"You're my wife." Royce cupped a hand around her cheek, making her look him in the eye as he spoke.

Selina paused for a while, still crying but also studying his face. "Elinor wasn't wrong."

"What?"

"Never once have you deceived me. In all your games and manipulations, you have always told me the truth of your intentions. You have my money; my usefulness has run out—"

"It's not about the money."

Selina almost hissed and picked up the gun, removing it from his reach. "Yes it is. That's what all of this was about! And now there's no one left with which to split your profits. We've destroyed them all."

Royce's voice was surprisingly even and gentle. "Selina. Please....give me the gun."

"Are you afraid I'll kill you too? Look at me," she cried. Shaking her shoulders, she gestured to herself in dismay. "Look at what I've become."

"Selina...Abram deserved what came to him. You did nothing but protect yourself. I am...I am the reason you had to...and you did not kill Elinor. I did. I couldn't allow her to hurt you too. That wasn't your fault."

Selina attempted to compose herself by inhaling but she only choked up more. He stepped just a bit closer to her, strategically moving closer to the gun, but not yet reaching for it.

"Is that why you didn't tell Barratt?"

"I—I don't..." Selina caught herself. The truth alarmed her. Her issues of trust and principle were the thin but stubborn obstacle preventing her from loving him.

"You protected me from speculation. I've been suspected of murder once, why not again? Why protect the villain who's taken....everything?"

"I don't—I just....I don't know."

"You have no reason to trust me, Selina. I have no expectations, no hope of....of reciprocation..." Royce stopped himself from continuing and shook his head. "And it doesn't matter. What matters," he smoothly reached for the gun, maintaining eye contact with her and slowing his verbal pace, "is that I prove to you that, while I may be driven by greed, I'm not the sort of man who lets harm befall his wife, no matter my ulterior motivations."

Selina exhaled, light tears falling from her eyes. She doesn't look convinced, more like surrendering. "I don't know what all you intended."

"Neither do I. But it certainly wasn't this."

Selina's lip quivered again as she looked away from him, and so he set the gun down on the table and gently pulled her in, allowing her to cry into his shoulder.

4
From the Mouths of Babes

That next morning, before setting out for the orphanage errand with Lady Selina, Barratt woke up to find a message had been left for him at the inn where he had been staying. It was another letter, another sin—completely expected considering Elinor's death. It bore the number 4, and inside, they had apparently arrived at the sin known as *ENVY*.

Barratt chuckled in spite of himself.

The innkeeper looked at him strangely. "Something funny, sir?"

"We seem to be getting closer, good man."

"Closer to what?"

"The end." Barratt tucked the letter in his pocket while the innkeeper frowned in confusion. "Which means my time is running short."

The second he walked into the police station and toward Constable Marley, he waved the letter in the air.

Marley sighed and his shoulders sank, appropriately contrasting Barratt's apparently entertained demeanor. "Another one? Does that make four now?"

"Elinor Abram died last night."

"Good heavens," Marley gasped.

"At the hands of Lady Selina Royce."

The constable stared blankly for a moment in shock. "And you've not arrested her."

Barratt laughed to himself. "Please. Arrest the Lady Selina and over half the county would be up in arms—not to mention, the better part of London. Besides, it was self defense, she claims."

"You doubt her?"

"Do I doubt Miss Abram accosted her? No. Elinor was desperate. I have no doubt there was a confrontation of sorts. Do I doubt that the elegant, demure Lady Selina clubbed a woman in the side of the head….it's difficult to say. Miss Abram was unarmed, and Mr. Royce was in the room…"

"You think Royce could've done it. Seems likely."

Barratt brushed this off. "It doesn't really matter."

"Doesn't it?" Marley squinted, cocking his head to one side.

"The important thing to note is that Miss Abram is dead. Envy, along with Wrath, Lechery, and the Sloth are all dead. Now we await Pride, Greed, and Gluttony."

"But how could it have all been done by one man?"

"Not one man. One puppet-master. We're not dealing with a serial murderer—each one appears to be an isolated incident, solely connected by these letters. Which suggests the writer of the letters is involved in the inner dealings of Everdon, one way or another."

"Do you think the dead maid is connected at all?"

Barratt brushed it off, this time with a wave of his hand. "No, no, no. There's no letter for her. All of this started after her death. The most likely candidate was in London at the time."

"And who might that be?"

Barratt grinned and the young desk clerk hurried into the room.

The clerk meekly interrupted. "Um, sir? Lady Selina and Mr. Royce are here to meet with you."

Barratt frowned. "Mr. Royce?"

"Yes, sir."

Barratt went to the small lobby to greet them, squinting at his friend in confusion. "Lady Selina, thank you for coming. Mr. Royce, I didn't expect you to join us this morning."

Royce smiled at him. "It felt appropriate my wife not embark on such a delicate outing alone."

"Of course. Considering the events of last night, I can understand why you'd want to....keep her close." Barratt looked at him suspiciously, not sympathetically. "Shall we?"

The three set off for the hospital, where all the children — healthy and injured both — were housed. Children ran freely around the building, the little ones being chased by nurses. Most took notice of Selina's arrival instantly and greeted her with hugs. Suddenly Barratt witnessed a previously foreign side of the Lady Selina. She was smiling, laughing, hugging, wiping the occasional dirt of a child's face. When he glanced at Royce he noticed a smile on his face as he watched her.

Barratt muttered to Royce. "I would have never suspected a woman so aloof and proper as Selina could be so....warmly maternal."

Royce watched his wife with such admiration, his smile would not fade. "It's more poetic that way; discreet compassion has its own allure," he replied. "She'd give them her own supper to keep them from starving."

Barratt mumbled softer. "S'pose she's not Pride, then."

"What was that?"

"We should speak to the older children first, if Lady Selina is finished entertaining the younglings."

Royce tapped Selina's elbow, prompting her to stand. "The inspector would like to speak to the older children."

"Of course." Selina nodded.

Barratt immediately headed for the child he talked to briefly last time. He's about 12-13 years old and clearly had an understood authority over the other children. All the children listened to him as he walked past them to his bed.

"Ollie," Selina called for him.

Ollie grinned at the sight of her. "Lady Selina."

"Inspector Barratt has a couple of questions for you...about Mr. Abram..."

Ollie's eyes widened, but settled on the familiar face.

Barratt moved straight to the point. "I'd like to know how many times Abram had been to the orphanage."

"Just the once." Ollie side-glanced at Selina, but then steadied his breathing and looked directly at Barratt. "He didn't seem like a man who was interested in spending time with orphans, sir."

"Did he come alone?"

"Yes."

"Did he meet anyone there? Or....follow someone?" Barratt sensed Royce stiffen.

"No, sir."

"Did he and Mr. Litchfield have a disagreement?"

Ollie shrugged. "Hard to know, sir."

"Did he seem like he intended to harm anyone?"

Ollie glanced again at Selina. "I didn't really talk to him, sir. Don't know who he'd come to harm."

Barratt sighed. "Had you ever met Miss Josephine Rodin?"

Royce's eyebrows wrinkled and he frowned, failing to see the relevance.

Ollie calmly and deliberately frowned. "Who's Miss Rodin?"

"Lady Selina's former maid." Barratt pointed to Selina, who also stared in confusion. "Did she ever visit the orphanage with Lady Selina?"

Ollie, still frowning, slowly shook his head. "Lady Selina only ever brought Miss Penelope."

Barratt sighed again, forcing patience. "Do you know how often Mr. Litchfield went to Everdon? Or when he would've encountered Miss Rodin?"

Selina cut off Ollie's half-hearted answer by putting a hand on the boy's shoulder. "Ollie's a little confused, Inspector. I did bring Miss Rodin to the orphanage. Remember? She was the girl with the lighter, sand-colored hair."

Ollie looked at her a moment and then eased his shoulders, taking the cue. "Oh yes, I remember."

Barratt smiled a little. "Who did she often interact with at the orphanage?"

"Well…" Ollie noticed Selina's eyes tighten with concern, as if she just realized something. "Lady Selina, of course. Some of the children. Litchfield was hardly there."

"Who was there, then?"

"Ollie was often left in charge in Litchfield's absence."

Ollie nodded after she said this, again, as if taking a cue. "Yes, I was."

Barratt leaned back a little, looking from Selina to Royce. "It seems Litchfield was terribly slothful in his duties." He eyed Royce's reaction to the word usage, only to be disappointed.

Instead, Selina was the one to react. "That particular word couldn't be more accurate."

Barratt looked back at her, curiously, and then rose.

Ollie softly asked, "Will you have lunch with us, Lady Selina?"

"Of course." Selina offered her hand and had him lead her to where the nurses had wheeled in some food for the kids.

"The children are remarkably well-coached."

Royce shrugged. "You wanted Selina's help."

"Indeed." Barratt tucked his notebook in his coat pocket, accepting the lack of progress.

"What makes you think Josephine Rodin's death had anything to do with the orphanage?"

Barratt grinned at Royce's curiosity, but was sure to only tease. "One or two anonymous tips I've received throughout recent events."

"These tips suggest they're all connected?"

"In a sense," the inspector shrugged one supposing shoulder, satisfied with Royce's frustration.

"How many?"

"Four. So far."

"Kincaid was ruled an accident," Royce began to contemplate Barratt's alleged cases. "Litchfield confessed to killing Abram, and burning down the orphanage. And Miss Rodin took her own life."

"No, no," Barratt shook a hand in the air. "Miss Rodin is unrelated. The fourth was Miss Abram's unfortunate demise."

Royce looked at him strangely and frowned. "I think someone is toying with you."

"Oh, most certainly," the inspector chuckled. "In any case, they've chosen a fascinating target around which to center this game of theirs."

In unison, they both sets of eyes moved toward Selina, who'd finished helping distribute lunches. She felt the attention from a distance and felt compelled to return to the conversation at hand.

"It seems the conclusion is unanimous, my lady," Barratt told her. "Mr. Litchfield killed Mr. Abram and set the orphanage ablaze. The children are better off because of it, I think. As, I hope, you are as well."

Barratt bowed to Selina and flashed Royce a knowing glance before taking his leave.

December 1889

Cynicism is intellectual dandyism
~George Meredith~

1

Diminishing Returns

With the impending holiday season, Rafferty thought it best to host his annual Christmas gathering before the Royces were expected to visit Lady Philippa's estate for the season. Inclusive as Rafferty was, he found it in his heart to invite the Honorable George Kincaid, despite his known coldness in the county's society. His attempts to ingratiate himself into the society surrounding his newly inherited estate had not been as productive as he'd hoped. His hopes were high that he would maintain an ally in Lady Selina, as did all the county.

As guests continued to arrive at the Rafferty home, Kincaid kept his distance from Selina, waiting for the opportune time to circle his social prey. Initially, she entered holding her husband's hand; if previous gatherings were any indication, Kincaid assumed he would have to navigate Royce's presence for the entirety of the evening as well. It was no matter, he thought. Royce was an interesting enough fellow.

What he failed to notice, however, was the limpness of Selina's grip. But Royce felt it. There was no leaning as there was before. She allowed him to hold her hand. She allowed him to lightly kiss her cheek as he sat her on the sofa. The smile plastered on her face was forced. Her demeanor was bland. While there was a lack of bitterness, there was also a lack of the luster he had so briefly seen in her. Deciding it best to grant her some space, Royce finally left her side, seeking out conversation with Lennox instead.

As the youth and children eagerly gathered around the table to play a friendly game of snapdragon, Selina abandoned her place on the couch to join Kincaid on the sidelines. Lanterns were dimmed, raisins were brought to the table by a young serving girl, and Rafferty granted his eldest son a bottle of brandy to light the raisins aflame.

George Kincaid chuckled at Rafferty's hesitant participation, but his eyes soon wandered from the game before them. "Sweeting seems a good man."

Selina nodded and smiled. "He's a very good man. Warm, generous, but a terrible business partner. I don't advise it."

"Noted. And what of Rafferty?"

"There have been stupider men. He's incredibly decent and mindful. He approaches money as he does women—with tender eagerness."

Kincaid noted this, now seeing Sophie and Rafferty exchange affectionate glances. "Don't you think it's a little soon?"

"Soon for what?"

"Henry had only just proposed," Kincaid whispered. "He sent word to us of his engagement not a month before he died."

"George, if you couldn't be bothered to respond to his announcement, you have no right to criticize the poor girl's ability to move on."

"Even so—"

He caught her warning expression, as if she'd readily scold him if he continued to insult Miss Campbell. He then paused, suddenly aware of the exhaustion he'd noticed in Selina's eyes. The children suddenly screamed gleefully because Penelope impressed them by holding the flaming raisin in her mouth the longest. The adults applauded, hardly paying much attention.

Kincaid then softened his tone. "Have you been well, Selina? Considering..."

"I've been just fine, George, thank you."

"That Royce is taking good care of you then?"

Selina glanced over at Royce, who happened to glance her way as well, bringing a smile to his face.

"He seems to be the good sort," Kincaid decided. "Cares about you a great deal."

She smirked lightly. "He's taken excellent care of Everdon."

"And what of its Lady?"

"He's doing his best. Any word from Francesca? I noticed she failed to attend her nephew's funeral."

Kincaid smirked this time. "Ah, you wish to avoid discussing your marital troubles. I can respect that, Selina. Only know that you're not entirely alone outside of Everdon. There's not a soul in the county that wouldn't kill for you."

Selina sipped her drink. "Well, I thank you. But I don't wish anyone to be killed. I only wish to have a merry Christmas and see to the end of the year."

"Cheers to that."

Royce's company was becoming just as sought after as his wife's. When Royce was finally not trapped into talking to someone, Lindon also approached him. "Would you care for a friendly game of chess, Mr. Royce?"

"Oh, I'm not quite—"

Lindon guided him to the chess table on the other end of the room while the bulk of the party moved on to another game. Royce sighed. He'd never played a game of chess in his life, but Lindon paid no mind and set up the board in any case.

"Such exquisite pieces." Lindon held up and admired the handcrafted set Rafferty owned.

"Rafferty doesn't skimp on quality."

"And such a regal game, too."

"Indeed."

Lindon moved his first pawn. "Your move."

Royce selected a pawn and mimicked Lindon's move. As the game continued, he carefully watched Lindon's face to gage where he could and couldn't move his pieces. Royce was a quick learner so he only seemed like a clumsy novice within the first few moves. When Lindon captured Royce's first piece, Lindon chuckled. The rest of the party began gathering around the piano while Sophie played Christmas hymns and Penelope and Henrietta sang.

"I used to play with Lord Edward Delamere. Do you know what he called this?" Lindon gestured to where Royce's captured piece now sat.

"The dungeon?"

"The cage. A dungeon prevents the captured from viewing the rest of the battle. But a cage…a cage is a subtle form of torture. The prisoner can view every move the enemy continues to make, watching each and every one of their comrades fall as they have."

"That's a rather dark view of chess."

"Yes, well, Edward was a peculiar man."

"And a sore loser, I imagine."

"Probably. But he never lost."

Royce studied Lindon's face and smiled. "I'm sure you saw to that."

Lindon chuckled again, still studying the board and moving pieces strategically. "My job at Everdon has always been to see to it that the reigning Delamere never loses. If a business failed, I softened the blow by allocating the appropriate safety net. If a knee was scraped, I tended to the wound. If baby was lost….I found them." He looked up at Royce directly. "Not a single piece was put in a cage on my watch….until a rather mischievous wordsmith galavanted his way onto the estate."

Royce almost smirked, but instead pressed his fist against his mouth thoughtfully, allowing Lindon to continue.

Lindon mumbled, so really only Royce can hear him. "Coercion, abuse—how was I to protect her from that?" His tone became a little clearer. "I should've expected her to be strong enough to take matters into her own hands…I only wish it hadn't been quite so damaging."

Royce leaned back in his chair. "Take matters into her own

hands." The two stared at each other for a moment until Royce sighed. His voice was now the muttered. "You knew about Abram. How?"

"You confirmed it just now. I suspected. I know the lecherous sort when I see them—Everdon seemed to attract them. The way he looked at her...I hoped when she found your pistol she'd keep it with her if she could. It seems I was right."

Royce paused with a pained expression. "She believes I've offed my accomplices for a greater portion of the profit."

Lindon saw how Royce was gazing over at Selina. "That's not why they're gone."

Royce looked back at him curiously.

Lindon just smiled and glanced again at Selina. "It was inevitable, I suppose."

"What do you mean?"

"Selina is a woman of many secrets, but one of them you both share."

"Do we?"

"Hers is hidden behind a sharp tongue and pompous demure, while yours is hidden behind your words and stories. You're a swindler, Royce, but you are first and foremost a writer. And writers are, by nature, desperate romantics."

Royce gave a small smile, acknowledging the truth of the statement.

"Understandably, she sees things differently."

Lindon was about to win the game, but he stopped and looked up at Royce. His tone softened. "I must know one thing."

"Of course."

"How did you know? About Selina?"

Royce sighed and took the blackmail letter out of his jacket. He didn't trust it in that desk drawer it was in before anymore—if Elinor found it, and broke through the lock, someone else could too. Lindon took the letter and opened it, angling away from the party. Even though they were some distance from the group, he didn't want to risk prying eyes.

The more Lindon read, however, the deeper he frowned and then mumbled. "I don't understand. And you never showed this to Selina?"

"She never asked for proof."

"It wouldn't have mattered to her. The idea of it was frightening enough. She wouldn't risk her livelihood—particularly Penelope's—even with a forged letter."

"Forged? How?"

"One glance at this and she'd have known it was not in her father's hand, nor mine."

Penelope approached the chess table, almost whispering. "Royce, Hettie let me have some of her sweets. Could you put it in your pocket before Selina sees?"

Royce took a second to look away from Lindon and address Penelope.

"What is that?" Lindon chuckled.

Penelope whispered. "Licorice. She bought them just yesterday."

Royce took them and put them in his pocket. "Selina won't be happy with me."

"Yes, well, I can't have her unhappy with me. She can get so cross with me sometimes. She'll forgive you much faster."

Royce smirked with doubt and he and Lindon chuckled a little.

Penelope nudged Royce's arm. "Now, I'm pretending to ask you to tell everyone a story, but I really would love that—so would you tell all of us a story. Have you finished the highwayman story?"

"I haven't quite figured out the ending yet."

"I can help you. The highwayman falls in love with the princess and together they become a lovely thieving team."

"Ah, there it is. Excellent." Royce stood to humor her and tell everyone a story.

"Actually, would you tell us the one about the goblin's market instead? You can work on a better ending for your highwayman."

349

"Whatever you wish, Nell." He and Lindon exchanged glances of understanding, at least reaching a mutual respect.

2
The Favorite

The only reason Lady Philippa cared for Christmas and its various festivities was that it brought the visit of Selina and Penelope. She frequently visited them throughout the year at Everdon, but she could never truly spoil them to her heart's content until they finally resided under her roof. Bridgestone, her family estate, welcomed the arrival of the girls each year, with an overabundance of decorations and gifts which made it inconvenient to walk through rooms.

"You didn't have to, Aunt," Selina always modestly assured her.

"Yes I did." Philippa patted Selina's cheek. "Now put on a smile or I'll send you back."

Selina genuinely obeyed, repaying her aunt with a tired, but sincere grin.

"And your gift is the presence of my company, Royce," Philippa moved past Selina to pat his cheek as well. "In addition to a new suit and boots, I suppose. One must always have at least one gift to open on Christmas."

"You're too kind." Royce chuckled, kissing her cheek in gratitude.

They suddenly heard children running upstairs, clattering loudly as they did so. To answer the unasked question, Philippa rolled her eyes and feigned annoyance. "I have a new housekeeper. And she has children, apparently."

"Oh, you love it," Selina nudged her and chuckled.

"I confess, I do miss the sound of children. They're far more entertaining around the holidays than you adults," she gestured to Selina and Royce. "And as long as they don't destroy my fine china and furniture, I suppose they'll do."

Penelope headed for the drawing room where she assumed her gifts were being stored. "What gifts do you have for me, aunt?"

Philippa moved her cane to stop her, scolding her with a light slap on the hand. "You must wait for Christmas Day, child." Penelope pouted for a moment, but conceded. "Now, go and get settled."

Obediently following Selina's signal, Helen trailed behind as the group moved upstairs to settle into the guest bedrooms. It didn't take long for Helen to realize there was only one room arranged for the couple. Helen hesitated at the new format, but tried to smile at the housekeeper as she was directed.

Royce pointed to the room. "You can set her luggage there, Miss Thomas."

"Of course, sir."

Selina, lagging behind just a bit, finally caught up to them and took notice of the sleeping arrangements.

Royce mumbled to Selina as she approached, "I can ask Lady Philippa for another room."

"No, no, that's not necessary."

Helen awkwardly began setting out Selina's clothes, pretending to be as invisible as was possible.

"Are you certain?" Royce questioned softly. "If you'd be more comfortable—"

"Yes," Selina snapped. "We're married. It's to be expected. I hardly sleep anyway. Aunt Philippa said she'd have tea ready for us." The lady then turned on her heel and returned downstairs.

The friction, and the defeat it brought to Royce's demeanor, did not escape Helen. In a weak attempt at comfort, she finally spoke.

"Have you finished your story, sir?"

Royce straightened his back, suddenly remembering she was there. "No, not yet."

"Perhaps that's what she needs."

He wrinkled his brow. "Selina?"

"Well, all that's been told of the highwayman so far is that he meant to rob the lady's mansion of all valuables. We haven't learned why he stayed. All the misfortune and horror—I don't know about the Lady Selina, but I'd sleep better knowing if there was hope at the end."

Royce stared thoughtfully for a moment, in no direction in particular. "How's your own story coming?"

"I think Lady Selina has more hope in it than I do. I still can't make sense of it. The format, the symbolism…"

"There's something to be said for simplicity as well, Miss Thomas. If it's unclear to you, it will be just as unclear to the rest of us. Try focusing on what you do know, and put aside what you don't." Royce nodded his head respectfully before leaving the room.

After tea, the housekeeper's children, who immediately took a shine to Selina, begged to go tobogganing on the hills in the back of the Bridgestone estate. Penelope and Helen quickly agreed, and so the remaining adults conceded. Penelope and Helen helped the younger children master the art of tobogganing, and after a couple attempts, they were all laughing and screaming and carrying on.

Royce joined them as well. The scared younger children were easily given courage by his impromptu character—a goblin, at Penelope's request—playfully put on an amusing voice, causing the children to giggle distractedly before being pushed down the hill. Screams and giggles repeated themselves as they each climbed up the hill, ready for more.

"What is that supposed to be?" Selina called out to the group.

Penelope shouted back. "He's a goblin—like in that market story with the two sisters and the sweets. Do you remember?"

Selina waved her off and let her play.

"My, he's as ridiculous as the children," Philippa clicked her tongue, pretending she didn't have the urge to laugh.

Selina smiled at the funny voices and animated expressions. "He is."

"Go, get on a toboggan, Selina."

"Oh no, I'm fine watching," Selina waved again, dismissively.

"No, child, you're not. Get out there and slide down that hill."

Selina looked at her stubbornly, but Philippa had a maternally threatening glare that Selina was never one to question. And so she stood. "Very well."

She walked over just as Royce pulled his toboggan to the top of the hill. He saw Selina joining them and looked pleasantly surprised. Philippa saw Selina gesture to her, assigning blame, and then Selina boarded the toboggan with Royce. To Philippa's delight, the two went down the hill twice together—both times, Selina laughed and smiled like she was a child again, which brought an even wider smile to Philippa's face. Finally, when the children noticed that Selina was joining the fun, they fought to have her on their toboggans as well. So Royce retreated to the top of the hill to stand next to Philippa's chair, and ended up sitting in the snow.

Royce smiled while he watched Selina. "I don't think I've heard her laugh like that."

Philippa's voice grew reminiscent. "She was raised well to be a responsible and loving caregiver. Poor girl was never a child. And Penelope gets to be forever a child. Neither seems fair...I pity the both of them. That fever nearly killed them both."

"Fever?"

"Penelope was gravely ill as a young child—almost a month, she was bedridden. It's the first vivid memory I have of Selina. When Penelope came out of it, with her mind in the state it was in....I saw the childhood drain out of Selina's eyes. No child should become a governess for her own cousin. It's never really changed over the years either, that." Philippa waved toward where Selina now helped

Penelope up from a nasty crash of the sled. "When her parents died, it
only became more....official rather than obligatory. Christmas is the
only season I've managed to tear her away from that and remember her
youth just a bit. It's what little girls need most—to play in the fresh air,
get mud-stains on their hems, run around until they're red in the face. I
always thought she'd have been better off running away from home.
And if her father hadn't stopped her, she would've been freed from all
this."

"With the Austrian prince?"

Philippa smiled proudly, which made Royce smile.
"Delameres have never shied away from scandal or rumors. The less
people truly know and the more they speculate, the more power and
intrigue you possess. Her father never saw things that way. Edward
and Angelica were an odd couple—preferred to remain as decent and
tastefully forthright as possible. Incredibly boring and not at all fun."
She clicked her tongue. "Sometimes I question that girl's genetics." She
pointed to Selina again. "She was always so unlike them. She has a
wild streak, that one. Always been my favorite."

"Mine too."

Philippa gave him a sly glance and smiled at the way the
charming man gazed.

Selina came to the room late that night, as Royce rinsed his
face in the bowl on the vanity in his corner of the room. Under her
arm, she carried a book, prepared to turn in for the night.

Royce glanced up at her. "I wondered where you'd gone."

Selina held up the book she chose. "The library here is not
nearly as organized as mine. And their librarian is no Croft. It took
time to find a good one."

Selina began to change into her night clothes Helen had laid
out for her—she had sent Helen to bed, as she had long drained her
energy with all of the day's tobogganing. Royce and Selina both sat on
their sides of the bed, comfortably settled.

As Selina started to crack open her story of choice, she pursed her lips in thought. "You seemed to speak to Aunt Philippa quite a bit today. And Lindon, before we left Everdon."

"People enjoy speaking with me. I'm told I'm a winning conversationalist." He teased. Selina paused and looked at him suspiciously. So he stopped the wide smiling and sobered a little. "I gave him the letter."

"Why would you do that?"

"Because I trust him."

Selina eyes widened in surprise as he spoke.

"It's information worth protecting," he went on. "Who better than Lindon to keep safe the secrets of Everdon?"

She stared a moment, dazed, but opened her book as if moving past it. From the corner of her eye, she noticed him retrieving his pistol from its box. "You brought that with you?"

"Yes, of course."

"Are you expecting more Abrams sneaking around?"

Royce chuckled, inspecting and wiping the gun as necessary. "There are monsters worse than the Abrams."

She lifted her eyebrows as he put the gun in the drawer of the bed stand beside him.

"And I won't be letting them get to you." Royce kissed her head. "Good night, Selina."

He blew out the candle next to him and rolled over to go to bed, leaving Selina with just her bedside candle, staring at the book page in pleasant confusion.

3
The Same Hand

In the week they remained at Aunt Philippa's, Selina slept better than she ever had before. Whether it was the loving atmosphere which her aunt provided, or that she was now lying beside a man who was finally in Lindon's confidence, or there was a weapon within reach she had regrettably become familiar with using. Whatever the reason, her energy upon her return was refreshed. There was an easy smile on her face as she beamed through the doors of Everdon, which did not go unnoticed by Lindon and Croft as they greeted her.

Croft stopped her in the hall while everyone else settled into unpacking from the long journey. "Good to see you in such high spirits, my lady. We've had several deliveries from London in your absence — gifts from publishing houses, all fresh prints for you to read."

"Oh, lovely." Croft smiled and started to follow him to the library.

Lindon stopped her with a tied bundle of letters. "These came for you as well."

Selina grabbed and fingered through the letters, attempting to read the sloppily scribbled words.

"The orphanage has been fully functional for the holidays," Lindon explained. "The children wanted to thank you both."

Selina smiled as she read a few of them. "I think they mean to thank Royce."

"Then you'd better pass on their gratitude," he suggested, rubbing her arm as he passed her.

Selina redirected away from the library, instead starting for Royce's room upstairs. When she let herself in, she saw Price standing near suitcases that laid open on the bed. He was mildly confused, but obediently at work. It took a moment for Selina to realize the source of Price's confusion: he was not unpacking Royce's luggage from the holiday trip—he was adding fresh clothes to a different empty case as Royce handed him more provisions to include.

"Um, the children sent you thank-you letters..." she started before giving up on guesswork, "What's this?"

Price raised his eyebrows, sensing a conversation he didn't care to hear. "Excuse me, sir. I'll just take these." He grabbed the dirty clothes and left the room to clean them.

"You're...you're leaving."

Royce remained focused on packing, not even glancing up as she entered the room. "Yes...it's...I think it's best I let the queen rule her kingdom again."

"I don't..."

"I'm going to Beechbury. Check on things there. See if I can settle into city life again. I've been out here too long, I think I've almost forgotten what it's like to thrive in a big city."

Selina watched him pack and cleared emotion out of her throat. "How-how long will you be gone?"

Royce shrugged, still not looking up. "A few weeks, at least. Perhaps a month or two."

"Two months?" Selina's voice broke.

This time he looked up at her.

She cleared her throat again. "I'd expected longer. London is filled with parties, plays, parlors...and friends. Who'd want to come back after that? Far more opportunities to spend your mounds of money than out here."

She straightened her back to feign indifference, but it was too late—he had already seen the fleeting expression of grief in her visage.

He sighed, pulling the cheque book from his pocket and placed it gently in her hands.

"What's this?" she stared blankly.

"The upper hand."

Royce kissed her forehead affectionately before closing his suitcase and leaving the room. On his way down the stairs, he passed Price once again. "Fetch me a carriage, Price. I'm ready—no need to attend to me."

Price frowned in uncertainty. "Are you quite sure, sir? You said you'd be gone for months, and the Beechbury staff are not as particular—"

"I'll be fine."

"But sir—"

Lindon approached them. "What's happening here?" he gestured to the bags in Royce's hands and the quizzical expression on Price's face. "Is there a problem?"

"I'll be going to Beechbury, Lindon. *Alone*." Royce emphasized to Price.

Lindon joined Price in his uncertain frown. "You've only just returned."

"Yes, that's right," Royce sighed, moving past the gentlemen, working his way closer to the front door.

"It's all right, Price," Lindon finally dismissed him. "Get back to your chores."

Price eyed both of them hesitantly. "Yes, sir."

When Price was out of earshot, Lindon then turned back to Royce with a more secretive tone this time. "Are you certain this is the best decision?"

"I am. You and I both know Selina's not well."

Lindon considered this but then shook his head. "She seems just fine to me since the holidays."

"And she'll continue to improve in my absence," he decided.

Lindon raised a doubtful brow, unconvinced. "You think she'll get worse?"

"I chose her, Lindon," he abruptly turned to the steward, his face inches from Lindon's. "She didn't choose me. I chose her. And if all of this has happened because…" He couldn't bring himself to recount his sins, so instead he swallowed hard and shook his head. "I could never forgive myself."

When Selina and Penelope suddenly descended from the staircase, Penelope landed right next to Royce, insistently tugging at his arm. "Royce, you can't leave without me! I haven't been to Beechbury since the spring—you must take me with you."

Lindon caught sight of the cheque book clutched in Selina's hands, and he smiled with a sudden idea. "Yes, I think he should take you with him," he nodded.

Royce glared at Lindon with quiet exasperation.

"Both of them? So soon after returning to Everdon?" Selina crossed her arms in front of her chest, hugging the cheque book.

"She's missed quite a bit of her usual socializing, Selina," Lindon advised. "I think the change of scenery would do her some good."

Lindon gave her a reassuring wink and gestured to a passing maid to see that Penelope's bags were repacked as well. Not long after Lindon's executive decision was made, Penelope's bags were packed and she'd redressed for travel, she eagerly took Royce's arm, ready to prance her way to the carriage.

Royce muttered to Lindon. "Take care of her."

Lindon winked. "Of course. We'll await your return, Mr. Royce." He then stood back with Selina and Price to watch as the party departed for Beechbury.

Selina mumbled as she watched her husband's carriage take him from her. "You were right, Lindon."

"Was I?"

"We have both ended up with the same hand."

January 1890

Of all acts of man repentance is the most divine. The greatest of all faults is to be conscious of none
~Thomas Carlyle~

1

The Lady Calls

After the New Year, the house was a little emptier, a little quieter, and for Selina, a little more restless. By the second night since Royce and Penelope's departure, the ghost of Everdon returned to haunt the halls in the night. Helen sighed in her bed as she heard Selina's footsteps pace the corridors; she missed the days in which she and her mistress both got some rest. When Selina was uneasy, the household was uneasy.

With little hope for sleep herself, Helen pulled her manuscript from her chest and decided to study the simpler parts of the plot. She remembered what Royce had said about focusing on the parts she did know, and putting aside what she did not.

Her difficulty resided in desperately seeking the unknown.

Such as the bird cage — *does the bird have a master? And what would happen if the master left the bird alone, with the cage open? Would the bird fly far away? Or would the bird step out of the cage and realize she missed the master?* No, she didn't like that. She preferred the bird getting herself out of the cage. It was far more victorious that way.

Now she feared she was overthinking. She would have dearly loved for the bird to simply tell her who caged her in the first place. It wouldn't be the person who walked away, leaving the cage ajar, she decided. No master of a bird would ever leave the cage open — they would keep it on a tight string for fear it would fly away.

So who trapped the bird? And then...who opened the door?

Croft found Selina in the library in the middle of the night
reading on the armchair in candlelight, ending one of her restless
midnight walks. She mindlessly sipped a glass of wine.

"And here we are again." Croft lit another candle.

"Did I wake you?"

"No, no, dear. I only got up for some tea." He showed her the
tea cup in his hand. "You seem lonely."

She lifted up her book. "Why would I be lonely?" Croft smiles
and she sighs. "I suppose I am, a bit. I'm accustomed to being alone,
but I've never...I've never felt like this before."

"Yes, Penelope's absence is highly unusual these days. It's
understandable we all feel a bit of emptiness."

Selina shrugged. "Her few years of boarding school
conditioned me to function without her here well enough."

Croft swallowed his sip of tea and hums. "Hm, you mean your
Mr. Royce then. Well, it appears he finally did the honorable thing and
granted you just a bit of peace. Feels appropriate, considering the
recent shadow he cast on Everdon."

Selina closed her book. "Everdon has a perpetual shadow, and
it has little to do with Royce. It only attracted him here. Some cages
seem quite appealing to arrogant animals who think they can conquer
it. And Royce is a very arrogant animal." Her tone carried hints of
admiration rather than bitterness.

Croft seemed a little troubled by this. "Hm."

"His arrival didn't darken the shadow— Josephine's death
did."

"So these recent misfortunes are your poor maid's fault, are
they?"

"None of this is her fault. Blaming her would be as silly as
blaming the curse of Everdon. Sometimes misfortune comes in morsels
—sometimes in hoards. Thus is life."

Croft good-naturedly lifted his cup. "Here's to an odd

assortment of misfortunes."

Selina lifted her wine glass and sipped. "The inspector believes they're all connected."

"Indeed he does. A man of his sort is always searching for patterns."

"Unless Josephine was killed by the same man who killed Henry, it's merely a terrible coincidence."

"You don't believe Miss Rodin took her own life, then."

She paused. "I knew Josephine. She was a young woman in love. She had no reason to want death. Someone did this to her— Barratt believes it was Henry, but I doubt that. He was wrathful, but hardly capable of killing a woman. And why would he? He barely knew her."

"The very wrathful don't need much provocation to lash out, Selina. I'm sure Inspector Barratt has weighed all the possibilities. I do wish he had taken my offer to read our copy of *The Murders of the Rue Morgue*. I think he would've discovered a very enlightening and intriguing lead."

Selina chuckled. "He hardly needs the encouragement. He only suspects Henry because he doesn't know of any other men in Josephine's life. I doubt he's even considered speaking with Mr. Bryant."

Croft raised an eyebrow and smiled. "Bryant. Litchfield's assistant? You don't say."

"I told you, she was a woman in love."

"I take it you didn't inform Inspector Barratt of this connection."

"He was determined to hunt for the father of her child amongst the nobles of the county. He needed only ask about the commoners and I would have told him." She sipped her wine, then paused, thoughtfully considering. "They were quite good together. He's not the murdering sort—he was practically beaming every time he saw her. Even after, I suspect, she found out she was carrying his child."

"Were you worried he'd fall under scrutiny?"

"Well, of course. You've met Inspector Barratt."

"You could protect him, as you did Mr. Royce."

Selina considered this as well. "I suppose you're right. Perhaps the information would help him solve Henry's murder as well."

"I thought Sir Henry's was ruled accidental? Did he not trip and fall?"

"Barratt hasn't closed a single case since he's arrived. I suspect he doubts Henry's death was an accident as much as I do."

Croft sipped his tea. "That certainly seems reasonable. The inspector appears to be a very thorough investigator. I don't envy his position."

Selina rose to leave, setting the book on the nearest desk.

"Finally turning in for the night?"

"Strategizing, dear Croft. In a few hours, I'll be calling on our thorough Inspector Barratt." Selina kissed Croft sweetly on the head. "Good night."

Croft smiled and lifted his tea cup to her in cheers again. "And good night to you, dear."

"And you felt the need to keep this information to yourself, why, my lady?"

The two of them sat in Barratt's office at the station, Selina poised for the challenge. "I'm sure you can understand my need for discretion. Never did I suspect the true father of her child killed her, nor was I willing to risk the exposure of his identity. However, I've decided, due to recent events, you might need just a little more assistance. And if Mr. Bryant becomes a suspect in your investigation, I will be providing legal representation for him. I want suspicion of Henry's guilt expunged—and the causes of both his and Miss Rodin's deaths re-evaluated."

Barratt almost chuckled. "I take it your husband has informed you of my suspicions."

"That all of these tragedies are somehow connected," her mouth shrugged at the notion.

"By you."

"I beg your pardon."

"Don't misunderstand, my lady. You are by no means a suspect. But I can guarantee you that every death over this last year has been connected. And you are the underlying factor."

"I fail to see how. Because I happen to live in this county and know those involved? Any number of residents here could fall under such suspicion."

"I said you were not a suspect, Lady Selina. And I meant it."

"Then what am I, exactly? A victim?"

"Hm, of sorts perhaps."

Selina lifted a brow. "I'm no one's victim, Inspector Barratt."

"Not in the traditional sense. I don't believe your life is in any sort of danger."

Selina was doubtful. "You don't believe?"

"I can assure you, Lady Selina, as soon as I know more valuable information, you will be the first informed."

Selina settled back into her seat, expectantly. "You seem to have informed Mr. Royce more than the woman around whom these things appear to occur. I don't believe you have substantial evidence to support this theory of yours."

"Your lady's maid is found dead in a river on your property. Your closest friend was killed after one of your own dinner parties. Mr. Abram, your guest, was shot and killed in your orphanage, which was then burned to the ground—also incidentally causing the death of the useless caretaker. Not two months later, Miss Abram allegedly attacks you and meets her end through your own act of self-defense. The word 'coincidence' cannot begin to account for all of these happenings, my lady."

"I'm certain I'm not the first to tell you that misfortune is a side effect of existence, Inspector," she offered.

Barratt studied her a moment. Her eyes were tight, as if afraid, but a smug expression properly feigned confidence. "Right, you are. This...new energy, my lady. Am I to assume you've been restored to full power now that your delinquent husband has abandoned his oppressive post? I imagine it must be quite freeing."

She smirked.

"Or perhaps more....peculiar?"

"Peculiar?" the smirk faded.

"The protector of Everdon has left the castle unguarded. Peculiar, for one so previously reluctant to let go of what he worked so hard to acquire."

Selina narrowed her eyes again as she stood to leave. "I expect to receive news as your investigation continues to unfold—regardless of my husband's presence at Everdon."

"As you wish, my lady."

She left him with a grin on his face and a fresh eagerness in his eye.

2

The Irresistible Charm of the Countryside

In Royce's absence, Lindon had thought it best to further investigate the puzzling origin of Royce's alleged source of blackmail. As he poured over old bookkeeping ledgers, sprawled on his desk in the library in no particular fashion, his face froze in perplexity.

"Everything all right, Mr. Lindon?" a concerned Croft hesitated to interrupt.

"Hm? Oh, yes. I just don't have a mind for numbers at the moment, apparently."

Croft chuckled while he shelved some books. Lindon pushed his chair further from the desk, lightly touching a locked drawer, to which only he held a key.

"Do you remember me ever leaving this drawer unlocked?"

Croft momentarily looked up. "The desk drawer? Not that I can recall. I don't know if I've ever seen it open, myself."

"Hm."

Croft paused. "Why do you ask? Is something wrong?"

"No, I suppose not. I can't understand....Mr. Royce spends a good deal of time in here, doesn't he?"

"As does the Lady Selina. I'm happy to say this is possibly the most favored room in Everdon."

Lindon opened the drawer and saw there were only financial papers—he never put anything related to the adoption or death of the previous baby in that library or anywhere at Everdon. He tightened his mouth. "Do you recall Mr. Royce ever mentioning association with any lawyers in London?"

Croft stopped what he was doing and slowly walked toward Lindon. "I'm not entirely certain what you're asking, but I have the stirring feeling you suspect something nefarious. Why would Mr. Royce be associated with lawyers?"

"Hm, he's always one to do his research before embarking on a project."

"Indeed. I believe he spent a few months on a ship while writing his latest work. That one with the naval captain."

Lindon muttered. "We should've gone to Winchester."

"What's troubling you, my friend?"

Lindon wrinkled his nose at the mild term of endearment, and remained pensively silent.

"Am I to believe you suspect our Mr. Royce of meaning Everdon harm?"

Lindon looked up at him. "You believe that?"

"You don't?"

"No. But that doesn't mean he once did. And he had help. I just can't wager a guess at who that might have been."

Croft's lip curled downward in distaste. "Well…the Abrams, surely."

"No, no, they were both too stupid to play a hand. Selina was untouchable to the likes of them."

"Hm, was."

"What does that mean?"

"You are not the only one who understands her, Lindon." Lindon shifted in his seat as Croft continued. "I've seen her decline as easily as you have. I saw Abram's wandering eyes….and hands. I saw the behavior of the presumptuous Miss Abram. They reached the untouchable Lady Selina, thanks to their good friend Darius Royce."

"You don't trust him."

"Do you?"

"I'm not entirely sure."

"Your instincts have always been accurate, Lindon. The day you trust him completely is the day my suspicions will yield."

"Selina's trust in him isn't enough?"

Croft's eyebrows wrinkled in concern. "Hm, perhaps I still see a child in her. A shrewd child, but not without naivete. Her trust in him waivers—I can see it—but I do believe she cares for him."

Lindon cleared throat. "He's her husband. I expect she does."

Croft smirked. "I suppose they're just a much more peculiar couple than the late Lord and Lady Delamere." He paused and then looked at Lindon with earnest eyes. "You would tell me….if Everdon was in danger….if Lady Selina was in danger….wouldn't you?"

Lindon stood and pushed the chair in. "I can assure you, Croft, there's no need to worry." He glanced out the window and saw Royce's carriage approach. "Well. Isn't this interesting…hardly lasted a fortnight."

Lindon exited the library and went to greet Royce and Penelope outside.

"Lindon! Look what Royce bought for me." Penelope slowly spun so Lindon could see her beautiful new coat.

"It's very lovely. Did you enjoy your time in London?"

"Oh yes, we saw a play nearly every night. And I was invited to a ball by one of Royce's friends," Penelope put on a grimace. "but Royce wouldn't let me go."

Lindon looked impressed at Royce, who just sighed with raised eyebrows—his friend was trouble and he had been protecting Penelope by actually parenting her. "I'm sure that was for the best."

Penelope pouted for a second, not getting sympathy from Lindon, but then shrugged. "I do love the coat. And our Beechbury cook, whatever her name was—"

"Maria." Royce answered for her.

Penelope kept going. "—has gotten much better at making

pastries. Oh, Mr. Croft, did you notice my new coat?" She walked past them to where Croft stood in the doorway after having followed Lindon outside

Lindon turned to Royce. "Such a short excursion."

"Well, it seems I'm no longer suited for city living."

"Yes, I imagine you missed the countryside...greatly."

"It has an irresistible charm." Royce glanced around, looking for Selina.

"Irresistible, yes. She's not at home."

"Hm?"

"That irresistible charm. She's out with Miss Thomas, getting some fresh air."

Royce sighed and adjusted his coat

"Who gave you the letter?"

"The letter? Oh...no one. I found it."

"You found it? Just lying around?"

Penelope ran past them. "Selina! Helen! You'll be ever so envious of my new coat."

Selina and Helen trekked up the path to the house, returning from their walk and pulling everyone's attention as Penelope called to them.

Royce lowered his voice to Lindon, still watching Selina. "It was in the book on my desk, the night before I was to leave Everdon." Lindon frowned.

As Selina and Helen neared, the Lady glanced curiously at her husband and his sudden arrival. Royce returned the expression as he took notice of the deepened bags under her eyes, and the way in which she leaned on Helen a little as they walked. The moment Helen stepped away to excitedly look at Penelope's coat, Selina swayed slightly until she gained more stable footing and approached Royce and Lindon. Meanwhile, Mrs. Melrose and Price hurried to their respective posts outside, upon noticing the carriage.

Selina gave a surprised smile. "You've returned."

"Penelope wanted to be home for her birthday," Royce

371

explained.

Penelope and Helen hurried back to Selina. "Royce thought celebrations here would be much more fun than Beechbury. What do you have planned?"

Selina stared at her a moment, almost as if she thought she just slept through a portion of the conversation. "Um, I had no idea you'd be back in time to celebrate at Everdon." Penelope looks temporarily disappointed. "But we've certainly planned a ball in shorter time, haven't we?"

Penelope smiled and embraced Selina. Selina hugged her back and kissed her head. While the love she expressed was genuine, onlookers only noticed the expression of exhausted resignation as she continued to cater to her ward's needs.

Mrs. Melrose approached and gently touched Penelope's arm. "Let's get you settled, Miss Ayres, and we can discuss planning the ball later."

"Of course, thank you. How were you while I was away?"

Melrose smiled maternally as she guided Nell to the house. "Oh I was quite alright, dear."

"Oh, Selina, I brought you a gift."

Selina smiled and nodded at Royce and Lindon. "Excuse me." She followed Nell to the house.

Helen started after Selina and Price mumbled to her as she passed, so she stopped.

Price spoke it in a low voice only Helen could hear. "She'll be the death of her, I'm sure of it." He moved to get Royce's bags from the carriage.

Royce turned back to Lindon. "You're right. I think I should've stayed in London a bit longer."

Lindon shook his head. "Don't be ridiculous. Didn't you see how pleased she was to see you?"

They both started walking to the house too.

"If I may, sir, Mr. Lindon is right." Both men pause and look at Helen trailing behind them, like they had forgotten she was there. "I don't think she's been able to sleep since you left, and I'm sure that's no coincidence."

Lindon looks at her in surprise. "She hasn't slept?"

"No, sir. She hasn't eaten much either. She's stubborn, pretending she's well and all that."

Lindon muttered and flashed Royce a concerned look. "As she does."

Later in the night, as the household slept, Helen's account of Selina's sleeping habits compelled Royce to catch a glimpse for himself. From the moment they'd returned from Beechbury, she'd been with Penelope, planning birthday celebrations. Helen had not exaggerated — Selina had not been sleeping.

Instead of sitting in her usual chair in the library, Royce found her outside on the back terrace. She held a book in her hand but she wasn't reading it—her eyes were on the stars. Beside her sat her usual glass of sherry and another glass filled with antacid Helen had fetched her for her stomach ache.

"And here I assumed Miss Thomas was prone to exaggeration." Royce startled her.

Selina's head snapped up at him, but she merely chuckled.

"She says you haven't been well."

Selina placed the book on the table next to her, gulped the antacid and stood up to face him. "I'm fine. Her concern is sweet, but unnecessary."

"Yes, she worries. As does Lindon. Perhaps if you slept through the night every now and again, they wouldn't have such concerns."

Selina sighed and took a few steps toward the garden, stopping near a rose bush before turning back to him. "I met with Inspector Barratt while you were away."

Royce grew a little anxious, walking toward her. "Did you?"

"He seems to believe all these…incidents are connected."

"Yes."

"And you agree with him."

"Of course. How could they not be?"

She studied his face a moment, not in suspicion, but for reassurance. "He doesn't....believe...that I'm in any danger."

Royce scoffed.

"You think otherwise?"

Royce stepped closer. "I know Barratt. When he digs, he never digs just a single hole. He'll explore multiple simultaneous avenues—there's no knowing what he might uncover in the process. He thinks he can solve anything, and his pride can be dangerous. He's clever enough, that if he gets too close....well, he wouldn't need an incriminating letter to bring down Everdon."

Selina's shoulders eased and she almost shrugged as she leaned against the statue next to the shrubbery. "Perhaps that's the intent." Royce frowned, she mumbled. "Would it really be so bad...?"

Royce took her hand. "You could never be so resigned."

"What would you do, if it all fell?"

"I would hope not all would fall."

"But, if it did. If all of this was taken away—if you were left penniless, stripped of all the wealth you've hoped for and worked to gain."

Royce paused. "Only you could take from me what I hope I've gained."

Selina looked at him strangely, not immediately understanding. Seeing her tired confusion, Royce leaned forward and tenderly kissed her.

"I've always longed for things, Selina.. But you're my first someone."

Selina smiled. "So that's why the highwayman stayed."

Royce pursed his lips and squared his shoulders. "It's never that simple. He stayed because there was more to be gained in the duration—a mansion is far more valuable than it's gold trinkets."

"So he left because the value ran short."

"One can only enjoy lavish luxury for so long."

Selina stopped leaning against the statue and stood straight, even taking a step closer. "But he came back."

He smiled. She moved toward him—not by coercion or obligation this time. This was what he had hoped for. "He did." He playfully scooped her up, as if intending to waltz. She even let out a surprised giggle when he grabbed her. "He realized the luxury he couldn't live without."

"Ridiculous," she muttered.

He grinned, swaying for a moment, to no music.

"Were there parties in London, then?"

"Hm, several. Music, dancing, and women."

"And you held them like this."

Royce pulled her in a little closer. "No, I never held them like this."

Selina started to smile wider, redness rising to her cheeks.

"Helen seems to think you missed me," he hummed in her ear.

Selina pulled her head back so she could look him in the eye while correcting him. "Liar. I didn't miss you for a single moment."

Royce smirked and she responded in kind. He tipped her chin slightly back to kiss her again.

"All right, then," she conceded before kissing him back. "Perhaps I missed you for all of them." Unlike previous intimacy, there was no air of obligation or social expectation. It was genuine, sincere, tender. A kiss worthy of a story's romantic leads crafted by Royce himself.

3

The Cost of Indulgence

Penelope's birthday was a two-day affair. It required a luncheon followed by ice skating on the lake to encompass the first day. Selina paced the celebrations over the course of the weekend, so as not to disrupt the staff too much with an immediate ball. The luncheon portion was simple — just food with guests who then all gathered outside at the lake on the property for ice skating, out of the house staff's way.

Nearly the whole county came to Penelope's ice skating celebration. Penelope wanted it to be grand, and so it was. Thankfully, the lake at Everdon was an ideal size for all those who chose to participate. However, the weather was unseasonably warm.

Selina didn't care for ice skating. As a child, she had once fallen into the frozen lake, and the fear of the water lingered. In fact, she was so anxious about it that she began standing by the edge of the lake, carefully watching Penelope.

Selina mumbled to Royce. "The weather's getting a bit warm."

Royce rubbed her hand, which rested on his arm. "The lake's been frozen long enough; it's perfectly safe."

Selina clutched her stomach lightly in pain.

Royce noticed and assumed it was due to her nerves. "It's all right, Selina. Here, we'll walk the perimeter if it'll put you at ease."

"I'm....I am at ease."

Royce looked at her doubtfully and started walking her
around the lake. Meanwhile, a few of the elder ladies of the county sat
on the sidelines, watching them walk away, before turning to one
another to exchange their usual gossip.

Mrs. Lennox started the whispering, as she usually did in
taking the lead. "Hm, Lady Selina seems afflicted."

"Afflicted?" Mrs. Sweeting was skeptical. She didn't often
encourage gossip but it inevitably happened around her, so she listened
in when the alleged truths were relevant to people she cared about.

"Mhm, afflicted with child, perhaps. Did you see the way she
held her stomach?"

Mrs. Fairfax chimed in. "She has seemed in poor health. I
remember being held up in bed for weeks when I was carrying
Stewart."

Suddenly haughty, straightening her back, Mrs. Lennox
turned up her nose. "They've been married for months, and at her age,
she ought to hurry it along."

Lindon considered this. It wasn't a ridiculous assumption.
According to Helen, Royce and Selina did well at Bridgestone—and
even shared a room. However, regardless of the lack of genetic
connection, he remembered that the late Lady Delamere got horribly
sick before each miscarriage. If Selina's other symptoms were any
indication of this, then he assumed she'd most likely lose the child.
Sarah Atwood herself had fallen ill during her pregnancy as well,
which weakened her enough to take her life during childbirth.

Mrs. Sweeting watched Selina with concern but gave a small,
maternal smile. "I certainly hope she's expecting. She'd be such a
loving mother—she's so good with those orphans in town."

"It would be a very attractive child, to say the least." Mrs.
Fairfax pointed. "Just look at them. Such a handsome couple."

Mrs. Lennox made an agreeable noise. "I wasn't so sure about
him at first, but I must say I agree with you. They're well-matched."

As Royce convinced Selina to go back to the house to rest,

Selina heard a light cracking and her eyes immediately snapped toward Penelope on the lake. Just as she expected, Penelope froze. She felt the ice cracking underneath her. Her eyes widened, her body tensed.

Lennox, who was skating with her just a bit ahead, stopped in his tracks and waved others away. "Miss Ayres, don't move."

Before Selina could react, Royce had moved to the edge of the lake. Within moments of silent panic, Penelope and Lennox were the only souls left on the lake.

Royce called out to her but with a very gentle tone. "Penelope, walk to me very slowly."

Penelope held eye contact with Royce. Royce nodded at Lennox, who made certain everyone had safely exited the lake. Penelope obediently took a couple of steps toward Royce.

"That's it. Just a bit closer."

Penelope suddenly froze again. The crack underneath her expanded. "I-I can't."

Royce took another couple of steps toward her instead. "Stay where you are—I'll get to you."

"No! No, no, don't. They're getting bigger."

"Look at me, just at me. I've got you." He reached his arms out. "Reach for my hands."

Penelope obeyed again and lunged forward, nearly jumping into Royce's arms. The cracks in the ice stretched to where Royce was standing, so he tossed Penelope onto shore while he slipped and fell on his back, into the cold water.

Crying and frightened, Penelope reached for Selina, who held her, but watched eagerly for Royce to get out of the water. She moved Penelope to the side a little, holding her hand but moving quickly to the edge of the lake. Royce pulled himself out of the water and sat on the shore, drenched. One of the servants fetched him a blanket to attempt to warm him.

"Oh Selina, that was the most terrifying—I nearly fell and froze to death!" Penelope tried to regain Selina's attention.

Lucky for Penelope, her friends hurried to her side and they were just as dramatic as she was, crowding around her and encouraging the attention. Royce was also collecting a crowd. Once Penelope was distracted by Henrietta, Selina rushed to Royce's side.

"Yes, yes, I'm all right." Royce's teeth chattered while Selina hugged him.

Selina stroked his face with condescending affection. "What was that you said about it being frozen long enough?"

They both laughed, but Royce's voice was strained by the cold.

Mary Kingston called out, "That was possibly the bravest thing I've ever seen, Mr. Royce."

"Oh no, it wasn't..." The frozen water had gotten the better of him before he could finish his humble thought.

"If Miss Ayres' love of sweets hadn't cracked the ice, we'd have never seen such a knight in shining armor."

Penelope scowled at her. Suddenly, her fawning friends weren't enough to appease her, so while Selina walked Royce up to the house, she hung on her guardian's arm—feeling a powerful need for maternal validation.

January 1890

February 1890

A ruffled mind makes a restless pillow
~Charlotte Bronte~

1

Nobody Likes a Fat Princess

The next evening marked the second and final day of Penelope's celebrations, as well as Penelope's favorite part: the ball. When guests began to funnel through the doors of Everdon, Helen noticed that the woman of honor was nowhere to be found. Discreetly, she assured Royce and Selina she would find her. And she did. The poor girl hid in the coat room, her knees propped up to hide her face.

Helen approached her gently, like she would a small animal. "Well, you can't very well enjoy a ball from behind all those coats, can you?"

Penelope lifted her head, her eyes puffy from the tears. "I changed my mind. I don't want a ball."

"All your guests have arrived, Miss Ayres."

"They saw me break the ice, all of them," she sobbed.

Helen understood now. She crouched down to her level. "You know, it was awfully warm out yesterday. Lady Selina worried about that ice. I don't think you had much to do with it."

"Why couldn't it have broken underneath Mary Kingston?"

Helen laughed. "That would've been funnier."

Penelope laughed a little as well. "Yes, it would have."

"I'm sure Mary Kingston doesn't have a line of gentlemen waiting to dance with her," Helen whispered, as if sharing exclusive gossip.

"She might."

Helen shook her head emphatically. "But it isn't her birthday ball."

Penelope sighed. "It isn't." She wiped her face. "Mustn't keep the gentlemen waiting. I just don't know if I have the energy."

"Would some candy from your stash be of any help?"

Penelope vehemently shook her head. "No, no. I'm going to be a fasting girl now. You know, the ones in the paper."

Helen frowned and wrinkled her nose. "A fasting girl? That doesn't sound at all appealing."

"I suppose you would think so. But nobody likes a fat princess." Penelope stood to compose herself before walking to the ballroom and taking Selina's arm, where she stood by Lindon and Royce.

Selina frowned. "Where've you been?"

"Getting ready," Penelope wiped her face and quickly bounded off after friends.

Selina made a pained expression as she watched Penelope prance away.

Lindon noted and wrinkled his brow in concern. "Are you well, Selina?"

"Yes, I'm fine. My head only aches. Oh, Sophie." Selina left the group to greet Sophie as she arrived, leaving Royce and Lindon.

"Has she been sleeping since your return, do you know?" Lindon mumbled to Royce.

Royce nodded. "She has. At least she's stayed resting in bed through the night. I've made sure of it."

Lindon raised his eyebrows, both surprised and impressed.

"She's even been eating more than she has been. I'm fairly certain she's found Penelope's well-hidden sweets stash."

Lindon chuckled. "Do you suppose she could be...?"

"What?"

"With child?"

Royce paused, his eyes widening a bit. "I don't...I don't

know," he stammered.

"If she is, be sure she takes care," Lindon's voice dropped with deep worry. "An ailing pregnancy took her mother."

Royce saw Selina touch her stomach again while she's talking to Sophie, and then lightly reach to rub her aching head.

He started moving toward her, now sharing in Lindon's concern. On his way to his wife's side, he passed Penelope looking distressed and heading for the hallway, despite Lennox's kind request for a dance.

Lennox shrugged helplessly. "I don't know what I could've said."

Royce glanced over at Mary Kingston and then patted Lennox on the shoulder. "Don't worry yourself, my friend. Young ladies aren't so simple." He then followed Penelope.

Penelope passed Croft on her way down the hall to the staircase.

"Miss Ayres—happy birthday to you."

She didn't answer, she just angled her face away from him and kept walking, hugging herself tightly in devastation.

Croft called after her again. "I say, Miss Ayres, are you all right?"

"I'm—I'm not feeling well. I want to go to bed."

Royce approached the pair as she answered. "Nell, come now. Lennox would like to have this next dance."

Penelope stifled her sob, but to no avail. "No."

Croft sighed. "She's unwell. She should rest. I do believe she seemed to have a stomach ache, the way she was walking, sir—perhaps a maid should fetch her a tonic."

Royce looked at him with a grimace. "Emotional abuse can have that effect."

"Hm, youth can be cruel, sir."

Before the ball had even seen its end, the police station in town received a message, a letter for Inspector Barratt. It bore the number 3, and the expected sin within: *GLUTTONY.*

"What's happening over at Everdon this evening?" Barratt simply shook his head.

Marley frowned in consideration. "I do believe it's Miss Ayres' birthday ball."

"Shall we give them another hour, then?"

Not more than an hour later, Barratt journeyed to Everdon. The ball was over and each room was being tidied and reset. The last of the guests had left, and being the good host he was, Royce lingered by the door to bid his farewells. He had sent Selina to bed early, as her energy had quickly waned throughout the evening.

"Ah, Mr. Royce—how were the festivities?"

"No one died, if that's what you're asking."

"And Miss Ayres? Did she enjoy herself?"

"She isn't dead either."

"I've received another tip and am here to do my due diligence. It doesn't always necessarily point to murder."

"History is against you, so you'll forgive me for doubting. Everyone is safe and sound."

"I'd only suggest you check on the young Miss Ayres before making such a claim."

Royce paused. "What's in your tip this time?"

"She simply seems the most likely candidate. Her inclination toward gluttony would make her a fairly easy target, were someone planning yet another nefarious act at Everdon."

"Gluttony."

Instead of responding with another question, Barratt stared at Royce for a moment with scrutiny. "Good night, Royce. Please give Lady Selina my best, and let her know I'm always at her service."

And then he left, as strangely and quickly as he had arrived.

2

Ask the Midwife

About a week passed since the ball, and there were no reports of unexpected deaths, much to Barratt's disappointment. The pensive inspector strolled aimlessly around the village, lost in thought, until he noticed the good-natured local physician, Doctor Davies, boarding a nearby carriage. Barratt overheard the driver confirm the destination of Everdon manner and he grinned hopefully.

"Everdon?" Barratt intruded.

Davies amiably glanced up at him and nodded. He was a very jolly man who bounced around with his medical bag in hand and a lilt in his step. "Yes—fourth day in a row, in fact. Checking on the young Miss Ayres."

Barratt smiled. "Do you mind if I accompany you? I was meaning to call on Everdon myself."

"But of course."

Both men boarded the carriage.

"Fourth day? How ill could this poor girl be?"

Davies shrugged. "Difficult to say. I've spent most of my visits in the parlor."

Barratt paused and frowned. "They call you to wait in the parlor."

"Yes. They see that I'm compensated, of course, but there's not been much healing done, I'm afraid. I haven't even seen the patient.

But the oddities of Everdon hardly surprise me any more."

"How long have you been the village physician?"

"Oh, decades. I remember when the miracle baby herself was born."

"Miracle baby?"

"The Lady Selina, of course. Poor child was grey and blue—not a breath in her. Midwife declared her stillborn. Within twenty-four hours, I checked in on Lady Delamere and, lo and behold, the infant made a full recovery! Miraculous." The good doctor shook his head in proud disbelief.

Barratt almost smiled, but stared thoughtfully out the window. "Miraculous indeed. What sort of explanation was offered, do you remember?

"Prayer and care, I'd say. If you ask the midwife—she's quite the religious woman, you know—she was praying loudly all through the delivery."

"Were you present during delivery then?"

"Lady Delamere was not in great health. I checked on her regularly before and during the pregnancy to tend to her. She was always a bit sickly—had a rather gloomy disposition and it weakened her stamina. As for the baby, I can only claim what the midwife told me. Apparently, she held the child for the whole of the night, weeping and praying and singing. Her tears and prayers must have given the child new life, if you believe in that sort of thing. Miraculous."

Barratt chuckled. Doctor Davies was so jolly and excitable. "Hm, yes, as you said. Miraculous. Is that midwife still alive, do you know?"

"Well, of course. She never left Everdon. She worked as Lady Delamere's lady's maid for over a decade, you know. Mrs. Melrose is now the head housekeeper, as I understand it."

Barratt leaned his head back against the carriage wall with that pensive smile on his face. It's all coming together. He's finally understanding what could make a woman like Selina crumble at the hands of a man like Royce.

When the two men arrived at Everdon, they were told to wait downstairs until Lady Selina could greet them.

"Doctor," Selina nodded in acknowledgment as he bowed, "and....Inspector. What a lovely surprise."

Barratt smiled and nodded. "I hope this isn't an intrusion. I only meant to call and check in on the state of things."

"Intrusion? It's practically become routine," Selina rolled her eyes as she turned to the staircase behind her. "Let me tell Penelope you're here, doctor."

Once the three ascended the staircase, Selina stopped outside Penelope's door. "Nell, Dr Davies is here."

Davies called through the door. "Good morning to you, Miss Ayres."

Penelope said sternly from behind the door. "No, I'm not well. He can't come in."

Davis sighed. "I can come back tomorrow, my lady."

Selina waved her hand at him. "Nonsense." She turned back to Penelope through the door. "As your guardian, your well-being is my responsibility. This became ridiculous two days ago, and I won't have it. I'll fetch Royce to help the good doctor hold you down while he administers the leeches."

Davies made a face. He whispered, "I haven't used leeches in years, my lady. I haven't any with me."

Selina touched a finger to her mouth to shush him. In seconds, Penelope opened the door with an urgent expression on her face. "Don't even think it."

Selina smiled. "Well good morning, Penelope. Can I come in?"

Penelope pouted. "You can. He can't."

Selina patted the doctor's arm. "Thank you so much for coming, Dr. Davies. Mr. Lindon will see that you're well paid for your troubles. Excuse me, gentlemen."

Selina left Barratt and Davies in the hallway. Davies chuckled and went to find Lindon. Selina shut the door behind her and looked at

Penelope, who sat on her bed, looking dejectedly at her hands.

"I haven't been ill."

"You don't say." Selina pulled her hands together in front of her.

"I....I don't want to be seen."

"Because of Miss Kingston."

"How did you know?"

She crossed the room and sat with Penelope on the bed. "Royce saw you leave your birthday ball. As it happens, he is a better guardian than I am."

"That's not true."

"But he was right. Miss Kingston's mockery went a bit too far this time."

Penelope's eyes welled. "I broke the ice. Anyone could have."

"That's true."

"She saw me eating at the ball....there were almond slices, and you know how much I adore those."

Selina put a reassuring hand on Nell's knee. "Almond slices are delicious, and Miss Kingston was wrong to mock you for enjoying them. But Nell....you're a woman now. You're not a child. Gorging yourself every moment you can is not how a woman behaves."

"So Mary Kingston was right. I'm getting quite large—"

"No, you're not. There's nothing wrong with your figure. It's your lack of self control that concerns me."

Nell looked at her hands again. "I shouldn't stash away candy and sweets then, should I?"

Selina chuckled. "No, you shouldn't. Not that there's much of that left anyway."

"Selina!"

"You're really not very good at hiding things."

Nell playfully nudged Selina, scolding her for eating her candy. Selina finally convinced her to leave her room, and so she emerged. She decided to retrieve the rest of her sweet stash before embarking on this new lifestyle change of self control.

When Croft noticed Penelope enter the library, with fresh energy and determination, he frowned in alarm."Miss Ayres? I thought you were horribly ill. Lady Selina called for Doctor Davies. We were all so very concerned."

"No, I'm quite well. I'm not at death's door."

Croft sighed. "I'm relieved to hear it."

"I was only devastated."

Croft frowned a little while watching her retrieve her stash. "I see. Well, it happens to the best of us, I suppose." He chuckled while she reached and shook his head as she scurried out of the library. He followed her out to the hallway where everyone stood.

The doctor chuckled and looked at Selina. "She's so like her aunt. Don't let your devastation linger too long, young lady, or your health will surely deteriorate."

Selina sadly smiled. "Dying slowly of a broken heart is a family trait, apparently."

Barratt made a face at this remark. "Might I inquire after Mr. Royce? I hoped to call on him today."

"He's doing some repairs over at the orphanage."

"Oh! I was so thrilled to hear you'd built another one. Such a generous soul." Davies gushed, lightly touching Selina's arm in admiration.

"No, the generous soul is entirely my husband's."

Barratt stared for a moment and smirked a little. "How incredibly thoughtful, to put so much effort into something he knew was dear to your heart."

Selina smiled. "Yes, it was. And he's taken care to see that it's properly maintained."

"What a relief that is. Mr. Litchfield was not at all fit to do so." Davies' mouth twisted to one side regretfully; he was not the sort of gentleman to enjoy speaking ill of the dead, even when the dead was a man such as Litchfield.

Barratt muttered and gradually grew in volume as he had Selina's full attention. "Those poor children. And after all the heart and soul you poured into their cause. How good it is to see orphans tended to with the care they deserve. Given a lovely home and all that."

Selina paused a moment to study him. "Of course."

Davies merrily smiled. "And who doesn't want the best for the children. Good man, Mr. Royce. You've married one of the honorable ones, my lady."

"It seems I have."

Davies, oblivious to the exchange of suspicious glances between the lady and the inspector, continued to grin. "Well, I'll be off," he sighed. "As usual, it's been a lovely visit. Inspector, would you like me to wait?"

"Yes, I'll be out at the carriage in a moment, please."

Davies bowed to Selina and headed to his carriage, leaving Selina and Barratt alone to stare at each other once again.

"What was it you wanted to discuss with my husband, Inspector?"

He shrugged, harmlessly. "Only to check on the state of things. I'm happy to see you yourself have improved in the time he's been here—if the improvement is genuine, that is."

"I'm afraid I don't understand."

"You can't deceive me, Lady Selina. I know my friend. Being married to Royce is no picnic, I'm sure. Particularly in light of the year you've had."

Selina chuckled. "It's not quite so bad," her eyes sparkled.

Barratt nodded and hummed a little. "Hm, he's charmed you, I see. So odd that it comes after the fact, isn't it? It's a wonder he was able to secure your hand in marriage at all. What tools could he have possibly used to pry his way into Everdon? He's always so very thorough." He paused a moment, then shook his head and tipped his hat. "Have a lovely day, Selina—pardon, *Lady* Selina."

3

At Death's Door

A day or two later, the household was readying for the morning's church service. The Delameres had built a chapel on Everdon's grounds, providing both private and convenient worship. The entire household had left ahead of the lord and lady of the house, at Royce's encouragement. Selina had dismissed Helen early, allowing her to prepare for the service herself. After the first of the party made their way to the chapel, Royce noticed Selina had taken far too long to finish preparations. He grew restless and finally decided to check on her progress. In her bedroom, Selina stood by her vanity, eyelids closed, breathing erratically, and gripping the edge of the worn copy of her family's Bible for dear life.

"Selina. Are you well?"

Her eyelids opened. Her complexion was grey and the bags under her eyes had deepened. "Yes, I'm fine. I'm almost ready."

"Everyone is at the chapel."

She stood a little straighter and started toward him, but couldn't make it farther than the end of her bed before she stopped to grab the bedpost. Painfully, she exhaled and shook her head.

Royce stepped toward her. "What's wrong?"

She shook her head and waved him off. "You've...you've never spoken....a word of my...origin to Inspector Barratt..."

"What? No, why would I?"

"He's just—he's had a way about him. He said some things the other day, as if he knew more than....well, more than either of us would like." Selina sways a little

Royce sat on her bed, holding a hand out for her to take. "Come here."

She walked around the corner of the bed to sit next to him, noticeably unsteady. At last she sat, but only when he guided her to the place beside him. She rested her head on his shoulder and he softly kissed her head, until her alarming warmth gave him pause.

Royce mumbled quietly. "Selina, you're feverish."

She didn't respond, feeling faint and hardly lucid. Gently, Royce laid her down on the bed before frantically calling for a passing maid.

"Fetch a doctor!"

Barratt's suspicions grew, following the peculiar conversation with the good doctor. He felt compelled to discover more of the Lady Selina's background; certainly he could stumble upon similar sources Royce must have used in his exploitation of the lady. He started toward Mr. Cuddy's place and the new orphanage. However, when he came within sight of the orphanage, he caught sight of Dr. Davies' carriage once again returning to Everdon. He attempted to match the pace of the carriage, until the coachman saw him and brought the horses to a gradual stop.

When the carriage stood still, Barratt peered inside and tipped his hat to Dr. Davies. "They'd better be paying you a pretty penny for all of Miss Ayres' devastations."

Davies expression this time was much more somber. "It's not Miss Ayres this time, Inspector. It seems our Lady Selina is at death's door."

Barratt frowned. She wasn't the victim he had expected. "Lady Selina?"

"Quite odd. I don't usually treat the lady — she's healthy as an ox, with a very impressive constitution. I'm sorry, Inspector, but time is of the essence, I'm afraid."

Barratt retreated from the carriage and it continued up the drive. Instead of following the path, the inspector continued toward the orphanage to speak to Cuddy. When he approached the freshly renovated building, he found himself almost impressed with Royce's attention to detail. The structure itself was well-constructed, well-furnished. The children seemed quite content as well, playing happily outside in the yard.

Barratt walked in to see Cuddy sitting in his office, joking with Ollie.

Cuddy smiled a friendly greeting. "Inspector Barratt! What can I do for you today?"

"I had a few questions for you — do you mind?"

"Of course not. Ollie." Cuddy gestured for Ollie to leave.

"Have you heard about Lady Selina falling ill?"

"What?" Cuddy moved to stand in surprise, but settled back down in his chair. "No, no I haven't. How odd!"

"She's never ill, is she?"

"No, she isn't. I don't believe I've ever heard of her being at all under the weather." Cuddy leaned back in chair pensively and started shaking his head. "Oh dear. Is she with child, I wonder....unpleasant childbirth is practically genetic."

"Lady Delamere, you mean."

"Of course."

"How long have you been with the family as a tenant?"

"I do believe you've asked me that before, Inspector. Around forty years, I said."

"So you remember Lady Selina's birth."

"Yes, of course."

"Doctor Davies describes it as a miracle birth. She should've been stillborn — is that right?"

Cuddy hesitated. "I suppose you could call it that, yes. I never knew the particulars, but I knew the Delameres desperately wanted a child, after having lost so many chances."

"Who's left from that time, do you know?"

"At Everdon? Mr. Lindon, Mrs. Melrose, that librarian and one of the cooks, I believe. I can't be sure. I haven't often been inside Everdon—and there was quite a turnover when Lady Selina took control of the estate, for the better, I'm sure." The old man paused a moment, rubbing the side of his face in contemplation. "I thought you were here to investigate a death, Inspector, not a birth."

"In a sense, all births connect with death in one way or another, don't they, Mr. Cuddy? It's quite poetic, actually. We all come into this world, experiencing forms of the same sorts of things and the same variety of sins….and then we leave this world. I aim to paint as full a picture as I can manage before coming to any definitive conclusions."

February 1890

March 1890

If there be no enemy there's no fight. If no fight, no victory and if no victory there is no
crown
~Thomas Carlyle~

1

Blame the Goblins

Selina's condition only worsened. The staff fretted up and down the halls; Everdon hadn't seen such uneasiness since the night Lady Delamere passed away. Whatever illness had stricken Selina had progressed quickly and then lingered. Some of the servants doubted she'd come out of it. Pulling her in and out of consciousness, her fever refused to break. While servants paced, Royce hardly left Selina's side, only resting his head against the wall in the hallway when mustering the strength to fetch her more water.

Helen, the romantic she was, found it overwhelmingly endearing the depth of Royce's apparent devastation. "He really loves her."

"Hm, perhaps you're right." Price was skeptical, but softening.

"She'll get better then, won't she?" She looked at him with a pained expression, desperate for any kind of hope.

"Because her husband loves her?" Price looked down at her in pity. "Child, the world works very differently. One cannot be saved simply because they are loved."

Helen walked toward Royce, who sat, exhausted, on the floor outside of Selina's room.

Royce didn't quite look up at her, but his eyes were desperate. "Miss Thomas…"

"Yes, sir?"

"Does….does she love me?"

Helen stared for a moment in confusion. "Has she never said?"

He slowly looked up at her. "She hasn't."

Helen hesitated. "I don't know if it's my place to say so, sir…"

"Say it anyway."

She paused again not knowing what to say, at first. She then remembered the heroine in her story. The one who had somehow taken on the metaphoric image of a caged bird. "She's not a particularly expressive lady, sir. And I don't know much of what love looks like. But those stolen glances when she thinks no one sees…the quiet longing in her eyes when she looks at you…the smirk she wears when she teases you…all of the subtle changes in her demeanor the longer you've been at Everdon. I don't know, sir. If I were to make a wager at what love looks like on Lady Selina, I'd imagine that's it."

Royce cleared tears from his throat and stood. "You just might make a writer yet."

He lightly nudged her arm as he passed her and moved in the direction of the kitchen to fetch Selina's water. Left pensive, Helen leaned against the wall before slowly stepping toward the lady's doorway and peeking inside. She was unsure what she had expected to see, but the sight of Selina's drained, almost lifeless form lying in the bed was far from what she had hoped. Cautiously, Mr. Croft approached with a similar intent.

Croft whispered to her. "How is our lady?"

"Not well." Helen slowly closed the door and turned to Croft and noticed how much of a toll Selina's condition had apparently taken on him as well. "Are you—are you well, Mr. Croft?"

"Only concerned." Croft sadly smiled. "Feels as though it was yesterday she was running through these halls, avoiding Lord Delamere's scolding."

Helen smiled just a little at the thought, but she'd found it harder to smile over the previous few days. "I've read many stories about ladies who meet misfortune. Some are saved and then pushed into the background of the hero's story. Some meet their end. Lady

Selina isn't like those ladies. She's stronger than that. She'll be all
right."

Croft sighed. "Miss Ayres wanted me to check in for her. I
suspect she's having a rather difficult time digesting….well, all of this."

"As are we all, it seems. If I were…" Helen trailed off,
stopping herself because she forgot she wasn't talking to Selina or
Royce.

"If you were what, Miss Thomas?"

"If I were….writing this part of the story, Mr. Royce would
find a-a cure or something. Or Melrose's prayers miraculously work.
Or perhaps…I would've written that she didn't fall ill to begin with."

Croft stared thoughtfully. "Yes, well, the characters never
quite do what you expect of them, do they? And you can't write them
back to life any more than you can rewrite their past."

Helen looked at him with shattered optimism. "I suppose we
can just move forward then."

Mrs. Melrose came to her with Penelope on her arm and an
exasperated expression on her face. "Miss Thomas, do take Miss Ayres
on a walk to get some fresh air."

Penelope mumbled. "Apparently my grief is irritating."

"No, dear, your idleness simply makes the grief all the worse.
One must keep busy—isn't that right, Miss Thomas?"

Helen understood. "Oh yes, of course. Come on, Nell, let's
walk to town."

Penelope agreed to go with her, and once they were outside
and making their way down the path, she became all the more
aggravated. Periodically, she stopped and turned to face Everdon
again, with a very concerned expression.

"She'll be all right." Helen repeated emptily, as she had far too
often recently.

Penelope eyes welled. "No, no, I don't think she will."

"You know nothing can best Selina. She's stronger than that."

"I can't—I don't think—I know what this is." Penelope started
hyperventilating.

Helen tried to steady her shoulders. "Penelope, Penelope,

calm down."

"No, no, they've poisoned her! I can't just leave!"

Helen was utterly confused by the hysterics, but Penelope continued to shout protests. Halfway to town, she had finally ceased the flailing and mad hysterics and had reduced to incoherent sobs instead. Thankfully, the young vicar, Mr. Holbrook, was walking along and heard Penelope's meltdown

"Oh dear. Miss Ayres, Miss Ayres—oh hello, Miss Thomas." Holbrook smiled at Helen, but then turns back to Nell. "What is it? What's the matter?"

"They're killing her! They've poisoned Selina! She told me not to, but then she did, and now she's—they've done it!"

At the word poison, Holbrook looked at Helen in alarm. "Um, considering the circumstances, Miss Thomas, perhaps we'd better get her to the inspector."

In the police station, Barratt sat Penelope gently by his desk. Looking her firmly but calmly in the eye, Barratt took her hand as she continued to hyperventilate. The trek to the station was no easy one, that was certain. Helen continued to pant and catch her breath as Barratt attempted to calm the young lady.

"Miss Ayres, I cannot help you if I cannot understand you. You must come up for air."

She tried to steady her breathing, even taking Helen's hand for support. Her grip was so tight, Helen could feel the fear Penelope struggled to articulate.

Barratt spoke softly, but with the same point-of-fact tone he bore in any interrogation. "What is that's upset you? Lady Selina's illness…?"

"They poisoned her. The goblins, they poisoned her!" Her hysterics began to rise once more as the pace of her words quickened. "She told me not to eat so much, but then she ate it instead—and now she's dying!"

"Goblins?" Barratt muttered. "What does that mean?"

The inspector glanced at Holbrook and Helen for assistance in translation, but Holbrook merely shrugged.

However, Helen's jaw fell slightly ajar as she reconsidered Penelope's words. "Oh dear."

"What is it?" Holbrook asked.

She cleared her throat; risking more false accusations was far from what she wanted. "I don't...I can't say. It can't be true anyway. I can't be wrong again and cause—"

"No need to fear implication, my dear." Barratt leaned back a bit and sighed. "I know who's done this."

2
Before the Fall

Barratt fetched a carriage and escorted Holbrook and the ladies back to Everdon. Mrs. Melrose greeted them immediately, noting the distressed expression on both young ladies' faces. Penelope's hysteria seemed to have worsened since embarking on the walk, and now Helen's expression followed suit.

"Is everything all right, Inspector?"

"I think Miss Ayres is in need of a sedative of some sort, Mrs. Melrose. And if possible, would you please fetch Mr. Royce for me?"

Mrs. Melrose frowned, but Helen gestured to the state Penelope's in and Melrose nodded and muttered an "of course" as she helped Helen take Penelope upstairs to Royce.

Barratt then cleared his throat, preparing to speak profound truths. "And Mrs. Melrose — I would suggest to Doctor Davies that he treat the Lady Selina with an antidote, as she's likely been poisoned."

Mrs. Melrose clutched her chest in disbelief. "Poisoned? Good heavens — why would anyone — I can't imagine..." she trailed off as she hurried upstairs.

After about ten minutes of Barratt waiting in the parlor, Royce finally came to meet him. Rundown, disheveled, and wrinkled with concern, Royce's appearance almost surprised Barratt.

Barratt furrowed his brow. "You look terrible."

"I'm not exactly in a position for social calls," he ran his fingers through his tousled hair. "Why would you tell Mrs. Melrose Selina's been poisoned?"

"How did you learn the circumstances of Selina's birth?"

Royce froze. "What?"

Barratt tucked his hands in his trouser pockets. He smiled humorlessly and shook his head. "It's all very crafty. Your intent to woo Miss Ayres was probably the most short-lived venture of yours that I've ever witnessed. Lady Selina was just so much more appealing. And once you gathered the necessary pieces of information—knowledge is power and all that—she simply crumbled at your feet. You were so determined to prove that she was human."

Royce snapped his head away from the inspector, silently threatening to leave. "You're grasping at straws."

Barratt held up a finger. "Securing her fortune wasn't enough. She had lived immortal too long. Humans have flaws, they have sins—they're more poetic that way, and she was no different. Kincaid saw through the charm. He may or may not have known how, but he suspected the blackmail, Royce, I have no doubt. You had to kill him."

"Haven't we done this before? Wouldn't it be just a bit too obvious?"

"Abram didn't care about the blackmail—the fool only cared about results. And he expected to be well-compensated for his troubles. I'd wager that nearly came at the expense of your lovely bride. How fortunate you kept her so armed."

"If I did all this—"

"Your pride was your downfall, my friend. I considered Kincaid to be an accident, Litchfield took the blame for Abram, Selina for Elinor—you thought yourself so impervious that you couldn't resist flaunting your successes, however anonymously." Smoothly, Barratt removed the assortment of letters from his coat pocket and held them to be seen. "You had to know I would see through it all."

Royce narrowed his eyes in confusion riddled with spite, cocking his head to one side. "This case has run you ragged. I think you need some rest. Why don't you—"

"Leave? Why—so you can finish killing your wife? You're a

manipulative snake, Royce. You scheme and you twist and....mind games are your forte. They always have been. Only this time, you've taken it too far. You've used every bit of cunning and energy within you to tear a woman apart."

"I wouldn't—"

"You would."

"Not to her!" Royce's voice rose in desperation. His breathing was uneven and his face reddened, as if his heart wasn't quite beating properly. His anguish was evident and his sincerity was just hopeless enough for Barratt to pause for a moment, reconsidering all of his alleged evidence.

The inspector then sighed. "You are right...you actually love this one...forgive me."

"How many letters?" Royce quietly asked, steadying his breath.

"I've spent so long believing it was you, I didn't—"

Royce grabbed him to get his attention. "How many letters? How many deaths?"

"Five." Barratt scrambled to hand them to him, nearly dropping two on the floor.

"Five letters or five bodies?"

Squinting raptly, he began to follow Royce's line of questioning. "Four deaths, five Letters. Not all were dead. That's why I...it's a mind game. Of course you would've been far too simple; how could I have been so dull? I should've known it wasn't you when it touched Selina directly."

"She isn't going to die."

"And you're so certain of that?"

Royce released an empty chuckle as his eyes fell to the ground. "Do you know what she said..." he started, "when I coerced her into sacrificing her own happiness for the sake of maintaining her fortune....when I stole her future—do you know what she said? She didn't fight, she didn't argue. *Very well*, she said." He cleared the emotion from his throat, finally bringing himself to look Barratt sternly in the eye. "Part of her died protecting the place...the people she cared about. I'm not going to let the rest of her die too."

"Cheers to that. We are finally in agreement."

"Who was the first letter?" Royce rubbed his forehead, feeling a headache emerging. "Wrath?"

"Kincaid, your first—his...the writer of...the first victim."

Royce frowned, clutching his chin. "Not the maid?"

"The letters didn't start until after Kincaid's death. And then, nearly all of them happened directly after the death of the respective sin."

"Nearly all of them?"

Barratt pointed to *GLUTTONY*.

Royce frowned again, but this time there was considerably less confusion in his tone. "You got the last letter before she fell ill."

"Yes."

He paused, exhaling sharply. "That letter wasn't meant for her."

"Well, now that I'm seeing reason, I fail to see how it would've applied to the Lady Selina in the first place." Barratt wiped the shame from his face with his hand.

"You received it the night of Penelope's birthday ball." Royce's voice when speaking Penelope's name was thick with regret.

"How did you know?"

"She's the only glutton I know."

"Selina was a mistake," Barratt muttered. He could hardly believe his own words. How could he have been so foolish as to make such detrimental assumptions?

"Mr. Royce!" Helen suddenly appeared with a huge smile on her face and a lilt in her step. "She's standing and out of bed."

Royce inhaled and shuffled the letters in his hands. "Thank you, Miss Thomas. See that the inspector gets a room made up for the night. It's getting late and you look worse than I do." He gestured to the ragged defeat settling into the lines on Barratt's face.

Helen obeyed and took Barratt to a guest room where he could rest and served something small to eat before bed.

Barratt settled in his room with his mind racing. When he

caught a glimpse of his own reflection in the vanity mirror, he decided defeat was not his best look. Royce was too simple of a solution. His raw impulsivity was bound to find a steady match, a deep infatuation to turn its ways. Lady Selina was certainly the sort of woman for whom any rogue would change his ways.

The list of viable suspects was running thin. All reasonable assumptions should have led to culprits who had recently found themselves forced to the grave. Perhaps it was always the unsuspecting. The trustworthy. The well-loved. The respectable. With the thought of Gilbert Lindon's face running through the inspector's mind, he dozed off to sleep.

Never to leave his room again.

Lady Selina was standing.

The good news was met by everyone with excitement. It was more progress than had been made in over a week. Royce walked alongside her around the room and down the hall, before she grew tired once again. Patience was needed, the doctor had said, but the results were promising nonetheless.

Royce and Selina sat up in her bed, her head resting on his shoulder as his arm wound around her. She munched on some toast while they sat quietly. Within minutes of finishing her toast, she had dozed off once again, but her breathing was infinitely better than it had been. Selina slept for a few hours before stirring. She woke up and realized Royce was still sitting wide awake, looking troubled. "Why aren't you sleeping? You look exhausted."

"Someone has to guard the castle," he sighed.

She sat up a little and faced him, propping herself up on the pillow. "Hm, my protector. The castle needs guarding?"

He forced a smile and stroked her hair. "Barratt thinks you were poisoned."

"And he promised so faithfully I was not to be a victim," she chuckled lightly, careful not to expel too much energy, no matter how amused. "Do you mean to say the great inspector was mistaken?"

"I think the killer was mistaken."

"There are many killers, darling—and I, among them."

He took her hand in his, kissing it before responding slowly. "And one puppet-master. One who's orchestrated around you from the beginning—since I found that letter."

Selina settled back into her position, resting her head on his shoulder again.

"It was fake," he confessed.

"Yes, it was. My father's hand wasn't nearly so neat."

The frown Royce attempted to mask now deepened. "Why did you accept it?"

"If you'd even suggested I was an impostor in certain company, I would have been ruined whether the claims were false or not. Besides, of all the scum in the world to have blackmailed me, at least you were one I was taken with." She peered up at him with the first smile she'd worn since her fever broke.

Royce chuckled and raised his eyebrows, responding to her sudden playfulness. "Is that right?"

"I told you," she intertwined her fingers in his, "if only you hadn't targeted Nell, we'd have been an ideal match from the start."

He smiled and kissed her hand again, but the smile soon faded. "Someone supplied that letter. And someone sent others to Barratt. I was played just as easily as he was."

"To what end?"

Royce wrinkled his forehead. "Barratt's letters suggest someone cared very much about the sins surrounding you. Henry, Litchfield, Abram, Elinor—"

"No one manipulated me into killing Abram, save Abram himself. You can't believe that was orchestrated."

"No, no…but anyone familiar with Abram, and with the knowledge that you had confiscated my pistol, could have easily drawn the correct conclusion. And Litchfield was such a fool—that sin practically disposes of itself. This is an observer. A subtle maestro who moves only a few pieces and then watches the rest of human nature unfold the results."

Selina was silent for a moment. "They knew you'd kill Elinor to protect me. But you didn't kill Henry."

"No. He was unstable that night; it could've been an accident. Unless the killer's motive was as mine was believed to be. Henry would have found the truth."

"The killer was protecting himself as well as me. But why give you a forged letter? If you'd gone back to London, the Abrams would have never come to Everdon. Henry would have never died. Litchfield would have drunken himself into a stupor of his own making without anyone's help. And I wouldn't have been...Nell. Nell's candy—she was meant to be poisoned, wasn't she?"

Royce slowed his vocal pace. "The fifth sin was Gluttony."

Selina's face tightened. She needn't be told for whom the poison had been intended. He stroked the back of her head to calm her and get her to lay back down while he himself stressed. He fell quiet for a moment, formulating, and then reached in his pocket for the letters. He showed her one of them.

"Is the same writing as your father's letter, do you remember?"

She glanced at it. "Yes. Neat and tidy."

Royce rose from the bed. "Sleep, Selina."

"Where are you going?"

"To protect the castle." He winked. "Stay here. Rest." Royce started for Barratt's room with his new theory.

He knocked, no answer.

He knocked again and called the inspector's name.

No answer.

Finally, in irritation, Royce slowly opened the door. There was an eerie stillness that gave Royce hesitation. The further he stepped into the room, the sooner he realized the source of the stillness. On the guest bed, Barratt laid under the blankets, restful, yet troubled as if sleeping—with the exception of a knife protruding from his chest.

Pinned beneath the knife was folded parchment like all the rest, this time bearing the number 2. Royce checked the body for a pulse before removing the letter from the knife. Scribbled on the inside of the parchment was the sin Royce himself would have chosen for

Barratt:
> *PRIDE.*

3
The Seventh Devil

The house was quiet. Everyone had finally rested and gone to bed, now that Selina was starting to come out of her illness. Royce had placed a blanket over Barratt's body for the time being, with plans to call the constable in the morning. For now, he had a more pressing matter to resolve, one that, in a rather poetic turn, Barratt had died before resolving.

Royce moved directly to the only other soul who seemed to be awake. With contemptuous arrogance as he entered the library, Royce dropped the sinful letters in the reading lap of Mr. Croft.

"These are yours."

Croft slowly looked up from his tea and his book and started to chuckle. "You never have disappointed me, Mr. Royce."

"You're missing one." Royce gestured glibly to the letters.

Croft mumbled almost to himself as he placed his teacup aside and fingered through the letters. "Selina has her demons, he always said. He was a clever man, rarely wrong. I told him seven. It's a fitting number, you know. Very suitable—and many pieces of poetry and prose proclaim as much. He never thought the number of demons made much difference; it was the overcoming of said demons that mattered most to Edward."

"Little did he know the devil himself would see to it that she faced them."

"No, no, these were the devils. Lady Selina is not infallible or untouchable. Nor has she ever been. She's always been tainted, fearful, cautious, vulnerable...to those who know just how carefully to attack her. You should be proud. You've bested Lady Selina in every possible way now. You married her, taking control of her estate. You made her fall in love with you, taking control of her heart. And now, with both, you are ultimately unstoppable. Mind, body, soul, and fortune. What more is there left in a woman?"

"I didn't come to—"

"You did," Croft slowly rose from his chair to face him. "Now, whether it became much more...well, that was entirely up to you, wasn't it? You asked me for a story. I asked what you lacked, and the first thing out of your mouth was the word treasure. I merely gave you the thing you wanted most."

Royce held up his hand lightly in protest. "You gave me Selina? No, no, you didn't give me anything but a book."

"A book…" the librarian nodded, advancing just a step or two, "about a haunted house and blackmail. A book which just so happened to contain the only piece of information that could have possibly been used to—how did you put it? Bring the Lady Selina to her knees. You blackmailed—nay, conquered the great lady of Everdon. That's what you wanted. You and your greed. Her entire estate at your fingertips— perhaps even her."

"No—" Royce's temper flared, but was cut by Croft's rebuttal.

"No, she came with time. I'll grant you that. She was never what you intended—the challenge, perhaps, but never the prize. You intended to fulfill a vice—arguably the most dangerous of them all. The root of all evil, I've considered you. After all, you brought all the rest with you."

"The rest of them."

"All your other deadly friends, waltzing on stage to throw tar at the lady's white feathers. Lechery, and his sister Envy, plotting to take what was not rightfully theirs. Pride, digging into the old wounds that brought her such pain. The others—Wrath, Gluttony, Slothfulness —you're not entirely to blame, but your spark ignited an explosion.

Fortunate for you there was someone to eat the sins seeking to tarnish her purity," Croft paused. "I do owe you some credit, however. You made for a better story. That's your niche, though isn't it? It always has been. To do the unexpected. And so it's been done. That first letter was meant to be yours." He looked down at the *WRATH* letter pensively. "Ah, Greed. If only Kincaid had been a more loathsome human being, or a more skilled killer. Apparently the villain had to live long enough to conquer as a hero."

"You thought you could get a man like Kincaid to kill me?" Royce scoffed, angling himself away from Croft in disbelief.

"That was my fault—anticipating a mild-mannered man's secret streak of rage to motivate him enough to murder…foolish. He's not quite as well-practiced as yourself."

Royce made a face of distaste.

"The streets of Whitechapel were not always kind to you, I understand."

Royce narrowed his eyes. "You killed him because he failed you."

"Oh heavens, no. He was an accident, don't you remember? Drunk with rage—it only takes a light tripping over a rock or a foot to cause a man of his height to hit a grounded rock like that and roll into a ditch."

"Just as predictable as a paranoid drunk believing he needed to dispose of the evidence of a crime he didn't commit."

Croft smiled. "The mere suggestion only an hour before would be enough to prompt him into rash actions. Very little influence on my part was necessary. Litchfield was simple. Almost as simple as little Miss Abram. A scorned woman is capable of a great many dangerous things. Your suspicions were warranted and expected—if she made one false move, which she did, your inclination toward greed would overtake you. You would do anything to protect your winnings."

This time, Royce almost smiled, squaring his shoulders. "You misjudged me."

"So it would seem."

"Just as you misjudged Penelope."

Croft's face hardened. "The girl hasn't shown restraint in her seventeen years of life. She had gorged herself on everything in her wake, and Selina could do very little to stop her. A single disparaging remark and suddenly self-control is of the essence."

"I told you, Croft. Youth can be cruel. If it's any consolation, your instincts regarding Abram proved correct."

Croft cleared his throat and looked down at the letters. "Yes, well, I never meant for Selina herself to pull the trigger."

"You thought I'd kill him too?"

Croft glanced back up at him. "You are not her only protector. Apparently there's no one better suited at spotting a predator at Everdon than our Mr. Lindon." He looked down again. "She didn't confide in him regarding the pistol as I expected. But, the sin was eaten nonetheless, so what complaint could there be?"

"Quite a few, from where I'm standing. Am I to assume then that the letters were for the goading benefit of the prideful detective insistent on involving himself in our affairs?"

Croft smirked. "Such frustration his soul must feel right this moment. To rest without knowing the truth. The unsolvable case of the seven sins. If only he'd known he was the sixth. And then, here you are, Mr. Royce. You were a broken cog in the machine I couldn't seem to fix or dispose of."

"Kincaid couldn't kill me, just as he couldn't kill Josephine."

"Ah, Josephine." Croft sighed almost regretfully.

Royce shifted his stance. It was his turn. "She reminded you too much of Sarah."

Croft slowly looked up at him with a fresh curiosity. The light panic in his eyes confirmed Royce's suspicions and fueled the remainder of his tale.

"Unlike Sarah, she'd fallen in love with the father of her child. Not that it mattered to you. A lady's maid, pregnant out of wedlock—it had been nearly thirty years, and you'd almost buried it all. Why did Josephine have to dig it back up again?"

Croft's expression settled into a reminiscent stare.

"You didn't mean to kill her. You meant to scare her away

from Everdon. You told her to leave—to run away with Bryant and hide. But she wouldn't, would she? Selina would have taken care of her. She would have seen that she and Bryant were married and that the child was well cared for. That wasn't good enough for you. You couldn't have that reminder of your past sins living at Everdon, walking the halls, borrowing your books for her mistress. Selina was enough of a haunting, I imagine."

Croft's lips began to curl into an ironic smile.

"A staged suicide would have worked, if Barratt hadn't been so thorough. His pride wouldn't let him accept that. So you needed something better. You needed a distraction. That's the only explanation I can find for why you would provide me with a forged letter revealing the deepest secret of the Delamere family—risking the financial destruction of the child you took under your twisted protection. Provide the villain with the key to Everdon, and draw everyone's gaze."

"It was impulsive, I'll admit." Croft nodded and shrugged, good-naturedly.

"It was selfish. And the moment you realized the harm you could have been inflicting, it was too late. I'd married her. I'd taken everything. And so, you had set out on your path to redemption, to destroy all of those devils you summoned."

"Ah, the devils you summoned. You kept the inspector here with his suspicions, you invited your scheming friends, you antagonized Sir Henry's rage, you enabled Miss Ayres' gluttony."

Royce took a step forward and held up a finger. "But I was summoned….by greed. By your greed. Rather poetic, isn't it, that the unresolved sin be greed? The root of all evil. The one who started it all. Greed which prompted Lechery, which was aggravated by the Envy felt when she favored another man. This overwhelmed the Glutton, the results of which brought a guilt which fueled his Wrath. And your Pride made you foolishly believe your problems would disappear with the personifications of your own sins." Pausing a moment, the shrewd wordsmith considered the outlier. "I suppose there's a Slothfulness to all of this, but my point lands, nonetheless."

Croft chuckled, shaking his head and stepping toward Royce. "It would be nice if it were all true. The new master of Everdon would certainly sleep better at night, I would think. But the story you've spun doesn't end quite the way you'd like. The hero and villain are one in the same. And unfortunately, they both must come to an end."

A bullet was fired and Royce and Croft both fell to the ground, one dead and one startled. Royce rose quickly and turned around to see Selina holding his pistol. He could hear Lindon running down the hallway to respond and he finally appeared in the doorway. Selina slowly walked toward Royce but she wasn't looking at him, she was looking at Croft's body.

When she heard Lindon enter the room, her dangerous eyes found him. "You knew. He....my mother—you knew."

"I suspected." Lindon corrected. His hands were raised defensively, as the gun followed her glare.

"And you let him stay." Selina's voice had an unhinged venom to it that alarmed Royce.

"Selina, give me the gun."

Lindon kept his voice level and steady as he clarified, "Edward let him stay. Edward trusted him...you trusted him. What could I do?"

Her eyes fell to Croft, welling at the sight of what she had done. What he had done. She let Royce gently peel the gun from her hand as she stood, shaking in shock.

"What can I do?" Lindon exhaled, almost helplessly.

"You can help me." Royce set the gun on the table, checked for a pulse, and began to lift Croft's body.

"Where are we taking him?"

"You'll see, just lift him."

"I'm afraid you were the seventh devil, Croft," Lindon grunted to the body as the two of them lifted him. "Perhaps you should have started with yourself."

"Inspector Barratt is dead upstairs," Royce stated plainly, as if rehearsing a script. "He was killed by the murderer Croft, who then fled, you understand?"

"Of course."

"Selina." She could hardly look at him. Royce signaled to Lindon and then gently set the body back down. "Darling, look at me." He gently took her hand and lifted her chin so she looked him in the eye. "He's gone. You won't see him again. All of this—it's over."

She nodded through her tears. "Just take him."

He kissed her forehead, softly stroking her cheek as he moved to fetch a wheelbarrow from the kitchen. With Lindon's assistance, Royce lifted the body into the wheelbarrow and discreetly wheeled the evidence out of the house and down to the stables.

Royce pointed to the pile of manure. "It'll destroy the evidence within a couple of months."

Lindon looked at him in slight alarm, but then exhaled with ease. "I'm disturbed and relieved to hear that you know that for certain. I'm sorry for ever being wrong about you, Royce."

"You were never wrong. We both just… changed."

The two lifted Croft onto the manure and used the nearby shovels to cover him completely and deeply so he sank to the bottom.

"You always suspected what he'd done. And you never once suspected he'd do all of this."

Lindon grunted with the force he exerted on the tool, and then dutifully shoveled. "I always thought he cared enough about his child to let things be. There were never any others….incidents. Though, I confess, I tended to avoid him on principle—"

"I would've killed him."

"I don't have that in me. Though, I never thought I'd have this in me either." He gestured to the disposal of the body. "But I could never look into the eyes of the man who….Sarah was very dear to me, you understand."

"I know. As is her daughter."

They finished their work and leaned the shovels back against a wall to survey the finished job. The body was no longer discernible amidst the feces, though the semblance of Croft's identity bore little difference in Lindon's eyes.

"What is she to do now?" Lindon muttered

Royce sighed and chuckled a little. "First, we must get Selina her own pistol. Clearly, she can wield her own."

Lindon chuckled too. A moment of solace passed between the respectable gentlemen before Royce sniffed the putrid smell around them and grimaced.

"But then…" he concluded, "we must never speak of any of this again. It never happened. Croft was never here. Everdon will hardly remember his name."

And then it was so. No one spoke of Croft. His fleeing from Everdon was widespread and accepted news for other staff as well as the villagers. Some weren't surprised he'd taunted authorities. Others hardly remembered who he was. And that's as it should have been.

Once Selina was fully recovered, she and Royce traveled to London to find Croft's replacement. Then, much like the year previous, Selina sat across from a young, bright-eyed recruit, eager to take up a post at Everdon, ignorant of all that had gone on before, and no remote inkling of what could possibly await them.

Epilogue
London 1930

"That's it?" A publisher, by the name of Francis Brady, pointed at the manuscript in front of him, looking expectantly at the older woman sitting across the desk from him. The ceiling fan in the publishing house buzzed while the two stared at one another, letting the question hang in the air for a moment or two.

"Um, what do you mean?" She leaned forward and squinted a little bit. Her greying hair was pulled into a loose bun on the top of her head, and it joined her in leaning forward in perplexity. Her colorfully framed spectacles were perched at the end of her nose, cupping the bottom of her large, inquisitive eyes.

"That's how it ends? They kill the librarian, and then just....hire a new one?"

The eccentric woman chuckled and traced a circle in the air with her pointer finger. "Beautifully cyclical ending, isn't it?"

For a moment, Brady considered this, but then sighed. "We can't accept this as non-fiction."

"You can't? Why not? It's true."

"No it isn't. There's no way to confirm this is the history of the Everdon estate."

"Yes, there is," she nodded emphatically. "I'm confirming it now."

Brady lifted a skeptical brow. "You're confirming it? You're Helen Thomas? Not…H.D. Strathers?"

Helen shrugged, erratically waving her hands. "Well, that's my pseudonym, obviously. But I can tell you that's what happened at Everdon in 1890."

Brady paused a moment and shook his head. "The Highwayman was written by Alfred Noyes—have you heard of him? 1906. Not by this Darius Royce in 1890. You must check your facts before marketing them as truth."

They stared at each other for a long moment—he waited for her to contradict him, and she attempted to concoct any way she possibly could.

Finally, she cracked a smile and chuckled. "But it's a good story, though, isn't it?"

Brady suppressed his own smile and leaned back in his office chair. "You certainly can spin a tale, can't you, Miss Strathers?"

"As it says," her lips stretched upward from ear to ear as she leaned forward, pointing once more to the manuscript on the desk, "I learned from the best."

Acknowledgments

Through the many, many versions of this story, there were so many patient ears I need to thank. Caitlin, my best friend, being the first. From the beginning, this was one of your favorites—despite all the murder and such—and your encouragement for me to finally finish it meant the world to me. I must also thank my beta readers, Sarah and Dylana, without whose feedback and strong opinions I may have never landed some of those gut-punching plot twists. You guys rock. And even though my time on Patreon has ended, my loyal patrons will always have a place in my heart—you beautiful souls fueled the creative fire that helped me finish this project. Lastly I'd love to give a shout-out to my fantastic editor, Kendra. You, my love, are an absolute BEAST for tackling such a hefty manuscript. Here's to many more to come!

About The Author

Renée Tamsin was raised in various parts of the Southern and Midwestern U.S. The one constant in her ever-changing environment was her stories. When not writing tales of adventure and intrigue, she's busy reading them.

Renée published her debut series *The Arkis Tales* in 2018, and continues to release installments of the fantasy saga, while working on projects such as this one on the side. *A Cage of Tarred Feathers* is the second of her serial novel publications initially released on Patreon, the first being *the bedtime prince*, which was published in 2021.

For exclusively signed copies and access to future serials, visit:
www.littlearkisshoppe.com

Like what you've read so far? Support Renée by leaving reviews and sharing her stories with friends and family.